This book belongs to

....

....

Classic Fairy Tales
from the
Brothers Grimm

Classic Fairy Tales
from the
Brothers Grimm

JACOB GRIMM &
WILHELM GRIMM

WORTH
PRESS

SIGNATURE CLASSICS

First published in 2019 by Worth Press Ltd, Bath, England
Email: worthpress@btconnect.com

Concept, design, introduction, reset text and coloured images of this edition
© Worth Press Ltd, 2019

British Library Cataloguing in Publication Data
A catalogue record for this book is available from the British Library

ISBN: 978-1-84931-167-0

10 9 8 7 6 5 4 3 2 1

Publisher's Note   Every effort has been made to ensure the accuracy of the information
presented in this book. The publisher will not assume liability for damages caused by
inaccuracies in the data and makes no warranty whatsoever expressed or implied. The
publisher welcomes comments and corrections from readers, emailed to worthpress@
btconnect.com, which will be considered for incorporation in future editions. Every effort
has been made to trace copyright holders and seek permission to use illustrative and
other material. The publisher wishes to apologize for any inadvertent errors or omissions
and would be glad to rectify these in future editions.

The images used in this book come from either the public domain or from the public
commons unless otherwise stated.

Page Resetting: IDSUK Ltd
Images coloured by Chandra Creative and Content Solutions
Cover and Front Matter Design: Jess Moon

Printed and bound in China

Contents

The Tales

Letter to the Reader

For over more than 160 years, the famous stories gathered by Jacob and Wilhelm Grimm remain unparalleled and are loved by people all over the world.

I was introduced to them by my parents when I was a child, because the stories of the brothers Grimm have meant so much to my family and to generations before. I really loved listening to them being read aloud as well as reading them for myself. I discovered ogres and giants, brave heroes and clever animals, princes, princesses and witches.

They have ever been a source of fascination and joy and I am sure will continue to be so for generations to come. It is therefore really exciting for me to help introduce this new collection of 64 wonderful tales.

These stories will bring the immense poetic richness and amazing fantasy of the Grimm' brothers fairy tales into the lives and hearts of both children and adults everywhere while reading or listening to them.

Lili Baumann, 18 years old

Dr Gail-Nina Anderson is a cultural historian, specializing in Victorian Romanticism and the Gothic genre across art history, film and literature. Based in Newcastle upon Tyne, she delivers seminar courses and a programme of public lectures for the city's historic Literary and Philosophical Society Library. She has curated and written the catalogues for two exhibitions of Victorian paintings at the University of Nottingham Gallery, and has published articles on topics as varied as *The Naked Lunch*, Arthur Machen, the ghost stories of E.F. Benson, John Martin and the fairy sculpture of Tessa Farmer. An active member of the Folklore Society, in 2013 she was invited to deliver the thirty-third Katharine Briggs Memorial Lecture, later published, on *Artlore: An Introduction to Recurring Motifs Generated by the Study of Fine Art*, a topic she is developing into a book. A regular contributor to the *Fortean Times* magazine, she has written for them on mermaid folklore, Count Dracula, and the network of links between vampire imagery and the Pre-Raphaelites. She still hopes to find the time to turn her PhD thesis into a book on mystic and mythic aspects in the work of Dante Gabriel Rossetti. A member of the Dracula Society and the M. R. James *Ghosts and Scholars* group, she occasionally writes ghost stories, and twice a year presides at *Phantoms at the Phil*, an evening of spooky tales specially written in honour of the library. Several of her stories have been published in anthologies, and a collection of her work is in the pipeline. Her secret vice is deltiology, and she is currently curating the third exhibition drawn from her massive collection of postcards.

David Stuart Davies is an author, playwright and editor. His fiction includes six novels featuring his wartime detective Johnny Hawke, Victorian puzzle solver Luther Darke, and nine Sherlock Holmes novels, the latest being *Sherlock Holmes and The Ripper Legacy*. His most recent novel is *Oliver Twist and The Mystery of Throate Manor*. His non-fiction work includes *Starring Sherlock Holmes*, detailing the film career of the Baker Street sleuth. David is regarded as an authority on Sherlock Holmes and is the author of three Holmes stage plays. David has also penned three dark gritty crime novels set in Yorkshire in the 1980s. He is a committee member of the Crime Writers' Association and edits their monthly publication *Red Herrings*. His collection of ghost and horror stories, *The Halloween Mask*, appeared in 2015, championed by Mark Gatiss who said they were 'pleasingly nasty'. David is General Editor of Wordsworth's Mystery & Supernatural series and also contributes a monthly blog on classic novels for the Wordsworth website. He is a past Fellow of the Royal Literary Fund and has appeared at many literary festivals and the Edinburgh Fringe performing his one-man presentation *The Game's Afoot – an evening with Sherlock Holmes and Arthur Conan Doyle*. David is also a member of the famed Detection Club.

The Romantic Revival
Gail-Nina Anderson

Let us start with the grandest symbol of the German Romantic spirit. Constructed throughout the 1870s and 1880s, the Palace of Neuschwanstein represents a dream of historicism and wishful thinking, with its baronial chambers, soaring turrets and commanding situation in the Alpine foothills of Bavaria. Actual mediaeval remains had to be destroyed to build it, however, and the history it embodies is a nineteenth-century dream, built around Wagnerian fantasies given shape by Ludwig II of Bavaria, the 'Swan King' who created this monument to an imagined version of the past. Neuschwanstein can be seen as anything from spiritually uplifting to simply kitsch – within months of Ludwig's mysterious death in 1886 it was opened to paying visitors, rapidly becoming a major tourist attraction.

This is the Romanticism that re-creates and embroiders past ages, that allows us to escape, however briefly, to a world where we can shed the mundane stress of modern life in favour of a more aesthetically intense experience (usually with due reference to changing expectations of hygiene and convenience, however. It comes as no surprise to learn that Neuschwanstein was equipped with flushing toilets.)

Alongside this there has flourished, since the late eighteenth century, a different strand of the Romantic, which looks to the apparently unchanging (again, wishful thinking may be involved) traditions of folk customs and superstitions, unwritten tales told down the generations, embodiments of unofficial beliefs and local traditions. There is a huge attraction in the notion that, as the corrective to a stiflingly bureaucratized urban world where ideas are increasingly pigeon-holed and labelled, we might feel a frisson of magic in a story or a song spontaneously created and reflecting a simpler, more wonder-filled attitude to life, where the strangest conjunctions remain possible.

To our contemporary society, where modern media strive to emphasize the individual, seek out extremes of behaviour, access the past or investigate the obscure and arcane, the question that might need asking is not so much *how* Romanticism emerged as a way of looking at the world, but *why* such an emergence was necessary at all, and why it seemed so distinctive that it could be seen as a whole new cultural attitude. The see-saw theory of history, whereby the tastes and attitudes of one cultural phase seem periodically doomed to inspire an adverse response in the next, has become something of a cliché, but one way to understand the significance of the Romantic is to see it as oppositional to the Classical. As the Age of Reason or the Enlightenment, the presiding philosophy of the eighteenth century was progressive, questioning what were seen as outmoded institutions and drawing on the perceived civic virtues of the Classical world to create a new society where rational thinking would replace superstition and a well-balanced sense of personal and social responsibility would be valued above the unruly possibilities of the emotional or sensational. Jane Austen's novel *Sense and Sensibility* (first published in 1811 though possibly begun as early as 1795) sets out the sort of character contrast this attitude inspired. However deeply her heroine Elinor feels, she remains rational, self-controlled, observant of social conventions and disinclined to jump to conclusions or rashly reveal her feelings. Some sympathy is reserved, however, for her sister Marianne who is at the mercy of her emotions, jumps swiftly to untenable assumptions and leaves herself vulnerable to disappointment and despair. Elinor's 'sense' is a Classical virtue, while Marianne's 'sensibility' typifies the Romantic personality.

The Romantic Movement might, then, be viewed as the re-assertion of subjective feelings unmitigated by purely rational restraints, and of free access to and expression of the emotions. At a fairly trivial level it must have been worrying for an older generation to see the discipline of classical metre displaced in favour of the archaic vernacular of ancient ballads, or the appreciation of a productive, ordered landscape give way to a taste for the decaying ruins of an earlier age, preferably viewed by moonlight or illuminated by lightning. There were deeper fears, though – Romanticism could be seen as socially regressive, as the encouragement of extreme states of mind or as so dangerously morbid that both physical and mental health might suffer. A suitably picturesque and twisting path – or perhaps that should be a tangled web – leads from such fears to the international and enduring acceptance of Grimms' Tales as a vital part of our cultural heritage.

One significant thread was the growth of antiquarianism, where it became fashionable to research the ancient ways of local and national history via obscure documents, monuments and oral tradition type. In England, the Society of Antiquaries had existed since the late sixteenth century, but the granting of a Royal Charter in 1751 formalized a learned group dedicated to illuminating the historical past, while more informal local research became an approved pastime for country parsons and squires. Traditional forms of literature that might once have been dismissed as crude made a popular reappearance, via such collections as the immensely influential *Reliques of Ancient English Poetry* published in 1765. The compiler of this collection of ballads, Bishop Thomas Percy, found many of them in a manuscript folio that a maid was dismembering to light the fire, and was thus able to introduce a new audience to a literature of illicit romance, chivalry, dragons, ghosts and Robin Hood. This manifestation of the literary via the antiquarian would flourish slightly later in Germany, where the Romantic cult of the Middle Ages created a huge taste for folk/fairy tales, local legends and ballads, traditional or re-invented. Indeed, in 1805 in Heidelberg the patrons of the Grimm brothers, Ludwig Achim von Arnim and Clemens Brentano, had already published a collection of songs and poems, *Des Knaben Wunderhorn: Alte deutsche Lieder (The Boy's Magic Horn: Old German Songs)*. Two further volumes followed in 1808, helping seal Germany's love affair with an idealized version of its own past. Although gathered from ancient sources, however, the contents of these volumes manifest a great amount of re-writing by their nineteenth-century editors – this is folklore and literature tidied up to suit the nationalistic yearnings of a new audience at odds with the mood of a changing modern world. The mixture was effective, however – Goethe considered that *Des Knaben Wunderhorn* 'has its place in every household'.

Alongside the apparent simplicity of the archaic, however, there also flourished pleasures more urban and romance more melodramatic, for this was also the period of when the theatre was hugely fashionable and, courtesy of actor-manager David Garrick, had become the location for what was virtually a cult of Shakespeare, formalizing his reputation as the greatest of English playwrights. Far from being seen as stuffy classics, the plays opened sensational windows on to a past where fairies, ghosts, predictions and visions appeared as part of our literary heritage. The revival of interest in the 'irrational' drama of Shakespeare spread across Europe, especially in Germany, where translations of his work were frequently performed. The influence of *Romeo and Juliet* can clearly be felt in Friedrich Maximilian Klinger's 1776 play *Sturm und Drang*, which lent its name to the proto-Romantic phase of German literary Romanticism. This 'Storm and Stress' (or 'Urge') movement saw a reaction against classical restraints of tone and language, emphasizing instead the sensational and the subjective and encompassing states of mind from the deeply introspective to the wildly unbalanced. Friedrich Schiller's intense and violent drama of 1781, *The Robbers*, for example, created an overnight sensation, while Goethe's hugely successful 1774 novel *The Sorrows of Young Werther* was blamed for inciting impressionable young men not simply to dress in the style of its melancholy hero, but even to commit suicide in the same manner. This led to the novel being banned in several places, and helps explain why, in his more classically attuned old age its author considered the Romantic movement to represent 'everything that is sick'. Not everyone agreed – in *Frankenstein* (1818) Mary Shelley's Monster reads *Werther* with sympathy as the story of a similarly outcast soul.

Readers across Europe became eager consumers of a new kind of literature which might go beyond the sensational to include elements of the supernatural drawn from the unofficial traditions of folklore. These helped create a new fascination with a past heavily coloured by what had previously been dismissed as 'mere' superstition (including, in the rather arid Protestant Anglicanism of eighteenth-century Britain, a prurient interest in what was viewed as corrupt mediaeval Roman Catholicism) and the Gothic genre was born. A figure who acts as a convenient focus for these disparate trends is Horace Walpole (1717–97), aristocrat, landowner and son of a prime minister. Waspish, sickly, addicted to gossip and of undefined sexuality, Walpole indulged in a creative form of antiquarianism that led him to collect, build and write out his mediaeval fantasies. His collection included ancient armour, Tudor miniatures and the 'black stone' with which the Elizabethan mage Dr Dee supposedly summoned spirits. Strawberry Hill, his modest Thames-side house at Twickenham, was imaginatively transformed into the first significant (if flimsy – the battlements were made of pasteboard) work in what became the Gothic Revival in architecture. In 1764 Walpole cemented his role as cover boy for the Gothic movement by publishing, anonymously, *The Castle of Otranto*, purportedly a translation from the Italian. The first edition of 500 copies sold so well that in a second edition, subtitled *A Gothic Tale* he admitted his sole authorship of this wildly extravagant story set (more or less) at the period of the Crusades. Apparently inspired by a dream in which he saw a giant armoured hand, Walpole concocted an outrageous piece of high-camp melodrama that, despite its earlier setting, obviously reflects his admiration for *Hamlet*. In a vast castle, the heir to an Italian principality is crushed to death by the unheralded appearance of a gigantic helmet, a fitting prelude to a plot that includes incestuous desire, a family curse, a perambulatory ancestral portrait, a usurped heir recognized by his birthmark, a mysterious friar, a bleeding statue and numerous untimely deaths. The tropes of the genre are gathered together so quickly and comprehensively that the Gothic novel seems to have sprung fully-formed from its progenitor's pen, but although many of these motifs were already culturally familiar through folklore, drama and early romances, the fact of Walpole's looking back to such sources and repackaging them for a new readership heralds the Romantic impulse. More exotic possibilities were explored by William Beckford, another wealthy eccentric of debated sexuality involved in collecting, politics and architecture – in this case the building of Fonthill Abbey. Constructed disastrously quickly, there was a fairy-tale quality to this pseudo-ecclesiastical edifice intended to resemble a mediaeval abbey – complete with tower and spire built to a structurally unsound height of about 27 metres (90 feet), which twice fell down and had to be rebuilt. Before being forced to sell it, Beckford lived there in solitary splendour, a rich recluse attempting to exist within his own fantasy. Despite demonstrating such a mediaeval affinity in his domestic arrangements, Beckford's Gothic novel Vathek, written in French and published in translation in 1786 (anonymously, and claiming to have come from an Arabic manuscript) presented a sinister tale of hedonism, pride and the occult set in the world of the *Arabian Nights*. This extra element of distance allowed for more extravagant degrees of transgression, with the characters choosing to interact with demons and djinns in a pursuit of pleasure and knowledge. The world of *Vathek* is overtly fantastic – portals open, inscriptions change and magic is a commodity, in contrast to the more established Gothic mode where the supernatural intrudes into a more-or-less recognizable world.

By the turn of the eighteenth/nineteenth centuries, Gothic sensationalism and sentiment had become overtly visible within mainstream western culture, with the French *roman noir* and German *schauerroman* developing national variants. When Mrs Ann Radcliffe produced her six popular novels between 1789 and 1802 (the last one, *Gaston de Blondeville*, appearing posthumously in 1826) she was consolidating these trends, with *The Mysteries of Udolpho* becoming the predominant example of literary Gothic at its height. Hers is a world of craggy continental landscapes where persecuted young lovers face terrifying dangers at the hands of charismatic villains eager to conceal the secrets of the past. Thrilling as her writing was, with a generation of young female readers held breathless with anticipation as they awaited the next volume from the circulating library, still it won the genre a level of respectability. Excepting some rather mild ghosts in her last novel, she only *flirts* with the supernatural, suggesting its presence then (infuriatingly to the modern reader) explaining it away. This was in contrast to the most notorious novel of the 1790s, *The Monk* by Matthew Lewis. This no-holds-barred rollercoaster ride through incest, murder, rape, transvestism, demonic seduction, Inquisitorial torture and the odd Bleeding Nun, all set in dangerously superstitious Madrid, can still shock, revelling as it does in the sort of visceral horror unknown to Mrs Radcliffe. First published in 1796 when its creator was only 20, it was a great success, winning praise from Lord Byron and the Marquis de Sade and earning its author the nickname 'Monk' Lewis.

Tradition, introspection, the sensational and the supernatural, then, are among the ingredients that present themselves to the Romantic author (or composer or visual artist – *The Nightmare*, first painted by Anglo-Swiss artist Henry Fuseli in 1781, could be seen as drawing on all these elements). As one might expect, however, within so disparate an index of possibilities different routes could be selected. Romantic writing in English, for example, might reasonably include the idiosyncratic personal mythologies of William Blake, the high-flown politicized verse of Percy Bysshe Shelley, the dream-like narratives of John Keats's poetry, the uncanny, fevered atmosphere created in the works of Edgar Allan Poe, or the epigrammatic introspection of Emily Dickinson. Even within the trio most usually cited as 'the British Romantic Poets', there are startling differences of approach. The poetry of Lord Byron, for example, is inextricably mixed with a life of celebrity and notoriety, weaving as it does an overtly masculine version of heroic romance in which the protagonist may be scholar or seducer, exotic potentate or fighter for freedom. This is the Romanticism of the grand gesture, whether dissolute, fearless or despairing. It almost unthinkingly dissolves the veil between worlds, engaging with eerie visions and cursed lives as readily as it does with Alpine scenery or satirical comment. Although no folklorist, Byron was, for example, sufficiently enthralled by Greek stories of vampire revenants to begin a short story on the theme. Left unfinished, its central idea was taken up by his one-time Physician John Polidori, whose 1819 novella *The Vampyre* became the effective progenitor of English vampire literature, an enduring Gothic/Romantic trope where Byronic imagery meets timeless folk beliefs, erotic metaphor and the frisson of terror by night. Byron's Romanticism was for the most part exotic, drawing from the attitudes of a privileged young aristocrat whose life became an unending Grand Tour – the great sweep of his writing is coloured by modern Greece and ancient Assyria, the decaying Venetian palazzo or the unnerving grandeur of the Swiss Alps. A vividly contrasting keynote of the Romantic sensibility can be found in the work of William Wordsworth and Samuel Taylor Coleridge, especially in their joint volume *Lyrical Ballads*, published in 1798. Despite Wordsworth's own foreign travel and (in youth at least) revolutionary sympathies, his most distinctive sentiments are drawn from the context of familiarity, as when he explores the emotional power of the English landscape in 'Tintern Abbey'. More innovatively, he pitches the tone of his poetical vocabulary to avoid the flowery formalities of earlier eighteenth-century verse, deliberately adopting a simplicity of language to suit the situations and characters of a simpler way of life, not noticeably modern, urbanized or overly-educated. He explained his poetical concept in the 'Advertisement' of the first edition:

'The majority of the following poems are to be considered as experiments. They were written chiefly with a view to ascertain how far the language of conversation in the middle and lower classes of society is adapted to the purpose of poetic pleasure.'

In other words, this was the poetry of the 'folk', dealing directly with those strata of society whose lives, usually rustic, went on unchanged, offering a basic panorama of the human condition informed by landscape and climate. Wordsworth's Romanticism was local, specific, rooted in areas he regularly walked and words he heard spoken. Along with Coleridge and Southey he is one of the 'Lake Poets', drawing from his immediate surroundings to give a sense of place and personality. Coleridge's main contribution to *Lyrical Ballads*, 'The Rime of the Ancient Mariner' offers a different side of the same coin by utilizing the deliberately archaic form of the narrative ballad to tell a weird tale of human interaction with a range of supernatural forces whose effects permeate the world both physically and spiritually. It is as though Coleridge continues a folk tradition rather than repeating it, with a poem that cries out for oral transmission to a wonder-struck audience, though actually written by a highly educated man and intended for publication.

By the time the Grimm bothers published the first edition of the first volume of their *'Kinder- und Hausmärchen'* (*'Children's and Household Tales'*) in 1812, they were contributing to an already well-rooted literary movement, predominant particularly in northern Europe. Its literature varied in tone, language, sentiment and function but could loosely be described as celebrating the unofficial voice by emphasizing the individual, traditional, emotional, local and even irrational. If the the Enlightenment had seen itself as the Age of Reason, the Romantic Movement chose instead to open the doors to the imagination, downplaying the idea of universal principles in favour of interior worlds. Grimms' *Tales* represents one of the most successful examples of playing to the imaginative impulse, as well as reinforcing the importance of regional identity and language. Of course, Jacob and Wilhelm Grimm did not compose these tales, but the antiquarian impulse to collect and collate the ancient, the vernacular and the orally-transmitted brings their endeavour firmly into line with a non-classical Romantic view of the past. Their desire to preserve a 'rustic tone' sits well with the ideas behind Wordsworth's *Lyrical Ballads,* as does the intention to record, via these stories, the authentic voices that originally told them.

Alas, by the early nineteenth century the purity of this endeavour was already difficult to maintain. Some of the tales were taken from books where they had already been collected and therefore subjected to editorial selection and possible manipulation (of which the Grimms themselves were also, inevitably, guilty). The idea that those gathered from oral tellings represented authentic peasant voices was also innaccurate, as educated and middle-class friends contributed remembered stories as well. Indeed, the most famous oral source, Dorothea Veihmann, was the widow of a tailor and of French descent, so her family traditions were unlikely to represent that untouched local identity the Grimms hoped to channel. The German-ness of the stories had, in Romantic fashion, always been essential to the project, as well as contributing to their immense popularity in America (via German settlers) and Britain (where Queen Victoria's German connections, consolidated by her marriage to Prince Albert of Saxe-Coburg and Gotha, effected a Germanophile culture). As all folklorists know, however, tales travel (perhaps even more so once they've been written down) and mutate with the passage of time and distance, so variant versions are the norm, and a German teller doesn't guarantee a German tale. Indeed, the Grimms included some stories from Charles Perrault's *Histoires ou contes du temps passé* of 1697, produced in the elevated style and courtly atmosphere suitable to the France of Louis XIV. Sometimes hints of a pre-Christian mythos are preserved, in the story of *Frau Holle*, for example, but any ideal of uncovering a pure German identity was thwarted from the start. A tale such as *Ashenputtel (Cinderella)* had already travelled from Graeco-Egyptian and Roman sources via Italian and French variants, carrying all the resonance of a myth rather than the nursery tale it subsequently became. If their specifically German nature was itself something of a Romantic myth, however, the content of the tales certainly nudged them towards an authentically Gothic mode. They may create a pristine world of royal palaces and simple peasants, but it is coloured by spells and curses. Here the dead speak, animals and humans shape-shift, family ties are twisted by jealousy, greed and desire, and a dangerous interaction with supernatural beings is a constant possibility. Any 'happy ever after' conclusions are hard won in a narrative context that often involves harsh treatment, emotional abuse and grotesque punishments

Although the stories were never intended to become bed-time reading for children (indeed, several are wildly unsuited to this purpose) their unplanned mutation from antiquarian status to fairy tales consolidates their Romantic status. Childhood could be seen as the ideal Romantic state, when imagination needed to flourish without rational repression and a simplicity of vision constantly made the world anew. This attitude coloured the work of Blake and Wordsworth, but it was the Brothers Grimm who (however unintentionally) helped create a Romantic literary form that would attract a readership of children, providing an 'authentic' voice for an audience in an 'unspoiled' state of imaginative receptivity.

By appealing directly to the imagination by way of the fantastic, by requiring a willing suspension of disbelief and by suggesting a universe of individual experiences not ratified by any central authority intent on rational justification, Kinder- und Hausmärchen (or let us accept the change in title brought about by massive international popularity and call the volume *Grimms' Fairy Tales*) took the Romantic impulse in a new direction.

The Brothers Grimm: The Unexpurgated Stories

David Stuart Davies

Jacob Grimm (4 January 1785 – 20 September 1863) and Wilhelm Grimm (24 February 1786 – 16 December 1859)

Enter any large bookstore and in the children's section you will find at least one prettily illustrated edition of Grimm's fairy tales, presented as a collection of charming stories for young minds. However, these editions will contain the sanitized versions of the Grimm brothers' tales – the original versions being very grim indeed.

The brothers were born in Hanau, Germany, and were part of a family of nine children, six of whom survived infancy. They grew up in the countryside while their father, Philipp Wilhelm Grimm, was employed by the Prince of Hessen between 1790 and 1796. However, events took the brothers down a different path when their father died in 1796 and the family had to leave their large house with servants and privileged lifestyle to move into a cramped urban residence. Further strain was put on their mother, Dorothea Grimm, when their grandfather died in 1798, leaving her struggling to support the children on her own.

The brothers studied at the Friedrichs-Gymnasium in Kassel and later they went to the University of Marburg and studied law, Jacob in 1802 and Wilhelm in 1803. At Marburg they came under the influence of the poet and novelist Clemens Brentano, who awakened in both a love of folk poetry, and Friedrich Karl von Savigny, co-founder of the historical school of jurisprudence, who taught them a method of antiquarian investigation that formed the real basis of all their later work.

Their interest in folklore, inspired by these mentors, led them to begin to collect and research stories and legends. Jacob was the more expert researcher, while it was Wilhelm's skill with interpreting these stories that helped to bring them alive and accessible to the general reader.

Jacob and Wilhelm first collected folk songs and tales for their friends, poet and folklorist Ludwig Achim von Arnim and Clemens Brentano. While doing so the brothers also studied critical essays which examined the essential difference between folk literature and other writing. To them, folk poetry was the only true poetry, expressing the eternal joys and sorrows, the hopes and fears, of humankind.

Not equipped with sound recording equipment, and relying sometimes on skeletal texts, the Grimms could not be utterly faithful to the words related to them, as later folklorists would insist upon. However they did their best, and they rewrote the tales in a good approximation of the straightforward style in which they were relayed originally.

Encouraged by Arnim, they published their collected tales in 1812 as the *Kinder- und Hausmärchen (Children's and Household Tales)*, implying in the title that the stories were meant for adults and children alike. In contrast to the extravagant fantasy of the Romantic school's poetical fairy tales, the 200 stories in this collection (including, among the most enduring, 'Snow-White,' 'Little Red Riding-Hood,' 'Sleeping Beauty', and 'Rumpelstiltskin') aimed at conveying a genuine reproduction of the teller's words and ways without censure. The collection also ensured that these ancient narratives achieved a literary posterity which would otherwise have been lost. Most of the stories were taken from oral recitations, though a few were from printed sources. The great merit of Wilhelm Grimm is that he gave the fairy tales a readable form without changing their folkloric character. The results were threefold: the collection enjoyed wide distribution in Germany and eventually in all parts of the globe; it became and remains a model for the collecting of folktales everywhere; and the Grimms' notes to the tales, along with other investigations, formed the basis for the science of the folk narrative and even of folklore itself. To this day the tales remain the earliest 'scientific' collection of folktales.

Despite the all-embracing title of the collection, however, a great number of these original stories were not intended for children. Von Armin was deeply concerned about the content of some of the tales, such as those which showed children being eaten, and suggested that they be removed. Instead, the brothers added an introduction with cautionary advice that parents steer children toward age-appropriate stories. Despite von Armin's unease, none of the tales was eliminated from the collection. It was the brothers' belief that all the tales were of value and reflected inherent cultural qualities. Furthermore, the stories were didactic in nature at a time when discipline of the young relied on fear. In her book *Legend & Belief – Dialectics of a Folklore Genre* (2001), acclaimed folklore scholar Linda Dégh maintained that tales such as 'Little Red Riding Hood' and 'Hansel and Gretel' were written to be 'warning tales' for children.

The stories in *Kinder- und Hausmärchen* include scenes of violence that have since been sanitized. For example, in the Grimms' original version of 'Snow-White', the queen is Little Snow-White's mother, not her stepmother, yet even so she orders her huntsman to kill her daughter and bring home the child's lungs and liver so that she can eat them. The story ends with the queen mother dancing at Snow-White's wedding wearing a pair of red-hot iron shoes that kill her.

In the story 'The Goose-Girl', a servant is stripped naked and pushed into a barrel 'studded with sharp nails' pointing inwards which tear her flesh and then she is rolled down the street. The Grimms' version of 'The Frog Prince' describes the princess throwing the frog against a wall instead of kissing him as she does in revised version. To some extent, the cruelty and violence may have been a reflection of the medieval culture from which the tales originated, such as scenes of witches burning, as described in the story 'The Six Swans'. The standard mantra of 'They all lived happily ever after' is decidedly absent from these fairy tales.

There is a story entitled 'How the Children Played at Slaughtering' which presents a veritable blood bath. The narrative stays true to its grisly title featuring a group of children playing at being a butcher and a pig. It ends in a dark and gruesome fashion: a boy cuts the throat of his little brother, only to be stabbed in the heart by his enraged mother. Unfortunately, in carrying out this violent punishment she left her other child alone in the bath at home, where he drowned. Unable to be cheered up by the neighbours, the woman hangs herself. When her husband gets home, he 'became so despondent that he died soon thereafter'. 'The Children of Famine' is just as disturbing: a mother threatens to kill her daughters because there is nothing else to eat. They offer her slices of bread, but fail to stave off her hunger: 'You've got to die or else we'll waste away,' she tells them. Their solution: 'We'll lie down and sleep, and we won't get up again until the Judgement Day arrives.' They do; 'no one could wake them from it. Meanwhile, their mother departed, and nobody knows where she went.'

Rapunzel, meanwhile, gives herself away to her captor when – after having a metaphorically 'merry time' in the tower with her prince – she asks: 'Tell me, Mother Gothel, why are my clothes becoming too tight? They don't fit me anymore.' This was changed in later editions to remove the implications of pre-marital sex and pregnancy. In the later editions, the text was also changed to suggest that a marriage had taken place. In the original story there is no reference to such a ceremony.

The wicked stepmother is a standard evil character in the realm of the fairy tale, but as already mentioned Snow-white's stepmother was originally her mother. Similarly, Hansel and Gretel's mother became their stepmother in the later version, supposedly making it more acceptable that the heartless creature is at liberty to abandon the children in the forest. Grimm scholar Jack Zipes believes that the brothers made these changes in later editions because they 'held motherhood sacred'. The blood tie created an innate sympathy and empathy with her children, a bond that was absent in the stepmother.

Cinderella's stepsisters go to extraordinary attempts to win the prince in the original Grimms' version of the tale, slicing off parts of their feet to fit the golden slipper – to no avail, in the end, because the prince spots the blood spilling out of the shoe. 'Here's a knife,' their mother urges. 'If the slipper is still too tight for you, then cut off a piece of your foot. It will hurt a bit. But what does that matter?'

Some are tales are not only brutal but strangely surrealistic such as 'The Strange Feast', in which the Liver Sausage invites the Blood Sausage to dinner. It is like a gory version of a Hieronymus Bosch painting.

Some critics say that the deaths of the brothers' father and grandfather are the reason for the Grimms' tendency to idealize and excuse fathers, as well as the predominance of female villains in the tales, such as the wicked stepmother and stepsisters in 'Cinderella', but this disregards the fact that they were collectors, not authors, of the tales. Another possible influence is found in stories such as 'The Twelve Brothers', which mirrors the brothers' family structure of several brothers facing and overcoming opposition. Autobiographical elements exist in some of the tales, and these narratives may have been a 'quest' to replace the family life lost after their father died. Many of the sibling stories follow a simple plot where the characters lose a home, work industriously at a specific task and, in the end, find a new home.

Stories featuring a spinning motif are broadly represented in *Kinder- und Hausmärchen*. In her essay 'Tale Spinners: Submerged Voices in Grimms' Fairy Tales', (*Fairy Tales & Society*, 1986) children's literature scholar Ruth B. Bottigheimer explains that these stories reflect the degree to which spinning was crucial in the life of women in the nineteenth century and earlier. Spinning, and particularly the spinning of flax, was commonly performed in the home by women. Many stories begin by describing the occupation of a main character, as in 'There once was a miller', yet spinning is never mentioned as an occupation, probably because the brothers did not consider it an occupation. Instead, spinning was a communal activity, frequently performed in a *Spinnstube* (spinning room), a place where women most likely kept the oral traditions alive by telling stories while engaged in tedious work. In the stories, a woman's personality is often represented by her attitude toward spinning; a wise woman might be a spinster and Bottigheimer explains that the spindle was the symbol of a 'diligent, well-ordered womanhood.' In some stories, such as Rumpelstiltskin, spinning is associated with a threat; in others, spinning might be avoided by a character who is either too lazy or not accustomed to spinning because of her high social status.

By 1857 the seventh edition of *Kinder- und Hausmärchen* had been published. Changes were made over the years based on reviews stating that some of the tales were not suitable for children, and that the tales were not sufficiently German. Other amendments, apart from changing wicked mothers to wicked stepmothers, included removing any sexual references and increasing violence when punishing the villains. The books were intended as serious works of folklore, and although the brothers were not the first to publish collections of such tales, they were the first to produce a book which was based on a serious formal academic study of folklore. However, as the brothers kept revising, re-editing and toning down the tales in subsequent editions, their fairy tales made them literary superstars of the Romantic age – culminating in the famous, decidedly child-friendly 7th edition of 1857. For more than 100 years, these later revised presentations of Grimms' fairy tales have delighted and enthralled children and adults alike. The censored stories in various translations based on 1857 edition, retold in quaint picture books, now bear little resemblance to the darker more brutal versions that appeared in the Grimms' two-volume editions of 1812 and 1815. The Disney studio in particular are responsible for sugaring the pill with their cartoon versions of *Snow White* (1937) and *Cinderella* (1950) which contained light-hearted comic characters, much humour and sentimental songs – the real darkness of the originals was largely expunged.

Over the years the tales have been put to many uses. Perhaps the most bizarre concerned the Nazis' interpretation of this revered collection. In the *Kinder- und Hausmarchen*, two of the stories have a Jew as a villain and are very anti-Semitic. Hitler used these tales to justify his persecution of Jews since the Grimms' stories clearly showed that the Jews were bad people.

Two of the greatest ballet scores are based on Grimms' tales: *Cinderella* with music by Sergei Prokofiev and *Sleeping Beauty* by Tchaikovsky.

Throughout their lives the Grimm brothers were very close, despite having very different personalities. Jacob was introspective and Wilhelm was outgoing. In 1825, Wilhelm married Henriette Dorothea (Dortchen) Wild, a long-time family friend and one of a group who supplied them with stories. Jacob never married but continued to live in the household with Wilhelm and Dortchen. The brothers were more than publishers of children's books, they were academics, linguists and cultural researchers. Their contribution to German literacy earned them a place on the 1000 Deutsche Mark note, the German currency before the Euro.

Both brothers died in Berlin, but live on through their stories of princes, princesses, witches, giants and dwarfs. Even though their undertaking was designed as a serious study of folklore, the stories have been adapted in a way that not only folklorists will enjoy, but anyone who wants to be transported to a magical world where anything is possible.

Their work is still recognized today for its groundbreaking literary endeavours. The tales are internationally renowned. The poet W. H. Auden praised the collection as one of the founding works of Western culture. He said: 'It is hardly too much to say that these tales rank next to the Bible in importance. The stories, and the figures themselves, have immense vitality, partly because no punches are pulled, and also because no emotion is unrepresented.' Novelist Margaret Atwood observed that: 'everyone should possess and know Grimm's Fairy Tales – one of the great books of the world'. The film maker Terry Gilliam, whose own nightmare fairy-tale movies have a tone and subject matter in common with the Grimms' wilder stories, stated that, 'the Brothers Grimm were responsible for fairy tales that informed my life and made it as interesting, or as confused, or as wondrous as it is . . . they scared the shit out of me when I was a kid and they also gave me some of the most pleasure in life'.

Whatever magic these stories perform on young and old alike, it remains as potent today as it was when the stories were written.

Principal Characters

The Valiant Little Tailor is a quick-thinking fellow who kills seven flies scavenging his jam with one swipe, so makes a belt proclaiming 'Seven at One Blow' (suggesting that he is a valiant hero who has defeated seven powerful enemies at once) and sets out to seek his fortune. With his wily ways and bravado, he succeeds in overcoming various adversaries through using his wits and cunning, and is taken into the king's employ. He wins the hand of the princess and half the kingdom. The princess eventually realizes he is not the hero she thought but a mere tailor, a trickster rather than a champion; the king promises her to get rid of him. Forewarned, however, the tailor succeeds in terrifying the servants sent to kill him. So the tailor stays, remaining a king in his own right.

With his fame and skills gaining momentum, the tailor augments his social standing and rises from peasant 'working' class to a role in the palace and then, ultimately, becomes a king. He is clever, upbeat and confident. He uses subterfuge, manipulation and cunning to trick his adversaries. He capitalizes on others' fears and mistaken first impressions. He is fearless and finds ways to outwit any opposition, including his wife's, and to overcome whatever obstacles present themselves. He remains cheery and in good spirits throughout his many adventures.

Rumpelstiltskin Research suggests this story originated around 4,000 years ago. The Grimms included a simpler version of the tale in the first edition of their collection *Kinder- und Hausmärchen* (*Children's and Household Tales*, 1812), and then added revised versions in succeeding editions. The name Rumpelstilzchen means 'little rattle stilt', a stilt being a post or pole that provides structural support. A *rumpelstilz* is a goblin that makes noises by rattling posts and rapping on planks, not unlike a poltergeist. Using personal names and titles is well established in psychology as a means of demonstrating power and adding value – often referred to as 'the Rumpelstiltskin Principle'.

A poor miller boasts that his beautiful daughter can spin straw into gold. The king summons her to his castle and locks her in a room filled with straw. He tells her to spin all the straw into gold, or she will have to die. This happens three nights in a row. Frightened and helpless, she is rescued by a strange little man who appears each night, offers to help and duly spins away, filling all the spools with gold. First she gives him

her necklace, second her ring. On the third night, the little man makes her promise that she will give him her first child. The king marries her and a year later she has a beautiful child. When the little man arrives claim him, the queen sobs so much that he gives her three days to discover his name. When she thwarts his plans, the little fellow is so furious that he stamps his foot into the ground right up to his waist and then rips himself in two.

The Goose-Girl is virtuous, honest and true to her word. Although she is a princess, she is humble and unassuming.

Riding on her magic talking horse, Falada, en route to meet her bridegroom, a princess is bullied by her attending maid and compelled to swap roles with her. She is forced to take an oath of secrecy and is

rendered even weaker and more powerless when her mother's protective charm falls in the river. On arrival in the distant kingdom, the maid usurps the princess's royal role beside the prince while the real princess is ordered to help guard the geese. To stop Falada talking and giving the game away, the maid has this magic horse killed. The princess rescues Falada's head and has it set above the gateway where he continues to talk to her. The princess's fellow goose guard, Conrad, watches her comb her lovely hair so she persuades the wind to blow away his hat to get rid of him. Conrad refuses to herd geese with her any longer and tells the king of her strange behaviour. Ultimately, the king discovers the truth, the maid is horribly punished and the prince and the true princess are married – to reign for many years.

Rapunzel is a German word that means rampion, field salad or lamb's lettuce. A woman persuades her husband to steal some delicious rapunzel from the garden of a powerful sorceress. Desperate for more, she begs him to go back to the garden, but this time the sorceress catches him and makes the hapless fellow promise to bring her the longed-for child that his wife is carrying. The sorceress takes their beautiful little girl, names her Rapunzel, and locks her in a tower deep in the forest. The tower has neither door nor steps so the witch has to climb up Rapunzel's splendid long hair through the window at the top. Rapunzel is very lonely living in the tower on her own and longs to experience the real

world. A prince hears her sweet singing and persuades Rapunzel to let him climb her braids. They fall in love and plan to weave a silk ladder to escape. The furious witch slashes off the girl's lovely hair and dumps her in the wilderness. The prince climbs the golden hair to find the witch waiting and throws himself back down into thorns which poke out his eyes. After wandering about miserably for years, he reaches the wilderness where Rapunzel lives with the twins that she has given birth to. As her tears fall into the prince's eyes, he regains his sight and then takes her to his kingdom to lived there happily together.

Little Red Riding-Hood was included in the first edition of the Grimm collection *Kinder- und Hausmärchen* (1812). The Grimm brothers later revised the story and it reached its best-known (and somewhat tamer) version in the 1857 edition.

Little Red Riding-Hood (or Little Red Cap, named for the red hat her grandmother gave her) is a sweet little girl, courageous, affectionate and inquisitive. On the way to visit her sick grandmother with gifts of cake and wine, she meets a wolf who persuades her to leave the path and pick flowers for Grandma – giving him time to get there first and eat up the old lady. When Little Red Riding-Hood arrives, the wolf – in Grandma's clothes and bed – entices the child over and gobbles her up whole, too. A passing huntsman discovers the snoring wolf, cuts him open to rescue the two victims and then Little Red Riding-Hood fills the beast's belly with large stones. When he wakes, the wolf tries to run away but the stones are so heavy he drops down dead. All are happy: the huntsman takes home the wolf's pelt; Grandma enjoys the cake and wine; and Little Red Riding-Hood thinks how lucky she has been to escape and that she will never leave the safe path again.

Little Snow-White The Grimms completed their final revision of the story in 1854. Later versions often omit the Queen's eating what she believes to be Snow White's organs – possibly emanating from Slavic mythology about witches eating human hearts. The princess's origins may derive from Maria Sophia Margarethe Catharina, Baroness von Erthal, born in Lohr in 1725; her domineering stepmother was said to use a magic mirror – still on view today in Lohr Castle's Spessart Museum.

A queen has a beautiful daughter, with skin as white as snow, lips as red as blood and ebony black hair. When her mother dies, the king marries a beautiful but evil, vain woman, whose magic mirror constantly reassures her that she is the fairest of all. One day the mirror announces that Snow-White is more beautiful. The queen commands a huntsman to kill Snow-White and bring back the child's lungs and liver. The huntsman takes pity on her and instead kills a young boar, taking its lungs and liver back to the queen. Snow-White flees through the forest until she reaches the cottage of the seven dwarfs who are at work digging for ore. She becomes their great friend and helper, cooking, keeping house and looking after them all. She is shown to be humble and unassuming, a hard worker, kind and sweet-natured. When the mirror tells the queen that her step-daughter is still alive, she makes three attempts to kill her, finally with a poisoned apple which does appear to succeed. The heartbroken dwarfs place Snow-White in a glass coffin where she remains until rescued and awakened by a handsome prince. When Snow-White's stepmother arrives at the wedding feast she is forced to dance in red-hot iron shoes until she falls down dead.

Little Briar Rose is the Grimm Brothers' version of Sleeping Beauty. Some translations call the princess Rosamond. She is described as beautiful, well-behaved, friendly and intelligent; everyone loves her. A frog tells the queen that she will have the child she so longs for. Within a year the

queen has a beautiful baby girl and a great celebration is held. Wise women present the child with magic gifts but the angry thirteenth uninvited one pronounces that: 'In the princess's fifteenth year she shall prick herself with a spindle and fall over dead.' The twelfth wise woman softens the curse, saying that the princess will not die but, instead, will sleep for a hundred years. The king orders all spindles to be burned but on her fifteenth birthday the princess discovers an old woman with a spindle at the top of an ancient tower and pricks her finger on the needle. She falls into a in a deep sleep, as does every living creature in the castle, which is soon hidden by the thorn hedge that grows around. Many years later, a prince broaches the thorn hedge; its beautiful flowers separate to let him through. He wakes the princess with a kiss and then, as everyone remerges from slumber, he marries her and they live happily ever after.

Cinderella's mother dies and her father remarries. The new wife treats Cinderella as a drudge. She is scorned by her stepmother and stepsisters and made to do all the hard work and to sleep in the cinders by the kitchen fire. Cinderella is hardworking and obedient; despite being treated so badly, she remains humble and kind. She is pious and good; her dying mother had told her to pray faithfully.

She desperately wants to go to the festival at the king's castle during which the prince will choose a bride. Despite her stepsisters' scorn, she gets there in the end, with the help of a magic hazel-tree together with various birds who help with her impossible tasks and provide ever more glorious gowns and slippers for three days in a row. Everyone at the castle is astonished at Cinderella's sweet beauty and she looks so unlike her former servant self that no one recognizes her. She dances with the prince and captures his heart but runs away as night approaches. The prince pursues her, but Cinderella hides in a pigeon coop and up a pear tree. She loses her shoe on the third night because the stairway has been smeared with pitch; this eventually enables the prince to track her down so that he can marry her.

Hansel and Gretel are two smart, resilient and courageous young children whose mother has died. During a time of famine, their heartless stepmother makes their poor woodcutter father take his children into the woods and leave them there to die. Hansel marks their way with white pebbles and he and Gretel are able to follow the trail home. The next day Hansel is unable to collect pebbles so marks their trail with bread crumbs, but the birds eat these so they are lost. The hungry children come across a gingerbread house; when they try to eat the roof, a hideous old witch emerges and lures them inside. She throws Hansel into a cage and feeds him, to fatten him up. She makes Gretel her slave.

Clever Hansel sticks out a bone when the semi-blind witch tests his finger she is repeatedly fooled into thinking Hansel is still too thin to eat. Eventually she decides to eat him anyway – and Gretel too – so she heats up the oven. Gretel manages to shove her into the oven and then frees Hansel. They discover the witch's treasure and escape. Their stepmother has died but their father is delighted to see them safe and sound, and they all live happily ever after with the witch's wealth.

Some commentators believe that the mother or stepmother and the witch are metaphorically the same woman.

A Brothers Grimm Timeline

	1785	**1786**	**1806**	**1812**

Grimm Brothers

Jacob Ludwig
Carl Grimm born
Hanau, Germany

Wilhelm Carl
Grimm born
Hanau, Germany

Volume 1 of *Kinder-
und Hausmärchen*
published

Jacob and Wilhelm
begin to collect folk
tales; *The Boy's Magic
Horn* published

UK and Ireland

First issue of the
*Daily Universal
Register*, later *The
Times*, published
in London

*The Marriage of
Figaro* premieres
in Vienna

Admiral Lord Nelson
is buried in St Paul's

John Stuart Mill born

Charles Dickens
born

Europe

First air crossing of
the English Channel
in a hydrogen
gas balloon

First ascent
of Mont Blanc

(1789)
French Revolution
begins

(1805)
Battle of Trafalgar

Napoleon crowned
king of Italy

Napoleon's invasion
of Russia begins

Rest of the World

Benjamin Franklin
invents bifocal lenses

(1787)
George Washington
presides over
convention which
creates new US
Constitution

(1805)
Lewis and Clark
reach the Pacific

War of 1812 when
US declares war
against Britain

	1785	**1786**	**1806**	**1812**

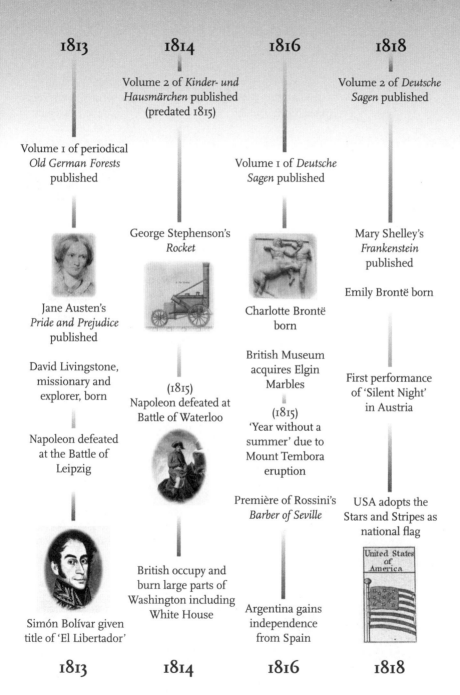

1813

Volume 1 of periodical
Old German Forests
published

Jane Austen's
Pride and Prejudice
published

David Livingstone,
missionary and
explorer, born

Napoleon defeated
at the Battle of
Leipzig

Simón Bolívar given
title of 'El Libertador'

1813

1814

Volume 2 of *Kinder- und
Hausmärchen* published
(predated 1815)

George Stephenson's
Rocket

(1815)
Napoleon defeated at
Battle of Waterloo

British occupy and
burn large parts of
Washington including
White House

1814

1816

Volume 1 of *Deutsche
Sagen* published

Charlotte Brontë
born

British Museum
acquires Elgin
Marbles

(1815)
'Year without a
summer' due to
Mount Tembora
eruption

Première of Rossini's
Barber of Seville

Argentina gains
independence
from Spain

1816

1818

Volume 2 of *Deutsche
Sagen* published

Mary Shelley's
Frankenstein
published

Emily Brontë born

First performance
of 'Silent Night'
in Austria

USA adopts the
Stars and Stripes as
national flag

1818

Grimm Brothers

1819

1823
First edition of
Grimm's Fary Tales
published in London

1825

1829
Jacob and Wilhelm
become professors
at the University
of Göttingen

UK and Ireland

Jacob and Wilhelm
receive honorary
doctorates from
the University of
Marburg

Wilhelm marries
Henriette
Dorothea Wild

William Webb Ellis
invents rugby

Panic of 1825,
first modern stock
market crash

Scotland Yard
formed in London

Peterloo Massacre in
Manchester

Stockton and
Darlington railway
opens

Europe

(1820)
Astronomical Society
of London

Decembrist uprising
against Tsar Nicholas
I in Russia

(1833)
Slavery abolished
in Britain and its
colonies

German astonomer
discovers Great
Comet of 1819

Rest of the World

Explorer James
Weddell reaches
further south than
any previous ship; a
record held for more
than 80 years

(1835)
HMS *Beagle* lands
in the Galapagos
Islands with Charles
Darwin on board

Sir Stamford Raffles
founds trading settlement
in Singapore

Thomas Kensett and
Ezra Daggett patent
method of storing
food in tin cans

1819

1823

1825

1829

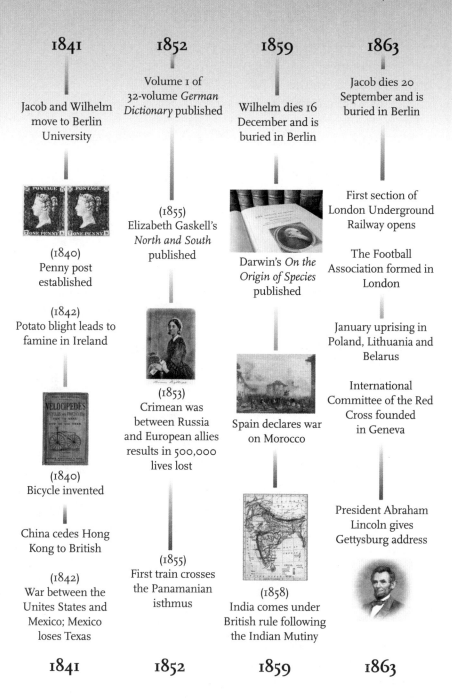

1841

Jacob and Wilhelm move to Berlin University

(1840)
Penny post established

(1842)
Potato blight leads to famine in Ireland

(1840)
Bicycle invented

China cedes Hong Kong to British

(1842)
War between the Unites States and Mexico; Mexico loses Texas

1852

Volume 1 of 32-volume *German Dictionary* published

(1855)
Elizabeth Gaskell's *North and South* published

(1853)
Crimean was between Russia and European allies results in 500,000 lives lost

(1855)
First train crosses the Panamanian isthmus

1859

Wilhelm dies 16 December and is buried in Berlin

Darwin's *On the Origin of Species* published

Spain declares war on Morocco

(1858)
India comes under British rule following the Indian Mutiny

1863

Jacob dies 20 September and is buried in Berlin

First section of London Underground Railway opens

The Football Association formed in London

January uprising in Poland, Lithuania and Belarus

International Committee of the Red Cross founded in Geneva

President Abraham Lincoln gives Gettysburg address

1841   1852   1859   1863

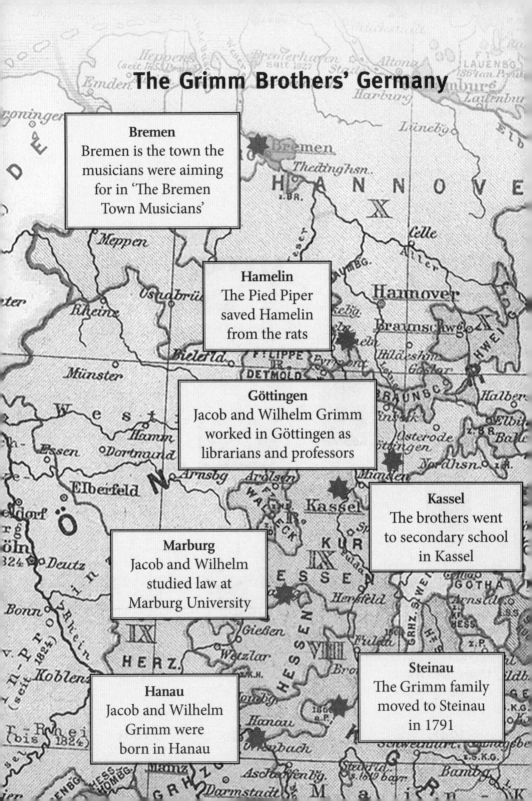

The Grimm Brothers' Germany

Bremen
Bremen is the town the musicians were aiming for in 'The Bremen Town Musicians'

Hamelin
The Pied Piper saved Hamelin from the rats

Göttingen
Jacob and Wilhelm Grimm worked in Göttingen as librarians and professors

Kassel
The brothers went to secondary school in Kassel

Marburg
Jacob and Wilhelm studied law at Marburg University

Hanau
Jacob and Wilhelm Grimm were born in Hanau

Steinau
The Grimm family moved to Steinau in 1791

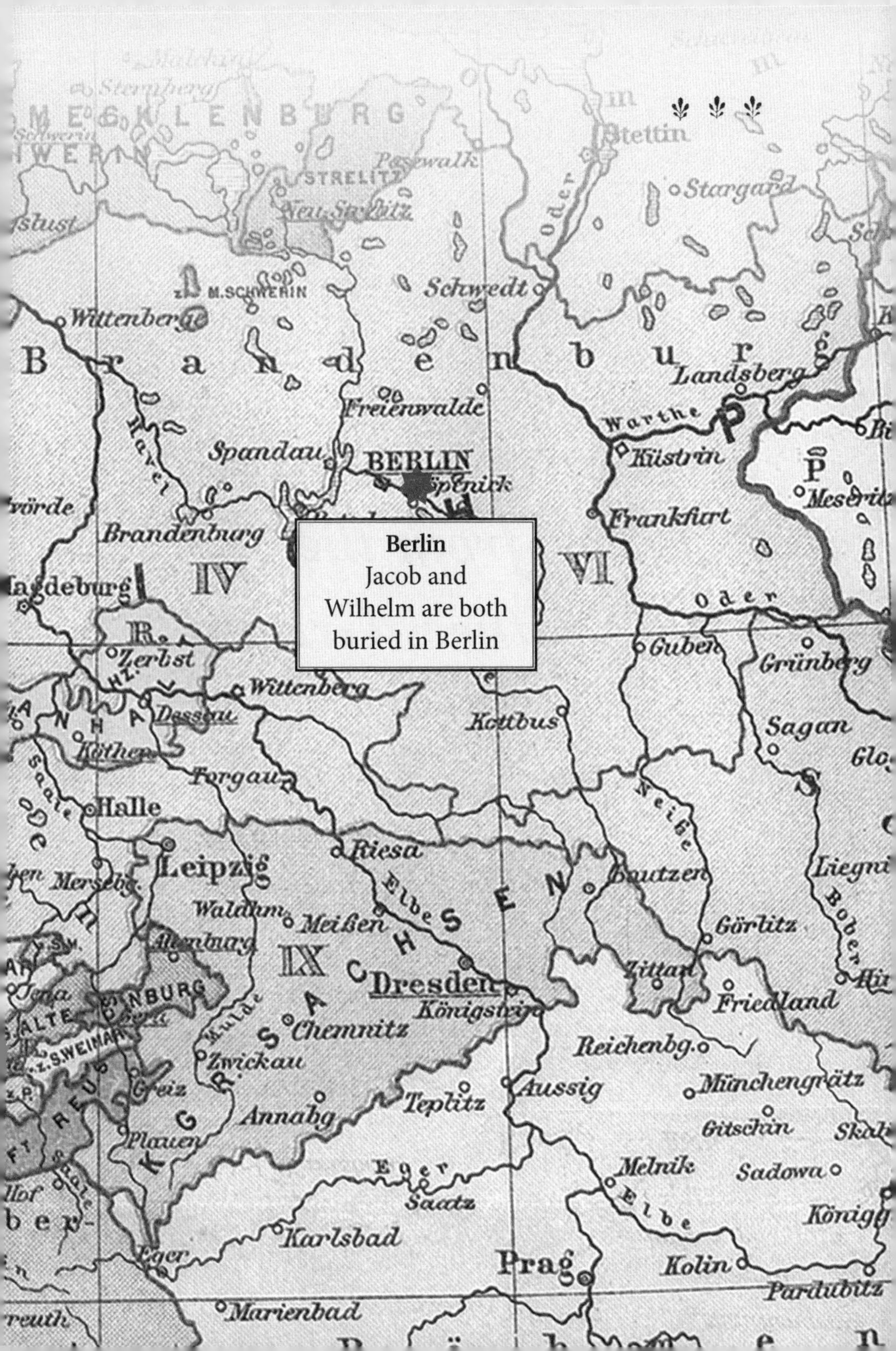

Berlin
Jacob and
Wilhelm are both
buried in Berlin

Classic Fairy Tales from the Brothers Grimm

The Valiant Little Tailor

One summer's morning a little tailor was sitting on his table by the window; he was in good spirits and sewed with all his might. A peasant woman came down the street crying, 'Good jams, cheap! Good jams, cheap!' This rang pleasantly in the tailor's ears; he stretched his delicate head out of the window, and called, 'Come up here, dear woman; here you will get rid of your goods.' The woman came up the three steps to the tailor with her heavy basket, and he made her unpack the whole of the pots for him. He inspected all of them, lifted them up, put his nose to them, and at length said, 'The jam seems to me to be good, so weigh me out four ounces, dear woman, and if it is a quarter of a pound that is of no consequence.' The woman, who had hoped to find a good sale, gave him what he desired, but went away quite angry and grumbling.

'Now, God bless the jam to my use,' cried the little tailor, 'and give me health and strength;' as he brought the bread out of the cupboard, cut himself a piece right across the loaf and spread the jam over it. 'This won't taste bitter,' said he, 'but I will just finish the jacket before I take a bite.' He laid the bread near him, sewed on, and in his joy, made bigger and bigger stitches. In the meantime the smell of the sweet jam rose to the wall, where the flies were sitting in great numbers, that they were attracted and descended on it in hosts.

'Hola! who invited you?' said the little tailor, and drove the unbidden guests away. The flies, however, did not understand and would not be turned away, but came back again in ever-increasing companies. The little tailor at last lost all patience, and got a bit of cloth from the hole under his work-table, and saying, 'Wait, and I will give it to you,' struck it mercilessly on them. When he drew it away and counted, there lay before him no fewer than seven, dead and with legs stretched out. He

1

could not help admiring his own bravery. 'The whole town shall know of this!' And the little tailor hastened to cut himself a sash, stitched it, and embroidered on it in large letters, 'Seven at one stroke!' 'Not just the town!' he continued, 'the whole world shall hear of it!' and his heart wagged with joy like a lamb's tail.

The tailor put on the sash, and resolved to go forth into the world, because he thought his workshop was too small for his valour. Before he went away, he searched in the house to see if there was anything which he could take with him but found nothing but an old cheese, which he put in his pocket. In front of the door he saw a bird which had caught itself in the thicket. It went into his pocket with the cheese. Now he took to the road boldly, and as he was light and nimble, he felt no fatigue.

The road led him up a mountain, and when he had reached the highest point of it, there sat a powerful giant looking about him quite comfortably. The little tailor went bravely up, spoke to him, and said, 'Good day, comrade, so thou art sitting there overlooking the wide-spread world! I am just on my way thither, and want to try my luck. Have you any inclination to go with me?'

The giant looked contemptuously at the tailor, and said, 'You ragamuffin! You miserable creature!'

'Oh, indeed?' answered the little tailor, and unbuttoned his coat, and showed the giant the sash, 'There you may read what kind of a man I am!'

The giant read, 'Seven at one stroke,' and thought that they had been men whom the tailor had killed, and began to feel a little respect for the tiny fellow. Nevertheless, he wished to try him first, and took a stone in his hand and squeezed it together so that water dropped out of it. 'Do the same,' said the giant, 'if you have the strength?'

'Is that all?' said the tailor, 'that is child's play with us!' and put his hand into his pocket, brought out the soft cheese, and pressed it until the liquid ran out of it. 'Faith, said he, 'that was a little better, wasn't it?'

The giant did not know what to say, and could not believe it of the little man. Then the giant picked up a stone and threw it so high that the eye could scarcely follow it.

'Now, little mite of a man, do that.'

'Well thrown,' said the tailor, 'but after all the stone came down to earth again; I will throw you one which shall never come back at all.' And he put his hand into his pocket, took out the bird, and threw it into the air. The bird, delighted with its liberty, rose, flew away and did not come back.

'How does that shot please you, comrade?' asked the tailor.

'You can certainly throw,' said the giant, 'but now we will see if you are able to carry anything properly.'

He took the little tailor to a mighty oak tree which lay felled on the ground, and said, 'If thou are strong enough, help me to carry the tree out of the forest.'

'Readily,' answered the little man; 'you take the trunk on your shoulders, and I will raise up the branches and twigs; after all, they are the heaviest.' The giant took the trunk on his shoulder, but the tailor seated himself on a branch, and the giant who could not look round, had to carry away the whole tree, and the little tailor into the bargain: he behind, was quite merry and happy, and whistled the song, 'Three tailors rode forth from the gate,' as if carrying the tree were child's play. The giant, after he had dragged the heavy burden part of the way, could go no further, and cried, 'Hark you, I shall have to let the tree fall!' The tailor sprang nimbly down, seized the tree with both arms as if he had been carrying it, and said to the giant, 'You are such a great fellow, and yet cannot even carry the tree!'

They went on together, and as they passed a cherry-tree, the giant laid hold of the top of the tree where the ripest fruit was hanging, bent it down, gave it into the tailor's hand, and bade him eat. But the little tailor was much too weak to hold the tree, and when the giant let it go, it sprang back again, and the tailor was hurried into the air with it. When he had fallen down again without injury, the giant said, 'What is this? Are you not strong enough to hold the weak twig?'

'There is no lack of strength,' answered the little tailor. 'Do you think that could be anything to a man who has struck down seven at one blow? I leapt over the tree because the huntsmen are shooting down there in the thicket. Jump as I did, if you can do it.'

The giant made the attempt, but could not get over the tree, and remained hanging in the branches, so that in this also the tailor kept the upper hand.

'If you are such a valiant fellow,' said the giant, 'come with me into our cavern and spend the night with us.' The little tailor was willing, and followed him. When they went into the cave, other giants were sitting by the fire, and each of them had a roasted sheep in his hand and was eating it. The little tailor looked round and thought, 'It is much more spacious here than in my workshop.' The giant showed him a bed, and said he was to lie down in it and sleep. The bed, however, was too big for the little tailor; he did not lie down in it, but crept into a corner. When it was midnight, and the giant thought that the little tailor was lying in a sound sleep, he got up, took a great iron bar, cut through the bed with one blow, and thought he had given the grasshopper his finishing stroke. With the earliest dawn the giants went into the forest, and had quite forgotten the little tailor, when all at once he walked up to them quite merrily and boldly. The giants were terrified, they were afraid that he would strike them all dead, and ran away in a great hurry.

The little tailor went onwards, always following his own pointed nose. After he had walked for a long time, he came to the courtyard of a royal palace, and as he felt weary, he lay down on the grass and fell asleep. While he lay there, the people came and inspected him on all sides, and read on his sash, 'Seven at one stroke.'

'Ah,' said they, 'What is a great warrior doing here in a time of peace? He must be a mighty lord.' They went and announced him to the king, and gave it as their opinion that if war should break out, this would be a weighty and useful man who ought on no account to be allowed to depart. The counsel pleased the King, and he sent one of his courtiers to the little tailor to offer him military service when he awoke. The ambassador remained standing by the sleeper, waited until he stretched his limbs and opened his eyes, and then conveyed to him this proposal.

'I have come here for this very reason,' the tailor replied. "I am ready to enter the King's service.' He was therefore honourably received and a special dwelling was assigned him.

The soldiers, however, were set against the little tailor, and wished him a thousand miles away.

'What is to be the end of this?' they said among themselves. 'If we quarrel with him, and he strikes about him, seven of us will fall at every blow; not one of us can stand against him.' They came therefore to a decision, went in a body to the King, and begged for their dismissal. 'We are not prepared,' said they, 'to stay with a man who kills seven at one stroke.'

The King was sorry that for the sake of one he should lose all his faithful servants, wished that he had never set eyes on the tailor, and would willingly have been rid of him again. But he did not venture to give dismiss the tailor, for he dreaded lest he should strike him and all his people dead, and place himself on the royal throne. He thought about it for a long time, and at last had an idea. He told the little tailor that as he was such a great warrior, he had one request to make to him. In a forest of his country lived two giants who caused great mischief with their robbing, murdering, ravaging, and burning, and no one could approach them without putting himself in danger of death. If the tailor conquered and killed these two giants, he would give him his only daughter to wife, and half of his kingdom as a dowry, likewise one hundred horsemen should go with him to assist him.

'That would indeed be a fine thing for a man like me!' thought the little tailor. 'One is not offered a beautiful princess and half a kingdom every day of one's life!' 'Oh, yes,' he replied, 'I will soon subdue the giants, and do not require the help of the hundred horsemen to do it; he who can hit seven with one blow has no need to be afraid of two.'

The little tailor went forth, and the hundred horsemen followed him. When he came to the outskirts of the forest, he said to his followers, 'Just stay waiting here, I alone will soon finish off the giants.' Then he bounded into the forest and looked about right and left. After a while he perceived both giants. They lay sleeping under a tree, and snored so that the branches waved up and down. The little tailor, not idle, gathered two pocketsful of stones, and with these climbed up the tree. When he was half-way up, he slipped down by a branch, until he sat just above the sleepers, and then let one stone after another fall on the breast of one of the giants. For a long time the giant felt nothing, but at last he awoke, pushed his comrade, and said, 'Why are you knocking me?'

'You must be dreaming,' said the other, 'I am not knocking you.' They lay down to sleep again, and then the tailor threw a stone down on the second.

'What is the meaning of this?' cried the other. 'Why are you pelting me?'

'I am not pelting you,' answered the first, growling. They disputed about it for a time, but as they were weary they let the matter rest, and their eyes closed once more. The little tailor began his game again, picked out the biggest stone, and threw it with all his might on the breast of the first giant.

'That is too bad!' cried he, and sprang up like a madman, and pushed his companion against the tree until it shook. The other paid him back in the same coin, and they got into such a rage that they tore up trees and fought each other so long, that at last they both fell down dead on the ground at the same time. Then the little tailor leapt down.

'It is a lucky thing,' said he, 'that they did not tear up the tree on which I was sitting, or I should have had to spring on to another like a squirrel; but we tailors are nimble.'

He drew out his sword and gave each of them a couple of thrusts in the breast, and then went out to the horsemen and said, 'The work is done; I have given both of them their finishing stroke, but it was hard work! They tore up trees in their sore need, and defended themselves with them, but all that is to no purpose when a man like myself comes, who can kill seven at one blow.'

'But are you not wounded?' asked the horsemen.

'You need not concern yourself about that,' answered the tailor. 'They have not bent one hair of mine.'

The horsemen would not believe him, and rode into the forest; there they found the giants swimming in their blood, and all round about lay the torn-up trees.

The little tailor demanded of the King the promised reward; he, however, repented of his promise, and again bethought himself how he could get rid of the hero.

'Before you receive my daughter, and the half of my kingdom," said the king, 'you must perform one more heroic deed. In the forest roams a unicorn which does great harm, and you must catch it first.'

'I fear one unicorn still less than two giants. Seven at one blow, is my kind of affair.'

He took a rope and an axe with him, went into the forest, and again bade those who were sent with him to wait outside. The unicorn soon came towards him, and rushed directly on the tailor, as if it would spit him on his horn without more ceremony.

'Softly, softly; it can't be done as quickly as that,' said he, and stood still and waited until the animal was quite close, and then sprang nimbly behind the tree. The unicorn ran against the tree with all its strength, and struck its horn so fast in the trunk that it had not strength enough to draw it out again, and thus it was caught.

'Now, I have got the bird,' said the tailor, and came out from behind the tree and put the rope round its neck, and then with his axe he hewed the horn out of the tree, and when all was ready he led the beast away and took it to the King.

The King still would not give him the promised reward, and made a third demand. Before the wedding the tailor was to catch him a wild boar that made great havoc in the forest, and the huntsmen should give him their help.

'Willingly,' said the tailor, 'that is child's play!'

He did not take the huntsmen with him into the forest, and they were well pleased that he did not, for the wild boar had several times received them in such a manner that they had no inclination to lie in wait for him. When the boar perceived the tailor, it ran on him with foaming mouth and whetted tusks, and was about to throw him to the ground, but the active hero sprang into a chapel which was near, and up to the window at once, and in one bound out again. The boar ran in after him, but the tailor ran round outside and shut the door behind it, and then the raging beast, which was much too heavy and awkward to leap out of the window, was caught. The little tailor called the huntsmen thither that they might see the prisoner with their own eyes.

The hero went to the king, who was now obliged to keep his promise whether he liked it or not, so gave the tailor his daughter and the half of his kingdom. Had he known that it was no warlike hero, but a little tailor who was standing before him, it would have gone to his heart still more than it did. The wedding was held with great magnificence and small joy, and out of a tailor a king was made.

After some time the young princess heard her husband say in his dreams at night, 'Boy, make me the doublet, and patch the pantaloons, or else I will rap the yard-measure over your ears.' Then she discovered in what state of life the young lord had been born, and next morning complained of her wrongs to her father, and begged him to help her to get rid of her husband, who was nothing else but a tailor. The King comforted her and said, 'Leave your bedroom door open tonight, and my servants shall stand outside, and when he has fallen asleep shall go in, bind him, and take him on board a ship which shall carry him away.' The woman was satisfied with this; but the King's armour-bearer, who had heard all, was friendly with the young lord, and informed him of the whole plot.

'I'll put a screw into that business,' said the little tailor. At night he went to bed with his wife at the usual time, and when she thought that he had fallen asleep, she got up, opened the door, and then lay down again.

The little tailor, who was only pretending to be asleep, began to cry out in a clear voice, 'Boy, make me the doublet and patch me the pantaloons, or I will rap the yard-measure over thine ears. I smote seven at one blow. I killed two giants, I brought away one unicorn and caught a wild boar, and am I to fear those who are standing outside the room?'

When these men heard the tailor speaking thus, they were overcome by a great dread, and ran as if the wild huntsman were behind them, and none of them would venture anything further against him. So the little tailor was a king and remained one, to the end of his life.

Rumpelstiltskin

Once upon a time there was a miller who was poor, but who had a beautiful daughter. Now it happened that he got into a conversation with the king, and to make an impression on him he said, 'I have a daughter who can spin straw into gold.'

The king said to the miller, 'That is an art that I really like. If your daughter is as skillful as you say, then bring her to my castle tomorrow, and I will put her to the test.'

When the girl was brought to him he led her into a room that was entirely filled with straw. Giving her a spinning wheel and a reel, he said, 'Get to work now. Spin all night, and if by morning you have not spun this straw into gold, then you will have to die.' Then he himself locked the room, and she was there all alone.

The poor miller's daughter sat there, and for her life she did not know what to do. She had no idea how to spin straw into gold. She became more and more afraid, and finally began to cry.

Then suddenly the door opened. A little man stepped inside and said, 'Good evening, Mistress Miller, why are you crying so?'

'Oh,' answered the girl, 'I am supposed to spin straw into gold, and I do not know how to do it.'

The little man said, 'What will you give me if I spin it for you?'

'My necklace,' said the girl.

The little man took the necklace, sat down before the spinning wheel, and whir, whir, whir, three times pulled, and the spool was full. Then he put another one on, and whir, whir, whir, three times pulled, and the second one was full as well. So it went until morning, and then all the straw was spun, and all the spools were filled with gold.

At sunrise the king came, and when he saw the gold he was surprised and happy, but his heart became even more greedy for gold. He had the miller's daughter taken to another room filled with straw. It was even larger, and he ordered her to spin it in one night, if she valued her life.

The girl did not know what to do, and she cried. Once again the door opened, and the little man appeared. He said, 'What will you give me if I spin the straw into gold for you?'

'The ring from my finger,' answered the girl.

The little man took the ring, and began once again to whir with the spinning wheel. By morning he had spun all the straw into glistening gold. The king was happy beyond measure when he saw it, but he still did not have his fill of gold. He had the miller's daughter taken to a still larger room filled with straw, and said, 'Tonight you must spin this too. If you succeed you shall become my wife.' He thought, 'Even if she is only a miller's daughter, I will not find a richer wife in all the world.'

When the girl was alone the little man returned for a third time. He said, 'What will you give me if I spin the straw this time?'

'I have nothing more that I could give you,' answered the girl.

'Then promise me, after you are queen, your first child.'

'Who knows what will happen,' thought the miller's daughter, and not knowing what else to do, she promised the little man what he demanded. In return the little man once again spun the straw into gold.

When in the morning the king came and found everything just as he desired, he married her, and the beautiful miller's daughter became queen.

A year later she brought a beautiful child to the world. She thought no more about the little man, but suddenly he appeared in her room and said, 'Now give me that which you promised.'

The queen took fright and offered the little man all the wealth of the kingdom if he would let her keep the child, but the little man said, 'No. Something living is dearer to me than all the treasures of the world.'

Then the queen began lamenting and crying so much that the little man took pity on her and said, 'I will give you three days' time. If by then you know my name, then you shall keep your child.'

The queen spent the entire night thinking of all the names she had ever heard. Then she sent a messenger into the country to inquire far and wide what other names there were. When the little man returned the next day she began with Kaspar, Melchior, Balzer, and said in order all the names she knew. After each one the little man said, 'That is not my name.'

The second day she sent inquiries into the neighbourhood as to what names people had. She recited the most unusual and most curious names to the little man: 'Is your name perhaps Beastrib? Or Muttoncalf? Or Legstring?'

But he always answered, 'That is not my name.'

On the third day the messenger returned and said, 'I have not been able to find a single new name, but when I was approaching a high mountain in the corner of the woods, there where the fox and the hare say goodnight, I saw a little house. A fire was burning in front of the house, and an altogether comical little man was jumping around the fire, hopping on one leg and calling out:

> 'Today I'll bake; tomorrow I'll brew,
> Then I'll fetch the queen's new child, too;
> It is good that no one knows my game,
> And that Rumpelstiltskin is my name.'

You can imagine how happy the queen was when she heard that name. Soon afterward the little man came in and asked, 'Now, Madame Queen, what is my name?'

She first asked, 'Is your name Kunz?'

'No.'

'Is your name Heinz?'

'No.'

'Is your name perhaps Rumpelstiltskin?'

'The devil told you that! The devil told you that!' shouted the little man, and with anger he stomped his right foot so hard into the ground that he fell in up to his waist. Then with both hands he took hold of his left foot and ripped himself up the middle in two.

Old Sultan

A farmer once had a faithful dog called Sultan, who had grown old and lost all his teeth, so that he could no longer hold anything tight in his mouth. One day the farmer was standing with his wife before the house-door, and said, 'To-morrow I intend to shoot Old Sultan, he is no longer of any use.'

His wife, who felt pity for the faithful beast, answered, 'He has served us so long, and been so faithful, that we might well give him his keep.'

'Eh! what?' said the man. 'You are not very sharp. He has not a tooth left in his mouth, and not a thief is afraid of him; now he may be off. If he has served us, he has had good feeding for it.'

The poor dog, who was lying stretched out in the sun not far off, had heard everything, and was sorry that the morrow was to be his last day. He had a good friend, the wolf, and he crept out in the evening into the forest to him, and complained of the fate that awaited him.

'Don't worry,' said the wolf, 'I will help you out of your trouble. I have thought of something. Tomorrow, early in the morning, your master is going with his wife to make hay, and they will take their little child with them, for no one will be left behind in the house. When they are working, they are used to lay the child under the hedge in the shade; you lay yourself there too, just as if you wished to guard it. Then I will come out of the wood, and carry off the child. You must rush swiftly after me, as if you would seize it again from me. I will let it fall, and you will take it back to its parents, who will think that you have saved it, and will be far too grateful to do you any harm; on the contrary, you will be in high favour, and they will never let you want for anything again.'

The plan pleased the dog, and it was carried out just as it was arranged. The father screamed when he saw the wolf running across the field with his child, but when Old Sultan brought it back, then he was full of joy, and stroked him and said, 'Not a hair of yours shall be hurt, you shall eat my bread free as long as you live.'

And to his wife he said, 'Go home at once and make Old Sultan some bread-sop that he will not have to bite, and bring the pillow out of my bed, I will give him that to lie upon.'

Henceforth Old Sultan was as well off as he could wish to be.

Soon afterwards the wolf visited him, and was pleased that everything had succeeded so well.

'But, my friend,' said he, 'you will just wink an eye if, when I have a chance, I carry off one of your master's fat sheep.'

'Don't be too sure of that,' answered the dog. 'I will remain true to my master; I cannot agree to that.'

The wolf, who thought that Old Sultan could not really mean that, came creeping about in the night and was going to take away the sheep. But the farmer, to whom the faithful Sultan had told the wolf's plan, caught him and dressed his hide soundly with the flail. The wolf had to back off, but he cried out to the dog:

'Just you wait, you scoundrel, you shall pay for this.'

The next morning the wolf sent the boar to challenge the dog to come out into the forest so that they might settle the affair. Old Sultan could find no one to stand by him but a cat with only three legs, and as they went out together the poor cat limped along, and at the same time stretched out her tail into the air with pain.

The wolf and his friend were already on the spot appointed, but when they saw their enemy coming they thought that he was bringing a sabre with him, for they mistook the outstretched tail of the cat for one. And when the poor beast hopped on its three legs, they could only think every time that it was picking up a stone to throw at them. So they were both afraid; the wild boar crept into the under-brush and the wolf jumped up a tree.

The dog and the cat, when they came up, wondered that there was no one to be seen. The wild boar, however, had not been able to hide himself altogether; and one of his ears was still to be seen. While the cat was looking carefully about, the boar moved his ear; the cat, who thought it was a mouse moving there, jumped upon it and bit it hard. The boar made a fearful noise and ran away, crying out:

'The guilty one is up in the tree.'

The dog and cat looked up and saw the wolf, who was ashamed of having shown himself so timid, and made friends again with the dog.

Snow-White and Rose-Red

There was once a poor widow who lived in a lonely cottage. In front of the cottage was a garden with two rose-trees, one of which bore white and the other red roses. She had two children who were like the two rose-trees, and one was called Snow-White, and the other Rose-Red. They were as good and happy, as busy and cheerful as ever two children in the world were, only Snow-White was more quiet and gentle than Rose-Red. Rose-Red liked better to run about in the meadows and fields seeking flowers and catching butterflies; but Snow-White sat at home with her mother, and helped her with her house-work, or read to her when the work was done.

The two children were so fond of each another that they always held each other by the hand when they went out together, and when Snow-White said, 'We will not leave each other,' Rose-Red answered, 'Never so long as we live,' and their mother would add, 'What one has she must share with the other.'

They often ran about the forest alone and gathered red berries, and no beasts did them any harm, but came close to them trustfully. The little hare would eat a cabbage-leaf out of their hands, the roe deer grazed by their side, the stag leapt merrily by them, and the birds sat still upon the boughs, and sang whatever they knew. No mishap overtook them; if they had stayed too late in the forest, and night came on, they laid themselves down near one another upon the moss, and slept until morning came, and their mother knew this and had no distress on their account.

Once when they had spent the night in the wood and the dawn had roused them, they saw a beautiful child in a shining white dress sitting near them. He got up and looked quite kindly at them, but said nothing and went away into the forest. And when they looked round they found that they had been sleeping quite close to a precipice, and would certainly have fallen into it in the darkness if they had gone only a few paces further. And their mother told them that it must have been the angel who watches over good children.

Snow-White and Rose-Red kept their mother's little cottage so neat that it was a pleasure to look inside it. In the summer Rose-Red took care of the house, and every morning laid a wreath of flowers by her mother's bed before she awoke, in which was a rose from each tree. In the winter Snow-White lit the fire and hung the kettle to boil. The kettle was of copper and shone like gold, so brightly was it polished. In the evening, when the snowflakes fell, the mother said, 'Go, Snow-White, and bolt the door,' and then they sat round the hearth, and the mother took her spectacles and read aloud out of a large book, and the two girls listened as they sat and span. And close by them lay a lamb upon the floor, and behind them upon a perch sat a white dove with its head hidden beneath its wings.

One evening, as they were thus sitting comfortably together, someone knocked at the door as if he wished to be let in. The mother said, 'Quick, Rose-Red, open the door, it must be a traveller who is seeking shelter.' Rose-Red went and pushed back the bolt, thinking that it was a poor man, but it was not; it was a bear that stretched his broad, black head within the door.

Rose-Red screamed and sprang back, the lamb bleated, the dove fluttered, and Snow-White hid herself behind her mother's bed. But the bear began to speak and said, 'Do not be afraid, I will do you no harm! I am half-frozen, and only want to warm myself a little.'

'Poor bear,' said the mother. 'Lie down by the fire, only take care that you do not burn your coat.' Then she cried, 'Snow-White, Rose-Red, come out, the bear will do you no harm, he means well.' So they both came out, and by-and-by the lamb and dove came nearer, and were not afraid of him. The bear said, 'Here, children, knock the snow out of my coat a little;' so they brought the broom and swept the bear's hide clean; and he stretched himself by the fire and growled contentedly and comfortably. It was not long before they grew quite at home, and played tricks with their clumsy guest. They tugged his hair with their hands, put their feet upon his back and rolled him about, or they took a hazel-switch and beat him, and when he growled they laughed. But the bear took it all in good part, only when they were too rough he called out, 'Leave me alive, children,

'Snowy-white, Rosy-red,
Will you beat your lover dead?'

When it was bed-time, and the others went to bed, the mother said to the bear, 'You can lie there by the hearth, and then you will be safe from the cold and the bad weather.' As soon as day dawned the two children let him out, and he trotted across the snow into the forest.

The bear came every evening at the same time, laid himself down by the hearth, and let the children amuse themselves with him as much as they liked; and they got so used to him that the doors were never fastened until their black friend had arrived.

When spring had come and all outside was green, the bear said one morning to Snow-White, 'Now I must go away, and cannot come back for the whole summer.'

'Where are you going, then, dear bear?' asked Snow-White. 'I must go into the forest and guard my treasures from the wicked dwarfs. In the winter, when the earth is frozen hard, they are obliged to stay below and cannot work their way through; but now, when the sun has thawed and warmed the earth, they break through it, and come out to pry and steal; and what once gets into their hands, and in their caves, does not easily see daylight again.'

Snow-White was quite sorry for his going away, and as she unbolted the door for him, and the bear was hurrying out, he caught against the bolt and a piece of his hairy coat was torn off, and it seemed to Snow-White as if she had seen gold shining through it, but she was not sure about it. The bear ran away quickly, and was soon out of sight behind the trees.

A short time afterwards the mother sent her children into the forest to get firewood. There they found a big tree which lay felled on the ground, and close by the trunk something was jumping backwards and forwards in the grass, but they could not make out what it was. When they came nearer they saw a dwarf with an old withered face and a long white beard a yard long. The end of the beard was caught in a crevice of the tree, and the little fellow was jumping backwards and forwards like a dog tied to a rope, and did not know what to do.

He glared at the girls with his fiery red eyes and cried, 'Why do you stand there? Can you not come here and help me?'

'What are you about there, little man?' asked Rose-Red.

'You stupid, prying goose!' answered the dwarf; 'I was going to split the tree to get a little wood for cooking. The little bit of food that one of us wants gets burnt up directly with thick logs; we do not swallow so much as you coarse, greedy folk. I had just driven the wedge safely in, and everything was going as I wished; but the wretched wood was too smooth and suddenly sprang asunder, and the tree closed so quickly that I could not pull out my beautiful white beard; so now it is tight in and I cannot get away, and the silly, sleek, milk-faced things laugh! Ugh! how odious you are!'

The children tried very hard, but they could not pull the beard out, it was caught too fast.

'I will run and fetch someone,' said Rose-Red.

'You senseless goose!' snarled the dwarf; 'why should you fetch someone? You are already two too many for me; can you not think of something better?'

'Don't be impatient,' said Snow-White, 'I will help you,' and she pulled her scissors out of her pocket, and cut off the end of the beard.

As soon as the dwarf felt himself free he laid hold of a bag which lay among the roots of the tree, and which was full of gold, and lifted it up, grumbling to himself, 'Uncouth people, to cut off a piece of my fine beard. Bad luck to you!' and then he swung the bag upon his back, and went off without even once looking at the children.

Some time after that Snow-White and Rose-Red went to catch a dish of fish. As they came near the brook they saw something like a large grasshopper jumping towards the water, as if it were going to leap in. They ran to it and found it was the dwarf.

'Where are you going?' said Rose-Red; 'you surely don't want to go into the water?'

'I am not such a fool!' cried the dwarf; 'don't you see that the accursed fish wants to pull me in?' The little man had been sitting there fishing, and unluckily the wind had twisted his beard with the fishing-line; just then a big fish bit, and the creature had not enough strength to pull it out; the fish kept the upper hand and pulled the dwarf towards him. He held on to all the reeds and rushes, but it was of little good, he was forced to follow the movements of the fish, and was in urgent danger of being dragged into the water.

The girls came just in time; they held him fast and tried to free his beard from the line, but all in vain, beard and line were entangled fast together. Nothing was left but to bring out the scissors and cut the beard, whereby a small part of it was lost. When the dwarf saw that he screamed out, 'Is that civil, you toad-stool, to disfigure one's face? Was it not enough to clip off the end of my beard? Now you have cut off the best part of it. I cannot let myself be seen by my people. I wish you had been made to run the soles off your shoes!' Then he took out a sack of pearls which lay in the rushes, and without saying a word more he dragged it away and disappeared behind a stone.

It happened that soon afterwards the mother sent the two children to the town to buy needles and thread, and laces and ribbons. The road led them across a heath upon which huge pieces of rock lay strewn here and there. Now they noticed a large bird hovering in the air, flying slowly round and round above them; it sank lower and lower, and at last settled near a rock not far off. Directly afterwards they heard a loud, piteous cry. They ran up and saw with horror that the eagle had seized their old acquaintance the dwarf, and was going to carry him off. The children, full of pity, at once took tight hold of the little man, and pulled against the eagle so long that at last he let his booty go.

As soon as the dwarf had recovered from his first fright he cried with his shrill voice, 'Could you not have done it more carefully! You dragged at my brown coat so that it is all torn and full of holes, you helpless clumsy creatures!' Then he took up a sack full of precious stones, and slipped away again under the rock into his hole. The girls, who by this time were used to his thanklessness, went on their way and did their business in the town.

As they crossed the heath again on their way home they surprised the dwarf, who had emptied out his bag of precious stones in a clean spot, and had not thought that anyone would come there so late. The evening sun shone upon the brilliant stones; they glittered and sparkled with all colours so beautifully that the children stood still and looked at them.

'Why do you stand gaping there?' cried the dwarf, and his ashen-gray face became copper-red with rage. He was going on with his bad words when a loud growling was heard, and a black bear came trotting towards them out of the forest. The dwarf sprang up in a fright, but he could not get to his cave, for the bear was already close.

'Dear Mr. Bear, spare me!' he cried in the dread of his heart. 'I will give you all my treasures; look, the beautiful jewels lying there! Grant me my life; what do you want with such a slender little fellow as I? you would not feel me between your teeth. Come, take these two wicked girls, they are tender morsels for you, fat as young quails; for mercy's sake eat them!'

The bear took no heed of his words, but gave the wicked creature a single blow with his paw, and he did not move again. The girls had run away, but the bear called to them, 'Snow-White and Rose-Red, do not be afraid; wait, I will come with you.' Then they knew his voice and waited, and when he came up to them suddenly his bearskin fell off, and he stood there, a handsome man, clothed all in gold. 'I am a king's son,' he said, 'and I was bewitched by that wicked dwarf, who had stolen my treasures; I have had to run about the forest as a savage bear until I was freed by his death. Now he has got his well-deserved punishment.'

Snow-White was married to him, and Rose-Red to his brother, and they divided between them the great treasure which the dwarf had gathered together in his cave. The old mother lived peacefully and happily with her children for many years. She took the two rose-trees with her, and they stood before her window, and every year bore the most beautiful roses, white and red.

The Fisherman and His Wife

There was once on a time a fisherman who lived with his wife in a miserable hovel close by the sea, and every day he went out fishing. And once as he was sitting with his rod, looking at the clear water, his line suddenly went down, far down below, and when he drew it up again he brought out a large flounder. Then the flounder said to him:

'Hark, you fisherman, I pray you, let me live, I am no flounder really, but an enchanted prince. What good will it do you to kill me? I should not be good to eat, put me in the water again, and let me go.'

'Come,' said the fisherman, 'there is no need for so many words about it a fish that can talk I should certainly let go, anyhow,' with that he put him back again into the clear water, and the flounder went to the bottom, leaving a long streak of blood behind him. Then the fisherman got up and went home to his wife in the hovel.

'Husband,' said the woman, 'have you caught nothing today?'

'No,' said the man, 'I did catch a flounder, who said he was an enchanted prince, so I let him go again.'

'Did you not wish for anything first?' said the woman.

'No,' said the man; 'what should I wish for?'

'Ah,' said the woman, 'it is surely hard to have to live always in this dirty hovel; you might have wished for a small cottage for us. Go back and call him. Tell him we want to have a small cottage, he will certainly give us that.'

'Ah,' said the man, 'why should I go there again?'

'Why,' said the woman, 'you did catch him, and you let him go again; he is sure to do it. Go at once.' The man still did not quite like to go, but did not like to oppose his wife, and went to the sea. When he got there the sea was all green and yellow, and no longer so smooth; so he stood still and said,

'Flounder, flounder in the sea,
Come, I pray thee, here to me;
For my wife, good Ilsabil,
Wills not as I'd have her will.'

Then the flounder came swimming to him and said:

'Well what does she want, then?'

'Ah,' said the man, 'I did catch you, and my wife says I really ought to have wished for something. She does not like to live in a wretched hovel any longer. She would like to have a cottage.'

'Go, then,' said the flounder, 'she has it already.'

When the man went home, his wife was no longer in the hovel, but instead of it there stood a small cottage, and she was sitting on a bench before the door. Then she took him by the hand and said to him:

'Just come inside, look, now isn't this a great deal better?' So they went in, and there was a small porch, and a pretty little parlour and bedroom, and a kitchen and pantry, with the best of furniture, and fitted up with the most beautiful things made of tin and brass, whatsoever was wanted. And behind the cottage there was a small yard, with hens and ducks, and a little garden with flowers and fruit.

'Look,' said the wife, 'is not that nice!'

'Yes,' said the husband, 'and so we must always think it – now we will live quite contented.' 'We will think about that,' said the wife. With that they ate something and went to bed.

Everything went well for a week or a fortnight, and then the woman said:

'Hark you, husband, this cottage is far too small for us, and the garden and yard are little; the flounder might just as well have given us a larger house. I should like to live in a great stone castle; go to the flounder, and tell him to give us a castle.'

'Ah, wife,' said the man, 'the cottage is quite good enough; why should we live in a castle?' 'What!' said the woman; 'just go, the flounder can do that.'

22

'No, wife,' said the man, 'the flounder has just given us the cottage, I do not like to go back so soon, it might make him angry.'

'Go,' said the woman, 'he can do it quite easily, and will be glad to do it; just you go to him.' The man's heart grew heavy, and he would not go. He said to himself, 'It is not right,' and yet he went. And when he came to the sea the water was quite purple and dark-blue, and grey and thick, and no longer so green and yellow, but it was still quiet. And he stood there and said:

> 'Flounder, flounder in the sea,
> Come, I pray thee, here to me;
> For my wife, good Ilsabil,
> Wills not as I'd have her will.'

'Well what does she want, then?' said the flounder.

'Alas,' said the man, half scared, 'she wants to live in a great stone castle.'

'Go to it, then, she is standing before the door,' said the flounder.

Then the man went away, intending to go home, but when he got there, he found a great stone palace, and his wife was just standing on the steps going in, and she took him by the hand and said, 'Come in.' So he went in with her, and in the castle was a great hall paved with marble, and many servants, who flung wide the doors; And the walls were all bright with beautiful hangings, and in the rooms were chairs and tables of pure gold, and crystal chandeliers hung from the ceiling, and all the rooms and bed-rooms had carpets, and food and wine of the very best were standing on all the tables, so that they nearly broke down beneath it. Behind the house, too, there was a great courtyard, with stables for horses and cows, and the very best of carriages; there was a magnificent large garden, too, with the most beautiful flowers and fruit-trees, and a park quite half a mile long, in which were stags, deer, and hares, and everything that could be desired.

'Come,' said the woman, 'isn't that beautiful?'

'Yes, indeed,' said the man, 'now let it be; and we will live in this beautiful castle and be content.'

'We will consider about that,' said the woman, 'and sleep upon it;' thereupon they went to bed.

Next morning the wife awoke first, and it was just daybreak, and from her bed she saw the beautiful country lying before her. Her husband was still stretching himself, so she poked him in the side with her elbow, and said:

'Get up, husband, and just peep out of the window. Look you, couldn't we be the king over all that land? Go to the flounder, we will be the king.'

'Ah, wife,' said the man, 'why should we be king? I do not want to be king.'

'Well,' said the wife, 'if you won't be king, I will; go to the flounder, for I will be king.'

'Ah, wife,' said the man, 'why do you want to be king? I do not like to say that to him.'

'Why not?' said the woman. 'Go to him this instant; I must be king!' So the man went, and was quite unhappy because his wife wished to be king. 'It is not right; it is not right,' thought he. He did not wish to go, but yet he went.

And when he came to the sea, it was quite dark-grey, and the water heaved up from below, and smelt putrid. Then he went and stood by it, and said:

> 'Flounder, flounder in the sea,
> Come, I pray thee, here to me;
> For my wife, good Ilsabil,
> Wills not as I'd have her will.'

'Well what does she want, then?' said the flounder.

'Alas,' said the man, 'she wants to be king.'

'Go to her; she is king already.'

So the man went, and when he came to the palace, the castle had become much larger, and had a great tower and magnificent ornaments, and the sentinel was standing before the door, and there were numbers of soldiers with kettle-drums and trumpets. And when he went inside the house, everything was of real marble and gold, with velvet covers and great golden tassels. Then the doors of the hall were opened, and there was the court in all its splendour, and his wife was sitting on a high throne of gold and diamonds, with a great crown of gold on her head, and a sceptre of pure gold and jewels in her hand, and on both sides of her stood her maids-in-waiting in a row, each of them always one head shorter than the last.

Then he went and stood before her, and said, 'Ah, wife, and now you are king.'

'Yes,' said the woman, 'now I am king.' So he stood and looked at her, and when he had looked at her thus for some time, he said:

'And now that you are King, let all else be, now we will wish for nothing more.'

'Nay, husband,' said the woman, quite anxiously, 'I find time pass very heavily, I can bear it no longer; go to the flounder – I am king, but I must be emperor, too.'

'Alas, wife, why do you wish to be emperor?'

'Husband,' said she, 'go to the flounder. I will be emperor.'

'Alas, wife,' said the man, 'he cannot make you emperor; I may not say that to the fish. There is only one emperor in the land. An emperor the flounder cannot make you! I assure you he cannot.'

'What!' said the woman, 'I am the king, and you are nothing but my husband; will you go this moment? go at once! If he can make a king he can make an emperor. I will be emperor; go instantly.' So he was forced to go. As the man went, however, he was troubled in mind, and thought to himself, 'It will not end well; it will not end well! Emperor is too shameless! The flounder will at last be tired out.'

With that he reached the sea, and the sea was quite black and thick, and began to boil up from below, so that it threw up bubbles, and such a sharp wind blew over it that it curdled, and the man was afraid. Then he went and stood by it, and said:

> 'Flounder, flounder in the sea,
> Come, I pray thee, here to me;
> For my wife, good Ilsabil,
> Wills not as I'd have her will.'

'Well what does she want, then?' said the flounder.

'Alas, flounder,' said he, 'my wife wants to be emperor.'

'Go to her," said the flounder; 'she is emperor already."

So the man went, and when he got there the whole palace was made of polished marble with alabaster figures and golden ornaments, and soldiers were marching before the door blowing trumpets, and beating cymbals and drums; and in the house, barons, and counts, and dukes were going about as servants. Then they opened the doors to him, which were of pure gold. And when he entered, there sat his wife on a throne, which was made of one piece of gold, and was quite two miles high; and she wore a great golden crown that was three yards high, and set with diamonds and carbuncles, and in one hand she had the sceptre, and in the other the imperial orb; and on both sides of her stood the yeomen of the guard in two rows, each being smaller than the one before him, from the biggest giant, who was two miles high, to the very smallest dwarf, just as big as my little finger. And before it stood a number of princes and dukes.

Then the man went and stood among them, and said:

'Wife, are you emperor now?'

'Yes,' said she, 'now I am Emperor.' Then he stood and looked at her well, and when he had looked at her thus for some time, he said, 'Ah, wife, be content, now that you are emperor.'

'Husband,' said she, why are you standing there? Now, I am emperor, but I will be pope too; go to the flounder.'

'Alas, wife,' said the man, 'what will you not wish for? You cannot be pope. There is but one in christendom. He cannot make you pope.'

'Husband,' said she, 'I will be Pope; go immediately, I must be Pope this very day.'

'No, wife,' said the man, 'I do not like to say that to him; that would not do, it is too much; the flounder can't make you pope.'

'Husband,' said she, 'what nonsense! If he can make an emperor he can make a pope. Go to him directly. I am emperor, and you are nothing but my husband; will you go at once?'

Then he was afraid and went; but he was quite faint, and shivered and shook, and his knees and legs trembled. And a high wind blew over the land, and the clouds flew, and towards evening all grew dark, and the leaves fell from the trees, and the water rose and roared as if it were boiling, and splashed upon the shore. And in the distance he saw ships which were firing guns in their sore need, pitching and tossing on the waves. And yet in the midst of the sky there was still a small bit of blue, though on every side it was as red as in a heavy storm. So, full of despair, he went and stood in much fear and said,

> 'Flounder, flounder in the sea,
> Come, I pray thee, here to me;
> For my wife, good Ilsabil,
> Wills not as I'd have her will.'

'Well what does she want, then?' said the flounder.

'Alas,' said the man, 'she wants to be the pope.'

'Go to her then,' said the flounder; 'she is the pope already.'

So he went, and when he got there, he saw what seemed to be a large church surrounded by palaces. He pushed his way through the crowd. Inside, however, everything was lighted up with thousands and thousands of candles, and his wife was clad in gold, and she was sitting on a much higher throne, and had three great golden crowns on, and round about her there was much ecclesiastical splendour; and on both sides of her was a row of candles the largest of which was as tall as the very tallest tower, down to the very smallest kitchen candle, and all the emperors and kings were on their knees before her, kissing her shoe.

'Wife,' said the man, and looked attentively at her, 'are you now the pope?'

'Yes,' said she, 'I am the pope.' So he stood and looked at her, and it was just as if he was looking at the bright sun. When he had stood looking at her thus for a short time, he said:

'Ah, wife, if you are Pope, do let well alone!' But she looked as stiff as a post, and did not move or show any signs of life. Then said he, 'Wife, now that you are pope, be satisfied, you cannot become anything greater now.'

'I will consider about that,' said the woman. Thereupon they both went to bed, but she was not satisfied, and greediness let her have no sleep, for she was continually thinking what there was left for her to be.

The man slept well and soundly, for he had run about a great deal during the day; but the woman could not fall asleep at all, and flung herself from one side to the other the whole night through, thinking always what more was left for her to be, but unable to call to mind anything else. At length the sun began to rise, and when the woman saw the red of dawn, she sat up in bed and looked at it. And when, through the window, she saw the sun thus rising, she thought, 'Cannot I, too, order the sun and moon to rise?'

'Husband,' she said, poking him in the ribs with her elbows, 'wake up! Go to the flounder, for I wish to be even as God is.' The man was still half asleep, but he was so horrified that he fell out of bed. He thought he must have heard amiss, and rubbed his eyes, and said, 'Alas, wife, what are you saying?'

'Husband,' said she, 'if I can't order the sun and moon to rise, and have to look on and see the sun and moon rising, I can't bear it. I shall not know what it is to have another happy hour, unless I can make them rise myself.' Then she looked at him so terribly that a shudder ran over him, and said, 'Go at once; I wish to be as powerful as God.'

'Alas, wife,' said the man, falling on his knees before her, the flounder cannot do that; he can make an emperor and a pope; I beseech you, go on as you are, and be the pope.' Then she fell into a rage, and her hair flew wildly about her head, and she cried:

'I will not endure this, I'll not bear it any longer; will you go?' He put on his trousers and ran away like a madman. But outside a great storm was raging, and blowing so hard that he could scarcely keep his feet; houses and trees toppled over, the mountains trembled, rocks rolled into the sea, the sky was pitch black, and it thundered and lightened, and the sea came in with black waves as high as church-towers and mountains, and all with crests of white foam at the top. Then he cried, but could not hear his own words:

> 'Flounder, flounder in the sea,
> Come, I pray thee, here to me;
> For my wife, good Ilsabil,
> Wills not as I'd have her will.'

'Well what does she want, then?' said the flounder.

'Alas,' said he, 'she wants to be like God.'

'Go to her, and you will find her back again in the dirty hovel.' And there they are living still at this very time.

The Seven Ravens

There was once a man who had seven sons, and last of all one daughter. Although the little girl was very pretty, she was so weak and small that they thought she could not live and they said she should at once be christened.

So the father sent one of his sons in haste to the spring to get some water, but the other six ran with him. Each wanted to be first at drawing the water, and so they were in such a hurry that all let their pitchers fall into the well, and they stood very foolishly looking at one another, and did not know what to do, for none dared go home.

In the meantime the father was uneasy, and could not tell what made the young men stay so long.

'Surely,' said he, 'the whole seven must have forgotten themselves over some game of play' – and when he had waited still longer and they yet did not come, he flew into a rage and wished them all turned into ravens. Scarcely had he spoken these words when he heard a croaking over his head, and looked up and saw seven ravens as black as coal flying round and round. Sorry as he was to see his wish so fulfilled, he did not know how what was done could be undone, and comforted himself as well as he could for the loss of his seven sons with his dear little daughter, who soon became stronger and every day more beautiful. For a long time she did not know that she had ever had any brothers, for her father and mother took care not to speak of them before her; but one day by chance she heard the people about her speak of them.

'Yes,' said they, 'she is beautiful indeed, but still 'tis a pity that her brothers should have been lost for her sake.'

Then she was much grieved, and went to her father and mother, and asked if she had had any brothers, and what had become of them.

So they dared no longer hide the truth from her, but said it was the will of heaven, and that her birth was only the innocent cause of it; but the little girl mourned sadly about it every day, and thought herself bound to do all she could to bring her brothers back; and she had neither rest nor ease, till at length one day she stole away, and set out into the wide world to find her brothers, wherever they might be, and free them, whatever it might cost her.

She took nothing with her but a little ring which her father and mother had given her, a loaf of bread in case she should be hungry, a little pitcher of water in case she should be thirsty, and a little stool to rest upon when she should be weary. Thus she went on and on, and journeyed till she came to the world's end; then she came to the sun, but the sun looked much too hot and fiery; so she ran away quickly to the moon, but the moon was cold and chilly, and said, 'I smell flesh and blood this way!' So she took herself away in a hurry and came to the stars, and the stars were friendly and kind to her, and each star sat upon his own little stool; but the morning star rose up and gave her a little piece of wood, and said:

'If you have not this little piece of wood, you cannot unlock the castle that stands on the glass mountain; it is there your brothers live.'

The little girl took the piece of wood, rolled it up in a little cloth, and went on again until she came to the glass mountain, and found the door to the castle shut. Then she felt for the little piece of wood; but when she unwrapped the cloth it was not there, and she saw she had lost the gift of the good stars. What was to be done? She wanted to save her brothers but had no key to the castle of the glass mountain; so this faithful little sister took a knife out of her pocket and cut off her little finger, that was just the size of the piece of wood she had lost, and put it in the door and opened it.

As she went in, a little dwarf came up to her.

'What are you seeking for?' he asked.

'I seek for my brothers, the seven ravens,' answered she.

'My masters are not at home,' the dwarf said; 'but if you will wait till they come, pray step in.'

31

Now the little dwarf was getting their dinner ready, and he brought their food upon seven little plates, and their drink in seven little glasses, and set them upon the table, and out of each little plate their sister ate a small piece, and out of each little glass she drank a small drop; but she let the ring that she had brought with her fall into the last glass.

All of a sudden she heard a fluttering and croaking in the air, and the dwarf said, 'Here come my masters.' When they came in, they wanted to eat and drink, and looked for their little plates and glasses.

'Who has eaten from my little plate?' they said one after the other. 'And who has been drinking out of my little glass? Caw! Caw! Well I ween mortal lips have this way been.'

When the seventh came to the bottom of his glass, and found there the ring, he looked at it, and knew that it was his father's and mother's.

'Oh, that our little sister would but come! Then we should be free,' he said.

When the little girl heard this (for she stood behind the door all the time and listened), she ran forward, and in an instant all the ravens took their right form again; and all hugged and kissed each other, and went merrily home.

The Twelve Dancing Princesses

There was once a king who had twelve daughters, each more beautiful than the last. They slept in twelve beds all in one big room and when they went to bed, the doors were shut and locked. And yet every morning when the door was unlocked again, their shoes were found to be quite worn through as if they had been danced in all night. Nobody could find out how it happened, or where the princesses had been.

So the king made it known to all the land that if any person could discover the secret and find out where it was that the princesses danced in the night, he would have the one he liked best to take as his wife, and would in due course inherit the kingdom. They could try three times, but, after three days and nights, whoever tried and did not succeed would be put to death.

A king's son soon came. He was well entertained, and in the evening was taken to the chamber next to the one where the princesses lay in their twelve beds. There he was to sit and watch where they went to dance; and, in order that nothing could happen without him hearing it, the door of his chamber was left open. But the king's son soon fell asleep; and when he awoke in the morning he found that the princesses had all been dancing, for the soles of their shoes were full of holes. The same thing happened the second and third night and so the king ordered his head to be cut off.

After him came several others; but they all had the same luck, and all lost their lives in the same way. Not one could find out the secret of the twelve dancing princesses.

Now it happened that a poor soldier, who had been wounded in battle and could fight no longer, passed through the country where this king reigned, and as he was travelling through a wood, he met an old woman, who asked him where he was going.

'I hardly know where I am going; I am just a poor soldier,' he said, and the two sat and chatted for a while. 'Is it true that there's a wife and a kingdom to be won here, if someone can find out where it is that the princesses dance? I think I should like to try for that and then in time I might be a king.'

'Well,' said the old woman, 'that is not a very hard task: only take care not to drink any of the wine which one of the princesses will bring to you in the evening; and as soon as she thinks you have drunk it all and leaves, you pretend to be fast asleep.'

The soldier thanked her kindly for her advice and she gave him a cloak, and said, 'As soon as you put that on you will become invisible, and you will then be able to follow the princesses wherever they go.'

33

Once the soldier heard all this good advice, he was determined to try his luck, so he went to the king, and said he was willing to undertake the task of discovering the secret of the twelve princesses.

He was as well received as the others had been, and the king ordered fine royal robes to be given him; and when the evening came he was led to the outer chamber. Just as he was going to lie down, the eldest of the princesses brought him a cup of wine; but the soldier threw it all away secretly, taking care not to drink a drop. Then he laid himself down on his bed, and in a little while began to snore very loudly as if he was fast asleep. When the twelve princesses heard this they laughed heartily.

'This fellow too might have done a wiser thing than lose his life in this way!' said the eldest. Then they rose and opened their drawers and boxes, and took out all their fine clothes, and dressed themselves at the mirror, and skipped about as if they were eager to begin dancing.

But the youngest said:

'I don't know why it is, but while you are so happy I feel very uneasy; I am sure some mischance will befall us.'

'You simpleton,' said the eldest, 'you are always afraid; have you forgotten how many princes and dukes have already watched in vain? And as for this soldier, even if I had not given him his sleeping draught, he would have slept soundly enough.'

When they were all ready, they went and looked at the soldier; but he slept on, and did not stir hand or foot: so they thought they were quite safe. Then the eldest went up to her own bed and clapped her hands, and the bed sank into the floor and a trap-door flew open. The soldier saw them going down through the trap-door one after another, the eldest leading the way; and thinking he had no time to lose, he jumped up, put on the cloak which the old woman had given him, and followed them. However, in the middle of the stairs he trod on the gown of the youngest princess, and she cried out to her sisters, 'All is not right; someone took hold of my gown.'

'You silly creature!' said the eldest, 'it is probably nothing but a nail in the wall.'

Down they all went, and at the bottom they found themselves in a most delightful grove of trees; and the leaves were all of silver, and glistened and sparkled beautifully. The soldier thought to take away some token of the place; so he broke off a little branch, and there came a loud noise from the tree. The youngest daughter was frightened again.

'I am sure all is not right – did not you hear that noise? That never happened before.' But the eldest said:

'It is only our princes, who are shouting for joy at our approach.'

They came to another grove of trees, where all the leaves were of gold; and afterwards to a third, where the leaves were all glittering diamonds. The soldier broke a branch from each; and every time there was a loud noise, which made the youngest sister tremble with fear. But the eldest still said it was only the princes, who were crying for joy.

They went on till they came to a great lake; and at the side of the lake there lay twelve little boats with twelve handsome princes in them, who seemed to be waiting there for the princesses. One of the princesses went into each boat, and the soldier stepped into the same boat as the youngest. As they were rowing over the lake, the prince who was in the boat with the youngest princess and the soldier said, 'The boat seems very heavy today. I do not know why it is, but though I am rowing with all my might we do not get on so fast as usual, and I am quite tired.'

'It is only the heat of the weather,' said the princess, 'I am very warm, too.'

On the other side of the lake stood a fine castle with all its windows lit up by candles and torches, and from which came the merry music of horns and trumpets. There they all landed, and went into the castle, and each prince danced with his princess; and the soldier, who was still invisible, danced with them too. When any of the princesses had a cup of wine set by her, he drank it all up, so that when she put the cup to her mouth it was empty. At this, too, the youngest sister was terribly frightened, but the eldest always told her not to be so nervous.

They danced on till three o'clock in the morning, and then all their shoes were worn out, so that they were obliged to leave. The princes rowed them back again over the lake (but this time the soldier placed himself in the boat with the eldest princess); and on the opposite shore they took leave of each other, the princesses promising to come again the next night.

When they came to the stairs, the soldier ran on before the princesses, and laid himself down. And as the twelve, tired sisters slowly came up, they heard him snoring in his bed and believed themselves to be safe. Then they undressed themselves, put away their fine clothes, pulled off their shoes, and went to bed.

In the morning the soldier said nothing about what had happened, but determined to see more of this strange adventure, and went again on the second and third nights. Everything happened just as before: the princesses danced till their shoes were worn to pieces, and then returned home. On the third night the soldier carried away one of the golden cups as a further token of where he had been.

As soon as the time came when he was to declare the secret, he was taken before the king with the three branches and the golden cup; and the twelve princesses stood listening behind the door to hear what he would say.

'Where do my twelve daughters dance at night?" the king asked him.

'With twelve princes in a castle underground,' answered the soldier. And then he told the king all that had happened, and showed him the three branches and the golden cup which he had brought with him.

The king called for the princesses, and asked them whether what the soldier said was true and when they saw that they were discovered, and that it was of no use to deny what had happened, they confessed it all.

So the king asked the soldier which of the princesses he would choose for his wife.

'I am not very young, so I will have the eldest,' he answered, and they were married that very day, and the soldier became the king's heir.

The Frog Prince

In the olden time, when wishing was having, there lived a king, whose daughters were all beautiful; but the youngest was so exceedingly beautiful that the Sun himself, although he saw her very, very often, was delighted every time she came out into the sunshine.

Near the castle of this king was a large and gloomy forest, where in the midst stood an old lime-tree, beneath whose branches splashed a little fountain; so, whenever it was very hot, the king's youngest daughter ran off into this wood, and sat down by the side of the fountain; and, when she felt dull, would often divert herself by throwing a golden ball up into the air and catching it again. And this was her favourite amusement.

Now, one day it happened that this golden ball, when the princess threw it into the air, did not fall down into her hand, but on to the grass; and then it rolled right into the fountain. The princess followed the ball with her eyes, but it disappeared beneath the water, which was so deep that she could not see to the bottom. Then she began to lament, and to cry more loudly and more loudly; and, as she cried, a voice called out, 'Why weepest thou, O princess? thy tears would melt even a stone to pity.'

She looked around to the spot whence the voice came, and saw a frog stretching his thick, ugly head out of the water.

'Ah! You old water-paddler,' said she, 'was it you that spoke? I am weeping for my golden ball which bounced away from me into the water.'

'Be quiet, and do not cry,' replied the Frog; 'I can give thee good assistance. But what wilt thou give me if I succeed in fetching thy plaything up again?'

'What would you like, dear Frog?' said she. 'My dresses, my pearls and jewels, or the golden crown which I wear?'

The Frog replied, 'Dresses, or jewels, or golden crowns, are not for me; but if thou wilt love me, and let me be thy companion and playmate, and sit at thy table, and eat from thy little golden plate, and drink out of thy cup, and sleep in thy little bed, – if thou wilt promise me all these things, then I will dive down and fetch up thy golden ball.'

'Oh, I will promise you all,' said she, 'if you will only get me my golden ball.' But she thought to herself, 'What is the silly Frog chattering about? Let him stay in the water with his equals; he cannot enter into society.'

Then the Frog, as soon as he had received her promise, drew his head under the water and dived down. Presently he swam up again with the golden ball in his mouth, and threw it on to the grass. The princess was full of joy when she again saw her beautiful plaything; and, taking it up, she ran off immediately.

'Stop! stop!' cried the Frog; 'take me with thee. I cannot run as thou canst.'

But this croaking was of no avail; although it was loud enough, the princess did not hear it, but, hastening home, soon forgot the poor Frog, who was obliged to leap back into the fountain.

The next day, when the princess was sitting at table with her father and all his courtiers, and was eating from her own little golden plate, something was heard coming up the marble stairs, splish-splash, splish-splash; and when it arrived at the top, it knocked at the door, and a voice said:

'Open the door, thou youngest daughter of the king!'

So she arose and went to see who it was that called to her; but when she opened the door and caught sight of the Frog, she shut it again very quickly and with great passion, and sat down at the table, looking exceedingly pale.

But the king perceived that her heart was beating violently, and asked her whether it were a giant who had come to fetch her away who stood at the door.

'Oh, no!' answered she; 'it is no giant, but an ugly Frog.'

'What does the Frog want with you?' said the king.

'Oh, dear father, yesterday when I was playing by the fountain, my golden ball fell into the water, and this Frog fetched it up again because I cried so much: but first, I must tell you, he pressed me so much, that I promised him he should be my companion. I never thought that he could come out of the water, but somehow he has managed to jump out, and now he wants to come in here.'

At that moment there was another knock, and a voice said:

> 'King's daughter, youngest,
> Open the door.
> Hast thou forgotten
> Thy promises made
> At the fountain so clear
> 'Neath the lime-tree's shade?
> King's daughter, youngest.
> Open the door.'

Then the king said, 'What you have promised, that you must perform; go and let him in.'

So the princess went and opened the door, and the Frog hopped in after her right up to her chair: and as soon as she was seated, he said, 'Lift me up;' but she hesitated so long that the king had to order her to obey. And as soon as the Frog sat on the chair he jumped on to the table and said, 'Now push thy plate near me, that we may eat together.' And she did so, but, as every one noticed, very unwillingly.

The Frog seemed to relish his dinner very much, but every bit that the princess ate nearly choked her, till at last the Frog said, 'I have satisfied my hunger, and feel very tired; wilt thou carry me upstairs now into thy chamber, and make thy bed ready that we may sleep together?' At this speech the princess began to cry, for she was afraid of the cold Frog, and dared not touch him; and besides, he actually wanted to sleep in her own beautiful, clean bed! But her tears only made the king very angry, and he said, 'He who helped you in the time of your trouble must not now be despised!' So she took the Frog up with two fingers, and put him into a corner of her chamber. But as she lay in her bed, he crept up to it, and said, 'I am so very tired that I shall sleep well; do take me up, or I will tell thy father.' This speech put the princess into a terrible passion, and catching the Frog up, she threw him with all her strength against the wall, saying 'Now will you be quiet, you ugly Frog!'

But as he fell he was changed from a Frog into a handsome Prince with beautiful eyes, who after a little while became her dear companion and betrothed. One morning, Henry, trusted servant of the Prince, came for them with a carriage. When his master was changed into a frog, trusty Henry had grieved so much that he had bound three iron bands around his heart, for fear it should break with grief and sorrow. The faithful Henry (who was also the trusty Henry) helped in the bride and bridegroom, and placed himself in the seat behind, full of joy at his master's release. They had not proceeded far when the Prince heard a crack as if something had broken behind the carriage; so he put his head out of the window and asked trusty Henry what was broken. Faithful Henry answered, 'It was not the carriage, my master, but an iron band which I bound around my heart when it was in such grief because you were changed into a frog.'

Twice afterwards on the journey there was the same noise, and each time the Prince thought that it was some part of the carriage that had given way; but it was only the breaking of the bands which bound the heart of the trusty Henry (who was also the faithful Henry), and who was thenceforward free and happy.

Cat and Mouse in Partnership

A certain cat had made the acquaintance of a mouse, and had said so much to her about the great love and friendship she felt for her, that at length the mouse agreed that they should live and keep house together.

'But we must make a provision for winter, or else we shall suffer from hunger,' said the cat, 'and you, little mouse, cannot venture everywhere, or you will be caught in a trap some day.'

The good advice was followed, and a pot of fat was bought, but they did not know where to put it. At length, after much consideration, the cat said, 'I know no place where it will be better stored up than in the church, for no one dares take anything away from there. We will set it beneath the altar, and not touch it until we are really in need of it.'

So the pot was placed in safety, but it was not long before the cat had a great yearning for it, and said to the mouse, 'I want to tell you something, little mouse; my cousin has brought a little son into the world, and has asked me to be godmother; he is white with brown spots, and I am to hold him over the font at the christening. Let me go out to-day, and you look after the house by yourself.'

'Yes, yes,' answered the mouse, 'by all means go, and if you get anything very good, think of me, I should like a drop of sweet red christening wine too.'

All this, however, was untrue; the cat had no cousin, and had not been asked to be godmother. She went straight to the church, stole to the pot of fat, began to lick at it, and licked the top of the fat off. Then she took a walk upon the roofs of the town, looked out for opportunities, and then stretched herself in the sun, and licked her lips whenever she thought of the pot of fat, and not until it was evening did she return home.

'Well, here you are again,' said the mouse, 'no doubt you have had a merry day.'

'All went off well,' answered the cat. 'What name did they give the child?'

'Top off!' said the cat quite coolly.

'Top off!' cried the mouse, 'that is a very odd and uncommon name, is it a usual one in your family?'

'What does it signify?' said the cat. 'It is no worse than Crumbstealer, as your god-children are called.'

Before long the cat was seized by another fit of longing. She said to the mouse, 'You must do me a favour, and once more manage the house for a day alone. I am again asked to be godmother, and, as the child has a white ring round its neck, I cannot refuse.'

The good mouse consented, but the cat crept behind the town walls to the church, and devoured half the pot of fat.

'Nothing ever seems so good as what one keeps to oneself,' said she, and was quite satisfied with her day's work.

When she went home the mouse inquired, 'And what was this child christened?'

'Half-done,' answered the cat. 'Half-done! What are you saying? I never heard the name in my life, I'll wager anything it is not in the calendar!'

The cat's mouth soon began to water for some more licking.

'All good things go in threes,' said she, 'I am asked to stand godmother again. The child is quite black, only it has white paws, but with that exception, it has not a single white hair on its whole body; this only happens once every few years, you will let me go, won't you?'

'Top-off! Half-done!' answered the mouse. They are such odd names, they make me very thoughtful.'

'You sit at home,' said the cat, 'in your dark-grey fur coat and long tail, and are filled with fancies, that's because you do not go out in the daytime.'

During the cat's absence the mouse cleaned the house and put it in order, but the greedy cat entirely emptied the pot of fat.

'When everything is eaten up one has some peace,' said she to herself, and well filled and fat she did not return home till night. The mouse at once asked what name had been given to the third child.

'It will not please you more than the others,' said the cat. 'He is called All-gone.'

'All-gone!' cried the mouse. 'That is the most suspicious name of all! I have never seen it in print. All-gone; what can that mean?' and she shook her head, curled herself up, and lay down to sleep.

From this time forth no one invited the cat to be god-mother, but when the winter had come and there was no longer anything to be found outside, the mouse thought of their provision, and said, 'Come cat, we will go to our pot of fat which we have stored up for ourselves – we shall enjoy that.'

'Yes,' answered the cat, 'you will enjoy it as much as you would enjoy sticking that dainty tongue of yours out of the window.'

They set out on their way, but when they arrived, the pot of fat certainly was still in its place, but it was empty.

'Alas!' said the mouse. 'Now I see what has happened, now it comes to light! You are a true friend! You have devoured all when you were standing godmother. First top off, then half done, then –'

'Will you hold your tongue!' cried the cat. 'One word more and I will eat you too.'

'All gone' was already on the poor mouse's lips; scarcely had she spoken it before the cat sprang on her, seized her, and swallowed her down. Verily, that is the way of the world.

The Goose-Girl

An old queen, whose husband had been dead some years, had a beautiful daughter. When she grew up, she was betrothed to a prince who lived a great way off; and as the time drew near for her to be married, she got ready to set off on her journey to his country. Then the queen, her mother, packed up a great many costly things – jewels, and gold, and silver, trinkets, fine dresses, and in short, everything that became a royal bride; for she loved her child very dearly; and she gave her a waiting-maid to ride with her, and give her into the bridegroom's hands; and each had a horse for the journey. Now the princess's horse was called Falada, and could speak.

When the time came for them to set out, the old queen went into her bed-chamber, and took a little knife, and cut off a lock of her hair, and gave it to her daughter, saying:

'Take care of it, dear child; for it is a charm that may be of use to you on the road.' Then they took a sorrowful leave of each other, and the princess put the lock of her mother's hair into her bosom, got upon her horse, and set off on her journey to her bridegroom's kingdom.

One day, as they were riding along by the side of a brook, the princess began to feel very thirsty, and said to her maid:

'Pray get down and fetch me some water in my golden cup out of yonder brook, for I want to drink.'

'Nay,' said the maid, 'if you are thirsty, get down yourself, and lie down by the water and drink; I shall not be your waiting-maid any longer.'

The princess was so thirsty that she got down, and knelt over the little brook and drank, for she was frightened, and dared not bring out her golden cup.

'Alas! What will become of me?' she said as she wept. And the lock of hair answered her, and said:

> 'Alas! Alas! If thy mother knew it,
> Sadly, sadly her heart would rue it.'

But the princess was very humble and meek, so she said nothing about her maid's ill behaviour, but got upon her horse again.

Then they rode further on their journey, till the day grew so warm, and the sun so scorching, that the bride began to feel very thirsty again; and at last, when they came to a river, she forgot her maid's rude speech, and said:

'Pray get down and fetch me some water to drink in my golden cup.'

But the maid answered her, and even spoke more haughtily than before:

'Drink if you will, but I shall not be your waiting-maid.'

The princess was so thirsty that she got off her horse and lay down, and held her head over the running stream.

'What will become of me?' she cried.

And the lock of hair answered her again:

> 'Alas! Alas! If thy mother knew it,
> Sadly, sadly her heart would rue it.'

And as she leaned down to drink, the lock of hair fell from her bosom and floated away with the water, without her seeing it, she was so much frightened. But her maid saw it, and was very glad, for she knew the charm, and saw that the poor bride would be in her power now that she had lost the hair. So when the bride had finished drinking, and would have got upon Falada again, the maid stopped her.

'I shall ride upon Falada,' she said, 'and you may have my horse instead.' So the princess was forced to give up her horse, and soon afterwards to take off her royal clothes, and put on her maid's old ones.

At last, as they drew near the end of the journey, this treacherous servant threatened to kill her mistress if she ever told anyone what had happened. But Falada saw it all, and marked it well. Then the waiting-maid got upon Falada, and the real bride was set upon the other horse, and they went on in this way till at last they came to the royal court. There was great joy at their coming, and the prince hurried to meet them, and lifted the maid from her horse, thinking she was the one who was to be his wife; and she was led upstairs to the royal chamber, but the true princess was told to stay in the court below.

The old king happened to be looking out of the window, and saw her in the yard below; and as she looked very pretty, and too delicate for a waiting-maid, he went into the royal chamber to ask the bride whom it was she had brought with her, that was left standing in the court below.

'I brought her with me for the sake of her company on the road,' said she. 'Pray give the girl some work to do, that she may not be idle.'

The old king could not for some time think of any work for her.

'I have a lad who takes care of my geese,' he said at last; 'she may go and help him.' Now the name of this lad, that the real bride was to help in watching the king's geese, was Curdken.

Soon after, the false bride said to the prince:

'Dear husband, pray do me one piece of kindness.'

'That I will,' said the prince.

'Then tell one of your slaughterers to cut off the head of the horse I rode upon, for it was very unruly, and plagued me sadly on the road.' But the truth was, she was very much afraid that Falada should speak, and tell all she had done to the princess. She carried her point, and the faithful Falada was killed; but when the true princess heard of it she wept, and begged the man to nail up Falada's head against a large dark gate in the city through which she had to pass every morning and evening, that there she might still see him sometimes. Then the slaughterer said he would do as she wished, so he cut off the head and nailed it fast under the dark gate.

Early the next morning, as the princess and Curdken went out through the gate, she said sorrowfully:

'Falada, Falada, there thou art hanging!"

and the head answered:

'Bride, bride, there thou are ganging!
Alas! Alas! If thy mother knew it,
Sadly, sadly her heart would rue it.'

Then they went out of the city, driving the geese. And when they came to the meadow, the princess sat down upon a bank there and let down her waving locks of hair, which were all of pure gold; and when Curdken saw it glitter in the sun, he ran up, and would have pulled some of the locks out; but she cried:

'Blow, breezes, blow!
Let Curdken's hat go!
Blow breezes, blow!
Let him after it go!
O'er hills, dales, and rocks,
Away be it whirl'd,
Till the golden locks
Are all comb'd and curl'd!'

Then there came a wind, so strong that it blew off Curdken's hat, and away it flew over the hills, and he after it; till, by the time he came back, she had done combing and curling her hair, and put it up again safely. Then he was very angry and sulky, and would not speak to her at all; but they watched the geese until it grew dark in the evening, and then drove them homewards.

The next morning, as they were going through the dark gate, the poor girl looked up at Falada's head, and cried –

'Falada, Falada, there thou art hanging!'

and it answered:

'Bride, bride, there thou are ganging!
Alas! Alas! If thy mother knew it,
Sadly, sadly her heart would rue it.'

Then she drove on the geese and sat down again in the meadow, and began to comb out her hair as before, and Curdken ran up to her, and wanted to take of it; but she cried out quickly:

'Blow, breezes, blow!
Let Curdken's hat go!
Blow breezes, blow!
Let him after it go!
O'er hills, dales, and rocks,
Away be it whirl'd,
Till the golden locks
Are all comb'd and curl'd!'

Then the wind came and blew off his hat, and off it flew a great distance over the hills and far away, so that he had to run after it: and when he came back, she had done up her hair again, and all was safe. So they watched the geese till it grew dark.

In the evening, after they came home, Curdken went to the old king.

'I cannot have that strange girl to help me to keep the geese any longer,' he said.

'Why?' inquired the king.

'Because she does nothing but tease me all day long.'

Then the king made him tell him all that had passed. And Curdken said, 'When we go in the morning through the dark gate with our flock of geese, she weeps, and talks with the head of a horse that hangs upon the wall, and says:

'Falada, Falada, there thou art hanging!'

and the head answers:

'Bride, bride, there thou are ganging!
Alas! alas! if thy mother knew it,
Sadly, sadly her heart would rue it.'

And Curdken went on telling the king what had happened upon the meadow where the geese fed; and how his hat was blown away, and he was forced to run after it, and leave his flock. But the old king told him to go out again as usual the next day: and when morning came, he placed himself behind the dark gate, and heard how the princess spoke, and how Falada answered; and then he went into the field and hid himself in a bush by the meadow's side, and soon saw with his own eyes how they drove the flock of geese, and how, after a little time, she let down her hair that glittered in the sun; and then he heard her say:

'Blow, breezes, blow!
Let Curdken's hat go!
Blow breezes, blow!
Let him after it go!
O'er hills, dales, and rocks,
Away be it whirl'd,
Till the golden locks
Are all comb'd and curl'd!'

And soon came a gale of wind, and carried away Curdken's hat, while the girl went on combing and curling her hair.

All this the old king saw; so he went home without being seen; and when the goose-girl came back in the evening, he called her aside, and asked her why she did so; but she burst into tears, and said:

'That I must not tell you or any man, or I shall lose my life.'

But the old king begged so hard that she had no peace till she had told him all, word for word: and it was very lucky for her that she did so, for the king ordered royal clothes to be put upon her, and he gazed with wonder, she was so beautiful. Then he called his son, and told him that he had only the false bride, for that she was merely a waiting-maid, while the true one stood by. And the young prince rejoiced when he saw her beauty, and heard how meek and patient she had been; and without saying anything, he ordered a great feast to be prepared for all his court. The bridegroom sat at the top, with the false princess on one side, and the true one on the other; but nobody knew her, for she was quite dazzling to their eyes, and was not at all like the little goose-girl, now that she had on her brilliant dress.

When they had eaten and drunk, and were very merry, the old king told all the story, as one that he had once heard of, and asked the true waiting-maid what she thought ought to be done to anyone who would behave thus.

'Nothing better,' said this false bride, 'than that she should be thrown into a cask stuck around with sharp nails, and that two white horses should be put to it, and should drag it from street to street till she is dead.'

'You are she!' said the old king; 'and since you have judged yourself, it shall be so done to you.'

Then the young king was married to his true wife, and they reigned over the kingdom in peace and happiness all their lives.

The Elves and the Shoemaker

There was once a shoemaker, who worked very hard and was very honest: but still he could not earn enough to live upon; and at last all he had in the world was gone, save just leather enough to make one pair of shoes.

Then he cut his leather out, all ready to make up the next day, meaning to rise early in the morning to his work. His conscience was clear and his heart light amidst all his troubles; so he went peaceably to bed, left all his cares to Heaven, and soon fell asleep. In the morning after he had said his prayers, he sat himself down to his work; when, to his great wonder, there stood the shoes all ready made, upon the table. The good man knew not what to say or think at such an odd thing happening. He looked at the workmanship; there was not one false stitch in the whole job; all was so neat and true, that it was quite a masterpiece.

The same day a customer came in, and the shoes suited him so well that he willingly paid a price higher than usual for them; and the poor shoemaker, with the money, bought leather enough to make two pairs more. In the evening he cut out the work, and went to bed early, that he might get up and begin betimes next day; but he was saved all the trouble, for when he got up in the morning the work was done ready to his hand. Soon in came buyers, who paid him handsomely for his goods, so that he bought leather enough for four pair more. He cut out the work again overnight and found it done in the morning, as before; and so it went on for some time: what was got ready in the evening was always done by daybreak, and the good man soon became thriving and well-off again.

One evening, about Christmas-time, as he and his wife were sitting over the fire chatting together, he said to her, 'I should like to sit up and watch tonight, that we may see who it is that comes and does my work for me.'

The wife liked the thought; so they left a light burning, and hid themselves in a corner of the room, behind a curtain that was hung up there, and watched what would happen.

As soon as it was midnight, there came in two little naked dwarfs; and they sat themselves upon the shoemaker's bench, took up all the work that was cut out, and began to ply with their little fingers, stitching and rapping and tapping away at such a rate, that the shoemaker was all wonder, and could not take his eyes off them. And on they went, till the job was quite done, and the shoes stood ready for use upon the table. This was long before daybreak; and then they bustled away as quick as lightning.

The next day the wife said to the shoemaker. 'These little wights have made us rich, and we ought to be thankful to them, and do them a good turn if we can. I am quite sorry to see them run about as they do; and indeed it is not very decent, for they have nothing upon their backs to keep off the cold. I'll tell you what, I will make each of them a shirt, and a coat and waistcoat, and a pair of pantaloons into the bargain; and do you make each of them a little pair of shoes."

The thought pleased the good cobbler very much; and one evening, when all the things were ready, they laid them on the table, instead of the work that they used to cut out, and then went and hid themselves, to watch what the little elves would do.

About midnight in they came, dancing and skipping, hopped round the room, and then went to sit down to their work as usual; but when they saw the clothes lying for them, they laughed and chuckled, and seemed mightily delighted. Then they dressed themselves in the twinkling of an eye, and danced and capered and sprang about, as merry as could be; till at last they danced out at the door, and away over the green.

The good couple saw them no more; but everything went well with them from that time forward, as long as they lived.

The Six Swans

A king was once hunting in a large wood, and pursued his game so hotly that none of his courtiers could follow him. But when evening approached he stopped, and looking around him perceived that he had lost himself. He tried to find a path out of the forest but could not find one, and presently he saw an old woman, with a nodding head, who came up to him.

'My good woman,' said he to her, 'can you show me the way out of the forest?'

'Oh, yes, my lord king,' she replied; 'I can do that very well, but upon one condition, which if you do not fulfil, you will never again get out of the wood, but will die of hunger.'

'What, then, is this condition?' asked the king.

'I have a daughter,' said the old woman, 'who is as beautiful as any one you can find in the whole world, and well deserves to be your bride. Now, if you will make her your queen, I will show you your way out of the wood.'

In the anxiety of his heart, the king consented, and the old woman led him to her cottage, where the daughter was sitting by the fire. She received the king as if she had expected him, and he saw at once that she was very beautiful, but yet she did not quite please him, for he could not look at her without a secret shuddering. However, he took the maiden upon his horse, and the old woman showed him the way, and the king arrived safely at his palace, where the wedding was to be celebrated.

The king had been married once before, and had seven children by his first wife, six boys and a girl, whom he loved above everything else in the world. He became afraid, soon, that the stepmother might not treat his children very well, and might even do them some great injury, so he took them away to a lonely castle which stood in the midst of a forest. The castle was so entirely hidden, and the way to it was so difficult to discover, that he himself could not have found it if a wise woman had not given him a ball of cotton which had the wonderful property, when he threw it before him, of unrolling itself and showing him the right path. The king went so often to see his dear children, that the queen, noticing his absence, became inquisitive, and wished to know what he went to fetch out of the forest. So she gave his servants a great quantity of money, and they disclosed to her the secret, and also told her of the ball of cotton which alone could show her the way. She had now no peace until she discovered where this ball was concealed, and then she made some fine silken shirts, and, as she had learnt of her mother, she sewed within each a charm.

One day soon after, when the king was gone out hunting, she took the little shirts and went into the forest, and the cotton showed her the path. The children, seeing someone coming in the distance, thought it was their dear father, and ran out full of joy. Then she threw over each of them a shirt, that, as it touched their bodies, changed them into swans, which flew away over the forest. The queen then went home quite contented, and thought she was free of her stepchildren; but the little girl had not met her with the brothers, and the queen did not know of her.

The following day the King went to visit his children, but he found only the maiden.

'Where are your brothers?' asked he.

'Ah, dear father,' she replied, 'they are gone away and have left me alone;' and she told him how she had looked out of the window and seen them changed into swans, which had flown over the forest; and then she showed him the feathers which they had dropped in the courtyard, and which she had collected together. The king was much grieved, but he did not think that his wife could have done this wicked deed, and, as he feared the girl might also be stolen away, he took her with him. She was, however, so much afraid of the stepmother, that she begged him not to stop more than one night in the castle.

The poor maiden thought to herself, 'This is no longer my place; I will go and seek my brothers;' and when night came she escaped and went deep into the wood. She walked all night long, and a great part of the next day, until she could go no further from weariness. Just then she saw a rough-looking hut, and going in, she found a room with six little beds, but she dared not get into one, so crept under, and laying herself upon the hard earth, prepared to pass the night there. Just as the sun was setting, she heard a rustling, and saw six white swans come flying in at the window. They settled on the ground and began blowing one another until they had blown all their feathers off, and their swan's down slipped from them like a shirt. Then the maiden knew them at once for her brothers, and gladly crept out from under the bed, and the brothers were not less glad to see their sister, but their joy was of short duration.

'You must not stay here,' said they to her; 'this is a robbers' hiding-place; if they should return and find you here, they would murder you.'

'Can you not protect me, then?' inquired the sister.

'No,' they replied; 'for we can only lay aside our swan's feathers for a quarter of an hour each evening, and for that time we regain our human form, but afterwards we resume our changed appearance.'

Their sister then asked them, with tears, 'Can you not be restored again?'

'Oh, no,' replied they; 'the conditions are too difficult. For six long years you must neither speak nor laugh, and during that time you must sew together for us six little shirts of star-flowers, and should there fall a single word from your lips, then all your labour will be in vain.' Just as the brothers finished speaking, the quarter of an hour elapsed, and they all flew out of the window again as swans.

The little sister, however, made a solemn resolution to rescue her brothers, or die in the attempt; and she left the cottage, and, penetrating deep into the forest, passed the night amid the branches of a tree. The next morning she went out and collected the star-flowers to sew together. She had no one to converse with and no reason to laugh, so there up in the tree she sat, intent upon her work.

After she had passed some time there, it happened that the king of that country was hunting in the forest, and his huntsmen came beneath the tree on which the maiden sat. 'Who are you?' they called up to her. But she gave no answer. 'Come down to us,' continued they; 'we will do you no harm.' She simply shook her head, and when they pressed her further with questions, she threw down to them her gold necklace, hoping therewith to satisfy them. They did not, however, leave her, and she threw down her girdle, but in vain! And even her rich dress did not make them desist. At last the huntsman himself climbed the tree and brought down the maiden, and took her before the king.

'Who are you?' asked the king. 'What are you doing in that tree?' But she did not answer; and then he questioned her in all the languages that he knew, but she remained dumb to all, as a fish. Since, however, she was so beautiful, the king's heart was touched, and he conceived for her a strong affection. Then he put around her his cloak, and, placing her before him on his horse, took her to his castle.

There he ordered rich clothing to be made for her, and, although her beauty shone as the sunbeams, not a word escaped her. The king placed her by his side at table, and there her dignified mien and manners so won upon him, that he said, 'This maiden will I marry, and no other in the world,' and after some days he wedded her.

Now, the King had a wicked stepmother, who was discontented with his marriage, and spoke evil of the young queen.

'Who knows where the wench comes from?' said she. 'She who cannot speak is not worthy of a king.'

A year after, when the queen brought her first-born into the world, the old woman took him away. Then she went to the king and complained that the queen was a murderess. The king, however, would not believe it, and suffered no one to do any injury to his wife, who sat composedly sewing at her shirts and paying attention to nothing else. When a second child was born, the false stepmother used the same deceit, but the king again would not listen to her words.

'She is too pious and good to act so,' he said. 'Could she but speak and defend herself, her innocence would come to light.'

But when again, the old woman stole away the third child, and then accused the queen, who answered not a word to the accusation, the king was obliged to give her up to be tried, and she was condemned to suffer death by fire.

When the time had elapsed, and the sentence was to be carried out, it happened that the very day had come round when her dear brothers should be set free; the six shirts were also ready, all but the last, which yet wanted the left sleeve. As she was led to the scaffold, she placed the shirts upon her arm, and just as she had mounted it, and the fire was about to be kindled, she looked around, and saw six swans come flying through the air. Her heart leapt for joy as she perceived her deliverers approaching, and soon the swans, flying towards her, alighted so near that she was enabled to throw over them the shirts, and as soon as she had done so, their feathers fell off and the brothers stood up alive and well; but the youngest was without his left arm, instead of which he had a swan's wing. They embraced and kissed each other, and the queen, going to the king, who was thunderstruck, was at last able to speak.

'Now may I speak, my dear husband, and prove to you that I am innocent and falsely accused,' she said to the king, and then she told him how the wicked woman had stolen away and hidden her three children. When she had concluded, the King was overcome with joy, and the wicked stepmother was led to the scaffold and bound to the stake and burnt to ashes. The king and queen for ever after lived in peace and prosperity with their six brothers.

The Golden Goose

There was once a man who had three sons. The youngest was called Dummling, and was on all occasions scorned and ill-treated by the whole family. It happened that the eldest took it into his head one day to go into the forest to cut wood; and his mother gave him a delicious meat pie and a bottle of wine to take with him, that he might sustain himself at his work. As he went into the forest, a little old man bid him good day, and said, 'Give me a little bit of meat from your plate, and a little wine out of your flask; I am very hungry and thirsty.' But this clever young man said, 'If give you my meat and wine, there would not be enough left for me; be off with you,' and he went on his way.

He soon began to chop down a tree; but he had not worked long before he missed his stroke, and cut himself, and was obliged to go home and have the wound bound up. Now, it was the little old man who caused him this mischief.

Next the second son went out to work; and his mother gave him, too, a meat pie and a bottle of wine. And the same little old man encountered him also, and begged him for something to eat and drink. But he, too, thought himself extremely clever, and said, 'Whatever you get, I shall be without; so go your way!' The little man made sure that he should have his reward; and the second stroke that he struck at a tree, hit him on the leg, so that he too had to be carried home.

Then Dummling said, 'Father, I should like to go and cut wood too.'

But his father replied, 'Your brothers have both maimed themselves; you had better stop at home, for you know nothing of the job.'

But Dummling begged so long that at length his father said, 'Just go then; you will be wiser when you have suffered for your foolishness.' And his mother gave him only some dry bread, and a bottle of sour ale; but when he went into the forest, he met the little old man, who said, 'Give me some meat and drink, for I am very hungry and thirsty.'

Dummling said, 'I have nothing but dry bread and sour beer; if that will do for you, we will sit down and eat it together.' So they sat down, and when the lad took out his bread, behold it was turned into a splendid meat pie, and his sour beer became delicious wine! They ate and drank heartily, and when they had finished, the little man said, 'As you have a kind heart, and have been willing to share everything with me I will bring good to you. There stands an old tree; chop it down, and you will find something at the root.' Then he took his leave and went his way.

Dummling set to work, and cut down the tree; and when it fell, he discovered in a hollow under the roots a goose with plumage of pure gold. He took it up, and went on to an inn, where he proposed sleep for the night. The landlord had three daughters, and when they saw the goose, they were very curious to find out what this wonderful bird could be, and wished very much to pluck one of the feathers out of its tail.

At last the eldest said, 'I must and will have a feather.' So she waited till his back was turned, and then caught hold of the goose by the wing; but to her great surprise, there she stuck, for neither hand nor finger could she pull away again. Presently in came the second sister, and thought to have a feather too; but the instant she touched her sister, there she too hung fast. At last came the third, and desired a feather; but the other two cried out, 'Keep away! for heaven's sake, keep away!' But she did not understand why she should keep away. 'If they are there,' thought she, 'I may as well be there too,' so she went up to them, but the moment she touched her sisters she stuck fast, and hung to the goose as they did. And so they had to spend the night with the goose.

The next morning Dummling set off with the goose under his arm, and took no heed of the three girls, but went out with them sticking fast behind; and wherever he journeyed, the three were obliged to follow wherever he went, whether they wished or not.

In the middle of a field the parson met them; and when he saw the procession, he said, 'Are you not ashamed of yourselves, you bold girls, to run after the young man like that over the fields? Is that proper behaviour?' He took the youngest by the hand to lead her away; but the moment he touched her he, too, hung fast, and followed in the procession.

Presently up came the clerk; and when he saw his master, the parson, running after the three girls, he was greatly surprised, and said, 'Hi, your reverence, whither away so fast? Don't forget there is a christening today.' Then he ran up, and caught the parson by the sleeve, and instantly he was fast too.

As the five were thus trotting along, one after another, they met two labourers with their mattocks coming from work; and the parson called out and begged them to set him and the clerk free. But hardly had they touched the clerk when they, too, joined the ranks, and so made seven, all running after Dummling and his goose.

Soon afterwards they came to a city, where a king reigned who had an only daughter. The princess was of so serious a turn of mind that no one could make her laugh; and the King had announced to all the world that whoever could make her laugh should have her for his wife. When Dummling heard this, he went to the palace with the goose and all its followers; and as soon as she saw the seven all hanging together, and running about, treading on each other's heels, she could not help bursting into a long and loud laugh, as if she would never stop. Then Dummling claimed her for his bride; the wedding took place, and he was heir to the kingdom, and lived long and happily with his wife.

The Devil with the Three Golden Hairs

There was once a poor woman who gave birth to a little son; and as he came into the world with a caul on, it was predicted that in his fourteenth year he would have the king's daughter for his wife. It happened that soon afterwards the king came into the village in disguise, and when he asked the people what news there was, they answered, 'A child has just been born with a caul on; whatever any one so born undertakes turns out well. It is prophesied, too, that in his fourteenth year he will have the king's daughter for his wife.'

The king, who had a bad heart, and was angry about the prophecy, went to the parents, and, seeming quite friendly, said, 'You poor people, let me have your child, and I will take care of it.' At first they refused, but when the stranger offered them a large amount of gold for it, and they thought, 'He is a luck-child, and everything must turn out well for him,' they at last consented, and gave him the child.

The king put the child in a box and rode away with it until he came to a deep river; then he threw the box into it and thought, 'I have freed my daughter from her unlooked-for suitor.'

The box, however, did not sink, but floated like a boat, and not a drop of water made its way into it. And it floated to within two miles of the king's chief city, where there was a mill, and it came to a stop at the mill-dam. A miller's boy, who by good luck was standing there, noticed it and pulled it out with a hook, thinking that he had found a great treasure, but when he opened it there lay a pretty boy inside, quite fresh and lively. He took him to the miller and his wife, and as they had no children they were glad, and said, 'God has given him to us.' They took great care of the foundling, and he grew up in all goodness.

It happened that the king was once caught in a storm and took refuge in the mill. He asked the mill-folk if the tall youth was their son. 'No,' answered they, 'he's a foundling. Fourteen years ago he floated down to the mill-dam in a box, and the mill-boy pulled him out of the water.'

Then the king knew that it was none other than the luck-child which he had thrown into the water, and he said, 'My good people, could not the youth take a letter to the queen; I will give him two gold pieces as a reward?'

'Just as the king commands,' answered they, and they told the boy to hold himself in readiness. Then the King wrote a letter to the queen, wherein he said, 'As soon as the boy arrives with this letter, let him be killed and buried, and all must be done before I come home.'

The boy set out with this letter; but he lost his way, and in the evening came to a large forest. In the darkness he saw a small light; he went towards it and reached a cottage. When he went in, an old woman was sitting by the fire quite alone. She started when she saw the boy, and said, 'Where do you come from, and where are you going?'

'I come from the mill,' he answered, 'and wish to go to the Queen, to whom I am taking a letter; but as I have lost my way in the forest I should like to stay here over night.'

'You poor boy,' said the woman, 'you have come into a den of thieves, and when they come home they will kill you.'

'Let them come,' said the boy, 'I am not afraid; but I am so tired that I cannot go any farther,' and he stretched himself upon a bench and fell asleep.

Soon afterwards the robbers came, and angrily asked what strange boy was lying there? 'Ah,' said the old woman, 'it is an innocent child who has lost himself in the forest, and out of pity I have let him come in; he has to take a letter to the Queen.' The robbers opened the letter and read it, and in it was written that the boy as soon as he arrived should be put to death. Then the hard-hearted robbers felt pity, and their leader tore up the letter and wrote another, saying, that as soon as the boy came, he should be married at once to the king's daughter. Then they let him lie quietly on the bench until the next morning, and when he awoke they gave him the letter, and showed him the right way.

And the queen, when she had received the letter and read it, did as was written in it, and had a splendid wedding-feast prepared, and the king's daughter was married to the luck-child, and as the youth was handsome and agreeable she lived with him in joy and contentment.

After some time the King returned to his palace and saw that the prophecy was fulfilled, and the luck-child married to his daughter. 'How has that come to pass?' said he; 'I gave quite another order in my letter.'

So the Queen gave him the letter, and said that he might see for himself what was written in it. The King read the letter and saw quite well that it had been exchanged for the other. He asked the youth what had become of the letter entrusted to him, and why he had brought another instead of it.

'I know nothing about it,' answered he; 'it must have been changed in the night, when I slept in the forest.'

The King said in a passion, 'You shall not have everything quite so much your own way; whoever marries my daughter must fetch me from hell three golden hairs from the head of the devil; bring me what I want, and you shall keep my daughter.' In this way the King hoped to be rid of him for ever.

But the luck-child answered, 'I will fetch the golden hairs, I am not afraid of the Devil;' whereupon he took leave of them and began his journey.

The road led him to a large town, where the watchman by the gates asked him what his trade was, and what he knew.

'I know everything,' answered the luck-child.

'Then you can do us a favour,' said the watchman, 'if you will tell us why our market-fountain, which once flowed with wine has become dry, and no longer gives even water?'

'You shall know that,' answered he; 'only wait until I come back.'

Then he went farther and came to another town, and there also the gatekeeper asked him what was his trade, and what he knew.

'I know everything,' answered he.

'Then you can do us a favour and tell us why a tree in our town which once bore golden apples now does not even put forth leaves?'

'You shall know that,' answered he; 'only wait until I come back.'

Then he went on and came to a wide river over which he must go. The ferryman asked him what his trade was, and what he knew.

'I know everything,' answered he.

'Then you can do me a favour,' said the ferryman, 'and tell me why I must always be rowing backwards and forwards, and am never set free?'

'You shall know that,' answered he; 'only wait until I come back.'

When he had crossed the water he found the entrance to Hell. It was black and sooty within, and the Devil was not at home, but his grandmother was sitting in a large arm-chair. 'What do you want?' said she to him, but she did not look so very wicked.

'I should like to have three golden hairs from the devil's head,' answered he, 'else I cannot keep my wife.'

'That is a good deal to ask for,' said she; 'if the devil comes home and finds you, it will cost you your life; but as I pity you, I will see if I cannot help you.'

She changed him into an ant and said, 'Creep into the folds of my dress, you will be safe there.'

'Yes,' answered he, 'so far, so good; but there are three things besides that I want to know: why a fountain which once flowed with wine has become dry, and no longer gives even water; why a tree which once bore golden apples does not even put forth leaves; and why a ferry-man must always be going backwards and forwards, and is never set free?'

'Those are difficult questions,' answered she, 'but only be silent and quiet and pay attention to what the devil says when I pull out the three golden hairs.'

As the evening came on, the devil returned home. No sooner had he entered than he noticed that the air was not pure.

'I smell man's flesh,' said he; 'all is not right here.'

Then he pried into every corner, and searched, but could not find anything. His grandmother scolded him.

'It has just been swept,' said she, 'and everything put in order, and now you are upsetting it again; you have always got man's flesh in your nose. Sit down and eat your supper.'

When he had eaten and drunk he was tired, and laid his head in his grandmother's lap, and before long he was fast asleep, snoring and breathing heavily. Then the old woman took hold of a golden hair, pulled it out, and laid it down near her.

'Oh!' cried the devil, 'what are you doing?'

'I have had a bad dream,' answered the grandmother, 'so I seized hold of your hair.'

'What did you dream then?' asked the devil.

'I dreamed that a fountain in a market-place from which wine once flowed was dried up, and not even water would flow out of it; what is the cause of it?'

'Oh, ho! if they did but know it,' answered the devil; 'there is a toad sitting under a stone in the well; if they killed it, the wine would flow again.'

He went to sleep again and snored until the windows shook. Then she pulled the second hair out.

'Ha! what are you doing?' cried the devil angrily.

'Do not take it ill,' said she, 'I did it in a dream.'

'What have you dreamt this time?' asked he.

'I dreamt that in a certain kingdom there stood an apple-tree which had once borne golden apples, but now would not even bear leaves. What, think you, was the reason?'

'Oh! If they did but know,' answered the devil, 'a rat is gnawing at the root; if they killed this they would have golden apples again, but if it gnaws much longer the tree will wither altogether. But leave me

65

alone with your dreams: if you disturb me in my sleep again you will get a box on the ear.'

The grandmother spoke gently to him until he fell asleep again and snored. Then she took hold of the third golden hair and pulled it out. The devil jumped up, roared out, and would have treated her ill if she had not quieted him once more and said, 'Who can help bad dreams?'

'What was the dream, then?' asked he, and was quite curious.

'I dreamt of a ferry-man who complained that he must always ferry from one side to the other, and was never released. What is the cause of it?'

'Ah! the fool,' answered the devil; 'when any one comes and wants to go across he must put the oar in his hand, and the other man will have to ferry and he will be free.'

As the grandmother had plucked out the three golden hairs, and the three questions were answered, she let the old serpent alone, and he slept until daybreak.

When the devil had gone out again the old woman took the ant out of the folds of her dress, and gave the luck-child his human shape again.

'There are the three golden hairs for you,' said she. 'What the Devil said to your three questions, I suppose you heard?'

'Yes,' answered he, 'I heard, and will take care to remember.'

'You have what you want,' said she, 'and now you can go your way.'

He thanked the old woman for helping him in his need, and left hell well content that everything had turned out so fortunately.

When he came to the ferry-man he was expected to give the promised answer.

'Ferry me across first,' said the luck-child, 'and then I will tell you how you can be set free,' and when he reached the opposite shore he gave him the devil's advice: 'Next time any one comes, who wants to be ferried over, just put the oar in his hand.'

He went on and came to the town wherein stood the unfruitful tree, and there too the watchman wanted an answer. So he told him what he had heard from the devil: 'Kill the rat which is gnawing at its root, and it will again bear golden apples.' Then the watchman thanked him, and gave him as a reward two asses laden with gold, which followed him.

At last he came to the town whose well was dry. He told the watchman what the devil had said: 'A toad is in the well beneath a stone; you must find it and kill it, and the well will again give wine in plenty.' The watchman thanked him, and also gave him two asses laden with gold.

At last the luck-child got home to his wife, who was heartily glad to see him again, and to hear how well he had prospered in every-thing. To the king he took what he had asked for, the devil's three golden hairs, and when the king saw the four asses laden with gold he was quite content, and said, 'Now all the conditions are fulfilled, and you can keep my daughter. But tell me, dear son-in-law, where did all that gold come from? this is tremendous wealth!' 'I was rowed across a river,' answered he, 'and got it there; it lies on the shore instead of sand.'

'Can I too fetch some of it?' said the king; and he was quite eager about it.

'As much as you like,' answered he. 'There is a ferry-man on the river; let him ferry you over, and you can fill your sacks on the other side.'

The greedy king set out in all haste, and when he came to the river he beckoned to the ferry-man to put him across. The ferry-man came and bade him get in, and when they got to the other shore he put the oar in his hand and sprang out. From this time forth the king had to ferry, as a punishment for his sins. Perhaps he is ferrying still? If he is, it is because no one has taken the oar from him.

Rapunzel

Once upon a time there lived a man and his wife who were very unhappy because they had no children. These good people had a little window at the back of their house, which looked into the most lovely garden, full of all manner of beautiful flowers and vegetables; but the garden was surrounded by a high wall, and no one dared to enter it, for it belonged to a witch of great power, who was feared by the whole world.

One day the woman stood at the window overlooking the garden, and saw there a bed full of the finest rampion: the leaves looked so fresh and green that she longed to eat them. The desire grew day by day, and just because she knew she couldn't possibly get any, she pined away and became quite pale and wretched. Then her husband grew alarmed and said:

'What ails you, dear wife?'

'Oh,' she answered, 'if I don't get some rampion to eat out of the garden behind the house, I know I shall die.'

The man, who loved her dearly, thought to himself, 'Come! rather than let your wife die you shall fetch her some rampion, no matter the cost.' So at dusk he climbed over the wall into the witch's garden, and, hastily gathering a handful of rampion leaves, he returned with them to his wife. She made them into a salad, which tasted so good that her longing for the forbidden food was greater than ever. If she were to know any peace of mind, there was nothing for it but that her husband should climb over the garden wall again, and fetch her some more. So at dusk over he got, but when he reached the other side he drew back in terror, for there, standing before him, was the old witch.

'How dare you,' she said, with a wrathful glance, 'climb into my garden and steal my rampion like a common thief? You shall suffer for your foolhardiness.'

'Oh!' he implored, 'pardon my presumption; necessity alone drove me to the deed. My wife saw your rampion from her window, and conceived such a desire for it that she would certainly have died if her wish had not been gratified.'

Then the Witch's anger was a little appeased, and she said:

'If it's as you say, you may take as much rampion away with you as you like, but on one condition only – that you give me the child your wife will shortly bring into the world. All shall go well with it, and I will look after it like a mother.'

The man in his terror agreed to everything she asked, and as soon as the child was born the Witch appeared, and having given it the name of Rapunzel, which is the same as rampion, she carried it off with her.

Rapunzel was the most beautiful child under the sun. When she was twelve years old the Witch shut her up in a tower, in the middle of a great wood, and the tower had neither stairs nor doors, only high up at the very top a small window. When the old Witch wanted to get in she stood underneath and called out:

'Rapunzel, Rapunzel, Let down your golden hair,' for Rapunzel had wonderful long hair, and it was as fine as spun gold. Whenever she heard the Witch's voice she unloosed her plaits, and let her hair fall down out of the window about twenty yards below, and the old Witch climbed up by it.

After they had lived like this for a few years, it happened one day that a Prince was riding through the wood and passed by the tower. As he drew near it he heard someone singing so sweetly that he stood still spell-bound, and listened. It was Rapunzel in her loneliness trying to while away the time by letting her sweet voice ring out into the wood. The Prince longed to see the owner of the voice, but he sought in vain for a door in the tower. He rode home, but he was so haunted by the song he had heard that he returned every day to the wood and listened. One day, when he was standing thus behind a tree, he saw the old Witch approach and heard her call out:

'Rapunzel, Rapunzel, Let down your golden hair.'

Then Rapunzel let down her plaits, and the Witch climbed up by them.

'So that's the staircase, is it?' said the Prince. 'Then I too will climb it and try my luck.'

So on the following day, at dusk, he went to the foot of the tower and cried:

'Rapunzel, Rapunzel, Let down your golden hair,' and as soon as she had let it down the Prince climbed up.

At first Rapunzel was terribly frightened when a man came in, for she had never seen one before; but the Prince spoke to her so kindly, and told her at once that his heart had been so touched by her singing, that he felt he should know no peace of mind till he had seen her. Very soon Rapunzel forgot her fear, and when he asked her to marry him she consented at once. 'For,' she thought, 'he is young and handsome, and I'll certainly be happier with him than with the old Witch.' So she put her hand in his and said:

'Yes, I will gladly go with you, only how am I to get down out of the tower? Every time you come to see me you must bring a skein of silk with you, and I will make a ladder of them, and when it is finished I will climb down by it, and you will take me away on your horse.'

They arranged that till the ladder was ready, he was to come to her every evening, because the old woman was with her during the day. The old Witch, of course, knew nothing of what was going on, till one day Rapunzel, not thinking of what she was about, turned to the Witch and said:

'How is it, good mother, that you are so much harder to pull up than the young Prince? He is always with me in a moment.'

'Oh! you wicked child,' cried the Witch. 'What is this I hear? I thought I had hidden you safely from the whole world, and in spite of it you have managed to deceive me.'

In her wrath she seized Rapunzel's beautiful hair, wound it round and round her left hand, and then grasping a pair of scissors in her right, snip snap, off it came, and the beautiful plaits lay on the ground. And, worse than this, she was so hard-hearted that she took Rapunzel to a lonely desert place, and there left her to live in loneliness and misery.

But on the evening of the day in which she had driven poor Rapunzel away, the Witch fastened the plaits on to a hook in the window, and when the Prince came and called out: 'Rapunzel, Rapunzel, Let down your golden hair,' she let them down, and the Prince climbed up as usual, but instead of his beloved Rapunzel he found the old Witch, who fixed her evil, glittering eyes on him, and cried mockingly:

'Ah, ah! you thought to find your lady love, but the pretty bird has flown and its song is dumb; the cat caught it, and will scratch out your eyes too. Rapunzel is lost to you for ever – you will never see her more.'

The Prince was beside himself with grief, and in his despair he jumped right down from the tower, and, though he escaped with his life, the thorns among which he fell pierced his eyes out. Then he wandered, blind and miserable, through the wood, eating nothing but roots and berries, and weeping and lamenting the loss of his lovely bride. So he wandered about for some years, as wretched and unhappy as he could well be, and at last he came to the desert place where Rapunzel was living. Of a sudden he heard a voice which seemed strangely familiar to him.

He walked eagerly in the direction of the sound, and when he was quite close, Rapunzel recognized him and fell on his neck and wept. But two of her tears touched his eyes, and in a moment they became quite clear again, and he saw as well as he had ever done. Then he led her to his kingdom, where they were received and welcomed with great joy, and they lived happily ever after.

King Thrushbeard

A king had a daughter who was beautiful beyond all measure, but so proud and haughty withal that no suitor was good enough for her. She sent away one after the other, and ridiculed them as well.

Once the king held a great feast and invited to it all the eligible young men from far and near. They were all marshalled in a row according to their rank and standing; first came the kings, then the grand-dukes, then the princes, the earls, the barons, and the gentry. Then the king's daughter was led through the ranks, but to every one she had some objection to make; one was too fat, 'The wine-cask,' she said. Another was too tall, 'Long and thin has little in.' The third was too short, 'Short and thick is never quick.' The fourth was too pale, 'As pale as death.' The fifth too red, 'A fighting-cock.' The sixth was not straight enough, 'A green log dried behind the stove.'

So she had something to say against everyone, but she made herself especially merry over a good king who stood quite high up in the row, and whose chin had grown a little crooked.

'Well,' she cried and laughed, 'he has a chin like a thrush's beak!' and from that time he got the name of King Thrushbeard. But the old king, when he saw that his daughter did nothing but mock the people, and despised all the suitors who were gathered there, was very angry, and swore that she should have for her husband the very first beggar that came to his doors.

A few days afterwards a fiddler came and sang beneath the windows, trying to earn a small alms.

'Let him come up,' the king said what he heard him. So the fiddler came in, in his dirty, ragged clothes, and sang before the king and his daughter, and when he had ended he asked for a trifling gift. The king said, 'Your song has pleased me so well that I will give you my daughter there, to wife.'

The king's daughter shuddered, but the king said:

'I have taken an oath to give you to the very first beggar-man, and I will keep it.'

All she could say was in vain; the priest was brought, and she had to let herself be wedded to the fiddler on the spot. When that was done the king said:

'Now it is not proper for you, a beggar-woman, to stay any longer in my palace, you may just go away with your husband.'

The beggar-man led her out by the hand, and she was obliged to walk away on foot with him. When they came to a large forest she asked:

'To whom does that beautiful forest belong?'

'It belongs to King Thrushbeard; if you had taken him, it would have been yours.'

'Ah, unhappy girl that I am, if I had but taken King Thrushbeard!'

Afterwards they came to a meadow, and she asked again, 'To whom does this beautiful green meadow belong?'

'It belongs to King Thrushbeard; if you had taken him, it would have been yours.'

'Ah, unhappy girl that I am, if I had but taken King Thrushbeard!'

Then they came to a large town, and she asked again, 'To whom does this fine large town belong?'

'It belongs to King Thrushbeard; if you had taken him, it would have been yours.'

'Ah, unhappy girl that I am, if I had but taken King Thrushbeard!'

'It does not please me,' said the fiddler, 'to hear you always wishing for another husband; am I not good enough for you?'

At last they came to a very little hut, and she said, 'Oh goodness! what a small house; to whom does this miserable, mean hovel belong?'

'That is my house and yours, where we shall live together,' the fiddler answered.

She had to stoop in order to go in at the low door.

'Where are the servants?' said the king's daughter.

'What servants?' answered the beggar-man; 'you must yourself do what you wish to have done. Just make a fire at once, and set on water to cook my supper, I am quite tired.'

But the king's daughter knew nothing about lighting fires or cooking, and the beggar-man had to lend a hand himself to get anything fairly done. When they had finished their scanty meal they went to bed; but he forced her to get up quite early in the morning in order to look after the house.

For a few days they lived in this way as well as might be, and came to the end of all their provisions. Then the man said:

'Wife, we cannot go on any longer eating and drinking here and earning nothing. You weave baskets.' He went out, cut some willows, and brought them home. Then she began to weave, but the tough willows wounded her delicate hands.

'I see that this will not do,' said the man; 'you had better spin, perhaps you can do that better.' She sat down and tried to spin, but the hard thread soon cut her soft fingers so that the blood ran down.

'See,' said the man, 'you are fit for no sort of work; I have made a bad bargain with you. Now I will try to make a business with pots and earthenware; you must sit in the market-place and sell the ware.'

'Alas,' thought she, 'if any of the people from my father's kingdom come to the market and see me sitting there, selling, how they will mock me!' But it was of no use, she had to yield unless she chose to die of hunger.

For the first time she succeeded well, for the people were glad to buy the woman's wares because she was good-looking, and they paid her what she asked; many even gave her the money and left the pots with her as well. So they lived on what she had earned as long as it lasted, then the husband bought a lot of new crockery. With this she sat down at the corner of the market-place, and set it out round about her ready for sale. But suddenly there came a drunken hussar galloping along, and he rode right amongst the pots so that they were all broken into a thousand bits. She began to weep, and did now know what to do for fear.

'Alas! what will happen to me?' cried she; 'what will my husband say to this?'

She ran home and told him of the misfortune.

'Who would seat herself at a corner of the market-place with crockery?' said the man; 'leave off crying, I see very well that you cannot do any ordinary work, so I have been to our king's palace and have asked whether they cannot find a place for a kitchen-maid, and they have promised me to take you; in that way you will get your food for nothing.'

The king's daughter was now a kitchen-maid, and had to be at the cook's beck and call, and do the dirtiest work. In both her pockets she fastened a little jar, in which she took home her share of the leavings, and upon this they lived.

It happened that the wedding of the king's eldest son was to be celebrated, so the poor woman went up and placed herself by the door of the hall to look on. When all the candles were lit, and people, each more beautiful than the other, entered, and all was full of pomp and splendour, she thought of her lot with a sad heart, and cursed the pride and haughtiness which had humbled her and brought her to so great poverty.

The smell of the delicious dishes which were being taken in and out reached her, and now and then the servants threw her a few morsels of them: these she put in her jars to take home.

All at once the king's son entered, clothed in velvet and silk, with gold chains about his neck. And when he saw the beautiful woman standing by the door he seized her by the hand, and would have danced with her; but she refused and shrank with fear, for she saw that it was King Thrushbeard, her suitor whom she had driven away with scorn. Her struggles were of no avail, he drew her into the hall; but the string by which her pockets were hung broke, the pots fell down, the soup ran out, and the scraps were scattered all about. And when the people saw it, there arose general laughter and derision, and she was so ashamed that she would rather have been a thousand fathoms below the ground. She sprang to the door and would have run away, but on the stairs a man caught her and brought her back; and when she looked at him it was King Thrushbeard again. He said to her kindly:

'Do not be afraid, I and the fiddler who has been living with you in that wretched hovel are one. For love of you I disguised myself so; and I also was the hussar who rode through your crockery. This was all done to humble your proud spirit, and to punish you for the insolence with which you mocked me.'

Then she wept bitterly and said, 'I have done great wrong, and am not worthy to be your wife.'

But he said, 'Be comforted, the evil days are past; now we will celebrate our wedding.'

Then the maids-in-waiting came and put on her the most splendid clothing, and her father and his whole court came and wished her happiness in her marriage with King Thrushbeard, and the joy now began in earnest. I wish you and I had been there too.

The Wolf and the Seven Little Kids

Once upon a time there was a mother goat who had seven little kids, and loved them with all the love of a mother for her children. One day she wanted to go into the forest and fetch some food. So she called all seven to her and said, 'Dear children, I have to go into the forest, be on your guard against the wolf; if he comes in, he will devour you all – skin, hair, and all. The wretch often disguises himself, but you will know him at once by his rough voice and his black feet.'

The kids said, 'Dear mother, we will take good care of ourselves; you may go away without any anxiety.' Then she went on her way with an easy mind.

It was not long before there was a knock at the door and a voice called, 'Open the door, dear children; your mother is here, and has brought something back with her for each of you.'

But the little kids knew that it was the wolf, by the rough voice; 'We will not open the door,' they cried, 'you are not our mother. She has a soft, pleasant voice, but your voice is rough; you are the wolf!' The wolf went away to a shopkeeper and bought himself a great lump of chalk, ate this and made his voice soft with it. Then he came back, knocked at the door of the house, and cried, 'Open the door, dear children, your mother is here and has brought something back with her for each of you.' But the wolf had laid his black paws against the window, and the children saw them and cried, 'We will not open the door, our mother doesn't have black feet like you; you are the wolf.'

Then the wolf ran to a baker and said, 'I have hurt my feet, rub some dough over them for me.'

When the baker had rubbed dough over his feet, he ran to the miller and said, 'Strew some white meal over my feet for me.' The miller thought to himself, 'The wolf wants to deceive someone,' and refused; but the wolf said, 'If you will not do it, I will eat you.' Then the miller was afraid, and made his paws white for him. Truly men are like that.

So now the wretch went for the third time to the house door, knocked at it and said, 'Open the door for me, children, your dear mother has come home, and has brought every one of you something back from the forest with her.'

The little kids cried, 'First show us your feet so we may know if you are our dear mother.' Then he put his paws in through the window, and when the kids saw that they were white, they believed that all he said was true, and opened the door. But who should come in but the wolf! They were terrified and ran to hide themselves. One sprang under the table, the second into the bed, the third into the stove, the fourth into the kitchen, the fifth into the cupboard, the sixth under the washing-bowl, and the seventh into the clock-case. But the wolf found them, and one after the other he swallowed them down his throat. The youngest, who was in the clock-case, was the only one he did not find.

When the wolf had satisfied his appetite he took himself off, laid himself down under a tree in the green meadow outside, and began to sleep.

Soon afterwards the old goat came home again from the forest. Ah! What a sight she saw there! The house-door stood wide open. The table, chairs, and benches were thrown down, the washing-bowl lay broken to pieces, and the quilts and pillows were pulled off the bed. She sought her children, but they were nowhere to be found. She called them one after another by name, but no one answered. At last, when she came to the youngest, a soft voice cried, 'Dear mother, I am in the clock-case.' She took the kid out, and it told her that the wolf had come and had eaten all the others. Then you may imagine how she wept over her poor children.

At length in her grief she went out, and the youngest kid ran with her. When they came to the meadow, there lay the wolf by the tree snoring so loudly that the branches shook. She looked at him and saw that something was moving and struggling in his gorged belly.

'Ah, heavens,' said she, 'is it possible that my poor children whom he has swallowed down for his supper, can be still alive?' Then the kid had to run home and fetch scissors, and a needle and thread, and the goat cut open the monster's stomach, and hardly had she make one cut, than one little kid thrust its head out, and when she cut farther, all six sprang out one after another, and were all still alive, and had suffered no injury whatever, for in his greediness the wolf had swallowed them down whole. What rejoicing there was! They embraced their dear mother, and jumped like a sailor at his wedding.

The mother, however, said, 'Now go and look for some big stones, and we will fill the wicked beast's stomach with them while he is still asleep.' Then the seven kids dragged the stones thither with all speed, and put as many of them into his stomach as they could get in; and the mother sewed him up again in the greatest haste, so that he was not aware of anything and never once stirred.

When the wolf at length woke, he got on his legs, and as the stones in his stomach made him very thirsty, he wanted to go to a well to drink. But when he began to walk and move about, the stones in his stomach knocked against each other and rattled. Then cried he,

> 'What rumbles and tumbles
> Against my poor bones?
> I thought it was six kids,
> But it's naught but big stones.'

He got to the well and when he stooped over the water to drink, the heavy stones made him fall in, and he drowned. When the seven kids saw that, they came running to the spot and cried aloud, 'The wolf is dead! The wolf is dead!' and danced for joy round about the well with their mother.

The Youth Who Went Forth to Learn What Fear Was

A certain father had two sons, the elder of whom was smart and sensible, and could do everything, but the younger was stupid and could neither learn nor understand anything, and when people saw him they said, 'There's a fellow who will give his father some trouble!' When anything had to be done, it was always the elder who had to do it; but if his father bade him fetch anything when it was late, or in the night-time, and the way led through the churchyard, or any other dismal place, he answered 'Oh, no, father, I'll not go there, it makes me shudder!' for he was afraid. Or when stories were told by the fire at night which made the flesh creep, the listeners sometimes said 'Oh, it makes us shudder!'

The younger sat in a corner and listened with the rest of them, and could not imagine what they could mean. 'They are always saying "it makes me shudder, it makes me shudder!" It does not make me shudder,' thought he. 'That, too, must be an art of which I understand nothing.'

One day his father said to him: 'Listen to me, you fellow in the corner there, you art growing tall and strong, and you too must learn something by which you can earn your living. Look how you brother works, but you don't do anything.'

'Well, father,' he replied, 'I am quite willing to learn something – indeed, if it could be managed, I should like to learn how to shudder. I don't understand that at all yet.'

The elder brother smiled when he heard that, and thought to himself, 'Good God, what a blockhead that brother of mine is! He will never be good for anything as long as he lives.'

The father sighed, and answered him, 'You shall soon learn what it is to shudder, but you will not earn your bread by that.'

Soon after this the sexton came to the house on a visit, and the father bewailed his trouble, and told him how his younger son was so backward in every respect that he knew nothing and learnt nothing.

'Just think,' said he, 'when I asked him how he was going to earn his bread, he actually wanted to learn to shudder.'

'If that be all,' replied the sexton, 'he can learn that with me. Send him to me, and I will soon polish him.'

The father was glad to do it, for he thought, 'It will train the boy a little.'

The sexton therefore took the boy into his house, and he had to ring the bell. After a day or two, the sexton awoke him at midnight, and bade him arise and go up into the church tower and ring the bell.

'You shall soon learn what shuddering is,' thought he, and secretly went there before him; and when the boy was at the top of the tower and turned round, about to take hold of the bell rope, he saw a white figure standing on the stairs opposite the sounding hole.

'Who is there?' cried he, but the figure made no reply, and did not move or stir.

'Give an answer,' cried the boy, 'or take yourself off, you have no business here at night.'

The sexton, however, remained standing motionless that the boy might think he was a ghost.

The boy cried a second time, 'What do you want here? Speak if you are an honest fellow, or I will throw you down the steps!'

The sexton thought, 'He can't intend to be as bad as his words,' uttered no sound and stood as if he were made of stone. Then the boy called to him for the third time, and as that was also to no purpose, he ran against him and pushed the ghost down the stairs, so that it fell down ten steps and remained lying there in a corner. Thereupon the boy rang the bell, went home, and without saying a word went to bed, and fell asleep. The sexton's wife waited a long time for her husband, but he did not come back. At length she became uneasy, and woke the boy, and asked, 'Do you know where my husband is? He climbed up the tower before you did.'

'No, I don't know,' replied the boy, 'but someone was standing by the sounding hole on the other side of the steps, and as he would neither give an answer nor go away, I took him for a scoundrel, and threw him downstairs, just go there and you will see if it was he. I should be sorry if it were.'

The woman ran away and found her husband, who was lying moaning in the corner, and had broken his leg. She carried him down, and then with loud screams she hastened to the boy's father.

'Your boy,' cried she, 'has been the cause of a great misfortune! He has thrown my husband down the steps and made him break his leg. Take the good-for-nothing fellow away from our house.'

The father was terrified, and scolded the boy. 'What wicked tricks are these?' said he. 'The devil must have put this into your head.'

'Father,' he replied, 'do listen to me. I am quite innocent. He was standing there by night like one who is intending to do some evil. I did not know who it was, and I entreated him three times either to speak or to go away.'

'Ah,' said the father, 'I have nothing but unhappiness with you. Go out of my sight. I will see you no more.'

'Yes, father, willingly, wait only until it is day. Then will I go forth and learn how to shudder, and then I shall, at any rate, understand one art which will support me.'

'Learn what you will,' said the father, 'it is all the same to me. Here are fifty coins for you. Take these and go into the world, and tell no one where you come from and who is your father, for I have reason to be ashamed of you.'

'Yes, father, it shall be as you will. If you desire nothing more than that, I can easily keep it in mind.'

When day dawned, therefore, the boy put his fifty coins into his pocket, and went forth on the great highway, and continually said to himself, 'If I could but shudder! If I could but shudder!' A man approached who heard this conversation which the youth was holding with himself, and when they had walked a little farther to where they could see the gallows, the man said to him, 'Look, there is the tree where seven men have married the ropemaker's daughter, and are now learning how to fly. Sit down below it, and wait till night comes, and you will soon learn how to shudder.'

'If that is all that is wanted,' answered the youth, 'it is easily done; but if I learn how to shudder as fast as that, you shall have my fifty coins. Just come back to me early in the morning.'

Then the youth went to the gallows, sat down below it, and waited till evening. As he was cold, he lit himself a fire, but at midnight the wind blew so sharply that in spite of his fire, he could not get warm. As the wind knocked the hanged men against each other, and they moved backwards and forwards, he thought to himself 'you are shivering below by the fire, but how those up above must freeze and suffer!' He felt pity for them, so he climbed the ladder and brought down all seven. Then he stirred the fire, blew it, and set them all round it to warm themselves. But they sat there and did not stir, and the fire caught their clothes. So he said, 'Take care, or I will hang you up again.' The dead men, however, did not hear, but were quite silent, and let their rags go on burning. On this he grew angry, and said, 'If you will not take care, I cannot help you, I will not be burnt with you,' and he hung them up again each in his turn. Then he sat down by his fire and fell asleep.

The next morning the man came to him and wanted to have the fifty coins, and said, 'Well, do you know how to shudder?'

'No,' answered he, 'how was I to get to know? Those fellows up there did not open their mouths, and were so stupid that they let the few old rags which they had on their bodies get burnt.'

Then the man saw that he would not get the fifty coins that day, and went away saying, 'One of this kind has never come my way before.'

The youth likewise went his way, and once more began to mutter to himself, 'Ah, if I could but shudder! Ah, if I could but shudder!' A waggoner who was striding behind him heard that and asked, 'Who are you?'

'I don't know,' answered the youth.

Then the waggoner asked, 'Where do you come from?'

'I know not.'

'Who is your father?'

'That I may not tell you.'

'What is it that you are always muttering between thy teeth?'

'Ah,' replied the youth, 'I do so wish I could shudder, but no one can teach me how to do it.' 'Give up your foolish chatter,' said the waggoner. 'Come with me, and I will see about some work for you.'

The youth went with the waggoner, and in the evening they arrived at an inn where they wished to pass the night. Then at the entrance of the room the youth again said quite loudly, 'If I could but shudder! If I could but shudder!' The innkeeper, who heard this, laughed and said, 'If that is your desire, there ought to be a good opportunity for you here.'

'Ah, be silent,' said his wife. 'So many inquisitive persons have already lost their lives, it would be a pity and a shame if such beautiful eyes as these should never see the daylight again.'

But the youth said, 'However difficult it may be, I will learn it and for this purpose indeed I have journeyed forth.'

He let the innkeeper have no rest until the man told him that not far from thence stood a haunted castle where any one could very easily learn what shuddering was, if he would but watch in it for three nights. The king had promised that anyone who would venture should have his daughter to wife, and she was the most beautiful maiden the sun shone on. Great treasures likewise lay in the castle, which were guarded by evil spirits, and these treasures would then be freed, and would make a poor man rich enough. Already many men had gone into the castle, but as yet none had come out again.

The youth went to the king next morning and said if he were allowed he would watch three nights in the haunted castle. The king looked at him and, as the youth pleased him, he said, 'You may ask for three things to take into the castle with you, but they must be things without life.'

'Then I ask for a fire, a turning lathe, and a cutting-board with a knife,' he replied.

The king had these things carried into the castle during the day. When night was drawing near, the youth went up and made himself a bright fire in one of the rooms, placed the cutting-board and knife beside it, and seated himself by the turning-lathe.

'Ah, if I could but shudder!' said he. 'But I shall not learn it here either.'

Towards midnight, he was poking his fire, when something cried suddenly from one corner, 'Au, miau! how cold we are!'

'You simpletons!' cried he, 'what are you crying about? If you are cold, come and take a seat by the fire and warm yourselves.'

And when he had said that, two great black cats came with one tremendous leap and sat down on each side of him, and looked savagely at him with their fiery eyes. After a short time, when they had warmed themselves, they said, 'Comrade, shall we have a game at cards?'

'Why not?' he replied. 'But just show me your paws.' Then they stretched out their claws. 'Oh,' said he, 'what long nails you have! Wait, I must first cut them for you.' Thereupon he seized them by the throats, put them on the cutting-board and screwed their feet fast. 'I have looked at your fingers,' said he, 'and my fancy for card-playing has gone,' and he struck them dead and threw them out into the water. But when he had made away with these two, and was about to sit down again by his fire, out from every hole and corner came black cats and black dogs with red-hot chains, and more and more of them came until he could no longer stir, and they yelled horribly, and got on his fire, pulled it to pieces, and tried to put it out. He watched them for a while quietly, but at last when they were going too far, he seized his cutting-knife, and cried, 'Away with you, vermin,' and began to cut them down. Part of them ran away, the others he killed, and threw out into the fish-pond.

When he came back he fanned the embers of his fire again and warmed himself. And as he sat, his eyes would keep open no longer, and he felt a desire to sleep. Then he looked round and saw a great bed in the corner. 'That is the very thing for me,' said he, and got into it. When he was just going to shut his eyes, however, the bed began to move of its own accord, and went over the whole of the castle. 'That's right,' said he, 'but go faster.' Then the bed rolled on as if six horses were harnessed to it, up and down, over thresholds and steps, but suddenly hop, hop, it turned over upside down, and lay on him like a mountain. But he threw quilts and pillows up in the air, got out and said, 'Now anyone who likes, may drive,' and lay down by his fire, and slept till it was day. In the morning the King came, and when he saw him lying there on the ground, he thought the evil spirits had killed him and he was dead. Then said he, 'After all it is a pity, he is a handsome man.'

The youth heard it, got up, and said, 'It has not come to that yet.'

The King was astonished, but very glad, and asked how he had fared.

'Very well indeed,' answered the youth; 'one night is past, the two others will get over likewise.' Then he went to the innkeeper, who opened his eyes very wide, and said, 'I never expected to see you alive again! Have you learnt how to shudder yet?'

'No,' said he, 'it is all in vain. If someone would but tell me.'

The second night he again went up into the old castle, sat down by the fire, and once more began his old song, 'If I could but shudder.' When midnight came, an uproar and noise of tumbling about was heard; at first it was low, but it grew louder and louder. Then it was quiet for awhile, and at length with a loud scream, half a man came down the chimney and fell before the lad.

'Hollo!' cried he. 'Another half belongs to this. This is too little!'

Then the uproar began again, there was a roaring and howling, and the other half fell down too.

'Wait,' said he, 'I will just blow up the fire a little for you.'

When he had done that and looked round again, the two pieces were joined together, and a frightful man was sitting in his place.

'That is no part of our bargain,' said the youth, 'the bench is mine.'

The man wanted to push him away; the youth, however, would not allow that, but thrust him off with all his strength, and seated himself again in his own place. Then still more men fell down, one after the other; they brought nine dead men's legs and two skulls, and set them up and played at nine-pins with them. The youth also wanted to play and said 'Hark you, can I join you?'

'Yes, if you have any money.'

'Money enough,' replied he, 'but your balls are not quite round.'

Then he took the skulls and put them in the lathe and turned them till they were round. 'There, now, they will roll better!' said he. 'Hurrah! Now it goes merrily!' He played with them and lost some of his money, but when it struck twelve, everything vanished from his sight. He lay down and quietly fell asleep. Next morning the King came to inquire after him. 'How has it fared with you this time?' asked he.

'I have been playing at nine-pins,' he answered, 'and have lost a couple of farthings.'

'Have you not shuddered then?'

'Shudder?' said he. 'No, I have made merry. If I did but know what it was to shudder!'

The third night he sat down again on his bench and said quite sadly, 'If I could but shudder.' When it grew late, six tall men came in and brought a coffin. Then said he, 'Ha, ha, that is certainly my little cousin, who died only a few days ago,' and he beckoned with his finger, and cried 'Come, little cousin, come.' They placed the coffin on the ground, so he went to it and took the lid off, and a dead man lay inside. He felt his face, but it was cold as ice. 'I will warm you a little,' said he, and went to the fire and warmed his hand and laid it on the dead man's face, which remained cold. Then he took him out, and sat down by the fire and rubbed his arms that the blood might circulate again. As this also did no good, he thought to himself 'when two people lie in bed together, they warm each other,' so he carried the dead man to the bed, covered him over and lay down by him. After a short time the dead man became warm too, and began to move. Then said the youth, 'See, little cousin, have I not warmed you?' The dead man, however, got up and cried, 'Now will I strangle you.'

'What!' said he, 'is that the way you thank me? You shall go into your coffin again,' and he took him up, threw him into it, and shut the lid. Then came the six men and carried him away again.

'I cannot manage to shudder,' said he. 'I shall never learn it here as long as I live.'

Then a man entered who was taller than all others, and looked terrible. He was old, however, and had a long white beard.

'You wretch,' cried he, 'you shalt soon learn what it is to shudder, for you shall die.'

'Not so fast,' replied the youth. 'If I am to die, I shall have to have a say in it.'

'I will seize you,' said the fiend.

'Softly, softly, do not talk so big. I am as strong as you, and perhaps even stronger.'

'We shall see,' said the old man. 'If you are stronger, I will let you go – come, we will try.' Then he led him by dark passages to a smith's forge, took an axe, and with one blow struck an anvil into the ground.

'I can do better than that,' said the youth, and went to the other anvil. The old man placed himself near and wanted to look on, and his white beard hung down. Then the youth seized the axe, split the anvil with one blow, and struck the old man's beard in with it.

'Now I have you,' said the youth. 'Now it is you who will have to die.'

Then he seized an iron bar and beat the old man till he moaned and entreated him to stop, and he would give him great riches. The youth drew out the axe and let him go. The old man led him back into the castle, and in a cellar showed him three chests full of gold.

'Of these,' said he, 'one part is for the poor, the other for the king, the third is yours.'

Then it struck twelve and the spirit disappeared; the youth, therefore, was left in darkness. 'I shall still be able to find my way out,' said he, and felt about, found the way into the room, and slept there by his fire.

Next morning the King came and said 'Now you must have learnt what shuddering is?'

'No,' he answered; 'what can it be? My dead cousin was here, and a bearded man came and showed me a great deal of money down below, but no one told me what it was to shudder.' 'Then,' said the King, 'you have delivered the castle, and shall marry my daughter.'

'That is all very well,' said the youth, 'but still I do not know what it is to shudder.'

Then the gold was brought up and the wedding celebrated; but however much the young prince loved his wife, and however happy he was, he still said always 'If I could but shudder – if I could but shudder.' And at last she was angry at this. Her waiting-maid said, 'I will find a cure for him; he shall soon learn what it is to shudder.'

She went out to the stream which flowed through the garden, and had a whole bucketful of gudgeons brought to her. At night when the young prince was sleeping, his wife was to draw the clothes off him and empty the bucketful of cold water with the gudgeons in it over him, so that the little fishes would sprawl about him. When this was done, he woke up and cried 'Oh, what makes me shudder so? What makes me shudder so, dear wife? Ah! now I know what it is to shudder!'

The Iron Stove

In the days when wishing was still of some use, a king's son was bewitched by an old witch and shut up in an iron stove in a forest. There he passed many years, and no one could deliver him. One day, a princess came into the forest, who had lost herself, and could not find her father's kingdom again. After she had wandered about for nine days, she at length came to the iron stove. Then a voice came forth from it, and asked her, 'Where did you come from, and where are you going?'

'I have lost my father's kingdom,' she answered, 'and cannot get home again.'

Then the voice inside the iron stove said: 'I will help you to get home again, and that indeed most swiftly, if you will promise to do what I desire of you. I am the son of a far greater king than your father, and I will marry you.'

Then was she afraid, and thought, 'Good heavens! What can I do with an iron stove?' But as she much wished to get home to her father, she promised to do as he desired. But he said, 'You shall return here, and bring a knife with you, and scrape a hole in the iron.' Then he gave her a companion who walked near her, but did not speak, but in two hours he took her home; there was great joy in the castle when the princess came home, and the old king fell on her neck and kissed her. She, however, was sorely troubled.

'Dear father, what I have suffered!' she said. 'I should never have got home again from the great wild forest, if I had not come to an iron stove, but I have been forced to give my word that I will go back to it, set it free, and marry it.'

Then the old king was so terrified that he all but fainted, for he had but this one daughter. They therefore resolved they would send, in her place, the miller's daughter, who was very beautiful. They took her there, gave her a knife, and said she was to scrape at the iron stove. So she scraped at it for four-and-twenty hours, but could not bring off the least morsel of it. When day dawned, a voice in the stove said:

'It seems to me it is day outside.'

'It seems so to me too,' she answered. 'I fancy I hear the noise of my father's mill.'

'So you are a miller's daughter! Then go thy way at once, and let the king's daughter come here.'

Then she went away at once, and told the old king that the man in the iron stove, would have none of her – he wanted the king's daughter. They, however, still had a swineherd's daughter, who was even prettier than the miller's daughter, and they determined to give her a piece of gold to go to the iron stove instead of the king's daughter. So she was taken thither, and she also had to scrape for four-and-twenty hours. She, too, made no impression on it. When day broke, a voice inside the stove cried:

'It seems to me it is day outside!'

'So it seems to me also,' she answered. 'I fancy I hear my father's horn blowing.'

'Then you are a swineherd's daughter! Go away at once, and tell the king's daughter to come, and tell her all must be done as promised, and if she does not come, everything in the kingdom shall be ruined and destroyed, and not one stone be left standing on another.' When the king's daughter heard that she began to weep, but now there was nothing for it but to keep her promise. So she took leave of her father, put a knife in her pocket, and went forth to the iron stove in the forest. When she got there, she began to scrape, and the iron gave way, and when two hours were over, she had already scraped a small hole. Then she peeped in, and saw a youth so handsome, and so brilliant with gold and with precious jewels, that her very soul was delighted. Now, therefore, she went on scraping, and made the hole so large that he was able to get out. Then said he:

'You are mine, and I am yours; you are my bride, and have released me.'

He wanted to take her away with him to his kingdom, but she entreated him to let her go once again to her father, and the king's son allowed her to do so, but she was not to say more to her father than three words, and then she was to come back again. So she went home, but she spoke more than three words, and instantly the iron stove disappeared, and was taken far away over glass mountains and piercing swords; but the king's son was set free and no longer shut up in it. After this she bade goodbye to her father, took some money with her, but not much, and went back to the great forest, and looked for the iron stove, but it was nowhere to be found. For nine days she sought it, and then her hunger grew so great that she did not know what to do, for she could no longer live. When it was evening, she seated herself in a small tree, and made up her mind to spend the night there, as she was afraid of wild beasts.

When midnight drew near she saw in the distance a small light, and thought, 'Ah, there I should be saved!' She got down from the tree, and went towards the light, but on the way she prayed. Then she came to a little old house, and much grass had grown all about it, and a small heap of wood lay in front of it. She wondered what sort of place she had come to and peeped in through the window, but she saw nothing inside but toads, big and little, except a table well covered with wine and roast meat, and the plates and glasses were of silver. Then she took courage, and knocked at the door. The fat toad cried,

> 'Little green waiting-maid,
> Waiting-maid with the limping leg,
> Little dog of the limping leg,
> Hop hither and thither,
> And quickly see who is without:'

and a small toad came walking by and opened the door to her. When she entered, they all bade her welcome, and she was forced to sit down.

'Where have you come from, and where are you going?' they asked.

Then she related all that had befallen her, and how because she had transgressed the order which had been given her not to say more than three words, the stove, and the king's son also, had disappeared, and now she was about to seek him over hill and dale until she found him. Then the old fat toad said,

> 'Little green waiting-maid,
> Waiting-maid with the limping leg,
> Little dog of the limping leg,
> Hop hither and thither,
> And bring me the great box.'

Then the little one went and brought the box. After this they gave her meat and drink, and took her to a well-made bed, which felt like silk and velvet, and she laid herself down and slept.

When morning came she arose, and the old toad gave her three needles out of the great box which she was to take with her; they would be needed by her, for she had to cross a high glass mountain, and go over three piercing swords and a great lake. If she did all this she would get her lover back again. Then she gave her three things, which she was to take the greatest care of, namely, three large needles, a plough-wheel, and three nuts. With these she travelled onwards, and when she came to the glass mountain which was so slippery, she stuck the three needles first behind her feet and then before them, and so got over it, and when she was over it, she hid them in a place which she marked carefully. After this she came to the three piercing swords, and then she seated herself on her plough-wheel and rolled over them. At last she arrived in front of a great lake, and when she had crossed it, she came to a large and beautiful castle.

She went and asked for a place; she was a poor girl, she said, and would like to be hired. She knew, however, that the king's son whom she had released from the iron stove in the great forest was in the castle. Then she was taken as a scullery-maid at low wages. But the king's son had another maiden by his side whom he intended to marry, for he thought that she had long been dead.

In the evening, when she had washed up and was done, she felt in her pocket and found the three nuts which the old toad had given her. She cracked one with her teeth, and was going to eat the kernel when lo and behold there was a stately royal garment in it! But when the bride heard of this she came and asked for the dress, and wanted to buy it, and said, 'It is not a dress for a servant-girl.' But the king's daughter said no, she would not sell it, but if the bride would grant her one thing she should have it, and that was, leave to sleep one night in her bridegroom's chamber. The bride gave her permission because the dress was so pretty, and she had never had one like it. When it was evening she said to her bridegroom:

'That silly girl will sleep in your room.'

'If you are willing so am I,' said he.

She, however, gave him a glass of wine in which she had poured a sleeping-draught. So the bridegroom and the scullery-maid went to sleep in the room, and he slept so soundly that she could not wake him. She wept the whole night and cried:

'I set you free when you were in an iron stove in the wild forest, I sought you, and walked over a glass mountain, and three sharp swords, and a great lake before I found you, and yet you will not hear me!'

The servants sat by the chamber-door, and heard how she thus wept the whole night through, and in the morning they told it to their lord. And the next evening when she had washed up, she opened the second nut, and a far more beautiful dress was within it, and when the bride beheld it, she wished to buy that also. But the girl would not take money, and begged that she might once again sleep in the bridegroom's chamber. Again the bride gave him a sleeping-drink, and he slept so soundly that he could hear nothing. But the scullery-maid wept the whole night long, and cried:

'I set you free when you were in an iron stove in the wild forest, I sought you, and walked over a glass mountain, and over three sharp swords and a great lake before I found you, and yet you will not hear me!'

The servants sat by the chamber-door and heard her weeping the whole night through, and in the morning informed their lord of it. And on the third evening, when she had washed up, she opened the third nut, and within it was a still more beautiful dress which was stiff with pure gold. When the bride saw that she wanted to have it, but the maiden only gave it up on condition that she might for the third time sleep in the bridegroom's apartment. The king's son was, however, on his guard, and threw the sleeping-draught away. Now, therefore, when she began to weep and to cry:

'Dearest love, I set you free when you were in the iron stove in the terrible wild forest,' the king's son leapt up and said, 'you are the true one, you are mine, and I am yours.' Thereupon, while it was still night, he got into a carriage with her, and they took away the false bride's clothes so that she could not get up. When they came to the great lake, they sailed across it, and when they reached the three sharp-cutting swords they seated themselves on the plough-wheel, and when they got to the glass mountain they thrust the three needles in it, and so at length they got to the little old house; but when they went inside that, it was a great castle, and the toads were all disenchanted, and were king's children, and full of happiness.

Then the wedding was celebrated, and the king's son and the princess remained in the castle, which was much larger than the castles of their fathers. As, however, the old king grieved at being left alone, they fetched him away, and brought him to live with them, and they had two kingdoms, and lived in happy wedlock.

> A mouse did run,
> This story is done.

Little Red Riding-Hood

Once upon a time there was a dear little girl who was loved by everyone who looked at her, but most of all by her grandmother, and there was nothing that she would not have given to the child. Once she gave her a little riding-hood of red velvet, which suited her so well that she would never wear anything else; so she was always called 'Little Red Riding-Hood.'

One day her mother said to her, 'Come, Little Red Riding-Hood, here is a piece of cake and a bottle of wine; take them to your grandmother, she is ill and weak, and they will do her good. Set out before it gets hot, and when you are going, walk nicely and quietly and do not run off the path, or you may fall and break the bottle, and then your grandmother will get nothing; and when you go into her room, don't forget to say, "Good-morning," and don't peep into every corner before you do it.'

'I will take great care,' said Little Red Riding-Hood to her mother, and gave her hand on it.

The grandmother lived out in the wood, half a league from the village, and just as Little Red Riding-Hood entered the wood, a wolf met her. Red Riding-Hood did not know what a wicked creature he was, and was not at all afraid of him.

'Good-day, Little Red Riding-Hood,' said he.

'Thank you kindly, wolf.'

'Where are you going so early, Little Red Riding-Hood?'

'To my grandmother's.'

'What have you got in your apron?'

'Cake and wine; yesterday was baking-day, so poor sick grand-mother is to have something good, to make her stronger.'

'Where does your grandmother live, Little Red Riding-Hood?'

'A good quarter of a league farther on in the wood; her house stands under the three large oak-trees, the nut-trees are just below; you surely must know it,' replied Little Red Riding-Hood.

The wolf thought to himself, 'What a tender young creature! what a nice plump mouthful –she will be better to eat than the old woman. I must act craftily, so as to catch both.' So he walked for a short time by the side of Little Red Riding-Hood, and then he said, 'See Little Red Riding-Hood, how pretty the flowers are about here – why do you not look round? I believe, too, that you do not hear how sweetly the little birds are singing; you walk gravely along as if you were going to school, while everything else out here in the wood is merry.'

Little Red Riding-Hood raised her eyes, and when she saw the sunbeams dancing here and there through the trees, and pretty flow-ers growing everywhere, she thought, 'Suppose I take grandmother a fresh nosegay; that would please her too. It is so early in the day that I shall still get there in good time;' and so she ran from the path into the wood to look for flowers. And whenever she had picked one, she fancied that she saw a still prettier one farther on, and ran after it, and so got deeper and deeper into the wood.

Meanwhile the wolf ran straight to the grandmother's house and knocked at the door.

'Who is there?'

'Little Red Riding-Hood,' replied the wolf. 'I am bringing cake and wine; open the door.'

'Lift the latch,' called out the grandmother, 'I am too weak, and cannot get up.'

The wolf lifted the latch, the door flew open, and without saying a word he went straight to the grandmother's bed, and devoured her. Then he put on her clothes, dressed himself in her cap, laid himself in bed and drew the curtains.

Little Red Riding-Hood, however, had been running about picking flowers, and when she had gathered so many that she could carry no more, she remembered her grandmother, and set out on the way to her.

She was surprised to find the cottage-door standing open, and when she went into the room, she had such a strange feeling that she said to herself, 'Oh dear! how uneasy I feel to-day, and at other times I like being with grandmother so much.' She called out, 'Good morning,' but received no answer; so she went to the bed and drew back the curtains. There lay her grandmother with her cap pulled far over her face, and looking very strange.

'Oh! grandmother,' she said, 'what big ears you have!'

'The better to hear you with, my child,' was the reply.

'But, grandmother, what big eyes you have!' she said.

'The better to see you with, my dear.'

'But, grandmother, what large hands you have!'

'The better to hug you with.'

'Oh! but, grandmother, what a terrible big mouth you have!'

'The better to eat you with!'

And scarcely had the wolf said this, than with one bound he was out of bed and swallowed up Little Red Riding-Hood.

When the wolf had appeased his appetite, he lay down again in the bed, fell asleep and began to snore very loud. The huntsman was just passing the house, and thought to himself, 'How the old woman is snoring! I must just see if she wants anything.' So he went into the room, and when he came to the bed, he saw that the wolf was lying in it.

'Do I find you here, you old sinner!' said he. 'I have long hunted you!'

Then just as he was going to fire at him, it occurred to him that the wolf might have devoured the grandmother, and that she might still be saved, so he did not fire, but took a pair of scissors, and began to cut open the stomach of the sleeping wolf. When he had made two snips, he saw the little red riding-hood shining, and then he made two snips more, and the little girl sprang out, crying, 'Ah, how frightened I have been! How dark it was inside the wolf;' and after that the aged grandmother came out alive also, but scarcely able to breathe. Red Riding-Hood, however, quickly fetched great stones with which they filled the wolf's body, and when he awoke, he wanted to run away, but the stones were so heavy that he fell down at once, and fell dead.

Then all three were delighted. The huntsman drew off the wolf's skin and went home with it; the grandmother ate the cake and drank the wine which Red Riding-Hood had brought, and revived, but Red Riding-Hood thought to herself, 'As long as I live, I will never by myself leave the path, to run into the wood, when my mother has forbidden me to do so.'

The Golden Bird

In the olden time there was a king, who had behind his palace a beautiful pleasure-garden in which there was a tree that bore golden apples. When the apples were getting ripe they were counted, but on the very next morning one was missing. This was told to the king, and he ordered that a watch should be kept every night beneath the tree.

The king had three sons, the eldest of whom he sent, as soon as night came on, into the garden; but when midnight came he could not keep himself from sleeping, and next morning again an apple was gone.

The following night the second son had to keep watch, it fared no better with him; as soon as twelve o'clock had struck he fell asleep, and in the morning an apple was gone.

Now it came to the turn of the third son to watch; and he was quite ready, but the king had not much trust in him, and thought that he would be of less use even than his brothers; but at last he let him go. The youth lay down beneath the tree, but kept awake, and did not let sleep master him. When it struck twelve, something rustled through the air, and in the moonlight he saw a bird coming whose feathers were all shining with gold. The bird alighted on the tree, and had just plucked off an apple, when the youth shot an arrow at him. The bird flew off, but the arrow had struck his plumage, and one of his golden feathers fell down. The youth picked it up, and the next morning took it to the king and told him what he had seen in the night. The king called his council together, and everyone declared that a feather like this was worth more than the whole kingdom.

'If the feather is so precious,' declared the king, 'one alone will not do for me; I must and will have the whole bird!'

The eldest son set out; he trusted to his cleverness and thought that he would easily find the golden bird. When he had gone some distance, he saw a fox sitting at the edge of a wood, so he cocked his gun and took aim at him.

'Don't shoot me!' cried the fox. 'And in return I will give you some good counsel. You are on the way to the golden bird; and this evening you will come to a village in which stand two inns opposite to one another. One of them is lighted up brightly, and all goes on merrily within, but do not go into it; go rather into the other, even though it seems a bad one.'

'How can such a silly beast give wise advice?' thought the king's son, and he pulled the trigger. But he missed the fox, who stretched out his tail and ran quickly into the wood.

So he pursued his way, and by evening came to the village where the two inns were; in one they were singing and dancing; the other had a poor, miserable look.

'I should be a fool, indeed,' he thought, 'if I were to go into the shabby tavern, and pass by the good one.' So he went into the cheerful one, lived there in riot and revel, and forgot the bird and his father, and all good counsels.

When some time had passed, and the eldest son for month after month did not come back home, the second set out, wishing to find the golden bird. The fox met him as he had met the eldest, and gave him the good advice of which he also took no heed. He came to the two inns, and his brother was standing at the window of the one from which came the music, and called out to him. He could not resist, but went inside and lived only for pleasure.

Again some time passed, and then the king's youngest son wanted to set off and try his luck, but his father would not allow it.

'It is of no use,' said he, 'he will find the golden bird still less than his brothers, and if a mishap were to befall him he knows not how to help himself; he is a little wanting at the best.' But at last, as he had no peace, he let him go.

Again the fox was sitting outside the wood, and begged for his life, and offered his good advice. The youth was good-natured, and said:

'Be easy, little fox, I will do you no harm.'

'You shall not repent it,' answered the fox; 'and that you may get on more quickly, get up behind on my tail.'

And scarcely had he seated himself when the fox began to run, and away he went over stock and stone till his hair whistled in the wind. When they came to the village the youth got off; he followed the good advice, and without looking round turned into the little inn, where he spent the night quietly. The next morning, as soon as he got into the open country, there sat the fox already, and said:

'I will tell you further what you have to do. Go on quite straight, and at last you will come to a castle, in front of which a whole regiment of soldiers is lying, but do not trouble yourself about them, for they will all be asleep and snoring. Go through the middle of them straight into the castle, and go through all the rooms, till at last you will come to a chamber where a golden bird is hanging in a wooden cage. Close by, there stands an empty gold cage for show, but beware of taking the bird out of the common cage and putting it into the fine one, or it may go badly with you.'

With these words the fox again stretched out his tail, and the king's son seated himself upon it, and away he went over stock and stone till his hair whistled in the wind.

When he came to the castle he found everything as the fox had said. The king's son went into the chamber where the golden bird was shut up in a wooden cage, while a golden one stood hard by; and the three golden apples lay about the room. 'But,' thought he, 'it would be absurd if I were to leave the beautiful bird in the common and ugly cage,' so he opened the door, laid hold of it, and put it into the golden cage. But at the same moment the bird uttered a shrill cry. The soldiers awoke, rushed in, and took him off to prison. The next morning he was taken before a court of justice, and as he confessed everything, was sentenced to death.

The king, however, said that he would grant him his life on one condition namely, if he brought him the golden horse which ran faster than the wind; and in that case he should receive, over and above, as a reward, the golden bird.

The king's son set off, but he sighed and was sorrowful, for how was he to find the golden horse? But all at once he saw his old friend the fox sitting on the road.

'Look you,' said the fox, 'this has happened because you did not give heed to me. However, be of good courage. I will give you my help and tell you how to get to the golden horse. You must go straight on, and you will come to a castle, where in the stable stands the horse. The grooms will be lying in front of the stable; but they will be asleep and snoring, and you can quietly lead out the golden horse. But of one thing you must take heed; put on him the common saddle of wood and leather, and not the golden one, which hangs close by, else it will go ill with you.'

Then the fox stretched out his tail, the king's son seated himself upon it, and away he went over stock and stone until his hair whistled in the wind.

Everything happened just as the fox had said; the prince came to the stable in which the golden horse was standing, but just as he was going to put the common saddle upon him, he thought, 'It will be a shame to such a beautiful beast, if I do not give him the good saddle which belongs to him by right.' But scarcely had the golden saddle touched the horse than he began to neigh loudly. The grooms awoke, seized the youth, and threw him into prison. The next morning he was sentenced by the court to death; but the king promised to grant him his life, and the golden horse as well, if he could bring back the beautiful princess from the golden castle. With a heavy heart the youth set out; yet luckily for him he soon found the trusty fox.

'I ought only to leave you to your ill-luck,' said the fox, 'but I pity you, and will help you once more out of your trouble. This road takes you straight to the Golden Castle, you will reach it by eventide; and at night when everything is quiet the beautiful princess goes to the bathing-house to bathe. When she enters it, run up to her and give her a kiss, then she will follow you, and you can take her away with you; only do not allow her to take leave of her parents first, or it will go ill with you.'

Then the fox stretched out his tail, the king's son seated himself upon it, and away the fox went, over stock and stone, till his hair whistled in the wind.

When he reached the golden castle it was just as the fox had said. He waited until midnight, when everything lay in deep sleep, and the beautiful princess was going to the bathing-house. Then he sprang out and gave her a kiss. She said that she would like to go with him, but she asked him pitifully, and with tears, to allow her first to take leave of her parents. At first he withstood her prayer, but when she wept more and more, and fell at his feet, he at last gave in. But no sooner had the maiden reached the bedside of her father than he and all the rest in the castle awoke, and the youth was laid hold of and put into prison.

The next morning the king said to him:

'Your life is forfeited, and you can only find mercy if you take away the hill which stands in front of my windows, and prevents my seeing beyond it; and you must finish it all within eight days. If you do that you shall have my daughter as your reward.'

The king's son began, and dug and shovelled without leaving off, but when after seven days he saw how little he had done, and how all his work was as good as nothing, he fell into great sorrow and gave up all hope. But on the evening of the seventh day the fox appeared and said:

'You do not deserve that I should take any trouble about you; but just go away and lie down to sleep, and I will do the work for you.'

The next morning when he awoke and looked out of the window the hill had gone. The youth ran, full of joy, to the king, and told him that the task was fulfilled, and whether he liked it or not, the king had to hold to his word and give him his daughter. So the two set forth together, and it was not long before the trusty fox came up with them.

'You have certainly got what is best,' said he, 'but the golden horse also belongs to the maiden of the golden castle.'

'How shall I get it?' asked the youth.

'That I will tell you,' answered the fox. 'First take the beautiful maiden to the king who sent you to the golden castle. There will be unheard-of rejoicing; they will gladly give you the golden horse, and will bring it out to you. Mount it as soon as possible, and offer your hand to all in farewell; last of all to the beautiful maiden. And as soon as you have taken her hand swing her up on to the horse, and gallop away, and no one will be able to bring you back, for the horse runs faster than the wind.'

All was carried out successfully, and the king's son carried off the beautiful princess on the golden horse. The fox did not remain behind, and he said to the youth, 'Now I will help you to get the golden bird. When you come near to the castle where the golden bird is to be found, let the maiden get down, and I will take her into my care. Then ride with the golden horse into the castle-yard; there will be great rejoicing at the sight, and they will bring out the golden bird for you. As soon as you have the cage in your hand gallop back to us and take the maiden away again.'

The plan succeeded, and the king's son turned to ride home with his treasures.

'Now you shall reward me for my help,' said the fox.

'What do you require for it?' asked the youth.

'When you get into the wood yonder, shoot me dead, and chop off my head and feet.'

'That would be fine gratitude,' said the king's son. 'I cannot possibly do that for you.'

'If you will not do it I must leave you,' said the fox, 'but before I go away I will give you a piece of good advice. Be careful about two things. Buy no gallows'-flesh, and do not sit at the edge of any well.' And then he ran into the wood.

The youth thought, 'That is a wonderful beast, though he has strange whims; who is going to buy gallows'-flesh? and the desire to sit at the edge of a well it has never yet seized me.'

He rode on with the beautiful maiden, and his road took him again through the village in which his two brothers had remained. There was a great stir and noise, and, when he asked what was going on, he was told that two men were going to be hanged. As he came nearer to the place he saw that they were his brothers, who had been playing all kinds of wicked pranks, and had squandered all their wealth. He inquired whether they could not be set free.

'If you will pay for them,' answered the people; 'but why should you waste your money on wicked men, and buy them free?'

He did not think twice about it, but paid for them, and when they were set free they all went on their way together.

They came to the wood where the fox had first met them, as it was cool and pleasant within it, the two brothers said, 'Let us rest a little by the well, and eat and drink.' He agreed, and while they were talking he forgot himself, and sat down upon the edge of the well without thinking of any evil. But the two brothers threw him backwards into the well, took the maiden, the horse, and the bird, and went home to their father.

'Here we bring you not only the golden bird,' said they; 'we have won the golden horse also, and the maiden from the golden castle.'

Then was there great joy; but the horse would not eat, the bird would not sing, and the maiden sat and wept.

But the youngest brother was not dead. By good fortune the well was dry, and he fell upon soft moss without being hurt, but he could not get out again. Even in this strait the faithful fox did not leave him: it came and leapt down to him and upbraided him for having forgotten its advice.

'But yet I cannot give it up like this,' he said; 'I will help you up again into daylight.' He bade him grasp his tail and keep tight hold of it; and then he pulled him up.

'You are not out of all danger yet,' said the fox. 'Your brothers were not sure of your death, and have surrounded the wood with watchers, who are to kill you if you let yourself be seen.' But a poor man was sitting upon the road, with whom the youth changed clothes, and in this way he got to the king's palace.

No one knew him, but the bird began to sing, the horse began to eat, and the beautiful maiden left off weeping.

'What does this mean?' asked the king, astonished.

'I do not know,' replied the maiden, 'but I have been so sorrowful and now I am so happy! I feel as if my true bridegroom had come.'

She told him all that had happened, although the other brothers had threatened her with death if she were to betray anything.

The king commanded that all people who were in his castle should be brought before him; and amongst them came the youth in his ragged clothes; but the maiden knew him at once and fell upon his neck. The wicked brothers were seized and put to death, but he was married to the beautiful maiden and declared heir to the king.

But how did it fare with the poor fox? Long afterwards the king's son was once again walking in the wood, when the fox met him and said:

'You have everything now that you can wish for, but there is never an end to my misery, and yet it is in your power to free me,' and again he asked him with tears to shoot him dead and chop off his head and feet. So the king's son did as the fox asked, and scarcely was it done when the fox was changed into a man, and was no other than the brother of the beautiful princess, who at last was freed from the magic charm which had been laid upon him. And now nothing more was wanting to their happiness as long as they lived.

The Bremen Town Musicians

There was a man who owned a donkey, which had carried his sacks to the mill industriously for many years, but whose strength had come to an end, so that the poor beast grew more and more unfit for work. The master determined to stop his food, but the donkey, discovering that there was no good intended to him, ran away and took the road to Bremen: 'There,' thought he, 'I can surely be a town musician.'

When he had gone a little way, he found a hound lying on the road and panting, like one who was tired with running.

'Hello! what are you panting so for, you big fellow?' asked the donkey.

'Oh!' said the dog, 'just because I am old, and get weaker every day, and cannot go out hunting, my master wanted to kill me, so I have taken leave of him; but how shall I gain my living now?'

'I'll tell you what,' said the donkey, 'I am going to Bremen to be town musician; come with me and take to music too. I will play the lute, and you shall beat the drum.'

The dog liked the idea, and they traveled on. It was not long before they saw a cat sitting by the road, making a face like three rainy days.

'Now then, what has gone wrong with you?' said the donkey.

'Who can be merry when his neck is in danger?' answered the cat. 'Because I am now getting old, and my teeth are blunt, and I like sitting before the fire and purring better than chasing the mice about, my mistress wanted to drown me. I have managed to escape, but good advice is scarce; tell me where am I to go?'

'Come with us two to Bremen; you understand serenading; you also can become a town musician.'

The cat thought it an excellent idea and went with them.

Soon after the three runaways came to a farmyard, and there sat a cockerel on the gate, crowing with might and main.

'You crow loud enough to deafen one,' said the donkey; 'what is the matter with you?'

'I prophesied fair weather,' said the cock, 'because it is our good mistress's washing-day, and she wants to dry the clothes; but because to-morrow is Sunday, and company is coming, the mistress has no pity on me, and has told the cook to put me into the soup to-morrow, and I must have my head cut off to-night: so now I am crowing with all my might as long as I can.'

'Oh, you old red-comb,' said the donkey, 'you had better come with us; we are going to Bremen, where you will certainly find something better than having your head cut off; you have a good voice, and if we all make music together, it will be something striking.'

The cock agreed to this plan and they went on, all four together.

But they could not reach the city of Bremen in one day, and by evening they had come to a wood, where they agreed to spend the night. The donkey and the dog laid themselves down under a great tree, but the cat and the cock went higher – the cock flying up to the topmost branch, where he was safest. Before he went to sleep he looked round on all four sides, and thought he saw in the distance a little spark burning; so he called out to his companions that there must be a house not far off, for he saw a light.

'If so, we had better get up and go on,' said the donkey, 'for the shelter here is bad.'

The hound thought that a few bones with some meat on would do him good too.

So they made their way to the place where the light was, and soon saw it shine brighter and grow larger, until they came to a well-lit robber's house. The donkey, as the biggest, went to the window and looked in.

'What do you see, my grey-horse?' asked the cock.

'What do I see?' answered the donkey; 'a table covered with good things to eat and drink, and robbers sitting at it enjoying themselves.'

'That would be the sort of thing for us,' said the cock.

'Yes, yes; ah, how I wish we were there!' said the donkey.

Then the animals took counsel together how they should manage to drive away the robbers, and at last they thought of a plan. The donkey was to place himself with his fore-feet upon the window-ledge, the hound was to jump on the donkey's back, the cat was to climb upon the dog, and lastly the cock was to fly up and perch upon the head of the cat. When this was done, at a given signal, they began to perform their music together: the donkey brayed, the hound barked, the cat mewed, and the cock crowed; then they burst through the window into the room, so that the glass clattered down. At this horrible din, the robbers sprang up, thinking that nothing less than a ghost was coming in, and fled in a great fright out into the forest. The four companions now sat down at the table, well content with what was left, and ate as if they were going to fast for a month.

As soon as the four musicians had finished, they put out the light, and each found for himself a sleeping-place according to his nature and to what suited him. The donkey laid himself down upon some straw in the yard, the hound behind the door, the cat upon the hearth near the warm ashes, and the cock perched himself upon a beam of the roof; and being tired from their long walk, they soon went to sleep.

When it was past midnight, and the robbers saw from afar that the light was no longer burning in their house, and all appeared quiet, the captain said, 'We ought not to have let ourselves be frightened out of our wits;' and ordered one of them to go and examine the house.

The messenger finding all still, went into the kitchen to light a candle, and, taking the glistening fiery eyes of the cat for live coals, he held a lucifer-match to them to light it. But the cat did not understand the joke, and flew in his face, spitting and scratching. He was dreadfully frightened, and ran to the back-door, but the dog, who lay there sprang up and bit his leg; and as he ran across the yard by the straw-heap, the donkey gave him a smart kick with its hind foot. The cock, too, who had been awakened by the noise, and had become lively, cried down from the beam, 'Cock-a-doodle-doo!'

Then the robber ran back as fast as he could to his captain, and said, 'Ah, there is a horrible witch sitting in the house, who spat on me and scratched my face with her long claws; and by the door stands a man with a knife, who stabbed me in the leg; and in the yard there lies a black monster, who beat me with a wooden club; and above, upon the roof, sits the judge, who called out, 'Bring the rogue here to me!' so I got away as well as I could.'

After this the robbers did not trust themselves in the house again; but it suited the four musicians of Bremen so well that they did not care to leave it any more and stayed there for the rest of their days, as the last person who told this story is ready to vouch for a fact.

The Little Brother and Sister

There was once a little brother who took his sister by the hand, and said:

'Since our own dear mother's death we have not had one happy hour; our stepmother beats us every day, and, when we come near her, kicks us away with her foot. Come, let us wander forth into the wide world.' So all day long they travelled over meadows, fields, and stony roads. By the evening they came into a large forest, and laid themselves down in a hollow tree, and went to sleep. When they awoke the next morning, the sun had already risen high in the heavens, and its beams made the tree so hot that the little boy said to his sister:

'I am so very thirsty, that if I knew where there was a brook, I would go and drink. Ah! I think I hear one running;' and so saying, he got up, and taking his sister's hand they went to look for the brook.

The wicked stepmother, however, was a witch, and had witnessed the departure of the two children: so, sneaking after them secretly, as is the habit of witches, she had enchanted all the springs in the forest.

Presently they found a brook, which ran trippingly over the pebbles, and the brother would have drunk out of it, but the sister heard how it said as it ran along, 'Who drinks of me will become a tiger!'

'I pray you, brother, drink not, or you will become a tiger, and tear me to pieces!' the sister exclaimed. So the brother did not drink, although his thirst was very great.

'I will wait till the next brook,' he said. As they came to the second, the sister heard it say, 'Who drinks of me becomes a wolf!' The sister ran up crying:

'Brother, do not, pray do not drink, or you will become a wolf and eat me up!' Then the brother did not drink, saying, 'I will wait until we come to the next spring, but then I must drink, you may say what you will; my thirst is much too great.'

Just as they reached the third brook, the sister heard the voice saying, 'Who drinks of me will become a fawn, who drinks of me will become a fawn!'

'Oh, my brother, do not drink,' she said, 'or you will be changed into a fawn, and run away from me!' But he had already kneeled down, and he drank of the water, and, as the first drops passed his lips, his shape took that of a fawn.

At first the sister wept over her little, changed brother, and he wept too, and knelt by her, very sorrowful; but at last the maiden said:

'Be still, dear little fawn, and I will never forsake you!' and, taking off her golden garter, she placed it around his neck, and, weaving rushes, made a belt to lead him with. This she tied to him, and taking the other end in her hand, she led him away, and they travelled

111

deeper and deeper into the forest. After they had gone a long distance they came to a little hut, and the maiden, peeping in, found it empty, and thought, 'Here we can stay and dwell.' Then she looked for leaves and moss to make a soft couch for the fawn, and every morning she went out and collected roots and berries and nuts for herself, and tender grass for the fawn. In the evening when the sister was tired, and had said her prayers, she laid her head upon the back of the fawn, which served for a pillow, on which she slept soundly. Had but the brother regained his own proper form, their lives would have been happy indeed.

Thus they dwelt in this wilderness, and some time had elapsed when it happened that the king of the country had a great hunt in the forest; and now sounded through the trees the blowing of horns, the barking of dogs, and the lusty cry of the hunters, so that the little fawn heard them, and wanted very much to join in.

'Ah!' said he to his sister, 'let me go to the hunt, I cannot restrain myself any longer;' and he begged so hard that at last she consented.

'But,' she told him, 'return again in the evening, for I shall shut my door against the wild huntsmen, and, that I may know you, do you knock, and say, "sister, dear, let me in," and if you do not speak I shall not open the door.'

As soon as she had said this, the little fawn sprang off quite glad and merry in the fresh breeze. The king and his huntsmen perceived the beautiful animal, and pursued him; but they could not catch him, and when they thought they certainly had him, he sprang away over the bushes, and got out of sight. Just as it was getting dark, he ran up to the hut, and, knocking, said, 'Sister mine, let me in.'

Then she unfastened the little door, and he went in, and rested all night long upon his soft couch. The next morning the hunt was commenced again, and as soon as the little fawn heard the horns and the tally-ho of the sportsmen he could not rest.

'Sister, dear, open the door; I must be off.'

'Return at evening, mind, and say the words as before,' she said as she opened the door.

When the king and his huntsmen saw him again, the fawn with the golden necklace, they followed him, close, but he was too nimble and quick for them. The whole day long they kept up with him, but towards evening the huntsmen made a circle around him, and one wounded him slightly in the hinder foot, so that he could run but slowly. Then one of them slipped after him to the little hut, and heard him say, 'Sister, dear, open the door,' and saw that the door was opened and immediately shut behind him. The huntsman, having observed all this, went and told the king what he had seen and heard.

'On the morrow I will pursue him once again,' the king said.

The sister, however, was terribly afraid when she saw that her fawn was wounded, and, washing off the blood, she put herbs upon the foot, and said, 'Go and rest upon your bed, dear fawn, that your wound may heal.'

It was so slight, that the next morning he felt nothing of it, and when he heard the hunting cries outside, he exclaimed:

'I cannot stop away – I must be there, and none shall catch me so easily again!' The sister wept very much and told him:

'Soon will they kill you, and I shall be here alone in this forest, forsaken by all the world: I cannot let you go.'

'I shall die here in vexation,' answered the fawn, 'if you do not, for when I hear the horn, I think I shall jump out of my skin.' The sister, finding she could not prevent him, opened the door, with a heavy heart, and the fawn jumped out, quite delighted, into the forest. As soon as the king perceived him, he said to his huntsmen:

'Follow him all day long till the evening, but let no one do him any harm.'

Then when the sun had set, the king asked his huntsman to show him the hut; and as they came to it he knocked at the door and said, 'Let me in, dear Sister.' Upon this the door opened, and, stepping in, the king saw a maiden more beautiful than he had ever beheld before. She was frightened when she saw not her fawn, but a man enter, who had a golden crown upon his head. But the king, looking at her with a kindly glance, held out to her his hand, saying, 'Will you go with me to my castle, and be my dear wife?'

'Oh, yes,' replied the maiden; 'but the fawn must go too: him I will never forsake.'

'He shall remain with you as long as you live, and shall never want,' the king replied.

The king took the beautiful maiden upon his horse, and rode to his castle, where the wedding was celebrated with great splendour and she became queen, and they lived together a long time; while the fawn was taken care of and played about the castle garden.

The wicked stepmother, however, on whose account the children had wandered forth into the world, had supposed that long ago the sister had been torn into pieces by the wild beasts, and the little brother in his fawn's shape hunted to death by the hunters. As soon, therefore, as she heard how happy they had become, and how everything prospered with them, envy and jealousy were aroused in her wicked heart, and left her no peace; and she was always thinking in what way she could bring misfortune upon them.

Her own daughter, who was as ugly as night, and had but one eye, for which she was continually reproached, said, 'The luck of being a queen has never happened to me.'

'Be quiet, now,' replied the old woman, 'and make yourself contented: when the time comes I will help and assist you.'

As soon, then, as the time came when the queen gave birth to a beautiful little boy, which happened when the king was out hunting, the old witch took the form of a chambermaid, and got into the room where the queen was lying.

'The bath is ready, which will restore you and give you fresh strength; be quick before it gets cold,' she said. Her daughter being at hand, they carried the weak queen between them into the room, and laid her in the bath, and then, shutting the door, they ran off; but first they made up an immense fire in the stove, which must soon suffocate the poor young queen.

When this was done, the old woman took her daughter, and, putting a cap upon her head, laid her in the bed in the queen's place. She gave her, too, the form and appearance of the real queen, as far as she was able; but she could not restore the lost eye, and, so that the king might not notice it, she turned her upon that side where there was no eye.

When midnight came, and everyone was asleep, the nurse, who sat by herself, wide awake, near the cradle, in the nursery, saw the door open and the true queen come in. She took the child in her arms, and rocked it a while, and then, shaking up its pillow, laid it down in its cradle, and covered it over again. She did not forget the fawn, either, but going to the corner where he was, stroked his head, and then went silently out of the door. The nurse asked in the morning of the guards if anyone had passed into the castle during the night.

'No, we have not seen anybody,' they answered.

For many nights afterwards the true queen came constantly, but never spoke a word; and the nurse saw her always, but she would not trust herself to speak about it to anyone. When some time had passed away, the queen one night began to speak, and said:

'How fares my child! how fares my fawn? Twice more will I come, but never again.'

The nurse made no reply; but, when she had disappeared, went to the King, and told him. 'Oh, mercy! What does this mean?' the king exclaimed. 'The next night I will watch myself by the child.'

So in the evening he went into the nursery, and about midnight the Queen appeared, and said:

'How fares my child! how fares my fawn? Once more will I come, but never again.'

And she nursed the child, as she usually did, and then disappeared. The King dared not speak; but he watched the following night, and this time she said:

'How fares my child! how fares my fawn? This time have I come, but never again.'

At these words the King could hold back no longer, but, springing up, cried, 'You can be no other than my dear wife!'

'Yes, I am your dear wife,' she answered; and at that moment her life was restored by God's mercy, and she was again as beautiful and charming as ever. She told the King the fraud which the witch and her daughter had practised upon him, and he had them both tried, and sentence was pronounced against them. The little fawn was disenchanted, and received once more his human form; and the brother and sister lived happily together to the end of their days.

Thumbling

There was once a poor woodman who sat in his cottage one evening, smoking his pipe by the fireside, while his wife sat and span.

'How sad it is, wife,' said he, as he puffed out a long curl of smoke, 'for you and me to sit here by ourselves, without any children to play about and amuse us! With us all is so quiet, and in other houses it is happy and merry.'

'Yes,' replied the wife, and sighed, 'how happy I should be even if we had only one child! Even if it were quite small, and only as big as a thumb, I should be quite satisfied, and we would love it with all our hearts.' Now it so happened that the woman fell ill, and after seven months her wish was fulfilled and she gave birth to a child, that was perfect in all its limbs, but no longer than a thumb. So they said, 'Well, we cannot say we have not got what we wished for, and little as he is, he shall be our dear child.' And because of his size, they called him Thumbling.

They did gave him plenty of food, yet the child did not grow taller, but remained just the same size as when he was born. Nevertheless, his eyes were sparkling and he soon showed himself to be a cleaver and nimble little, who always knew well what he was about.

One day, the woodman was getting ready to go into the forest to cut wood, when he said as if to himself, 'How I wish that there was someone who would bring the cart to me!'

'Oh father,' cried Thumbling, 'I will bring the cart, rely on that; it shall be in the forest at the time you want it.'

The man smiled and said, 'How can that be done, when you are far too small to lead the horse by the reins?'

'That's of no consequence, father; if my mother will only harness it, I shall sit in the horse's ear and call out to him which way to go.'

'Well,' answered the man, ' we will try it for once.'

When the time came, the mother harnessed the horse, and placed Thumbling in its ear, and then the little fellow cried, 'Gee up, gee up!' The horse went quite properly as if with its master, and the cart went the right way into the forest. It so happened that just as he was turning a corner, and the little one was crying, 'Gently, gently!' two strange men came towards him.

'My word!' said one of them. 'What is this? There is a cart coming, and a driver is calling to the horse and still he is not to be seen!'

'That can't be right,' said the other, 'we will follow the cart and see where it stops.'

They followed the cart right into the forest, to the exact place where the wood had been cut. When Thumbling saw his father, he cried to him, 'See, father, here I am with the cart; now take me down.'

The father got hold of the horse with his left hand and with the right took his little son out of the ear. He put his son on the ground, where Thumbling sat down on a straw, as merry as you please.

When the two strange men saw him, they did not know what to say for astonishment. Then one of them took the other aside and said, 'Hark, the little fellow would make our fortune if we exhibited him in a large town, for money. We will buy him.' They went to the woodman and said, 'Sell us the little man. He shall be well treated with us.'

'No,' replied the father, 'he is the apple of my eye, and all the money in the world cannot buy him from me.'

Thumbling, however, when he heard of the bargain, had crept up the folds of his father's coat, placed himself on his shoulder, and whispered in his ear, 'Father do take their money, I will soon come back again.' So the father at last said with him to the two men for a handsome bit of money.

'Where would you like to sit?' they asked Thumbling.

'Oh just set me on the rim of your hat, and then I can walk about there and look at the country as we go along.'

They did as he wished, and when Thumbling had taken leave of his father, he went away with them. They walked until it was dusk, and then the little fellow said, 'Let me get down, I am tired.'

The man took his hat off, and put the little fellow on the ground by the wayside, and he leapt and crept about a little between the lumps of earth, and then he suddenly slipped into a mouse-hole which he had sought out. 'Good evening, gentlemen, just go home without me,' he cried to them, and mocked them. They ran over and stuck their sticks into the mouse-hole, but it was all in vain. Thumbling crept still farther in, and as it soon became quite dark, they were forced to go home with their vexation and their empty purses.

When Thumbling saw that they were gone, he crept back out of the subterranean passage. 'It is so dangerous to walk on the ground in the dark,' said he; 'how easily a neck or a leg is broken!' Fortunately he bumped into an empty snail-shell. 'Thank goodness!' said he. 'I can sleep in here safely,' and got into it.

Not long afterwards, when he was just going to sleep, he heard two men go by, and one of them was saying, 'How shall we contrive to get into the rich pastor's house to rob his silver and gold?'

'I could tell thee that,' cried Thumbling, interrupting them.

'What was that?' said one of the thieves in fright, 'I heard someone speaking.'

They stood still listening, and Thumbling spoke again, and said, 'Take me with you, and I'll help you.'

'But where are you?'

'Just look on the ground, and hear where my voice comes from,' he replied.

The thieves found him eventually, and lifted him up. 'You little imp, what can you do to help us?' they said.

'A great deal,' said he. 'I will creep into the pastor's room through the iron bars, and will reach out to you whatever you want to have.'

'Come then,' they said, 'and we will see what you can do.'

When they got to the pastor's house, Thumbling crept into the room, but instantly called out as loud as he could, 'Do you want to have everything that is here?'

The thieves were alarmed, and said, 'Speak softly, so as not to wake anyone!'

Thumbling however, behaved as if he had not understood this, and cried again, 'What do you want? Do you want to have everything that is here?'

The maid, who slept in the next room, heard this and sat up in bed, and listened. The thieves in their fright had run some distance away, but at last they took courage, and thought, 'The little rascal wants to make fools of us.' So they came back and whispered to him, 'Come, be serious, and pass something out to us.'

Then Thumbling again cried as loudly as he could, 'I will pass everything out to you, just hold out your hands.' The maid, who was listening, heard this quite distinctly, and jumped out of bed and rushed to the door. The thieves took flight, and ran as if a wolf were behind them, but as the maid could not see anything, she went to find a light. When she came back with it, Thumbling, unperceived, took himself off to the barn, and the cook, after she had examined every corner and found nothing, lay down in her bed again, and believed that, after all, she had only been dreaming with her eyes and ears open.

Thumbling had climbed up among the hay and found a beautiful place to sleep in; there he intended to rest until day, and then go home again to his parents. But he had other things to go through. Truly, there is much affliction and misery in this world! When day dawned, the maid arose from her bed to feed the cows. Her first walk was into the barn, where she laid hold of an armful of hay, and precisely that very one in which poor Thumbling was lying asleep. He, however, was sleeping so soundly that he was aware of nothing, and did not awake until he was in the mouth of the cow, who had picked him up with the hay.

'Ah, heavens!' cried he, 'how have I come to tumble into the mill?' But he soon discovered where he was. Then he had to be careful not to let himself fall between the teeth and be dismembered, but he was nevertheless forced to slip down into the stomach with the hay. 'In this little room the windows are forgotten,' said he, 'and no sun shines in, neither will a candle be brought.' His quarters were especially unpleasing to him, and the worst was, more and more hay was always coming in by the door, and the space grew less and less. Then at length in his anguish, he cried as loud as he could, 'Don't bring me any more hay! Don't bring me any more hay!'

The maid was just milking the cow, and when she heard someone speaking and saw no one, and realized that it was the same voice that she had heard in the night, she was so terrified that she slipped off her stool, and spilt the milk. She ran in great haste to her master, and said, 'Oh heavens, pastor, the cow has been speaking!'

'You are surely mad,' replied the pastor; but he went with her to the byre to see what was there. Hardly, had he set his foot inside when Thumbling again cried, 'Don't bring me any more hay! Don't bring me any more hay!'

Then the pastor himself was alarmed, and thought that an evil spirit had gone into the cow, and ordered her to be killed. She was killed, but the stomach, with Thumbling in it, was thrown on the rubbish heap. Thumbling had great difficulty in working his way out, but at last, just as he was going to thrust his head out, a new misfortune occurred. A hungry wolf ran to the rubbish heap, and swallowed the whole stomach at one gulp.

Thumbling did not lose courage. 'Perhaps,' thought he, 'the wolf will listen to what I have got to say,' and he called to him from out of his stomach, 'Dear wolf, I know of a magnificent feast for you.'

'Where's that?' said the wolf.

'In such and such a house,' said Thumbling, describing his own father's house. 'You must creep into it through the kitchen-sink, and will find cakes, and bacon, and sausages, and as much of them as you can eat.'

The wolf did not need to be told this twice, squeezed himself in at night through the sink, and ate to his heart's content in the larder. When he had eaten his fill, he wanted to go out again, but he had become so big that he could not go out by the same way. Thumbling had counted on this, and now began to make a violent noise in the wolf's body, and raged and screamed as loudly as he could.

'Will you be quiet,' said the wolf, 'you will wake up the people!'

'What's that to me?' replied the little fellow. 'You have eaten your fill, and now it's my turn to make merry,' and began once more to shout with all his strength.

At last his father and mother were aroused by it, and ran to the room and looked in through the opening in the door. When they saw that a wolf was inside, the husband ran and fetched his axe, and the wife the scythe.

'Stay behind me,' said the man, when they entered the room. 'When I have knocked him out, you must cut his body to pieces.'

Thumbling heard his parents, voices and cried, 'Dear father, I am here; I am in the wolf's body.'

'Thank God!' said the father, full of joy. 'Our dear child has found us again.' And he told his wife not to use her scythe, in case Thumbling should be hurt by it. After that he raised his arm, and struck the wolf such a blow on his head that he fell down dead, and then they got knives and scissors and cut his body open and drew the little fellow forth.

'Ah,' said the father, 'we have been so worried for you."

'Yes father, I have gone about the world a great deal. Thank heaven, I breathe fresh air again!'

'Where have you been, then?'

'Ah, father, I have been in a mouse's hole, in a snail's shell, in a cow's stomach, and then in a wolf's; and now I am safely home again and will stay with you.'

'And we will not sell you again, no, not for all the riches in the world,' said his parents, and they embraced and kissed their dear Thumbling. They gave him plenty to eat and to drink, and had some new clothes made for him, for his own had been spoiled on his journey. So Thumbling stayed happily at home with his parents, for though he had been on a great journey with many adventures, he was always agreed that, after all, there's no place like home!

Little Snow-White

Once upon a time in the middle of winter, when the flakes of snow were falling like feathers from the sky, a queen sat at a window sewing, and the frame of the window was made of black ebony. And whilst she was sewing and looking out of the window at the snow, she pricked her finger with the needle, and three drops of blood fell upon the snow. And the red looked pretty upon the white snow, and she thought to herself, 'Would that I had a child as white as snow, as red as blood, and as black as the wood of the window-frame.' Soon after that she had a little daughter, who was as white as snow, and as red as blood, and her hair was as black as ebony; and she was therefore called Little Snow-White. And when the child was born, the queen died.

After a year had passed the king took to himself another wife. She was a beautiful woman, but proud and haughty, and she could not bear that anyone else should surpass her in beauty. She had a wonderful looking-glass, and when she stood in front of it and looked at herself in it, and said:

> 'Looking-glass, looking-glass, on the wall,
> Who in this land is the fairest of all?'

The looking-glass answered:

> 'Thou, O Queen, are the fairest of all!'

Then she was satisfied, for she knew that the looking-glass spoke the truth.

But Snow-White was growing up, and grew more and more beautiful; and when she was seven years old she was as beautiful as the day, and more beautiful than the queen herself. And once when the queen asked her looking-glass:

> 'Looking-glass, looking-glass, on the wall,
> Who in this land is the fairest of all?'

It answered:

> 'Thou art fairer than all who are here, Lady Queen.
> But more beautiful still is Snow-White, as I ween.'

Then the Queen was shocked, and turned yellow and green with envy. From that hour, whenever she looked at Snow-White, her heart heaved in her breast, she hated the girl so much. And envy and pride grew higher and higher in her heart like a weed, so that she had no peace day or night. She called a huntsman, and said, 'Take the child away into the forest; I will no longer have her in my sight. Kill her, and bring me back her heart as a token.'

The huntsman obeyed, and took her away; but when he had drawn his knife, and was about to pierce Snow-White's innocent heart, she began to weep, and said, 'Ah dear huntsman, leave me my life! I will run away into the wild forest, and never come home again.'

And as she was so beautiful the huntsman had pity on her and said, 'Run away, then, you poor child.' 'The wild beasts will soon have devoured you,' thought he, and yet it seemed as if a stone had been rolled from his heart since it was no longer needful for him to kill her. A young boar just then came running by so he stabbed it, and cut out its heart and took it to the queen as proof that the child was dead. The cook had to salt this, and the wicked queen ate it, and thought she had eaten the heart of Snow-White.

But now the poor child was all alone in the great forest, and so terrified that she looked at every leaf of every tree, and did not know what to do. Then she began to run, and ran over sharp stones and through thorns, and the wild beasts ran past her, but did her no harm.

She ran as long as her feet would go until it was almost evening; then she saw a little cottage and went into it to rest herself. Everything in the cottage was small, but neater and cleaner than can be told. There was a table on which was a white cover, and seven little plates, and on each plate a little spoon; moreover, there were seven little knives and forks, and seven little mugs. Against the wall stood seven little beds side by side, and covered with snow-white counterpanes.

Little Snow-White was so hungry and thirsty that she ate some vegetables and bread from each plate and drank a drop of wine out of each mug, for she did not wish to take all from one only. Then, as she was so tired, she laid herself down on one of the little beds, but none of them suited her; one was too long, another too short, but at last she found that the seventh one was right, and so she remained in it, said a prayer and went to sleep.

When it was quite dark the owners of the cottage came back; they were seven dwarfs who dug and delved in the mountains for ore. They lit their seven candles, and as it was now light within the cottage they saw that someone had been there, for everything was not in the same order in which they had left it.

The first said, 'Who has been sitting on my chair?'

The second, 'Who has been eating off my plate?'

The third, 'Who has been taking some of my bread?'

The fourth, 'Who has been eating my vegetables?'

The fifth, 'Who has been using my fork?'

The sixth, 'Who has been cutting with my knife?'

The seventh, 'Who has been drinking out of my mug?'

Then the first looked round and saw that there was a little hole on his bed, and he said, 'Who has been getting into my bed?' The others came up and each called out, 'Somebody has been lying in my bed too.' But the seventh when he looked at his bed saw little Snow-White, who was lying fast asleep. And he called the others, who came running up, and they cried out with astonishment, and brought their seven little candles and let the light fall on little Snow-White.

'Oh, heavens! oh, heavens!' cried they, 'what a lovely child!' and they were so glad that they did not wake her up, but let her sleep on in the bed. And the seventh dwarf slept with his companions, one hour with each, and so got through the night.

When it was morning little Snow-White awoke, and was frightened when she saw the seven dwarfs. But they were friendly and asked her what her name was.

'My name is Snow-White,' she answered.

'How have you come to our house?' asked the dwarfs.

Then she told them that her step-mother had wished to have her killed, but that the huntsman had spared her life, and that she had run for the whole day, until at last she had found their dwelling. The dwarfs said, 'If you will take care of our house, cook, make the beds, wash, sew, and knit, and if you will keep everything neat and clean, you can stay with us and you shall want for nothing.'

'Yes,' said Snow-White, 'with all my heart,' and she stayed with them. She kept the house in order for them; in the mornings they went to the mountains and looked for copper and gold, in the evenings they came back, and then their supper had to be ready. The girl was alone the whole day, so the good dwarfs warned her and said, 'Beware of your step-mother, she will soon know that you are here; be sure to let no one come in.'

But the queen, believing that she had eaten Snow-White's heart, could not but think that she was again the first and most beautiful of all; and she went to her looking-glass and said:

> 'Looking-glass, looking-glass, on the wall,
> Who in this land is the fairest of all?'

And the glass answered:

> 'Oh, Queen, thou art fairest of all I see,
> But over the hills, where the seven dwarfs dwell,
> Snow-White is still alive and well,
> And none is so fair as she.'

Then she was astounded, for she knew that the looking-glass never spoke falsely, and she knew that the huntsman had betrayed her, and that little Snow-White was still alive.

And so she thought and thought again how she might kill her, for so long as she was not the fairest in the whole land, envy let her have no rest. And when she had at last thought of something to do, she painted her face, and dressed herself like an old pedlar-woman, and no one could have known her. In this disguise she went over the seven mountains to the seven dwarfs, and knocked at the door and cried, 'Pretty things to sell, very cheap, very cheap.'

Little Snow-White looked out of the window and called out, 'Good-day my good woman, what have you to sell?'

'Good things, pretty things,' she answered; 'stay-laces of all colours,' and she pulled out one which was woven of bright-coloured silk. 'I may let the worthy old woman in,' thought Snow-White, and she unbolted the door and bought the pretty laces.

'Child,' said the old woman, 'what a fright you look; come, I will lace you properly for once.' Snow-White had no suspicion, but stood before her, and let herself be laced with the new laces. But the old woman laced so quickly and so tightly that Snow-White lost her breath and fell down as if dead.

'Now I am the most beautiful,' said the Queen to herself, and ran away.

Not long afterwards, in the evening, the seven dwarfs came home, but how shocked they were when they saw their dear little Snow-White lying on the ground, and that she neither stirred nor moved, and seemed to be dead. They lifted her up, and, as they saw that she was laced too tightly, they cut the laces; then she began to breathe a little, and after a while came to life again. When the dwarfs heard what had happened they said, 'The old pedler-woman was no one else than the wicked queen; take care and let no one come in when we are not with you.'

But the wicked woman when she had reached home went in front of the glass and asked:

> 'Looking-glass, looking-glass, on the wall,
> Who in this land is the fairest of all?'

And it answered as before:

> 'Oh, Queen, thou art fairest of all I see,
> But over the hills, where the seven dwarfs dwell,
> Snow-White is still alive and well,
> And none is so fair as she.'

When she heard that, all her blood rushed to her heart with fear, for she saw plainly that little Snow-White was again alive. 'But now,' she said, 'I will think of something that shall put an end to you,' and by the help of witchcraft, which she understood, she made a poisonous comb. Then she disguised herself and took the shape of another old woman. So she went over the seven mountains to the seven dwarfs, knocked at the door, and cried, 'Good things to sell, cheap, cheap!' Little Snow-White looked out and said, 'Go away; I cannot let any one come in.'

'I suppose you can look,' said the old woman, and pulled the poisonous comb out and held it up. It pleased the girl so well that she let herself be beguiled, and opened the door. When they had made a bargain the old woman said, 'Now I will comb you properly.' Poor little Snow-White had no suspicion, and let the old woman do as she pleased, but hardly had she put the comb in her hair than the poison in it took effect, and the girl fell down senseless.

'You paragon of beauty,' said the wicked woman, you are done for now,' and she went away.

But fortunately it was almost evening, when the seven dwarfs came home. When they saw Snow-White lying as if dead upon the ground they at once suspected the step-mother, and they looked and found the poisoned comb. Scarcely had they taken it out when Snow-White came to herself, and told them what had happened. Then they warned her once more to be upon her guard and to open the door to no one.

The queen, at home, went in front of the glass and said:

> 'Looking-glass, looking-glass, on the wall,
> Who in this land is the fairest of all?'

Then it answered as before:

> 'Oh, Queen, thou art fairest of all I see,
> But over the hills, where the seven dwarfs dwell,
> Snow-White is still alive and well,

And none is so fair as she.'

When she heard the glass speak thus she trembled and shook with rage. 'Snow-White shall die,' she cried, 'even if it costs me my life!'

Thereupon she went into a quite secret, lonely room, where no one ever came, and there she made a very poisonous apple. Outside it looked pretty, white with a red cheek, so that everyone who saw it longed for it; but whoever ate a piece of it must surely die.

When the apple was ready she painted her face, and dressed herself up as a country-woman, and so she went over the seven mountains to the seven dwarfs. She knocked at the door. Snow-White put her head out of the window and said, 'I cannot let anyone in; the seven dwarfs have forbidden me.' 'It is all the same to me,' answered the woman, 'I shall soon get rid of my apples. There, I will give you one.'

'No,' said Snow-White, 'I dare not take anything.'

'Are you afraid of poison?' said the old woman. 'Look, I will cut the apple in two pieces; you eat the red cheek, and I will eat the white.'

The apple was so cunningly made that only the red cheek was poisoned. Snow-White longed for the fine apple, and when she saw that the woman ate part of it she could resist no longer, and stretched out her hand and took the poisonous half. But hardly had she a bit of it in her mouth than she fell down dead. Then the queen looked at her with a dreadful look, and laughed aloud and said, 'White as snow, red as blood, black as ebony-wood! This time the dwarfs cannot wake you up again.'

And when she asked of the Looking-glass at home:

> 'Looking-glass, looking-glass, on the wall,
> Who in this land is the fairest of all?'

It answered at last:

> 'Oh, Queen, in this land thou art fairest of all.'

Then her envious heart had rest, so far as an envious heart can have rest.

The dwarfs, when they came home in the evening, found Snow-White lying upon the ground; she breathed no longer and was dead. They lifted her up, looked to see whether they could find anything poisonous, unlaced her, combed her hair, washed her with water and wine, but it was all of no use; the poor child was dead, and remained dead. They laid her upon a bier, and all seven of them sat round it and wept for her, and wept three days long.

Then they were going to bury her, but she still looked as if she were living, and still had her pretty red cheeks. They said, 'We could not bury her in the dark ground,' and they had a transparent coffin of glass made, so that she could be seen from all sides, and they laid her in it, and wrote her name upon it in golden letters, and that she was a king's daughter. Then they put the coffin out upon the mountain, and one of them always stayed by it and watched it. And birds came too, and wept for Snow-White; first an owl, then a raven, and last a dove.

And now Snow-White lay a long, long time in the coffin, and she did not change, but looked as if she were asleep; for she was as white as snow, as red as blood, and her hair was as black as ebony.

It happened that a king's son came into the forest, and went to the dwarfs' house to spend the night. He saw the coffin on the mountain, and the beautiful Snow-White within it, and read what was written upon it in golden letters.

'Let me have the coffin, I will give you whatever you want for it,' he said to the dwarfs.

'We will not part with it for all the gold in the world,' the dwarfs answered.

'Let me have it as a gift, for I cannot live without seeing Snow-White. I will honour and prize her as my dearest possession.' As he spoke in this way the good dwarfs took pity upon him, and gave him the coffin.

The king's son had the coffin carried away by his servants on their shoulders. It happened that they stumbled over a tree-stump, and with the shock the poisonous piece of apple which Snow-White had bitten off came out of her throat. And before long she opened her eyes, lifted up the lid of the coffin, sat up, and was once more alive.

'Oh, heavens, where am I?' she cried.

The king's son, full of joy, said, 'You are with me,' and told her what had happened, and said, 'I love you more than everything in the world; come with me to my father's palace, you shall be my wife.'

And Snow-White was willing, and went with him, and their wedding was held with great show and splendour. But Snow-White's wicked step-mother was also bidden to the feast. When she had arrayed herself in beautiful clothes she went before the Looking-glass, and said:

'Looking-glass, looking-glass, on the wall,
Who in this land is the fairest of all?'

The glass answered:

'Oh, Queen, of all here the fairest art thou,
But the young queen is fairer by far as I trow.'

Then the wicked woman uttered a curse, and was so wretched, so utterly wretched, that she knew not what to do. At first she would not go to the wedding at all, but she had no peace, and must go to see the young queen. And when she went in she knew Snow-White; and she stood still with rage and fear, and could not stir. But iron slippers had already been put upon the fire, and they were brought in with tongs, and set before her. Then she was forced to put on the red-hot shoes, and dance until she dropped down dead.

Mother Holle

Once upon a time there was a widow who had two daughters; one of them was beautiful and industrious, the other ugly and lazy. The mother, however, loved the ugly and lazy one best, because she was her own daughter, and so the other, who was only her stepdaughter, was made to do all the work of the house, and was quite the Cinderella of the family. Her stepmother sent her out every day to sit by the well in the high road, there to spin until she made her fingers bleed. Now it chanced one day that some blood fell on to the spindle, and as the girl stopped over the well to wash it off, the spindle suddenly sprang out of her hand and fell into the well. She ran home crying to tell of her misfortune, but her stepmother spoke harshly to her, and gave her a violent scolding.

'As you have let the spindle fall into the well you may go yourself and fetch it out,' she said unkindly.

The girl went back to the well not knowing what to do, and at last in her distress she jumped into the water after the spindle.

She remembered nothing more until she awoke and found herself in a beautiful meadow, full of sunshine, and with countless flowers blooming in every direction. She walked over the meadow, and presently she came upon a baker's oven full of bread.

'Take us out, take us out, or alas! we shall be burnt to a cinder,' the loaves cried out to her; 'we were baked through long ago.' So she took the bread-shovel and drew them all out. She went on a little farther, till she came to a tree full of apples.

'Shake me, shake me, I pray,' cried the tree; 'My apples, one and all, are ripe.' So she shook the tree, and the apples came falling down upon her like rain; but she continued shaking until there was not a single apple left upon it. Then she carefully gathered the apples together in a heap and walked on again.

The next thing she came to was a little house, and there she saw an old woman looking out, with such large teeth, that she was terrified, and turned to run away. But the old woman called after her:

'What are you afraid of, dear child? Stay with me; if you will do the work of my house properly for me, I will make you very happy. You must be very careful, however, to make my bed in the right way, for I wish you always to shake it thoroughly, so that the feathers fly about; then they say, down there in the world, that it is snowing; for I am Mother Holle.' The old woman spoke so kindly that the girl summoned up courage and agreed to enter into her service.

She took care to do everything according to the old woman's bidding and every time she made the bed she shook it with all her might, so that the feathers flew about like so many snowflakes. The old woman was as good as her word: she never spoke angrily to her, and gave her roast and boiled meats every day.

So she stayed on with Mother Holle for some time, and then she began to grow unhappy. She could not at first tell why she felt sad, but she became conscious at last of great longing to go home; then she knew she was homesick, although she was a thousand times better off with Mother Holle than with her stepmother and sister. After waiting awhile, she went to Mother Holle and said:

'I am so homesick, that I cannot stay with you any longer, for although I am so happy here, I must return to my own people.'

Then Mother Holle said, 'I am pleased that you should want to go back to your own people, and as you have served me so well and faithfully, I will take you home myself.'

Thereupon she led the girl by the hand up to a broad gateway. The gate was opened, and as the girl passed through, a shower of gold fell upon her, and the gold clung to her, so that she was covered with it from head to foot.

'That is a reward for your industry,' said Mother Holle, and as she spoke she handed her the spindle which had dropped into the well.

The gate was then closed, and the girl found herself back in the old world close to her mother's house. As she entered the courtyard, the cock who was perched on the well, called out:

'Cock-a-doodle-doo! Your golden daughter's come back to you.'

Then she went in to her stepmother and sister, and as she was so richly covered with gold, they gave her a warm welcome. She related to them all that had happened, and when the mother heard how she had come by her great riches, she thought she should like her ugly, lazy daughter to go and try her fortune. So she made the sister go and sit by the well and spin, and the girl pricked her finger and thrust her hand into a thorn-bush, so that she might drop some blood on to the spindle; then she threw it into the well, and jumped in herself. Like her sister she awoke in the beautiful meadow, and walked over it till she came to the oven.

'Take us out, take us out, or alas! we shall be burnt to a cinder; we were baked through long ago,' cried the loaves as before. But the lazy girl answered, 'Do you think I am going to dirty my hands for you?' and walked on. Presently she came to the apple-tree.

'Shake me, shake me, I pray; my apples, one and all, are ripe,' it cried. But she only answered, 'A nice thing to ask me to do, one of the apples might fall on my head,' and passed on.

At last she came to Mother Holle's house, and as she had heard all about the large teeth from her sister, she was not afraid of them, and engaged herself without delay to the old woman. The first day she was very obedient and industrious, and exerted herself to please Mother Holle, for she thought of the gold she should get in return. The next day, however, she began to dawdle over her work, and the third day she was more idle still; then she began to lie in bed in the mornings and refused to get up. Worse still, she neglected to make the old woman's bed properly, and forgot to shake it so that the feathers might fly about. So Mother Holle very soon got tired of her, and told her she might go. The lazy girl was delighted at this, and thought to herself, 'The gold will soon be mine.' Mother Holle led her, as she had led her sister,

to the broad gateway; but as she was passing through, instead of the shower of gold, a great bucketful of pitch came pouring over her.

'That is in return for your services,' said the old woman, and she shut the gate.

So the lazy girl had to go home covered with pitch, and the cock on the well called out as she saw her:

'Cock-a-doodle-doo! Your dirty daughter's come back to you.'

But, try what she would, she could not get the pitch off and it stuck to her as long as she lived.

The Dog and the Sparrow

A sheep-dog had not a good master, but, on the contrary, one who let him suffer hunger. As he could stay no longer with him, he went quite sadly away. On the road he met a sparrow who said:

'Brother dog, why are you so sad?'

'I am hungry, and have nothing to eat,' replied the dog.

'Dear brother, come into the town with me, and I will satisfy your hunger,' said the sparrow.

So they went into the town together, and when they came in front of a butcher's shop the sparrow said to the dog, 'Stay there, and I will pick a bit of meat down for you,' and he alighted on the stall, looked about him to see that no one was observing him, and pecked and pulled and tore so long at a piece which lay on the edge, that it slipped down. Then the dog seized it, ran into a corner, and devoured it.

'Now come with me to another shop,' said the sparrow, 'and then I will get you one more piece that you may be satisfied.' When the dog had devoured the second piece as well, the sparrow asked, 'Brother dog, have you now had enough?'

'Yes, I have had meat enough,' he answered, 'but I have had no bread yet.'

'You shall have that too – come with me,' said the sparrow. Then he took him to a baker's shop, and pecked at a couple of little buns till they rolled down, and as the dog wanted still more, he led him to another stall, and again got bread for him. When that was consumed, the sparrow said:

'Brother dog, have you now had enough?'

'Yes, thank you' he replied, 'now we will walk awhile outside the town.' Then they both went out on to the highway. It was, however, warm weather, and when they had walked a little way the dog said, 'I am tired, and would like to sleep.'

'Well, do sleep,' answered the sparrow, 'and in the meantime I will seat myself on a branch.'

So the dog lay down on the road, and fell fast asleep. While he lay sleeping there, a waggoner came driving by, who had a cart with three horses, laden with two barrels of wine. The sparrow saw that he was not going to turn aside, but was staying in the wheel track in which the dog was lying, so it cried, 'Waggoner, don't do it, or I will make you poor.' The waggoner, however, growled to himself, 'You will not make me poor,' and cracked his whip and drove the cart over the dog, and the wheels killed him.

'You have run over my brother dog and killed him,' cried the sparrow. 'It shall cost you your cart and horses.'

'Cart and horses indeed!' said the waggoner. 'What harm can you do me?' and drove onwards. Then the sparrow crept under the cover of the cart, and pecked so long at the same bung-hole that he got the bung out, and then all the wine ran out without the driver noticing it. But once when he was looking behind him he saw that the cart was dripping, and looked at the barrels and saw that one of them was empty.

'Unfortunate fellow that I am!' cried he.

'Not unfortunate enough yet,' said the sparrow, and flew on to the head of one of the horses and pecked his eyes out. When the driver saw that, he drew out his axe and wanted to hit the sparrow, but the sparrow flew into the air, and he hit his horse on the head, and it fell down dead.

'Oh, what an unfortunate man I am!' cried he.

'Not unfortunate enough yet,' said the sparrow, and when the driver drove on with the two hoses, the sparrow again crept under the cover, and pecked the bung out of the second cask, so all the wine was spilt. When the driver became aware of it, he again cried, 'Oh, what an unfortunate man I am,' but the sparrow replied, 'Not unfortunate enough yet,' and seated himself on the head of the second horse, and pecked his eyes out. The driver ran up to it and raised his axe to strike, but the sparrow flew into the air and the blow struck the horse, which fell.

'Oh, what an unfortunate man I am.'

'Not unfortunate enough yet,' said the sparrow, and lighted on the third horse's head, and pecked out his eyes. The driver, in his rage, struck at the sparrow without looking round, and did not hit him but killed his third horse likewise.

'Oh, what an unfortunate man I am!' cried he.

'Not unfortunate enough yet,' answered the sparrow. 'Now will I make you unfortunate in your home,' and flew away.

The driver had to leave the waggon standing, and full of anger and vexation went home.

'Ah,' said he to his wife, 'what misfortunes I have had! My wine has run out, and the horses are all three dead!'

'Alas, husband,' she answered, 'what a malicious bird has come into the house! It has gathered together every bird there is in the world, and they have fallen on our corn up there, and are devouring it.' Then he went upstairs, and thousands and thousands of birds were sitting in the loft and had eaten up all the corn, and the sparrow was sitting in the middle of them.

'Oh, what an unfortunate man I am!' cried the driver again.

'Not unfortunate enough yet!' answered the sparrow. 'Waggoner, it shall cost you your life as well,' and flew out.

Then the waggoner had lost all his property, and he went downstairs into the room, sat down behind the stove and was quite furious and bitter. But the sparrow sat outside in front of the window, and cried, 'Waggoner, it shall cost you your life.' Then the waggoner snatched the axe and threw it at the sparrow, but it only broke the window, and did not hit the bird. The sparrow now hopped in, placed itself on the stove and cried, 'Waggoner, it shall cost you your life.' The latter, quite mad and blind with rage, smote the stove in twain, and as the sparrow flew from one place to another so it fared with all his household furniture, looking-glass, benches, table, and at last the walls of his house, and yet he could not hit the bird. At length, however, he caught it with his hand.

'Shall I kill it?' his wife said.

'No,' cried he, 'that would be too merciful. It shall die much more cruelly,' and he took it and swallowed it whole. The sparrow, however, began to flutter about in his body, and fluttered up again into the man's mouth; then it stretched out its head, and cried, 'Waggoner, it shall still cost you your life.'

The driver gave the axe to his wife, and said, 'Wife, kill the bird in my mouth for me.' The woman struck, but missed her blow, and hit the waggoner right on his head, so that he fell dead. But the sparrow flew up and away.

Sleeping Beauty
(Little Briar Rose)

In times past there lived a king and queen, who said to each other every day of their lives, 'Would that we had a child!' and yet they had none. But it happened once that when the queen was bathing, there came a frog out of the water, and he squatted on the ground, and said to her, 'Thy wish shall be fulfilled; before a year has gone by, thou shalt bring a daughter into the world.'

And as the frog foretold, so it happened; and the queen bore a daughter so beautiful that the king could not contain himself for joy, and he ordained a great feast. Not only did he bid to it his relations, friends, and acquaintances, but also the wise women, that they might be kind and favourable to the child. There were thirteen of them in his kingdom, but as he had only provided twelve golden plates for them to eat from, one of them had to be left out.

However, the feast was celebrated with all splendour; and as it drew to an end, the wise women stood forward to present to the child their wonderful gifts: one bestowed virtue, one beauty, a third riches, and so on, whatever there is in the world to wish for. And when eleven of them had said their say, in came the uninvited thirteenth, burning to revenge herself, and without greeting or respect, she cried with a loud voice, "In the fifteenth year of her age the princess shall prick herself with a spindle and shall fall down dead." And without speaking one more word she turned away and left the hall. Everyone was terrified at her saying, when the twelfth came forward, for she had not yet bestowed her gift, and though she could not do away with the evil prophecy, yet she could soften it, so she said, 'The princess shall not die, but fall into a deep sleep for a hundred years.'

Now the king, being desirous of saving his child even from this misfortune, gave commandment that all the spindles in his kingdom should be burnt up. The maiden grew up, adorned with all the gifts of the wise women; and she was so lovely, modest, sweet, and kind and clever, that no one who saw her could help loving her. It happened one day, she being already fifteen years old, that the king and queen rode abroad, and the maiden was left behind alone in the castle. She wandered about into all the nooks and corners, and into all the chambers and parlours, as the fancy took her, till at last she came to an old tower. She climbed the narrow winding stair which led to a little door, with a rusty key sticking out of the lock; she turned the key, and the door opened, and there in the little room sat an old woman with a spindle, diligently spinning her flax.

'Good day, mother,' said the princess, 'what are you doing?'

'I am spinning,' answered the old woman, nodding her head.

'What thing is that that twists round so briskly?' asked the maiden, and taking the spindle into her hand she began to spin; but no sooner had she touched it than the evil prophecy was fulfilled, and she pricked her finger with it. In that very moment she fell back upon the bed that stood there, and lay in a deep sleep.

And this sleep fell upon the whole castle; the king and queen, who had returned and were in the great hall, fell fast asleep, and with them the whole court. The horses in their stalls, the dogs in the yard, the pigeons on the roof, the flies on the wall, the very fire that flickered on the hearth, became still, and slept like the rest; and the meat on the spit ceased roasting, and the cook, who was going to pull the scullion's hair for some mistake he had made, let him go, and went to sleep. And the wind ceased, and not a leaf fell from the trees about the castle. Then round about that place there grew a hedge of thorns thicker every year, until at last the whole castle was hidden from view, and nothing of it could be seen but the vane on the roof.

And a rumour went abroad in all that country of the beautiful sleeping Rosamond, for so was the princess called; and from time to time many kings' sons came and tried to force their way through the hedge; but it was impossible for them to do so, for the thorns held fast together like strong hands, and the young men were caught by them, and not being able to get free, there died a lamentable death.

Many a long year afterwards there came a king's son into that country, and heard an old man tell how there should be a castle standing behind the hedge of thorns, and that there a beautiful enchanted princess named Rosamond had slept for a hundred years, and with her the king and queen, and the whole court. The old man had been told by his grandfather that many kings' sons had sought to pass the thorn-hedge, but had been caught and pierced by the thorns, and had died a miserable death.

Then said the young man, 'Nevertheless, I do not fear to try; I shall win through and see the lovely Rosamond.'

The good old man tried to dissuade him, but he would not listen to his words. For now the hundred years were at an end, and the day had come when Rosamond should be awakened. When the prince drew near the hedge of thorns, it was changed into a hedge of beautiful large flowers, which parted and bent aside to let him pass, and then closed behind him in a thick hedge. When he reached the castle-yard, he saw the horses and brindled hunting-dogs lying asleep, and on the roof the pigeons were sitting with their heads under their wings. And when he came indoors, the flies on the wall were asleep, the cook in the kitchen had his hand uplifted to strike the scullion, and the kitchen-maid had the black fowl on her lap ready to pluck.

Then he mounted higher, and saw in the hall the whole court lying asleep, and above them, on their thrones, slept the king and the queen. And still he went farther, and all was so quiet that he could hear his own breathing; and at last he came to the tower, and went up the winding stair, and opened the door of the little room where Rosamond lay. And when he saw her looking so lovely in her sleep, he could not turn away his eyes; and presently he stooped and kissed her.

And she awaked, and opened her eyes, and looked very kindly on him. And she rose, and they went forth together, and the king and the queen and whole court woke up, and gazed on each other with great eyes of wonderment. And the horses in the yard got up and shook themselves, the hounds sprang up and wagged their tails, the pigeons on the roof drew their heads from under their wings, looked round, and flew into the field, the flies on the wall crept on a little farther, the kitchen fire leapt up and blazed, and cooked the meat, the joint on the spit began to roast, the cook gave the scullion such a box on the ear that he roared out, and the maid went on plucking the fowl.

Then the wedding of the Prince and Rosamond was held with all splendour, and they lived very happily together until their lives' end.

The Glass Mountain

Once upon a time there was a Glass Mountain at the top of which stood a castle made of pure gold, and in front of the castle there grew an apple-tree on which there were golden apples.

Anyone who picked an apple gained admittance into the golden castle, and there in a silver room sat an enchanted Princess of surpassing fairness and beauty. She was as rich as she was beautiful, for the cellars of the castle were full of precious stones, and great chests of the finest gold stood round the walls of all the rooms.

Many knights had come from afar to try their luck, but it was in vain they attempted to climb the mountain. In spite of having their horses shod with sharp nails, no one managed to get more than half-way up, and then they all fell back right down to the bottom of the steep slippery hill. Sometimes they broke an arm, sometimes a leg, and many a brave man had broken his neck even.

The beautiful Princess sat at her window and watched the bold knights trying to reach her on their splendid horses. The sight of her always gave men fresh courage, and they flocked from the four quarters of the globe to attempt the work of rescuing her. But all in vain, and for seven years the Princess had sat now and waited for some one to scale the Glass Mountain.

A heap of corpses both of riders and horses lay round the mountain, and many dying men lay groaning there unable to go any farther with their wounded limbs. The whole neighbourhood had the appearance of a vast churchyard.

In three more days the seven years would be at an end, when a knight in golden armour and mounted on a spirited steed was seen making his way towards the fatal hill. Sticking his spurs into his horse he made a rush at the mountain, and got up half-way, then he calmly turned his horse's head and came down again without a slip or stumble. The following day he started in the same way; the horse trod on the glass as if it had been level earth, and sparks of fire flew from its hoofs. All the other knights gazed in astonishment, for he had almost gained the summit, and in another moment he would have reached the apple-tree; but of a sudden a huge eagle rose up and spread its mighty wings, hitting as it did so the knight's horse in the eye. The beast shied, opened its wide nostrils and tossed its mane, then rearing high up in the air, its hind feet slipped and it fell with its rider down the steep mountain side. Nothing was left of either of them except their bones, which rattled in the battered golden armour like dry peas in a pod.

And now there was only one more day before the close of the seven years. Then there arrived on the scene a mere schoolboy – a merry, happy-hearted youth, but at the same time strong and well-grown. He saw how many knights had broken their necks in vain, but undaunted he approached the steep mountain on foot and began the ascent.

For long he had heard his parents speak of the beautiful Princess who sat in the golden castle at the top of the Glass Mountain. He listened to all he heard, and determined that he too would try his luck. But first he went to the forest and caught a lynx, and cutting off the creature's sharp claws, he fastened them on to his own hands and feet. Armed with these weapons he boldly started up the Glass Mountain.

The sun was nearly going down, and the youth had not got more than half-way up. He could hardly draw breath he was so worn out, and his mouth was parched by thirst. A huge black cloud passed over his head, but in vain did he beg and beseech her to let a drop of water fall on him. He opened his mouth, but the black cloud sailed past and not as much as a drop of dew moistened his dry lips. His feet were torn and bleeding, and he could only hold on now with his hands. Evening closed in, and he strained his eyes to see if he could behold the top of the mountain. Then he gazed beneath him, and what a sight met his eyes! A yawning abyss, with certain and terrible death at the bottom, reeking with half-decayed bodies of horses and riders! And this had been the end of all the other brave men who like himself had attempted the ascent.

It was almost pitch dark now, and only the stars lit up the Glass Mountain. The poor boy still clung on as if glued to the glass by his blood-stained hands. He made no struggle to get higher, for all his strength had left him, and seeing no hope he calmly awaited death. Then all of a sudden he fell into a deep sleep, and forgetful of his dangerous position, he slumbered sweetly. But all the same, although he slept, he had stuck his sharp claws so firmly into the glass that he was quite safe not to fall.

Now the golden apple-tree was guarded by the eagle which had overthrown the golden knight and his horse. Every night it flew round the Glass Mountain keeping a careful look-out, and no sooner had the moon emerged from the clouds than the bird rose up from the apple-tree, and circling round in the air, caught sight of the sleeping youth.

Greedy for carrion, and sure that this must be a fresh corpse, the bird swooped down upon the boy. But he was awake now, and perceiving the eagle, he determined by its help to save himself.

The eagle dug its sharp claws into the tender flesh of the youth, but he bore the pain without a sound, and seized the bird's two feet with his hands. The creature in terror lifted him high up into the air and began to circle round the tower of the castle. The youth held on bravely. He saw the glittering palace, which by the pale rays of the moon looked like a dim lamp; and he saw the high windows, and round one of them a balcony in which the beautiful Princess sat lost in sad thoughts. Then the boy saw that he was close to the apple-tree, and drawing a small knife from his belt, he cut off both the eagle's feet. The bird rose up in the air in its agony and vanished into the clouds, and the youth fell on to the broad branches of the apple-tree.

Then he drew out the claws of the eagle's feet that had remained in his flesh, and put the peel of one of the golden apples on the wound, and in one moment it was healed and well again. He pulled several of the beautiful apples and put them in his pocket; then he entered the castle. The door was guarded by a great dragon, but as soon as he threw an apple at it, the beast vanished.

At the same moment a gate opened, and the youth perceived a courtyard full of flowers and beautiful trees, and on a balcony sat the lovely enchanted Princess with her retinue.

As soon as she saw the youth, she ran towards him and greeted him as her husband and master. She gave him all her treasures, and the youth became a rich and mighty ruler. But he never returned to the earth, for only the mighty eagle, who had been the guardian of the Princess and of the castle, could have carried on his wings the enormous treasure down to the world. But as the eagle had lost its feet it died, and its body was found in a wood on the Glass Mountain.

One day when the youth was strolling about in the palace garden with the Princess, his wife, he looked down over the edge of the Glass Mountain and saw to his astonishment a great number of people gathered there. He blew his silver whistle, and the swallow who acted as messenger in the golden castle flew past.

'Fly down and ask what the matter is,' he said to the little bird, who sped off like lightning and soon returned saying: 'The blood of the eagle has restored all the people below to life. All those who have perished on this mountain are awakening up to-day, as it were from a sleep, and are mounting their horses, and the whole population are gazing on this unheard-of wonder with joy and amazement.'

The White Snake

A long time ago there lived a king who was famed for his wisdom through all the land. Nothing was hidden from him, and it seemed as if news of the most secret things was brought to him through the air. But he had a strange custom; every day after dinner, when the table was cleared, and no one else was present, a trusty servant had to bring him one more dish. It was covered, however, and even the servant did not know what was in it, neither did anyone know, for the king never took off the cover to eat of it until he was quite alone.

This had gone on for a long time, when one day the servant, who took away the dish, was overcome with such curiosity that he could not help carrying the dish into his room. When he had carefully locked the door, he lifted up the cover, and saw a white snake lying on the dish. But when he saw it he could not deny himself the pleasure of tasting it, so he cut of a little bit and put it into his mouth. No sooner had it touched his tongue than he heard a strange whispering of little voices outside his window. He went and listened, and then noticed that it was the sparrows who were chattering together, and telling one another of all kinds of things which they had seen in the fields and woods. Eating the snake had given him the power of understanding the language of animals.

Now it so happened that on this very day the queen lost her most beautiful ring, and suspicion of having stolen it fell upon this trusty servant, who was allowed to go everywhere. The king ordered the man to be brought before him, and threatened with angry words that unless he could before the morrow point out the thief, he himself should be looked upon as guilty and executed. In vain he declared his innocence; he was dismissed with no better answer.

In his trouble and fear he went down into the courtyard and took thought how to help himself out of his trouble. Now some ducks were sitting together quietly by a brook and taking their rest; and, while they were making their feathers smooth with their bills, they were having a confidential conversation together. The servant stood by and listened. They were telling one another of all the places where they had been waddling about all the morning, and what good food they had found; and one said in a pitiful tone:

'Something lies heavy on my stomach; as I was eating in haste I swallowed a ring which lay under the queen's window.'

The servant at once seized her by the neck, carried her to the kitchen, and said to the cook:

'Here is a fine duck; pray, kill her.'

'Yes,' said the cook, and weighed her in his hand; 'she has spared no trouble to fatten herself, and has been waiting to be roasted long enough.' So he cut off her head, and as she was being dressed for the spit, the queen's ring was found inside her.

The servant could now easily prove his innocence; and the king, to make amends for the wrong, allowed him to ask a favour, and promised him the best place in the court that he could wish for. The servant refused everything, and only asked for a horse and some money for travelling, as he had a mind to see the world and go about a little. When his request was granted, he set out on his way, and one day came to a pond, where he saw three fishes caught in the reeds and gasping for water. Now, though it is said that fishes are dumb, he heard them lamenting that they must perish so miserably, and, as he had a kind heart, he got off his horse and put the three prisoners back into the water. They leapt with delight, put out their heads, and cried to him:

'We will remember you and repay you for saving us!'

He rode on, and after a while it seemed to him that he heard a voice in the sand at his feet. He listened, and heard an ant-king complain:

'Why cannot folks, with their clumsy beasts, keep off our bodies? That stupid horse, with his heavy hoofs, has been treading down my people without mercy!' So he turned on to a side path and the ant-king cried out to him:

'We will remember you – one good turn deserves another!'

The path led him into a wood, and there he saw two old ravens standing by their nest and throwing out their young ones.

'Out with you, you idle, good-for-nothing creatures!' cried they; 'we cannot find food for you any longer; you are big enough and can provide for yourselves.'

But the poor young ravens lay upon the ground, flapping their wings, and crying:

'Oh, what helpless chicks we are! We must shift for ourselves, and yet we cannot fly! What can we do, but lie here and starve?'

So the good young fellow alighted and killed his horse with his sword, and gave it to them for food. Then they came hopping up to it, satisfied their hunger, and cried:

'We will remember you – one good turn deserves another!'

And now he had to use his own legs, and when he had walked a long way, he came to a large city. There was a great noise and crowd in the streets, and a man rode up on horseback, crying aloud:

'The king's daughter wants a husband; but whoever seeks her hand must perform a hard task, and if he does not succeed he will forfeit his life.'

Many had already made the attempt, but in vain; nevertheless when the youth saw the king's daughter he was so overcome by her great beauty that he forgot all danger, went before the king and declared himself a suitor. So he was led out to the sea, and a gold ring was thrown into it, before his eyes; then the king ordered him to fetch this ring up from the bottom of the sea, and added:

'If you come up again without it you will be thrown in again and again until you perish amid the waves.'

All the people grieved for the handsome youth; then they went away, leaving him alone by the sea. He stood on the shore and considered what he should do; suddenly he saw three fishes come swimming towards him, and they were the very fishes whose lives he had saved. The one in the middle held a mussel in its mouth, which it laid on the shore at the youth's feet, and when he had taken it up and opened it, there lay the gold ring in the shell. Full of joy he took it to the king and expected that he would grant him the promised reward.

But when the proud princess perceived that he was not her equal in birth, she scorned him, and required him first to perform another task. She went down into the garden and strewed with her own hands ten sackfuls of millet seed on the grass; then she said:

'Tomorrow morning before sunrise these must be picked up, and not a single grain be wanting.'

The youth sat down in the garden and considered how it might be possible to perform this task, but he could think of nothing, and there he sat sorrowfully awaiting the break of day, when he should be led to his death. But as soon as the first rays of the sun shone into the garden he saw all the ten sacks standing side by side, quite full, and not a single grain was missing. The ant-king had come in the night with thousands and thousands of ants, and the grateful creatures had by great industry picked up all the millet seeds and gathered them into the sacks.

Presently the king's daughter herself came down into the garden and was amazed to see that the young man had done the task she had given him. But she could not yet conquer her proud heart, and said:

'Although he has performed both the tasks, he shall not be my husband until he has brought me the Golden Apple from the Tree of Life.'

The youth did not know where the Tree of Life stood, but he set out, and would have gone on for ever, as long as his legs would carry him, though he had no hope of finding it. After he had wandered through three kingdoms, he came one evening to a wood, and lay down under a tree to sleep. But he heard a rustling in the branches, and a golden apple fell into his hand. At the same time three ravens flew down to him, perched themselves upon his knee, and said:

'We are the three young ravens whom you saved from starving; when we had grown big, and heard that you were seeking the Golden Apple, we flew over the sea to the end of the world, where the Tree of Life stands, and have brought you the apple.'

The youth, full of joy, set out homewards, and took the Golden Apple to the king's beautiful daughter, who had now no more excuses left to make. They cut the Apple of Life in two and ate it together; and then her heart became full of love for him, and they lived in undisturbed happiness to a great age.

Jorinda and Joringel

There was once an old castle in the middle of a large and thick forest, and in it an old woman who was a witch dwelt all alone. During the day she changed herself into a cat or a screech owl, but in the evening she took her proper shape again as a human being. She could lure wild beasts and birds to her, and then she killed and boiled and roasted them. If anyone came within one hundred paces of the castle he was obliged to stand still and could not stir from the place until she bade him be free. But whenever an innocent maiden came within this circle, she changed her into a bird, and shut her up in a wicker-work cage, and carried the cage into a room in the castle. She had about seven thousand cages of rare birds in the castle.

Now, there was once a maiden who was called Jorinda, who was fairer than all other girls. She and a handsome youth named Joringel had promised to marry each other. They were still in the days of betrothal, and their greatest happiness was being together. One day in order that they might be able to talk together in quiet they went for a walk in the forest.

'Take care,' said Joringel, 'that you do not go too near the castle.'

It was a beautiful evening; the sun shone brightly between the trunks of the trees into the dark green of the forest, and the turtle-doves sang mournfully upon the young boughs of the birch trees. They wandered so far that they lost their way. Jorinda wept now and then: she sat down in the sunshine and was sorrowful. Joringel was sorrowful too; they were as sad as if they were about to die. They looked around them and were quite at a loss, for they did not know by which way they should go home. The sun was still half above the mountain and half set.

Joringel looked through the bushes, and saw the old walls of the castle close at hand. He was horror-stricken and filled with deadly fear. Jorinda was singing:

> 'My little bird, with the necklace red,
> Sings sorrow, sorrow, sorrow,
> He sings that the dove must soon be dead,
> Sings sorrow, sor – jug, jug, jug.'

Joringel looked for Jorinda. She was changed into a nightingale, and sang, 'jug, jug, jug.' A screech-owl with glowing eyes flew three times round about her, and three times cried, 'to-whoo, to-whoo, to-whoo!'

Joringel could not move: he stood there like a stone, and could neither weep nor speak, nor move hand or foot.

The sun had now set. The owl flew into the thicket, and directly afterwards there came out of it a crooked old woman, yellow and lean, with large red eyes and a hooked nose, the point of which reached to her chin. She muttered to herself, caught the nightingale, and took it away in her hand.

Joringel could neither speak nor move from the spot; the nightingale was gone. At last the woman came back, and said in a hollow voice:

'Greet thee, Zachiel. If the moon shines on the cage, Zachiel, let him loose at once.' Then Joringel was freed. He fell on his knees before the woman and begged that she would give him back his Jorinda, but she said that he should never have her again, and went away. He called, he wept, he lamented, but all in vain.

'Ah, what is to become of me?' he cried.

Joringel went away, and at last came to a strange village; there he kept sheep for a long time. He often walked round and round the castle, but not too near to it. One night, he dreamt one night that he found a blood-red flower, in the middle of which was a beautiful large pearl; that he picked the flower and went with it to the castle, and that everything he touched with the flower was freed from enchantment; he also dreamt that by means of it he recovered his Jorinda.

In the morning, when he awoke, he began to seek over hill and dale if he could find such a flower. He sought until the ninth day, and then, early in the morning, he found the blood-red flower. In the middle of it there was a large dew-drop, as big as the finest pearl.

Day and night he journeyed with this flower to the castle. When he was within a hundred paces of it he was not held fast, but walked on to the door. Joringel was full of joy; he touched the door with the flower, and it sprang open. He walked in through the courtyard, and listened for the sound of the birds. At last he heard it. He went on and found the room it came from, and there the witch was feeding the birds in the seven thousand cages.

When she saw Joringel she was angry, very angry, and scolded and spat poison and gall at him, but she could not come within two paces of him. He did not take any notice of her, but went and looked at the cages with the birds; but there were many hundred nightingales, how was he to find his Jorinda again?

Just then he saw the old woman quietly take away a cage with a bird in it, and go towards the door. Swiftly he sprang towards her, touched the cage with the flower, and also the old woman. She could now no longer bewitch any one; and Jorinda was standing there, clasping him round the neck, and she was as beautiful as ever.

The Four Skilful Brothers

There was once a poor man who had four sons, and when they were grown up, he said to them, 'My dear children, you must now go out into the world, for I have nothing to give you, so set out, and go to some distance and learn a trade, and see how you can make your way.'

So the four brothers took their sticks, bade their father farewell, and went through the town gate together. When they had travelled about for some time, they came to a crossway which branched off in four different directions. Then said the eldest:

'Here we must separate, but on this day in four years, we will meet each other again at this spot, and in the meantime we will seek our fortunes.'

Then each of them went his way, and the eldest met a man who asked him where he was going, and what he was intending to do.

'I want to learn a trade,' he replied. Then the man said, 'Come with me, and be a thief.'

'No,' he answered, 'that is not regarded as a reputable trade, and the end of it is that one has to swing on the gallows.'

'Oh,' said the man, 'you need not be afraid of the gallows; I will only teach you to get such things as no other man could ever lay hold of, and no one will ever detect you.' So he allowed himself to be talked into it, and while with the man became an accomplished thief, and so dexterous that nothing was safe from him, if he once desired to have it.

The second brother met a man who put the same question to him, asking where he was going and what he wanted to learn in the world.

'I don't know yet,' he replied.

'Then come with me, and be an astronomer; there is nothing better than that, for nothing is hid from you.' He liked the idea, and became such a skilful astronomer that when he had learnt everything, and was about to travel onwards, his master gave him a telescope and said to him:

'With that you can see whatever takes place either on earth or in heaven, and nothing can remain concealed from you.'

A huntsman took the third brother into training, and gave him such excellent instruction in everything which related to huntsmanship, that he became an experienced hunter. When he went away, his master gave him a gun and said, 'It will never fail you; you are certain to hit whatever you aim at.'

The youngest brother also met a man who spoke to him and inquired what his intentions were.

'Would you not like to be a tailor?' said he.

'Not that I know of,' said the youth; 'sitting doubled up from morning till night, driving the needle and the goose backwards and forwards, is not to my taste.'

'Oh, but you are speaking in ignorance,' answered the man; 'with me you would learn a very different kind of tailoring, which is respectable and proper, and for the most part very honourable.'

So he let himself be persuaded, and went with the man, and learnt his art from the very beginning. When they parted, the man gave the youth a needle, and said, 'With this you can sew together whatever is given you, whether it is as soft as an egg or as hard as steel; and it will all become one piece of stuff, so that no seam will be visible.'

When the appointed four years were over, the four brothers arrived at the same time at the crossroads, embraced and kissed each other, and returned home to their father.

'So now,' said he, quite delighted, 'the wind has blown you back again to me.'

They told him of all that had happened to them, and that each had learnt his own trade. Now they were sitting just in front of the house under a large tree, and the father said, 'I will put you all to the test, and see what you can do.'

Then he looked up and said to his second son, 'Between two branches up at the top of this tree, there is a chaffinch's nest, tell me how many eggs there are in it?' The astronomer took his glass and looked up.

'There are five,' he said.

'Fetch the eggs down without disturbing the bird which is sitting hatching them,' the father then said to the eldest.

The skilful thief climbed up, and took the five eggs from beneath the bird, which never observed what he was doing, and remained quietly sitting where she was, and brought them down to his father. The father took them, and put one of them on each corner of the table, and the fifth in the middle, and said to the huntsman:

'With one shot you shall shoot me the five eggs in two, through the middle.'

The huntsman aimed, and shot the eggs, all five as the father had desired, and that with one shot. He certainly must have had some of the powder for shooting round corners.

'Now it's your turn,' said the father to the fourth son. 'You shall sew the eggs together again, and the young birds that are inside them as well, and you must do it so that they are not hurt by the shot.'

The tailor brought his needle and sewed them as his father wished. When he had done this the thief had to climb up the tree again, and carry them to the nest, and put them back again under

155

the bird without her being aware of it. The bird sat her full time, and after a few days the young ones crept out, and they had a red line round their necks where they had been sewn together by the tailor.

'Well,' said the old man to his sons, 'I begin to think you are worth more than breen clover; you have used your time well and learnt something good. I can't say which of you deserves the most praise. That will be proved if you have but an early opportunity of using your talents.'

Not long after this, there was a great uproar in the country, for the king's daughter was carried off by a dragon. The king was full of trouble about it, both by day and night, and caused it to be proclaimed that whoever brought her back should have her to wife.

'This would be a fine opportunity for us to show what we can do!' the four brothers said to each other, and resolved to go forth together and free the king's daughter.

'I will soon know where she is,' said the astronomer, and looked through his telescope. 'I see her already, she is far away from here on a rock in the sea, and the dragon is beside her watching her.'

Then he went to the king, and asked for a ship for himself and his brothers, and sailed with them over the sea until they came to the rock. There the king's daughter was sitting, and the dragon was lying asleep on her lap.

'I dare not fire, I should kill the beautiful maiden at the same time,' said the huntsman.

'Then I will try my art,' said the thief, and he crept over and stole her away from under the dragon, so quietly and dexterously, that the monster never remarked it, but went on snoring. Full of joy, they hurried off with her on board ship, and steered out into the open sea; but the dragon, who when he awoke had found no princess there, followed them, and came snorting angrily through the air. Just as he was circling above the ship, and about to descend on it, the huntsman shouldered his gun, and shot him to the heart. The monster fell down dead, but was so large and powerful that his fall shattered the whole ship. Fortunately, however, they laid hold of a couple of planks, and swam about the wide sea. They were in great peril, but the tailor, who was not idle, took his wondrous needle, and with a few stitches sewed the planks together, and they seated themselves upon them, and collected together all the fragments of the vessel. Then he sewed these so skilfully together, that in a very short time the ship was once more seaworthy, and they could go home again in safety.

When the king once more saw his daughter, there were great rejoicings.

'One of you shall have her to wife,' he said to the four brothers, 'but which of you it is to be you must settle among yourselves.'

Then a warm contest arose among them, for each of them preferred his own claim.

'If I had not seen the princess, all your arts would have been useless, so she is mine,' said the astronomer.

'What would have been the use of your seeing, if I had not got her away from the dragon? So she is mine,' said the thief.

'You and the princess, and all of you, would have been torn to pieces by the dragon if my ball had not hit him, so she is mine,' said the huntsman.

'And if I, by my art, had not sewn the ship together again, you would all of you have been miserably drowned, so she is mine,' the tailor said.

'Each of you has an equal right,' said the king, so I shall have to decide. 'As all of you cannot have the maiden, none of you shall have her, but I will give to each of you, as a reward, half a kingdom.'

The brothers were pleased with this decision.

'It is better this way than that we should be at variance with each other,' they said.

Then each of them received half a kingdom, and they lived with their father in the greatest happiness as long as it pleased God.

Sweetheart Roland

There was once on a time a woman who was a real witch and had two daughters, one ugly and wicked, and this one she loved because she was her own daughter, and one beautiful and good, and this one she hated, because she was her stepdaughter. The stepdaughter once had a pretty apron, which the other fancied so much that she became envious, and told her mother that she must and would have that apron.

'Be quiet, my child,' said the old woman, 'and you shalt have it. Your stepsister has long deserved death, tonight when she is asleep I will come and cut her head off. Only be careful that you are at the far-side of the bed, and push her well to the front.'

It would have been all over with the poor girl if she had not just then been standing in a corner, and heard everything. All day long she dared not go out of doors, and when bed-time had come, the witch's daughter got into bed first, so as to lie at the far side, but when she was asleep, the other pushed her gently to the front, and took for herself the place at the back, close by the wall. In the night, the old woman came creeping in, she held an axe in her right hand, and felt with her left to see if anyone was lying at the outside, and then she grasped the axe with both hands, and cut her own child's head off.

When she had gone away, the girl got up and went to her sweetheart, who was called Roland, and knocked at his door. When he came out, she said to him, 'Hear me, dearest Roland, we must fly in all haste; my stepmother wanted to kill me, but has struck her own child. When daylight comes, and she sees what she has done, we shall be lost.'

'But,' said Roland, 'first you need to take away her magic wand, or we cannot escape if she pursues us.'

The maiden fetched the magic wand, and she took the dead girl's head and dropped three drops of blood on the ground, one in front of the bed, one in the kitchen, and one on the stairs. Then she hurried away with her lover. When the old witch got up next morning, she called her daughter, and wanted to give her the apron, but she did not come.

'Where are you?' the witch then cried.

'Here, on the stairs, I am sweeping,' answered the first drop of blood. The old woman went out, but saw no one on the stairs.

'Where are you?' she cried again.

'Here in the kitchen, I am warming myself,' cried the second drop of blood. She went into the kitchen, but found no one.

'Where are you?' she cried for a third time.

'Ah, here in the bed, I am sleeping.' cried the third drop of blood. She went into the room to the bed. What did she see there? Her own child, whose head she had cut off, bathed in her blood. The witch fell into a passion, sprang to the window, and as she could look forth quite far into the world, she perceived her stepdaughter hurrying away with her sweetheart Roland.

'That shall not serve you,' cried she, 'even if you have got a long way off, you shall still not escape me.'

She put on her many league boots, in which went an hour's walk at every step, and it was not long before she overtook them. The girl, however, when she saw the old woman striding towards her, changed, with her magic wand, her sweetheart Roland into a lake, and herself into a duck swimming in the middle of it. The witch placed herself on the shore, threw bread-crumbs in, and gave herself every possible trouble to entice the duck; but the duck did not let herself be enticed, and the old woman had to go home at night as she had come. On this the girl and her sweetheart Roland resumed their natural shapes again, and they walked on the whole night until daybreak. Then the maiden changed herself into a beautiful flower which stood in the midst of a briar hedge, and her sweetheart Roland into a fiddler. It was not long before the witch came striding up towards them, and said to the musician, 'Dear musician, may I pluck that beautiful flower for myself?'

'Oh, yes,' he replied, 'I will play to you while you do it.'

As she was hastily creeping into the hedge and was just going to pluck the flower, for she well knew who the flower was, he began to play, and whether she would or not, she was forced to dance, for it was a magical dance. The quicker he played, the more violent springs was she forced to make, and the thorns tore her clothes from her body, and pricked her and wounded her till she bled, and as he did not stop, she had to dance till she lay dead on the ground.

'Now I will go to my father and arrange for the wedding,' Roland said when they were delivered.

'Then in the meantime I will stay here and wait for you,' said the girl, 'and that no one may recognize me, I will change myself into a red stone landmark.'

Then Roland went away, and the girl stood like a red landmark in the field and waited for her beloved. But when Roland got home, he fell into the snares of another, who prevailed on him so far that he forgot the maiden. The poor girl remained there a long time, but at length, as he did not return at all, she was sad, and changed herself into a flower, and thought, 'Someone will surely come this way, and trample me down.'

It befell, however, that a shepherd kept his sheep in the field, and saw the flower, and as it was so pretty, plucked it, took it with him, and laid it away in his chest. From that time forth, strange things happened in the shepherd's house. When he arose in the morning, all the work was already done, the room was swept, the table and benches cleaned, the fire on the hearth was lighted, and the water was fetched, and at noon, when he came home, the table was laid, and a good dinner served. He could not conceive how this came to pass, for he never saw a human being in his house, and no one could have concealed himself in it. He was certainly pleased with this good attendance, but still at last he was so afraid that he went to a wise woman and asked for her advice.

'There is some enchantment behind it,' said the wise woman. 'Listen very early one morning if anything is moving in the room, and if you see anything, let it be what it may, throw a white cloth over it, and then the magic will be stopped.'

The shepherd did as she bade him, and next morning just as day dawned, he saw the chest open, and the flower come out. Swiftly he sprang towards it and threw a white cloth over it. Instantly the transformation came to an end, and a beautiful girl stood before him, who owned to him that she had been the flower, and that up to this time she had attended to his housekeeping. She told him her story, and as she pleased him he asked her if she would marry him.

'No,' she answered, for she wanted to remain faithful to her sweetheart Roland, although he had deserted her, but she promised not to go away, but to keep house for the shepherd for the time being.

And now the time drew near when Roland's wedding was to be celebrated, and then, according to an old custom in the country, it was announced that all the girls were to be present at it, and sing in honour of the bridal pair. When the faithful maiden heard of this, she grew so sad that she thought her heart would break, and she would not go thither, but the other girls came and took her. When it came to her turn to sing, she stepped back, until at last she was the only one left, and then she could not refuse. But when she began her song, and it reached Roland's ears, he sprang up.

'I know that voice,' he cried. 'That is the true bride, I will have no other!' Everything he had forgotten, and which had vanished from his mind, had suddenly come home again to his heart. Then the faithful maiden held her wedding with her sweetheart Roland, and grief came to an end and joy began.

The Little Peasant

There was a certain village wherein no one lived but really rich peasants, and just one poor one, whom they called the little peasant. He had not even so much as a cow, and still less money to buy one, and yet he and his wife did so wish to have one. One day he said to her, 'Hark you, I have a good thought, there is our gossip the carpenter, he shall make us a wooden calf, and paint it brown, so that it look like any other, and in time it will certainly get big and be a cow.'

The woman also liked the idea, and their gossip the carpenter cut and planed the calf, and painted it as it ought to be, and made it with its head hanging down as if it were eating.

Next morning when the cows were being driven out, the little peasant called the cow-herd and said, 'Look, I have a little calf there, but it is still small and has still to be carried.'

'All right,' said the cow-herd, and took it in his arms and carried it to the pasture, and set it among the grass. The little calf always remained standing like one which was eating, and the cow-herd said, 'It will soon run alone, just look how it eats already!' At night when he was going to drive the herd home again, he said to the calf, 'If you can stand there and eat your fill, you can also go on your four legs; I don't care to drag you home again in my arms.'

But the little peasant stood at his door, and waited for his little calf, and when the cow-herd drove the cows through the village, and the calf was missing, he inquired where it was.

'It is still standing out there eating. It would not stop and come with us,' the cow-herd answered.

'Oh, but I must have my beast back again,' the little peasant said. Then they went back to the meadow together, but someone had stolen the calf, and it was gone.

'It must have run away,' the cow-herd said.

'Don't tell me that,' said the peasant, and led the cow-herd before the mayor, who for his carelessness condemned him to give the peasant a cow for the calf which had run away. And now the little peasant and his wife had the cow for which they had so long wished, and they were heartily glad, but they could give it nothing to eat, so it soon had to be killed. They salted the flesh, and the peasant went into the town and wanted to sell the skin there, so that he might buy a new calf with the proceeds. On the way he passed by a mill, and there sat a raven with broken wings, and out of pity he took him and wrapped him in the skin. As, however, the weather grew so bad and there was a storm of rain and wind, he could go no farther, and turned back to the mill and begged for shelter. The miller's wife was alone in the house.

'Lay yourself on the straw there', she said to the peasant, and gave him a slice of bread with cheese on it. The peasant ate it, and lay down with his skin beside him, and it appeared to the woman that he was tired out and had gone to sleep.

The parson then came to the door, and the miller's wife welcomed him in and said:

'My husband is out, so we will have a feast.'

The peasant listened, and when he heard about feasting he was vexed that he had been forced to make shift with a slice of bread with cheese on it. Then the woman served up four different things, roast meat, salad, cakes, and wine. Just as they were about to sit down and eat, there was a knocking outside.

'Oh, heavens! It is my husband!' the woman said. She quickly hid the roast meat inside the tiled stove, the wine under the pillow, the salad on the bed, the cakes under it, and the parson in the cupboard in the entrance. Then she opened the door for her husband.

'Thank heaven, you are back again! There is such a storm, it looks as if the world were coming to an end.' The miller saw the peasant lying on the straw, and asked, 'What is that fellow doing there?'

'Ah,' said the wife, 'the poor knave came in the storm and rain, and begged for shelter, so I gave him a bit of bread and cheese and showed him where the straw was.'

'I have no objection,' said the man, 'but be quick and get me something to eat.'

'But I have nothing but bread and cheese,' said the woman.

'I am contented with anything,' replied the husband, 'so far as I am concerned, bread and cheese will do,' and looked at the peasant and said, 'Come and eat some more with me.' The peasant did not require to be invited twice, but got up and ate. After this the miller saw the skin in which the raven was, lying on the ground.

'What have you there?' he asked.

'I have a soothsayer inside it,' answered the peasant.

'Can he foretell anything to me?' said the miller.

'Why not?' answered the peasant, 'but he only says four things, and the fifth he keeps to himself.' The miller was curious.

'Let him foretell something for once,' he said.

Then the peasant pinched the raven's head, so that he croaked and made a noise like krr, krr.

'What did he say?'

'In the first place, he says that there is some wine hidden under the pillow,' the peasant answered.

'Bless me!' cried the miller, and went there and found the wine. 'Now go on,' said he. The peasant made the raven croak again, and said:

'In the second place, he says that there is some roast meat in the tiled stove.'

'Upon my word!' cried the miller, and went thither, and found the roast meat. The peasant made the raven prophesy still more.

'Thirdly, he says that there is some salad on the bed.'

'That would be a fine thing!' cried the miller, and went there and found the salad. At last the peasant pinched the raven once more till he croaked, and said, 'Fourthly, he says that there are some cakes under the bed.'

'That would be a fine thing!' cried the miller, and looked there, and found the cakes.

And now the two sat down to the table together, but the miller's wife was frightened to death, and went to bed and took all the keys with her. The miller would have liked much to know the fifth, but the little peasant said:

'First, we will quickly eat the four things, for the fifth is something bad.' So they ate, and after that they bargained how much the miller was to give for the fifth prophesy, until they agreed on three hundred coins. Then the peasant once more pinched the raven's head till he croaked loudly. The miller asked, 'What did he say?' the miller asked.

'He says that the Devil is hiding outside there in the cupboard in the entrance,' replied the peasant.

'The Devil must go out,' cried the miller, and opened the house door; then the woman was forced to give up the keys, and the peasant unlocked the cupboard. The parson ran out as fast as he could.

'It was true; I saw the black rascal with my own eyes,' said the miller.

The peasant, however, made off next morning by daybreak with the three hundred coins. At home the small peasant gradually launched out; he built a beautiful house, and the other peasants said, 'The small peasant has certainly been to the place where golden snow falls, and people carry the gold home in shovels.' Then the small peasant was brought before the Mayor and bidden to say from whence his wealth came.

'I sold my cow's skin in the town, for three hundred coins,' he answered.

When the peasants heard that, they too wished to enjoy this great profit, and ran home, killed all their cows, and stripped off their skins in order to sell them in the town to the greatest advantage. The Mayor, however, said, 'But my servant must go first.' When she came to the merchant in the town, he did not give her more than two coins for a skin, and when the others came, he did not give them so much, and said, 'What can I do with all these skins?'

Then the peasants were vexed that the small peasant should have thus overreached them, wanted to take vengeance on him, and accused him of this treachery before the Mayor. The innocent little peasant was unanimously sentenced to death, and was to be rolled into the water, in a barrel pierced full of holes. He was led forth, and a priest was brought who was to say a mass for his soul. The others were all obliged to retire to a distance, and when the peasant looked at the priest, he recognized the man who had been with the miller's wife.

'I set you free from the cupboard,' he said to him, 'set me free from the barrel.'

At this same moment up came, with a flock of sheep, a shepherd who the peasant knew had long been wishing to be Mayor, so he cried with all his might:

'No, I will not do it; if the whole world insists on it, I will not do it!'

The shepherd hearing that, came up to him, and asked:

'What are you about? What is it that you will not do?'

'They want to make me Mayor,' the peasant said, 'if I will but put myself in the barrel, but I will not do it.'

'If nothing more than that is needful in order to be Mayor, I would get into the barrel at once,' the shepherd.

'If you will get in, you will be Mayor,' said the peasant.

The shepherd was willing, and got in, and the peasant shut the top down on him; then he took the shepherd's flock for himself, and drove it away. The parson went to the crowd, and declared that the mass had been said. Then they came and rolled the barrel towards the water. When the barrel began to roll, the shepherd cried:

'I am quite willing to be Mayor.' They believed no otherwise than that it was the peasant who was saying this, and answered, 'That is what we intend, but first you shalt look about you a little down below there,' and they rolled the barrel down into the water.

After that the peasants went home, and as they were entering the village, the small peasant also came quietly in, driving a flock of sheep and looking quite contented. Then the peasants were astonished, and said:

'Peasant, where do you come from? Have you come out of the water?'

'Yes, truly,' replied the peasant, 'I sank deep, deep down, until at last I got to the bottom; I pushed the bottom out of the barrel, and crept out, and there were pretty meadows on which a number of lambs were feeding, and I brought this flock away with me from there.'

'Are there any more there?' asked the peasants.

'Oh, yes,' said he, 'more than I could do anything with.' Then the peasants made up their minds that they too would fetch some sheep for themselves, a flock apiece, but the Mayor said:

'I come first.'

So they went to the water together, and just then there were some of the small fleecy clouds in the blue sky, which are called little lambs, and they were reflected in the water, whereupon the peasants cried, 'We already see the sheep down below!' The Mayor pressed forward and said:

'I will go down first, and look about me, and if things promise well I'll call you.' So he jumped in; splash! went the water; he made a sound as if he were calling them, and the whole crowd plunged in after him as one man. Then the entire village was dead, and the small peasant, as sole heir, became a rich man.

The Water of Life

There was once a king who had an illness, and no one believed that he would come out of it with his life. He had three sons who were much distressed about it, and went down into the palace-garden and wept. There they met an old man who inquired as to the cause of their grief. They told him that their father was so ill that he would most certainly die, for nothing seemed to cure him.

'I know of one more remedy,' the old man said, 'and that is the water of life; if he drinks of it he will become well again; but it is hard to find.'

'I will manage to find it,' said the eldest, and went to the sick king, and begged to be allowed to go forth in search of the water of life, for that alone could save him.

'No,' said the king, 'the danger of it is too great. I would rather die.'

But he begged so long that the king consented. The prince thought in his heart, 'If I bring the water, then I shall be best beloved of my father, and shall inherit the kingdom.' So he set out, and when he had ridden forth a little distance, a dwarf stood there in the road who called to him and said:

'Whither away so fast?'

'Silly shrimp,' said the prince, very haughtily, 'it is nothing to do with you,' and rode on.

But the little dwarf was angry at this, and had wished an evil wish. Soon after this the prince entered a ravine, and the further he rode the closer the mountains drew together, and at last the road became so narrow that he could not advance a step further; it was impossible either to turn his horse or to dismount from the saddle, and he was shut in there as if in prison. The sick king waited long for him, but he came not.

Then the second son said:

'Father, let me go forth to seek the water,' and thought to himself, 'If my brother is dead, then the kingdom will fall to me.'

At first the king would not allow him to go either, but at last he yielded, so the prince set out on the same road that his brother had taken, and he too met the dwarf, who stopped him to ask, whither he was going in such haste.

'Little shrimp,' said the prince, 'that is nothing to you,' and rode on without giving him another look. But the dwarf bewitched him, and he, like the other, rode into a ravine, and could neither go forwards nor backwards. So fare haughty people.

As the second son also remained away, the youngest begged to be allowed to go forth to fetch the water, and at last the king was obliged to let him go. When he met the dwarf and the latter asked him whither he was going in such haste, he stopped and gave him an explanation.

'I am seeking the water of life, for my father is sick unto death,' he said.

'Do you know, then, where that is to be found?'

'No,' said the prince. 'As you have borne yourself as is seemly, and not haughtily like your false brothers, I will give you the information and tell you how you may obtain the water of life. It springs from a fountain in the courtyard of an enchanted castle, but you will not be able to make your way to it, if I do not give you an iron wand and two small loaves of bread. Strike thrice with the wand on the iron door of the castle and it will spring open: inside lie two lions with gaping jaws, but if you throw a loaf to each of them, they will be quieted. Then hasten to fetch some of the water of life before the clock strikes twelve, else the door will shut again, and you will be imprisoned.'

The prince thanked him, took the wand and the bread, and set out on his way. When he arrived at the castle, everything was as the dwarf had said. The door sprang open at the third stroke of the wand, and when he had appeased the lions with the bread, he entered the castle, and came to a large and splendid hall, wherein sat some enchanted princes whose rings he drew off their fingers. A sword and a loaf of bread were lying there, which he carried away. After this, he entered a chamber, in which was a beautiful maiden who rejoiced when she saw him, kissed him, and told him that he had delivered her, and should have the whole of her kingdom, and that if he would return in a year their wedding should be celebrated; likewise she told him where the spring of the water of life was, and that he was to hasten and draw some of it before the clock struck twelve. Then he went onwards, and at last entered a room where there was a beautiful newly-made bed, and as he was very weary, he felt inclined to rest a little. So he lay down and fell asleep.

When he awoke, it was striking a quarter to twelve. He sprang up in a fright, ran to the spring, drew some water in a cup which stood near, and hastened away. But just as he was passing through the iron door, the clock struck twelve, and the door fell to with such violence that it carried away a piece of his heel. He, however, rejoicing at having obtained the water of life, went homewards, and again passed the dwarf. When the latter saw the sword and the loaf, he said, 'With these you have won great wealth; with the sword you can slay whole armies, and the bread will never come to an end.'

But the prince would not go home to his father without his brothers.

'Dear dwarf,' he said, 'can you not tell me where my two brothers are? They went out before I did in search of the water of life, and have not returned.'

'They are imprisoned between two mountains,' said the dwarf. 'I have condemned them to stay there, because they were so haughty.'

Then the prince begged until the dwarf released them; but he warned him, however, and said:

'Beware of them, for they have bad hearts.'

When his brothers came, the youngest prince rejoiced, and told them how things had gone with him, that he had found the water of life and had brought a cupful away with him, and had rescued a beautiful princess, who was willing to wait a year for him, and then their wedding was to be celebrated and he would obtain a great kingdom. After that they rode on together, and chanced upon a land where war and famine reigned, and the king already thought he must perish, for the scarcity was so great. Then the prince went to him and gave him the loaf, wherewith he fed and satisfied the whole of his kingdom, and then the prince gave him the sword also wherewith he slew the hosts of his enemies, and could now live in rest and peace. The prince then took back his loaf and his sword, and the three brothers rode on.

But after this they entered two more countries where war and famine reigned and each time the prince gave his loaf and his sword to the kings, and had now delivered three kingdoms, and after that they went on board a ship and sailed over the sea. During the passage, the two eldest conversed apart and said:

'The youngest has found the water of life and not we, for that our father will give him the kingdom the kingdom which belongs to us, and he will rob us of all our fortune.'

They then began to seek revenge, and plotted with each other to destroy him. They waited until they found him fast asleep, then they poured the water of life out of the cup, and took it for themselves, but into the cup they poured salt sea-water. Now therefore, when they arrived home, the youngest took his cup to the sick king in order that he might drink out of it, and be cured. But scarcely had he drunk a very little of the salt sea-water than he became still worse than before. And as he was lamenting over this, the two eldest brothers came, and accused the youngest of having intended to poison him, and said that they had brought him the true water of life, and handed it to him. He had scarcely tasted it, when he felt his sickness departing, and became strong and healthy as in the days of his youth. After that they both went to the youngest, and mocked him.

'You certainly found the water of life,' they said, 'but you have had the pain, and we the gain; you should have been sharper, and should have kept your eyes open. We took it from you while you were asleep at sea, and when a year is over, one of us will go and fetch the beautiful princess. But beware that you do not disclose aught of this to our father; indeed he does not trust you, and if you say a single word, you shall lose your life into the bargain, but if you keep silent, you shall have it as a gift.'

The old king was angry with his youngest son, and thought he had plotted against his life. So he summoned the court together and had sentence pronounced upon his son, that he should be secretly shot. And once when the prince was riding forth to the chase, suspecting no evil, the king's huntsman had to go with him, and when they were quite alone in the forest, the huntsman looked so sorrowful that the prince said to him:

'Dear huntsman, what ails you?'

'I cannot tell you, and yet I ought,' replied the huntsman.

'Say openly what it is, I will pardon you,' said the prince.

'Alas!' said the huntsman, 'I am to shoot you dead, the king has ordered me to do it.'

Then the prince was shocked.

'Dear huntsman, let me live; there, I give you my royal garments; give me your common ones in their stead.'

'I will willingly do that,' said the huntsman, 'indeed I should not have been able to shoot you.'

Then they exchanged clothes, and the huntsman returned home; the prince, however, went further into the forest. After a time three waggons of gold and precious stones came to the king for his youngest son, which were sent by the three kings who had slain their enemies with the prince's sword, and maintained their people with his bread, and who wished to show their gratitude for it.

'Can my son have been innocent?' the old king then thought, and said to his people, 'Would that he were still alive, how it grieves me that I have suffered him to be killed!'

'He still lives,' said the huntsman, 'I could not find it in my heart to carry out your command,' and told the king how it had happened. Then a stone fell from the king's heart, and he had it proclaimed in every country that his son might return and be taken into favour again.

The princess, however, had a road made up to her palace which was quite bright and golden, and told her people that whosoever came riding straight along it to her, would be the right wooer and was to be admitted, and whoever rode by the side of it, was not the right one, and was not to be admitted. As the time was now close at hand, the eldest thought he would hasten to go to the king's daughter, and give himself out as her deliverer, and thus win her for his bride, and the kingdom to boot. Therefore he rode forth, and when he arrived in front of the palace, and saw the splendid golden road, he thought, it would be a sin and a shame if he were to ride over that, and turned aside, and rode on the right side of it. But when he came to the door, the servants told him that he was not the right man, and was to go away again. Soon after this the second prince set out, and when he came to the golden road, and his horse had put one foot on it, he thought, it would be a sin and a shame to tread a piece of it off, and he turned aside and rode on the left side of it, and when he reached the door, the attendants told him he was not the right one, and he was to go away again.

When at last the year had entirely expired, the third son likewise wished to ride out of the forest to his beloved, and with her forget his sorrows. So he set out and thought of her so incessantly, and wished to be with her so much, that he never noticed the golden road at all. So his horse rode onwards up the middle of it, and when he came to the door, it was opened and the princess received him with joy, and said he was her deliverer, and lord of the kingdom, and their wedding was celebrated with great rejoicing. When it was over she told him that his father invited him to come to him, and had forgiven him. So he rode thither, and told him everything; how his brothers had betrayed him, and how he had nevertheless kept silence. The old king wished to punish them, but they had put to sea, and never came back as long as they lived.

The Blue Light

Once upon a time there was a soldier who for many years had served the king faithfully, but when the war came to an end could serve no longer because of the many wounds which he had received.

'You may return to your home,' said the king to him, 'I need you no longer, and you will not receive any more money, for I only pay wages to those who render me service for them.'

The soldier did not know how to earn a living, went away greatly troubled, and walked the whole day, until in the evening he entered a forest. When darkness came on, he saw a light, which he went up to, and came to a house wherein lived a witch.

'Do give me one night's lodging, and a little to eat and drink,' said he to her, 'or I shall starve.'

'Oho!' she answered, 'who gives anything to a runaway soldier? Yet will I be compassionate, and take you in, if you will do what I wish.'

'What do you wish?' asked the soldier.

'That you should dig all round my garden for me, tomorrow.'

The soldier consented, and next day laboured with all his strength, but could not finish it by the evening.

'I see well enough,' said the witch, 'that you can do no more today, but I will keep you yet another night, in payment for which you must tomorrow chop me a load of wood, and make it small.'

The soldier spent the whole day in doing it, and in the evening the witch proposed that he should stay one night more.

'Tomorrow, you shall only do me a very trifling piece of work. Behind my house, there is an old dry well, into which my light has fallen, it burns blue, and never goes out, and you shall bring it up again for me.'

174

Next day the old woman took him to the well and let him down in a basket. He found the blue light, and made her a signal to draw him up again. She did draw him up, but when he came near the edge, she stretched down her hand and wanted to take the blue light away from him.

'No,' said he, perceiving her evil intention, 'I will not give you the light until I am standing with both feet upon the ground.'

The witch fell into a passion, let him down again into the well, and went away.

The poor soldier fell without injury on the moist ground, and the blue light went on burning, but of what use was that to him? He saw very well that he could not escape death. He sat for a while very sorrowfully, then suddenly he felt in his pocket and found his tobacco pipe, which was still half full.

'This shall be my last pleasure,' thought he, pulled it out, lit it at the blue light and began to smoke. When the smoke had circled about the cavern, suddenly a little dwarf stood before him, and said, 'Lord, what are thy commands?'

'What commands have I to give you?' replied the soldier, quite astonished.

'I must do everything you bid me,' said the little man.

'Good,' said the soldier; 'then in the first place help me out of this well.'

The little man took him by the hand, and led him through an underground passage, but he did not forget to take the blue light with him. On the way the dwarf showed him the treasures which the witch had collected and hidden there, and the soldier took as much gold as he could carry.

'Now go and bind the old witch, and carry her before the judge,' he said to the little man when he was above ground again. In a short time, she, with frightful cries, was carried past by the little man, as swift as the wind on a wild tom-cat, nor was it long after that before the little man reappeared.

'It is all done,' said he, 'and the witch is already hanging on the gallows. What further commands has my lord?'

'At this moment, none,' answered the soldier; 'You can return home, only be at hand immediately, if I summon you.'

'Nothing more is needed than that you should light your pipe at the blue light, and I will appear before you at once.' And he vanished from sight.

The soldier returned to the town from which he had come. He went to the best inn, ordered himself handsome clothes, and then bade the landlord furnish him a room as handsomely as possible. When it was ready and the soldier had taken possession of it, he summoned the little mannikin and said:

'I have served the king faithfully, but he has dismissed me, and left me to hunger, and now I want to take my revenge.'

'What am I to do?' asked the little man.

'Late at night, when the king's daughter is in bed, bring her here in her sleep, she shall do servant's work for me.'

'That is an easy thing for me to do,' said the mannikin, 'but a very dangerous thing for you, for if it is discovered, you will fare ill.' When twelve o'clock had struck, the door sprang open, and the mannikin carried in the princess.

'Aha! are you there?' cried the soldier, 'get to your work at once! Fetch the broom and sweep the chamber.' When she had done this, he ordered her to come to his chair, and then he stretched out his feet and said, 'Pull off my boots for me,' and then he threw them in her face, and made her pick them up again, and clean and brighten them. She, however, did everything he bade her, without opposition, silently and with half-shut eyes. When the first cock crowed, the mannikin carried her back to the royal palace, and laid her in her bed.

Next morning when the princess arose, she went to her father, and told him that she had had a very strange dream. 'I was carried through the streets with the rapidity of lightning,' said she, 'and taken into a soldier's room, and I had to wait upon him like a servant, sweep his room, clean his boots, and do all kinds of menial work. It was only a dream, and yet I am just as tired as if I really had done everything.'

'The dream may have been true,' said the king, 'and we need to find where you were taken. Fill your pocket full of peas, and make a small hole in it, and then if you are carried away again, they will fall out and leave a track in the streets.' But unseen by the king, the mannikin was standing beside him when he said that, and heard all. At night when the sleeping princess was again carried through the streets, some peas certainly did fall out of her pocket, but they made no track, for the crafty mannikin had just before scattered peas in every street there was. And again the princess was compelled to do servant's work until cock-crow.

Next morning the king sent his people out to seek the track, but it was all in vain, for in every street poor children were sitting, picking up peas, and saying, 'It must have rained peas, last night.'

'We must think of something else,' said the king. 'Keep your shoes on when you go to bed, and before you come back from the place where you are taken, hide one of them there, I will soon contrive to find it.' The mannikin heard this plot, and at night when the soldier again ordered him to bring the princess, revealed it to him, and told him that he knew of no expedient to counteract this stratagem, and that if the shoe were found in the soldier's house it would go badly with him.

'Do what I bid you,' replied the soldier, and again this third night the princess was obliged to work like a servant, but before she went away, she hid her shoe under the bed.

Next morning the king had the entire town searched for his daughter's shoe. It was found at the soldier's, and the soldier himself, who at the entreaty of the dwarf had gone outside the gate, was soon brought back, and thrown into prison. In his flight he had forgotten the most valuable things he had, the blue light and the gold, and had only one ducat in his pocket. And now loaded with chains, he was standing at the window of his dungeon, when he chanced to see one of his comrades passing by. The soldier tapped at the pane of glass, and this man came up to him.

'Be so kind as to fetch me the small bundle I have left lying in the inn, and I will give you a ducat for doing it,' he said.

His comrade ran thither and brought him what he wanted. As soon as the soldier was alone again, he lit his pipe and summoned the mannikin.

'Have no fear,' said the latter to his master. 'Go wherever they take you, and let them do what they will, only take the blue light with you.'

Next day the soldier was tried, and though he had done nothing wicked, the judge condemned him to death. When he was led forth to die, he begged a last favour of the king.

'What is it?' asked the king.

'That I may smoke one more pipe on my way.'

'You may smoke three,' answered the king, 'but do not imagine that I will spare your life.'

Then the soldier pulled out his pipe and lit it at the blue light, and as soon as a few wreaths of smoke had ascended, the mannikin was there with a small cudgel in his hand, and said, 'What does my lord command?'

'Strike down to earth that false judge there, and his constable, and spare not the king who has treated me so ill.'

Then the mannikin fell on them like lightning, darting this way and that way, and whoever was so much as touched by his cudgel fell to earth, and did not venture to stir again. The king was terrified; he threw himself on the soldier's mercy, and merely to be allowed to live at all, gave him his kingdom for his own, and the princess to wife.

Hans the Hedgehog

There was once a countryman who had money and land in plenty, but however rich he was, one thing was still wanting in his happiness: he had no children. Often when he went into the town with the other peasants they mocked him and asked why he had no children. At last he became angry, and when he got home he said, 'I will have a child, even if it be a hedgehog.'

Then his wife had a child, that was a hedgehog in the upper part of his body, and a boy in the lower, and when she saw the child, she was terrified.

'See, there you have brought ill-luck on us,' she said.

'What can be done now? Said the man. 'The boy must be christened, but we shall not be able to get a godfather for him.'

'And we cannot call him anything else but Hans the Hedgehog,' said his wife.

When he was christened, the parson said, 'He cannot go into any ordinary bed because of his spikes.' So a little straw was put behind the stove, and Hans the Hedgehog was laid on it. His mother could not suckle him, for he would have pricked her with his quills. So he lay there behind the stove for eight years, and his father was tired of him and thought:

'If he would but die!'

He did not die, however, but remained lying there. Now it happened that there was a fair in the town, and the peasant was about to go to it, and asked his wife what he should bring back with him for her.

'A little meat and a couple of white rolls which are wanted for the house,' said she. Then he asked the servant, and she wanted a pair of slippers and some stockings with clocks. At last he said also:

'And what wilt thou have, Hans my Hedgehog?'

'Dear father,' he said, 'do bring me bagpipes.'

When, therefore, the father came home again, he gave his wife what he had bought for her; meat and white rolls, and then he gave the maid the slippers, and the stockings with clocks; and, lastly, he went behind the stove, and gave Hans the Hedgehog the bagpipes. And when Hans the Hedgehog had the bagpipes, he said, 'Dear father, do go to the forge and get the cock shod, and then I will ride away, and never come back again.'

On this, the father was delighted to think that he was going to get rid of him, and had the cock shod for him, and when it was done, Hans the Hedgehog got on it, and rode away, but took swine and asses with him which he intended to keep in the forest. When they got there he made the cock fly on to a high tree with him, and there he sat for many a long year, and watched his asses and swine until the herd was quite large, and his father knew nothing about him. While he was sitting in the tree, however, he played his bagpipes, and made music which was very beautiful.

Once a king came travelling by who had lost his way and heard the music. He was astonished at it, and sent his servant to look all round and see from where this music came. He spied about, but saw nothing but a little animal sitting up aloft on the tree, which looked like a cock with a hedgehog on it which made this music. Then the king told the servant he was to ask why he sat there, and if he knew the road which led to his kingdom. So Hans the Hedgehog descended from the tree, and said he would show the way if the king would write a bond and promise to him whatever he first met in the royal courtyard as soon as he arrived at home.

'I can easily do that,' thought the king. 'Hans the Hedgehog understands nothing, and I can write what I like.'

So the king took pen and ink and wrote something, and when he had done it, Hans the Hedgehog showed him the way, and he got safely home. But his daughter, when she saw him from afar, was so overjoyed that she ran to meet him, and kissed him. Then he remembered Hans the Hedgehog, and told her what had happened, and that he had been forced to promise whatsoever first met him when he got home, to a very strange animal which sat on a cock as if it were a horse, and made beautiful music, but that instead of writing that he should have what he wanted, he had written that he should not have it. Thereupon the princess was glad, and said he had done well, for she never would have gone away with the Hedgehog.

Hans the Hedgehog, however, looked after his asses and pigs, and was always merry and sat on the tree and played his bagpipes.

Now it came to pass that another king came journeying by with his attendants and runners, and he also had lost his way, and did not know how to get home again because the forest was so large. He likewise heard the beautiful music from a distance, and asked his runner what that could be, and told him to go and see. Then the runner went under the tree, and saw the cock sitting at the top of it, and Hans the Hedgehog on the cock.

'What are you about up there?' the runner asked him.

'I am keeping my asses and my pigs; but what is your desire?' replied Hans.

The messenger said that they had lost their way, and could not get back into their own kingdom, and asked if he would not show them the way. Then Hans the Hedgehog got down the tree with the cock, and told the aged king that he would show him the way, if he would give him for his own whatsoever first met him in front of his royal palace.

'Yes,' said the king, and wrote a promise to Hans the Hedgehog that he should have this. That done, Hans rode on before him on the cock, and pointed out the way, and the king reached his kingdom again in safety. When he got to the courtyard, there were great rejoicings. Now he had an only daughter who was very beautiful; she ran to meet him, threw her arms round his neck, and was delighted to have her old father back again. She asked him where in the world he had been so long. So he told her how he had lost his way, and had very nearly not come back at all, but that as he was travelling through a great forest, a creature, half hedgehog, half man, who was sitting astride a cock in a high tree, and making music, had shown him the way and helped him to get out, but that in return he had promised him whatsoever first met him in the royal court-yard, and how that was she herself, which made him unhappy now. But on this she promised that, for love of her father, she would willingly go with this Hans if he came.

Hans the Hedgehog, however, took care of his pigs, and the pigs multiplied until they became so many in number that the whole forest was filled with them. Then Hans the Hedgehog resolved not to live in the forest any longer, and sent word to his father to have every sty in the village emptied, for he was coming with such a great herd that all might kill who wished to do so. When his father heard that, he was troubled, for he thought Hans the Hedgehog had died long ago. Hans the Hedgehog, however, seated himself on the cock, and drove the pigs before him into the village, and ordered the slaughter to begin. Ha! but there was a killing and a chopping that might have been heard two miles off! After this Hans the Hedgehog said:

'Father, let me have the cock shod once more at the forge, and then I will ride away and never come back as long as I live.'

Then the father had the cock shod once more, and was pleased that Hans the Hedgehog would never return again.

Hans the Hedgehog rode away to the first kingdom. There the king had commanded that whosoever came mounted on a cock and had bagpipes with him should be shot at, cut down, or stabbed by every-one, so that he might not enter the palace. When, therefore, Hans the Hedgehog came riding thither, they all pressed forward against him with their pikes, but he spurred the cock and it flew up over the gate in front of the king's window and lighted there, and Hans cried that the king must give him what he had promised, or he would take both his life and his daughter's. Then the king began to speak his daughter fair, and to beg her to go away with Hans in order to save her own life and her father's. So she dressed herself in white, and her father gave her a carriage with six horses and magnificent attendants together with gold and possessions. She seated herself in the carriage, and placed Hans the Hedgehog beside her with the cock and the bagpipes, and then they took leave and drove away, and the king thought he should never see her again. He was however, deceived in his expectation, for when they were at a short distance from the town, Hans the Hedgehog took her pretty clothes off, and pierced her with his hedgehog's skin until she bled all over.

'That is the reward of your falseness,' said he, 'go your way, I will not have you!' and on that he chased her home again, and she was disgraced for the rest of her life.

Hans the Hedgehog, however, rode on further on the cock, with his bagpipes, to the dominions of the second king to whom he had shown the way. This one, however, had arranged that if any one resembling Hans the Hedgehog should come, they were to present arms, give him safe conduct, cry long life to him, and lead him to the royal palace.

But when the king's daughter saw him she was terrified, for he looked quite too strange. She remembered however, that she could not change her mind, for she had given her promise to her father. So Hans the Hedgehog was welcomed by her, and married to her, and had to go with her to the royal table, and she seated herself by his side, and they ate and drank.

When the evening came and they wanted to go to sleep, she was afraid of his quills, but he told her she was not to fear, for no harm would befall her, and he told the old king that he was to appoint four men to watch by the door of the chamber, and light a great fire, and when he entered the room and was about to get into bed, he would creep out of his hedgehog's skin and leave it lying there by the bedside, and that the men were to run nimbly to it, throw it in the fire, and stay by it until it was consumed.

When the clock struck eleven, he went into the chamber, stripped off the hedgehog's skin, and left it lying by the bed. Then came the men and fetched it swiftly, and threw it in the fire; and when the fire had consumed it, he was delivered, and lay there in bed in human form, but he was coal-black as if he had been burnt. The king sent for his physician who washed him with precious salves, and anointed him, and he became white, and was a handsome young man. When the king's daughter saw that she was glad, and the next morning they arose joyfully, ate and drank, and then the marriage was properly solemnized, and Hans the Hedgehog received the kingdom from the aged king.

When several years had passed he went with his wife to his father, and said that he was his son. The father, however, declared he had no son he had never had but one, and he had been born like a hedgehog with spikes, and had gone forth into the world. Then Hans made himself known, and the old father rejoiced and went with him to his kingdom.

> My tale is done,
> And away it has run
> To little August's house.

The King of the Golden Mountain

There was once a merchant who had two children, a boy and a girl. When they were both still very young, and could not walk, two richly laden ships of his sailed forth to sea with all his property on board. Just as he was expecting to make much money from the rich cargoes, news came that both ships had sunk to the bottom of the sea, and now, instead of being a rich man he was a poor one, and had nothing left but one field outside the town.

In order to drive his misfortune a little out of his thoughts, he went out to this field, and as he was walking forwards and backwards in it, a little mannikin stood suddenly by his side, and asked why he was so sad, and what he was taking so much to heart.

'If you could help me I would willingly tell you,' said the merchant.

'Who knows?' replied the little man. 'Perhaps I can help you.'

Then the merchant told him that all he possessed had gone to the bottom of the sea, and that he had nothing left but this field.

'Do not trouble thyself,' said the dwarf. 'If you will promise to give me the first thing that rubs itself against thy leg when you are at home again, and to bring it here to this place in twelve years' time, you shalt have as much money as you want.'

'What can that be but my dog?' thought the merchant, so he said yes, gave the little man a written and sealed promise, and went home.

When he reached home, his little boy was so delighted that he held by a bench, tottered up to him and seized him fast by the legs. The father was shocked, for he remembered his promise, and now knew what he had pledged himself to do; as however, he still found no money in his chest, he thought the dwarf had only been jesting. A month afterwards he went up to the garret, intending to gather together some old tin and to sell it, and saw a great heap of money lying. Then he was happy again, made purchases, became a greater merchant than before, and felt that this world was well-governed. In the meantime, the boy grew tall, and at the same time sharp and clever. But the nearer the twelfth year approached the more anxious grew the merchant, so that his distress might be seen in his face.

One day his son asked what ailed him, but the father would not say. The boy, however, persisted so long, that at last he told him that without being aware of what he was doing, he had promised him to a little mannikin, and had received much money for doing so. He also said that he had set his hand and seal to this, and that now when twelve years had gone by he would have to give him up.

'Oh, father, do not be uneasy, all will go well,' said the son. 'The little man has no power over me.'

The son had himself blessed by the priest, and when the time came, father and son went together to the field, and the son made a circle and placed himself inside it with his father. Then came the little man and said to the old man, 'Have you brought with you that which you have promised me?' He was silent, but the son asked:

'What do you want here?'

'I have to speak with your father, and not with you,' said the little man.

The son replied, 'You have betrayed and misled my father,' replied the son. 'Give back the writing.'

'No,' said the mannikin, 'I will not give up my rights.'

They spoke together for a long time after this, but at last they agreed that the son, as he did not belong to the enemy of mankind, nor yet to his father, should seat himself in a small boat, which should lie on water which was flowing away from them, and that the father should push it off with his own foot, and then the son should remain given up to the water. So the son took leave of his father, placed himself in a little boat, and the father had to push it off with his own foot. The boat capsized so that the keel was uppermost, and the father believed his son was lost and went home and mourned for him.

The boat, however, did not sink, but floated quietly away, and the boy sat safely inside it, and it floated thus for a long time, until at last it stopped by an unknown shore. Then he landed and saw a beautiful castle before him and set out to go to it. But when he entered it, he found that it was bewitched. He went through every room, but all were empty until he reached the last, where a snake lay coiled in a ring. The snake, however, was an enchanted maiden, who rejoiced to see him.

'Have you come, oh, my deliverer?' she said. 'I have already waited twelve years for you; this kingdom is bewitched, and you must set it free.'

'How can I do that?' he inquired.

'Tonight come twelve men covered with chains who will ask what you are doing here; keep silent; give them no answer, and let them do what they will with you; they will torment you, beat you, stab you; let everything pass, only do not speak; at twelve o'clock, they must go away again. On the second night twelve others will come; on the third, four-and-twenty, who will cut off your head, but at twelve o'clock their power will be over, and then if you have endured all, and have not spoken the slightest word, I shall be released. I will come to you, and will have, in a bottle, some of the water of life. I will rub you with that, and then you will come to life again, and be as healthy as before.'

'I will gladly set you free,' he said.

And everything happened just as he had said; the men could not force a single word from him, and on the third night the snake became a beautiful princess, who came with the water of life and brought him back to life again. So she threw herself into his arms and kissed him, and there was joy and gladness in the whole castle. After this their marriage was celebrated, and he was king of the Golden Mountain.

They lived very happily together, and the queen bore a fine boy. Eight years had already gone by, when the king bethought him of his father; his heart was moved, and he wished to visit him. The queen, however, did not want him to go away.

'I know beforehand that it will cause my unhappiness,' she said, but he suffered her to have no rest until she consented. At their parting she gave him a wishing-ring, and said:

'Take this ring and put it on your finger, and then you will immediately be transported wherever you would like to be, only you must promise me not to use it in wishing me away from this place and with your father.'

That he promised her, put the ring on his finger, and wished himself at home, just outside the town where his father lived. Instantly he found himself there, and made for the town, but when he came to the gate, the sentries would not let him in, because he wore such strange and yet such rich and magnificent clothing. Then he went to a hill where a shepherd was watching his sheep, changed clothes with him, put on the old shepherd's coat, and then entered the town without hindrance. When he came to his father, he made himself known to him, but he did not at all believe that the shepherd was his son, and said he certainly had had a son, but that he was dead long ago; however, as he saw he was a poor, needy shepherd, he would give him something to eat.

'I really am your son,' the shepherd said to his parents. 'Do you know of no mark on my body by which you could recognize me?'

'Yes,' said his mother, 'our son had a raspberry mark under his right arm.' He slipped back his shirt, and they saw the raspberry under his right arm, and no longer doubted that he was their son. Then he told them that he was King of the Golden Mountain, and a king's daughter was his wife, and that they had a fine son of seven years old. Then said the father, 'That is certainly not true,' said his father. 'It is a fine kind of a king who goes about in a ragged shepherd's coat.'

On this the son fell in a passion, and without thinking of his promise, turned his ring round, and wished both his wife and child with him. They were there in a second, but the queen wept, and reproached him, and said that he had broken his word, and had brought misfortune upon her.

'I have done it thoughtlessly, and not with evil intention,' he said and tried to calm her, and she pretended to believe this; but she had mischief in her mind. Then he led her out of the town into the field, and showed her the stream where the little boat had been pushed off, and then he said, 'I am tired; sit down, I will sleep awhile on thy lap.' And he laid his head on her lap, and fell asleep. When he was asleep, she first drew the ring from his finger, then she drew away the foot which was under him, leaving only the slipper behind her, and she took her child in her arms, and wished herself back in her own kingdom. When he awoke, there he lay quite deserted, and his wife and child were gone, and so was the ring from his finger, the slipper only was still there as a token.

'Home to your parents you can not return,' thought he, 'they would say that you were a wizard; you must be off, and walk on until you arrive in your own kingdom.'

So he went away and came at length to a hill by which three giants were standing, disputing with each other because they did not know how to divide their father's property. When they saw him passing by, they called to him and said little men had quick wits, and that he was to divide their inheritance for them. The inheritance, however, consisted of a sword, which had this property that if any one took it in his hand, and said, 'All heads off but mine,' every head would lie on the ground; secondly, of a cloak which made any one who put it on invisible; thirdly, of a pair of boots which could transport the wearer to any place he wished in a moment.

'Give me the three things that I may see if they are still in good condition,' he said.

They gave him the cloak, and when he had put it on, he was invisible and changed into a fly. Then he resumed his own form and said, 'The cloak is a good one, now give me the sword.'

'No, we will not give you that,' they said; 'if you were to say, "All heads off but mine", all our heads would be off, and you alone would be left with yours.'

Nevertheless they gave it to him with the condition that he was only to try it against a tree. This he did, and the sword cut in two the trunk of a tree as if it had been a blade of straw. Then he wanted to have the boots likewise, but they said, 'No, we will not give them; if you had them on thy feet and were to wish yourself at the top of the hill, we should be left down here with nothing.'

'Oh, no,' said he, 'I will not do that.'

So they gave him the boots as well. And now when he had got all these things, he thought of nothing but his wife and his child, and said as though to himself, 'Oh, if I were but on the Golden Mountain,' and at the same moment he vanished from the sight of the giants, and thus their inheritance was divided. When he was near his palace, he heard sounds of joy, and fiddles, and flutes, and the people told him that his wife was celebrating her wedding with another. Then he fell into a rage.

'False woman, she betrayed and deserted me whilst I was asleep!' he said. So he put on his cloak, and unseen by all went into the palace. When he entered the dining-hall a great table was spread with delicious food, and the guests were eating and drinking, and laughing, and jesting. She sat on a royal seat in the midst of them in splendid apparel, with a crown on her head. He placed himself behind her, and no one saw him. When she put a piece of meat on a plate for herself, he took it away and ate it, and when she poured out a glass of wine for herself, he took it away and drank it. She was always helping herself to something, and yet she never got anything, for plate and glass disappeared immediately. Then dismayed and ashamed, she arose and went to her chamber and wept, but he followed her there.

'Has the devil power over me, or did my deliverer never come?' she said.

Then he struck her in the face, and said, 'Did thy deliverer never come? It is he who has you in his power, you traitor. Have I deserved this from you?' Then he made himself visible, went into the hall, and cried, 'The wedding is at an end, the true king has returned.'

The kings, princes, and councillors who were assembled there, ridiculed and mocked him, but he did not trouble to answer them, and said, 'Will you go away, or not?' On this they tried to seize him and pressed upon him, but he drew his sword and said, 'All heads off but mine,' and all the heads rolled on the ground, and he alone was master, and once more King of the Golden Mountain.

Cinderella

The wife of a rich man fell sick, and as she felt that her end was drawing near, she called her only daughter to her bedside and said, 'Dear child, be good and pious, and then the good God will always protect you, and I will look down on you from heaven and be near you.' Then she closed her eyes and died. Every day the maiden went out to her mother's grave, and wept, and she remained pious and good. Winter came the snow spread a white sheet over the grave, and when the spring sun had drawn it off again, the man had taken another wife.

The woman had brought two daughters into the house with her, who were beautiful and fair of face, but vile and black of heart. Now began a bad time for the poor step-child.

'Is the stupid goose to sit in the parlour with us?' said they. 'He who wants to eat bread must earn it; out with the kitchen-wench.' They took her pretty clothes away from her, put an old grey bedgown on her, and gave her wooden shoes.

'Just look at the proud princess, how decked out she is!' they cried, and laughed, and led her into the kitchen. There she had to do hard work from morning till night, get up before daybreak, carry water, light fires, cook and wash. Besides this, the sisters did her every imaginable injury – they mocked her and emptied her peas and lentils into the ashes, so that she was forced to sit and pick them out again. In the evening when she had worked till she was weary she had no bed to go to, but had to sleep by the fireside in the ashes. And as on that account she always looked dusty and dirty, they called her Cinderella.

It happened that the father was once going to the fair, and he asked his two step-daughters what he should bring back for them.

'Beautiful dresses,' said one.

'Pearls and jewels,' said the second.

'And you, Cinderella,' said he, 'what will you have?'

'Father, break off for me the first branch which knocks against your hat on your way home.' So he bought beautiful dresses, pearls and jewels for his two step-daughters, and on his way home, as he was riding through a green thicket, a hazel twig brushed against him and knocked off his hat. Then he broke off the branch and took it with him. When he reached home he gave his step-daughters the things which they had wished for, and to Cinderella he gave the branch from the hazel-bush. Cinderella thanked him, went to her mother's grave and planted the branch on it, and wept so much that the tears fell down on it and watered it. And it grew, however, and became a handsome tree. Three times a day Cinderella went and sat beneath it, and wept and prayed, and a little white bird always came on the tree, and if Cinderella expressed a wish, the bird threw down to her what she had wished for.

One day the king announced a festival which was to last three days, and to which all the beautiful young girls in the country were invited, in order that his son might choose himself a bride. When the two step-sisters heard that they too were to appear among the number, they were delighted, called Cinderella and said, 'Comb our hair for us, brush our shoes and fasten our buckles, for we are going to the festival at the King's palace.'

Cinderella obeyed, but wept, because she too would have liked to go with them to the dance, and begged her step-mother to allow her to do so.

'You go, Cinderella!' said she; 'You are dusty and dirty and would go to the festival? You have no clothes and shoes, and yet would dance!'

As, however, Cinderella went on asking, the step-mother at last said, 'I have emptied a dish of lentils into the ashes for you, if you have picked them out again in two hours, you shall go with us.'

The maiden went through the back door into the garden, and called, 'You pigeons, you turtle-doves, and all you birds beneath the sky, come and help me to pick "the good into the pot, the bad into the crop".'

Then two white pigeons came in by the kitchen-window, and afterwards the turtle-doves, and at last all the birds beneath the sky, came whirring and crowding in, and alighted among the ashes. And the pigeons nodded with their heads and began pick, pick, pick, pick, and the rest began also pick, pick, pick, pick, and gathered all the good grains into the dish. Hardly had one hour passed before they had finished, and all flew out again. Then the girl took the dish to her step-mother, and was glad, and believed that now she would be allowed to go with them to the festival.

But the step-mother said, 'No, Cinderella, you have no clothes and you cannot dance; you would only be laughed at.' And as Cinderella wept at this, the step-mother said, 'If you can pick two dishes of lentils out of the ashes for me in one hour, you shall go with us.' And she thought to herself, 'that she most certainly cannot do.'

When the step-mother had emptied the two dishes of lentils amongst the ashes, the maiden went through the back-door into the garden and cried, 'You pigeons, you turtle-doves, and all you birds under heaven, come and help me to pick "The good into the pot, the bad into the crop".' Then two white pigeons came in by the kitchen-window, and afterwards the turtle-doves, and at length all the birds beneath the sky, came whirring and crowding in, and alighted amongst the ashes. And the doves nodded with their heads and began pick, pick, pick, pick, and the others began also pick, pick, pick, pick, and gathered all the good seeds into the dishes, and before half an hour was over they had already finished, and all flew out again. Then the maiden carried the dishes to the step-mother and was delighted, and believed that she might now go with them to the festival. But the step-mother said, 'All this will not help you; you are not going with us, for you have no clothes and cannot dance; we should be ashamed of you!' With this she turned her back on Cinderella, and hurried away with her two proud daughters.

As no one was now at home, Cinderella went to her mother's grave beneath the hazel-tree, and cried,

> 'Shiver and quiver, little tree,
> Silver and gold throw down over me.'

Then the bird threw a gold and silver dress down to her, and slippers embroidered with silk and silver. She put on the dress with all speed, and went to the festival. Her step-sisters and the step-mother however did not know her, and thought she must be a foreign princess, for she looked so beautiful in the golden dress. They never once thought of Cinderella, and believed that she was sitting at home in the dirt, picking lentils out of the ashes. The prince went to meet her, took her by the hand and danced with her. He would dance with no other maiden, and never let go of her hand, and if anyone else came to ask her to dance, he said, 'This is my partner.'

She danced till it was evening, and then she wanted to go home. But the king's son said, 'I will go with you and bear you company,' for he wished to see to whom the beautiful maiden belonged. She escaped from him, however, and sprang into the pigeon-house. The king's son waited until her father came, and then he told him that the strange maiden had leapt into the pigeon-house. The old man thought, 'Can it be Cinderella?' and they had to bring him an axe and a pickaxe that he might hew the pigeon-house to pieces, but no one was inside it. When they got home Cinderella lay in her dirty clothes among the ashes, and a dim little oil-lamp was burning on the mantlepiece, for Cinderella had jumped quickly down from the back of the pigeon-house and had run to the little hazel-tree, and there she had taken off her beautiful clothes and laid them on the grave, and the bird had taken them away again, and then she had placed herself in the kitchen amongst the ashes in her grey gown.

Next day, when the festival began afresh, and her parents and the step-sisters had gone once more, Cinderella went to the hazel-tree and said,

'Shiver and quiver, my little tree,
Silver and gold throw down over me.'

Then the bird threw down a much more beautiful dress than on the previous day. And when Cinderella appeared at the festival in this dress, everyone was astonished at her beauty. The prince had waited until she came, and instantly took her by the hand and danced with no one but her. When others came and invited her to dance, he said, 'She is my partner.'

When evening came she wished to leave, and the prince followed her and wanted to see into which house she went. But she sprang away from him, and into the garden behind the house. Therein stood a beautiful tall tree on which hung the most magnificent pears. She clambered so nimbly between the branches like a squirrel that the prince did not know where she was gone. He waited until her father came, and said to him, 'The stranger-maiden has escaped from me, and I believe she has climbed up the pear-tree.' The father thought, 'Can it be Cinderella?' and had an axe brought and cut the tree down, but no one was on it. And when they got into the kitchen, Cinderella lay there amongst the ashes, as usual, for she had jumped down on the other side of the tree, had taken the beautiful dress to the bird on the little hazel-tree, and put on her grey gown.

On the third day, when the parents and sisters had gone away, Cinderella went once more to her mother's grave and said to the little tree:

> 'Shiver and quiver, my little tree,
> Silver and gold throw down over me.'

And now the bird threw down to her a dress which was more splendid and magnificent than any she had yet had, and the slippers were golden. And when she went to the festival in the dress, no one knew how to speak for astonishment. The prince danced with her only, and if any one invited her to dance, he said, 'She is my partner.'

When evening came, Cinderella wished to leave, and the prince was anxious to go with her, but she escaped from him so quickly that he could not follow her. The prince had, however, caused the whole staircase to be smeared with pitch, and there, when she ran down, the maiden's left slipper remained stuck. The prince picked it up, and it was small and dainty, and all golden. Next morning, he went with it to the father, and said to him, 'No one shall be my wife but she whose foot this golden slipper fits.' Then the two sisters were glad, for they had pretty feet. The eldest went with the shoe into her room and wanted to try it on, and her mother stood by. But she could not get her big toe into it, and the shoe was too small for her. Then her mother gave her a knife and said, 'Cut the toe off; when you are queen thou will have no more need to go on foot.' The maiden cut the toe off, forced the foot into the shoe, swallowed the pain, and went out to the prince. Then he took her on his horse as his bride and rode away with her. They were, however, obliged to pass the grave, and there, on the hazel-tree, sat the two pigeons and cried,

> 'Turn and peep, turn and peep,
> There's blood within the shoe,
> The shoe it is too small for her,
> The true bride waits for you.'

Then he looked at her foot and saw how the blood was streaming from it. He turned his horse round and took the false bride home again, and said she was not the true one, and that the other sister was to put the shoe on. Then this one went into her chamber and got her toes safely into the shoe, but her heel was too large. So her mother gave her a knife and said, 'Cut a bit off your heel; when you are queen you will have no more need to go on foot.' The maiden cut a bit off her heel, forced her foot into the shoe, swallowed the pain, and went out to the prince. He took her on his horse as his bride, and rode away with her, but when they passed by the hazel-tree, two little pigeons sat on it and cried,

> 'Turn and peep, turn and peep,
> There's blood within the shoe,
> The shoe it is too small for her,
> The true bride waits for you.'

He looked down at her foot and saw how the blood was running out of her shoe, and how it had stained her white stocking. Then he turned his horse and took the false bride home again.

'This also is not the right one,' said he, 'have you no other daughter?'

'No,' said the man. 'There is still a little stunted kitchen-wench which my late wife left behind her, but she cannot possibly be the bride.'

The prince said he was to send her up to him; but the mother answered, 'Oh, no, she is much too dirty, she cannot show herself!'

He absolutely insisted on it, and Cinderella had to be called. She first washed her hands and face clean, and then went and bowed down before the prince, who gave her the golden shoe. Then she seated herself on a stool, drew her foot out of the heavy wooden shoe, and put it into the slipper, which fitted like a glove. And when she rose up and the prince looked at her face he recognized the beautiful maiden who had danced with him and cried, 'That is the true bride!'

The step-mother and the two sisters were terrified and became pale with rage; he, however, took Cinderella on his horse and rode away with her. As they passed by the hazel-tree, the two white doves cried—

'Turn and peep, turn and peep,
No blood is in the shoe,
The shoe is not too small for her,
The true bride rides with you.'

And when they had cried that, the two came flying down and placed themselves on Cinderella's shoulders, one on the right, the other on the left, and remained sitting there.

When the wedding with the prince was be celebrated, the two false sisters came and wanted to get into favour with Cinderella and share her good fortune. When the betrothed couple went to church, the elder was at the right side and the younger at the left, and the pigeons pecked out one eye of each of them. Afterwards as they came back, the elder was at the left, and the younger at the right, and then the pigeons pecked out the other eye of each. And thus, for their wickedness and falsehood, they were punished with blindness as long as they lived.

Hansel and Gretel

Once upon a time there dwelt near a large wood a poor woodcutter, with his wife and two children by his former marriage, a little boy called Hansel, and a girl named Gretel. He was so poor that he never had much food; and once, when there was a great famine in the land, he no money to buy even his daily bread; and as he lay thinking in his bed one evening, rolling about for trouble, he sighed.

'What will become of us?' he said to his wife. 'How can we feed our children, when we don't have enough to eat ourselves?'

'Know, then, my husband,' answered she, 'we will lead them away, quite early in the morning, into the thickest part of the wood, and there make them a fire, and give them each a little piece of bread; then we will go to our work, and leave them alone, so they will not find the way home again, and we shall be freed from them. With luck they may find someone who can look after them better than we can.'

'No, wife,' replied he, 'that I can never do. How can you bring your heart to leave my children all alone in the wood, for the wild beasts will soon come and tear them to pieces?'

'Oh, you fool!' said she, 'then we must all four die of hunger; you had better plane the coffins for us.'

She left him no peace till he consented, saying, 'Ah, but I shall regret the poor children.'

The two children, however, had not gone to sleep for very hunger, and so they overheard what the stepmother said to their father.

Gretel wept bitterly, and said to Hansel, 'What will become of us?'

'Go to sleep, Gretel,' said he; 'do not cry – I will help you.'

And as soon as their parents had fallen asleep, he got up, put on his coat, and, unbarring the back door, slipped out. The moon shone brilliantly, and the white pebbles which lay before the door seemed like silver pieces, they glittered so brightly. Hansel stooped down, and put as many into his pocket as it would hold; and then going back, he said to Gretel, 'Be comforted, dear sister, and sleep in peace; God will not forsake us.' And so saying, he went to bed again.

The next morning, before the sun arose, the wife went and awoke the two children.

'Get up, you lazy things; we are going into the forest to chop wood.' Then she gave them each a piece of bread, saying, 'There is something for your dinner; do not eat it before the time, for you will get nothing else.'

Gretel took the bread in her apron, for Hansel's pocket was full of pebbles; and so they all set out upon their way. When they had gone a little distance, Hansel stood still, and peeped back at the house; and this he repeated several times, till his father said, 'Hansel, what are you peeping at, and why do you lag behind? Take care, and remember your legs.'

'Ah, father,' said Hansel, 'I am looking at my white cat sitting upon the roof of the house, and trying to say goodbye.'

'You silly boy!' said the wife, 'that is not a cat; it is only the sun shining on the white chimney.'

In reality Hansel was not looking at a cat; but every time he stopped, he dropped a pebble out of his pocket upon the path.

When they came to the middle of the forest, the father told the children to collect wood, and he would make them a fire, so that they should not be cold. So Hansel and Gretel gathered together quite a little mountain of twigs. Then they set fire to them; and as the flame burnt up high, the wife said, 'Now, you children, lie down near the fire, and rest yourselves, while we go into the forest and chop wood; when we are ready, I will come and call you.'

Hansel and Gretel sat down by the fire, and when it was noon, each ate the piece of bread; and because they could hear the blows of an axe, they thought their father was near: but it was not an axe, but a branch which he had bound to a withered tree, so as to be blown to and fro by the wind. They waited so long that at last their eyes closed from weariness, and they fell fast asleep. When they awoke, it was quite dark, and Gretel began to cry, 'How shall we get out of the wood?'

But Hansel tried to comfort her by saying, 'Wait a little while till the moon rises, and then we will quickly find the way.'

The moon soon shone forth, and Hansel, taking his sister's hand, followed the pebbles, which glittered like new-coined silver pieces, and showed them the path. All night long they walked on, and as day broke they came to their father's house. They knocked at the door, and when the wife opened it, and saw Hansel and Gretel, she exclaimed, 'You wicked children! why did you sleep so long in the wood? We thought you were never coming home again.' But their father was very glad, for it had grieved his heart to leave them all alone.

Not long afterward there was again great scarcity in every corner of the land; and one night the children overheard their stepmother saying to their father, 'Everything is again consumed; we have only half a loaf left, and then the food is ended: the children must be sent away. We will take them deeper into the wood, so that they may not find the way out again; it is the only means of escape for us.'

But her husband felt heavy at heart, and thought, 'It were better to share the last crust with the children.' His wife, however, would listen to nothing that he said, and scolded and reproached him without end. He who says A must say B too; and he who consents the first time must also the second.

The children, however, had heard the conversation as they lay awake, and as soon as the old people went to sleep Hansel got up, intending to pick up some pebbles as before; but the wife had locked the door, so that he could not get out. Nevertheless, he comforted Gretel, saying, 'Do not cry; sleep in quiet; the good God will not forsake us.'

Early in the morning the stepmother came and pulled them out of bed, and gave them each a slice of bread, which was still smaller than the former piece. On the way, Hansel broke his in his pocket, and, stooping every now and then, dropped a crumb upon the path.

'Hansel, why do you stop and look about?' said the father; 'keep in the path.'

'I am looking at my little dove,' answered Hansel, 'nodding a good-bye to me.'

'Foolish child!' said the wife, 'that is no dove, but only the sun shining on the chimney.'

But Hansel still kept dropping crumbs as he went along.

The mother led the children deep into the wood, where they had never been before, and there making an immense fire, she said to them, 'Sit down here and rest, and when you feel tired you can sleep for a little while. We are going into the forest to hew wood, and in the evening, when we are ready, we will come and fetch you.'

When noon came Gretel shared her bread with Hansel, who had strewn his on the path. Then they went to sleep; but the evening arrived and no one came to visit the poor children, and in the dark night they awoke, and Hansel comforted his sister by saying, 'Only wait, Gretel, till the moon comes out, then we shall see the crumbs of bread which I have dropped, and they will show us the way home.'

The moon shone and they got up, but they could not see any crumbs, for the thousands of birds which had been flying about in the woods and fields had picked them all up.

Hansel kept saying to Gretel, 'We will soon find the way'; but they did not, and they walked the whole night long and the next day, but still they did not come out of the wood; and they got so hungry, for they had nothing to eat but the berries which they found upon the bushes. Soon they got so tired that they could not drag themselves along, so they lay down under a tree and went to sleep.

It was now the third morning since they had left their father's house, and they still walked on; but they only got deeper and deeper into the wood, and Hansel saw that if help did not come very soon they would die of hunger. At about noonday they saw a beautiful snow-white bird sitting upon a bough, which sang so sweetly that they stood still and listened to it. It soon ceased, and spreading its wings flew off; and they followed it until it arrived at a cottage, upon the roof of which it perched; and when they went close up to it they saw that the cottage was made of bread and cakes, and the window-panes were of clear sugar.

'We will go in there,' said Hansel, 'and have a glorious feast. I will eat a piece of the roof, and you can eat the window. Will they not be sweet?'

So Hansel reached up and broke a piece off the roof, in order to see how it tasted, while Gretel stepped up to the window and began to bite it.

Then a sweet voice called out in the room, 'Tip-tap, tip-tap, who raps at my door?' and the children answered, 'the wind, the wind, the child of heaven'; and they went on eating without interruption. Hansel thought the roof tasted very nice, so he tore off a great piece; while Gretel broke a large round pane out of the window, and sat down quite contentedly. Just then the door opened, and a very old woman, walking upon crutches, came out. Hansel and Gretel were so frightened that they let fall what they had in their hands; but the old woman, nodding her head, said, 'Ah, you dear children, what has brought you here? Come in and stop with me, and no harm shall befall you'; and so saying she took them both by the hand, and led them into her cottage. A good meal of milk and pancakes, with sugar, apples, and nuts, was spread on the table, and in the back room were two nice little beds, covered with white, where Hansel and Gretel laid themselves down, and thought themselves in heaven. The old woman behaved very kindly to them, but in reality she was a wicked witch who waylaid children, and built the bread-house in order to entice them in, but as soon as they were in her power she killed them, cooked and ate them, and made a great festival of the day. Witches have red eyes, and cannot see very far; but they have a fine sense of smelling, like wild beasts, so that they know when children approach them.

When Hansel and Gretel came near the witch's house she had laughed wickedly, saying, 'Here come two who shall not escape me.' And early in the morning, before they awoke, she went up to them, and saw how lovingly they lay sleeping, with their chubby red cheeks, and she mumbled to herself, 'That will be a good bite.'

Then she took up Hansel with her rough hands, and shut him up in a little cage with a lattice-door; and although he screamed loudly it was of no use. Gretel came next, and, shaking her till she awoke, the witch said, 'Get up, you lazy thing, and fetch some water to cook something good for your brother, who must remain in that stall and get fat; when he is fat enough I shall eat him.'

Gretel began to cry, but it was all useless, for the old witch made her do as she wished. So a nice meal was cooked for Hansel, but Gretel got nothing but a crab's claw.

Every morning the old witch came to the cage and said, 'Hansel, stretch out your finger that I may feel whether you are getting fat.'

But Hansel used to stretch out a bone, and the old woman, having very bad sight, thought it was his finger, and wondered very much that he did not get fatter. When four weeks had passed, and Hansel still kept quite lean, she lost all her patience, and would not wait any longer.

'Gretel,' she called out in a passion, 'get some water quickly; be Hansel fat or lean, this morning I will kill and cook him.'

Oh, how the poor little sister grieved, as she was forced to fetch the water, and fast the tears ran down her cheeks! 'Dear good God, help us now!' she exclaimed. 'Had we only been eaten by the wild beasts in the wood, then we should have died together.'

But the old witch called out, 'Leave off that noise; it will not help you a bit.'

So early in the morning Gretel was forced to go out and fill the kettle, and make a fire. 'First, we will bake, however,' said the old woman; 'I have already heated the oven and kneaded the dough'; and so saying, she pushed poor Gretel up to the oven, out of which the flames were burning fiercely. 'Creep in,' said the witch, 'and see if it is hot enough, and then we will put in the bread'; but she intended when Gretel got in to shut up the oven and let her bake, so that she might eat her as well as Hansel.

Gretel perceived what her thoughts were, and said, 'I do not know how to do it; how shall I get in?'

'You stupid goose,' said she, 'the opening is big enough. See, I could even get in myself!' and she got up, and put her head into the oven.

Then Gretel gave her a push, so that she fell right in, and then shutting the iron door she bolted it! Oh! how horribly she howled; but Gretel ran away, and left the ungodly witch to burn to ashes.

Now she ran to Hansel, and, opening his door, called out, 'Hansel, we are saved; the old witch is dead!' So he sprang out, like a bird out of his cage when the door is opened; and they were so glad that they fell upon each other's neck, and kissed each other over and over again.

And now, as there was nothing to fear, they went into the witch's house, where in every corner were caskets full of pearls and precious stones. 'These are better than pebbles,' said Hansel, putting as many into his pocket as it would hold; while Gretel thought, 'I will take some too,' and filled her apron full.

'We must be off now,' said Hansel, 'and get out of this enchanted forest.'

But when they had walked for two hours they came to a large piece of water.

'We cannot get over,' said Hansel; 'I can see no bridge at all.'

'And there is no boat, either,' said Gretel; 'but there swims a white duck, and I will ask her to help us over.' And she sang:

> 'Little Duck, good little Duck,
> Gretel and Hansel, here we stand;
> There is neither stile nor bridge,
> Take us on your back to land.'

So the duck came to them, and Hansel sat himself on, and bade his sister sit behind him.

'No,' answered Gretel, 'that will be too much for the duck; she shall take us over one at a time.' This the good little bird did, and when both were happily arrived on the other side, and had gone a little way, they came to a well-known wood, which they knew the better every step they went, and at last they perceived their father's house. Then they began to run, and, bursting into the house, they fell into their father's arms. He had not had one happy hour since he had left the children in the forest; and his wife was dead. Gretel shook her apron, and the pearls and precious stones rolled out upon the floor, and Hansel threw down one handful after the other out of his pocket. Then all their sorrows were ended, and they lived together in great happiness.

The Griffin

There was once upon a time a king, but where he reigned and what he was called, I do not know. He had no son, but an only daughter who had always been ill, and no doctor had been able to cure her. Then it was foretold to the king that his daughter eating an apple could make her well again. So he ordered it to be proclaimed throughout the whole of his kingdom, that whoever brought his daughter an apple with which she could eat herself well, should have her as his wife, and be king. This became known to a peasant who had three sons, and he said to the eldest, 'Go out into the garden and take a basketful of those beautiful apples with the red cheeks and carry them to the court; perhaps eating one of them will make the king's daughter well again, and then you will marry her and be king.' The lad did so, and set out.

When he had gone a short way he met a little iron man who asked him what he had there in the basket, to which replied Uele, for so was he named:

'Frogs' legs.'

'Well, so shall it be, and remain,' the little man said to this, and went away. At length Uele arrived at the palace, and made it known that he had brought apples which would cure the king's daughter if she ate them. This delighted the king hugely, and Uele was brought before him; but, alas! when he opened the basket, instead of having apples in it he had frogs' legs which were still kicking about. On this the king grew angry, and had Uele driven out of the palace. When he got home he told his father how it had fared with him.

Then the father sent the next son, who was called Seame, but all went with him just as it had gone with Uele. He also met the little iron man, who asked what he had there in the basket.

'Hogs' bristles,' Seame said.

'Well, so shall it be, and remain,' the iron man said.

When Seame got to the king's palace and said he brought apples with which the king's daughter might eat herself well, they did not want to let him go in, and said that one fellow had already been there, and had treated them as if they were fools. Seame, however, maintained that he certainly had the apples, and that they ought to let him go in. At length they believed him, and led him to the king. But when he uncovered the basket, he had but hogs' bristles. This enraged the king most terribly, so he caused Seame to be whipped out of the house. When he got home he related all that had befallen him, then the youngest boy, whose name was Hans, but who was always called Stupid Hans, came and asked his father if he might go with some apples.

'Oh!' said the father, 'you wouldst be just the right fellow for such a thing! If the clever ones can't manage it, what can you do?' The boy did not believe him, however, and said, 'Indeed, father, I wish to go.'

'Just get away, you stupid fellow, you must wait till you are wiser,' said the father to that, and turned his back. Hans, however, pulled at the back of his smock and said, 'Indeed, father, I wish to go.'

'Well, then, so far as I am concerned you may go, but you will soon come home again!' replied the old man in a spiteful voice.

The boy, however, was tremendously delighted and jumped for joy.

'Well, act like a fool! You grow more stupid every day!' said the father again. Hans, however, did not care about that, and did not let it spoil his pleasure, but as it was then night, he thought he might as well wait until the morrow, for he could not get to court that day. All night long he could not sleep in his bed, and if he did doze for a moment, he dreamt of beautiful maidens, of palaces, of gold, and of silver, and all kinds of things of that sort.

Early in the morning, he went forth on his way, and directly afterwards the little shabby-looking man in his iron clothes came to him and asked what he was carrying in the basket. Hans gave him the answer that he was carrying apples with which the king's daughter was to eat herself well. 'Then,' said the little man, 'so shall they be, and remain.'

But at the court they would none of them let Hans go in, for they said two had already been there who had told them that they were bringing apples, and one of them had frogs' legs, and the other hogs' bristles. Hans, however, resolutely maintained that he most certainly had no frogs' legs, but some of the most beautiful apples in the whole kingdom. As he spoke so pleasantly, the door-keeper thought he could not be telling a lie, and asked him to go in, and he was right, for when Hans uncovered his basket in the king's presence, golden-yellow apples came tumbling out.

The king was delighted, and caused some of them to be taken to his daughter, and then waited in anxious expectation until news should be brought to him of the effect they had. Before much time had passed by, news was brought to him: but who do you think it was who came? It was his daughter herself! As soon as she had eaten of those apples, she was cured, and sprang out of her bed. The joy the king felt cannot be described! But now he did not want to give his daughter in marriage to Hans, and said he must first make him a boat which would go quicker on dry land than on water. Hans agreed to the conditions, and went home, and related how it had fared with him.

Then the father sent Uele into the forest to make a boat of that kind. He worked diligently, and whistled all the time. At mid-day, when the sun was at the highest, came the little iron man and asked what he was making. Uele gave him for answer, 'Wooden bowls for the kitchen.'

'So it shall be, and remain,' the iron man said.

By evening Uele thought he had now made the boat, but when he wanted to get into it, he had nothing but wooden bowls.

The next day Seame went into the forest, but everything went with him just as it had done with Uele.

On the third day Stupid Hans went. He worked away most industriously, so that the whole forest resounded with the heavy strokes, and all the while he sang and whistled right merrily. At mid-day, when it was the hottest, the little man came again, and asked what he was making.

'A boat which will go quicker on dry land than on the water,' replied Hans, 'and when I have finished it, I am to have the king's daughter for my wife.'

'Well,' said the little man, 'such an one shall it be, and remain.'

In the evening, when the sun had turned into gold, Hans finished his boat, and all that was wanted for it. He got into it and rowed to the palace. The boat went as swiftly as the wind.

The king saw it from afar, but would not give his daughter to Hans yet, and said he must first take a hundred hares out to pasture from early morning until late evening, and if one of them got away, he should not have his daughter. Hans was contented with this, and the next day went with his flock to the pasture, and took great care that none of them ran away.

Before many hours had passed a servant came from the palace, and told Hans that he must give her a hare instantly, for some visitors had come unexpectedly. Hans, however, was very well aware what that meant, and said he would not give her one; the king might set some hare soup before his guest next day. The maid, however, would not believe in his refusal, and at last she began to get angry with him. Then Hans said that if the king's daughter came herself, he would give her a hare. The maid told this in the palace, and the daughter did go herself.

In the meantime, however, the little man came again to Hans, and asked him what he was doing there. Hans said he had to watch over a hundred hares and see that none of them ran away, and then he might marry the king's daughter and be king.

'Good,' said the little man, 'here is a whistle for you, and if one of them runs away, just whistle with it, and then it will come back again.'

When the king's daughter came, Hans gave her a hare into her apron; but when she had gone about a hundred steps with it, he whistled, and the hare jumped out of the apron, and before she could turn round was back to the flock again. When the evening came the hareherd whistled once more, and looked to see if all were there, and then drove them to the palace. The king wondered how Hans had been able to take a hundred hares to graze without losing any of them; he would, however, not give him his daughter yet, and said he must now bring him a feather from the Griffin's tail.

Hans set out at once, and walked straight forwards. In the evening he came to a castle, and there he asked for a night's lodging, for at that time there were no inns. The lord of the castle promised him that with much pleasure, and asked where he was going.

'To the Griffin,' Hans answered.

'Oh! To the Griffin! They tell me he knows everything, and I have lost the key of an iron money-chest; so you might be so good as to ask him where it is.'

'Yes, indeed,' said Hans, 'I will do that.'

Early the next morning he went onwards, and on his way arrived at another castle in which he again stayed the night. When the people who lived there learnt that he was going to the Griffin, they said they had in the house a daughter who was ill, and that they had already tried every means to cure her, but none of them had done her any good, and he might be so kind as to ask the Griffin what would make their daughter healthy again.

Hans said he would willingly do that, and went onwards. Then he came to a lake, and instead of a ferry-boat, a tall, tall man was there who had to carry everybody across. The man asked Hans whither he was journeying.

'To the Griffin,' said Hans. 'Then when you get to him,' said the man, 'just ask him why I am forced to carry everybody over the lake.' 'Yes, indeed, most certainly I'll do that,' said Hans. Then the man took him up on his shoulders, and carried him across. At length Hans arrived at the Griffin's house, but the wife only was at home, and not the Griffin himself. Then the woman asked him what he wanted? Thereupon he told her everything; that he had to get a feather out of the Griffin's tail, and that there was a castle where they had lost the key of their money-chest, and he was to ask the Griffin where it was, that in another castle the daughter was ill, and he was to learn what would cure her, and then not far away there was a lake and a man beside it, who was forced to carry people across it, and he was very anxious to learn why the man was obliged to do it.

'But look here, my good friend,' the woman said, 'no Christian can speak to the Griffin; he devours them all; but if you like, you can lie down under his bed, and in the night, when he is quite fast asleep, you can reach out and pull a feather out of his tail, and as for those things which you are to learn, I will ask about them myself.' Hans was quite satisfied with this, and got under the bed.

In the evening, the Griffin came home, and as soon as he entered the room, said, 'Wife, I smell a Christian.'

'Yes,' said the woman, 'one was here today, but he went away again;' and on that the Griffin said no more.

In the middle of the night when the Griffin was snoring loudly, Hans reached out and plucked a feather from his tail. The Griffin woke up instantly, and said, 'Wife, I smell a Christian, and it seems to me that somebody was pulling at my tail.'

'You must have been dreaming,' his wife said. 'I told you before that a Christian was here today, but that he went away again. He told me all kinds of things: that in one castle they had lost the key of their money-chest, and could find it nowhere.'

'Oh! the fools!' said the Griffin; 'the key lies in the wood-house under a log of wood behind the door.'

'And then he said that in another castle the daughter was ill, and they knew no remedy that would cure her.'

'Oh! the fools!' said the Griffin; 'under the cellar-steps a toad has made its nest of her hair, and if she got her hair back she would be well.'

'And then he also said that there was a place where there was a lake and a man beside it who was forced to carry everybody across.'

'Oh, the fool!' said the Griffin; 'if he only put one man down in the middle, he would never have to carry another across.'

Early the next morning the Griffin got up and went out. Then Hans came forth from under the bed, and he had a beautiful feather, and had heard what the Griffin had said about the key, and the daughter, and the ferry-man. The Griffin's wife repeated it all once more to him that he might not forget it, and then he went home again.

First he came to the man by the lake, who asked him what the Griffin had said, but Hans replied that he must first carry him across, and then he would tell him. So the man carried him across, and when he was over Hans told him that all he had to do was to set one person down in the middle of the lake, and then he would never have to carry over any more. The man was hugely delighted, and told Hans that out of gratitude he would take him once more across, and back again. But Hans said no, he would save him the trouble, he was quite satisfied already, and pursued his way.

Then he came to the castle where the daughter was ill; he took her on his shoulders, for she could not walk, and carried her down the cellar-steps and pulled out the toad's nest from beneath the lowest step and gave it into her hand, and she sprang off his shoulder and up the steps before him, and was quite cured. Then the father and mother were rejoiced beyond measure, and they gave Hans gifts of gold and of silver, and anything else he wished for, they gave him.

And when he got to the other castle he went at once into the woodhouse, and found the key under the log of wood behind the door, and took it to the lord of the castle. He also was not a little pleased, and gave Hans as a reward much of the gold that was in the chest, and all kinds of things besides, such as cows, and sheep, and goats. When Hans arrived before the king, with all these things – with the money, and the gold, and the silver and the cows, sheep and goats, the king asked him how he had come by them. Hans told him that the Griffin gave everyone whatever he wanted. So the king thought he himself could make such things useful, and set out on his way to the Griffin; but when he got to the lake, it just so happened that he was the very first who arrived there after Hans, and the man put him down in the middle of it and went away, and the king was drowned. Hans, however, married the daughter, and became king.

The Hare and the Hedgehog

This story, my dear young folks, seems to be false, but it really is true, for my grandfather, from whom I have it, used always, when relating it, to say, it must be true, my son, or else no one could tell it to you. The story is as follows.

One Sunday morning about harvest time, just as the buckwheat was in bloom, the sun was shining brightly in heaven, the east wind was blowing warmly over the stubble-fields, the larks were singing in the air, the bees buzzing among the buckwheat, the people in their Sunday clothes were all going to church, and all creatures were happy, and the hedgehog was happy too. The hedgehog, however, was standing by his door with his arms akimbo, enjoying the morning breezes, and slowly trilling a little song to himself, which was neither better nor worse than the songs which hedgehogs are in the habit of singing on a blessed Sunday morning.

Whilst he was thus singing half aloud to himself, it suddenly occurred to him that, while his wife was washing and drying the children, he might very well take a walk into the field, and see how his turnips were getting on. The turnips, in fact, were close beside his house, and he and his family were accustomed to eat them, for which reason he looked upon them as his own.

No sooner said than done. The hedgehog shut the house door behind him, and took the path to the field. He had not gone very far from home, and was just turning round the sloe-bush which stands there outside the field, to go up into the turnip-field, when he observed the hare who had gone out on business of the same kind, namely, to visit his cabbages. When the hedgehog caught sight of the hare, he bade him a friendly good morning. But the hare, who was in his own way a distinguished gentleman, and frightfully haughty, did not return the hedgehog's greeting, but said to him, assuming at the same time a very contemptuous manner:

'How do you happen to be running about here in the field so early in the morning?'

'I am taking a walk,' said the hedgehog.

'A walk,' said the hare, with a smile. 'It seems to me that you might use your legs for a better purpose.'

This answer made the hedgehog furiously angry, for he can bear anything but a reference to his legs, just because they are short and crooked by nature. So now the hedgehog said to the hare:

'You seem to imagine that you can do more with your legs than I with mine.'

'That is just what I do think,' said the hare.

'That can be put to the test,' said the hedgehog. 'I wager that if we run a race, I will outstrip you.'

'That is ridiculous. You with your short legs, said the hare, but for my part I am willing, if you have such a monstrous fancy for it. What shall we wager?'

'A golden louis-d'or and a bottle of brandy,' said the hedgehog.

'Done,' said the hare. 'Shake hands on it, and then we may as well begin at once.'

'Nay,' said the hedgehog, 'There is no such great hurry. I am still fasting, I will go home first, and have a little breakfast. In half-an-hour I will be back again at this place.' The hedgehog then departed, for the hare was quite satisfied with this.

On his way the hedgehog thought to himself, 'the hare relies on his long legs, but I will contrive to get the better of him. He may be a great man, but he is a very silly fellow, and he shall pay for what he has said.' So when the hedgehog reached home, he said to his wife: 'Dress yourself quickly; you must go out to the field with me.'

'What is going on, then?' asked his wife.

'I have made a wager with the hare, for a gold louis-d'or and a bottle of brandy. I am to run a race with him, and you must be present.'

'Good heavens, husband,' the wife now cried, 'Are you not right in your mind, have you completely lost your wits? What can make you want to run a race with the hare?'

'Hold your tongue, woman,' said the hedgehog. 'That is my affair. Don't begin to discuss things which are matters for men. Be off, dress yourself, and come with me.'

What could the hedgehog's wife do? She was forced to obey him, whether she liked it or not. So when they had set out on their way together, the hedgehog said to his wife:

'Now, pay attention to what I am going to say. Look you, I will make the long field our race-course. The hare shall run in one furrow, and when the hare arrives at the end of the furrow on the other side of you, you must cry out to him, "I am here already".' Then they reached the field, and the hedgehog showed his wife her place, and then walked up the field. When he reached the top, the hare was already there.

'Shall we start?' asked the hare.

'Certainly,' said the hedgehog.

Then each placed himself in his own furrow. The hare counted, once, twice, thrice, and away, and went off like a whirlwind down the field. The hedgehog, however, only ran about three paces, and then he crouched down in the furrow, and stayed quietly where he was. When the hare therefore arrived at full speed at the lower end of the field, the hedgehog's wife met him with the cry, 'I am here already.'

The hare was shocked but thought no other than that it was the hedgehog himself who was calling to him, for the hedgehog's wife looked just like her husband. The hare, however, thought to himself, that has not been done fairly, and cried:

'It must be run again, let us have it again!' And once more he went off like the wind in a storm, so that he seemed to fly. But the hedgehog's wife stayed quietly in her place. So when the hare reached the top of the field, the hedgehog himself cried out to him, 'I am here already.'

The hare, quite beside himself with anger, cried, 'It must be run again, we must have it again!'

'All right,' answered the hedgehog, 'For my part I am happy to race just as often as you choose.'

So the hare ran seventy-three times more, and the hedgehog always held out against him, and every time the hare reached either the top or the bottom, either the hedgehog or his wife said, 'I am here already.'

At the seventy-fourth time, however, the hare could no longer reach the end. In the middle of the field he fell to the ground, blood streamed out of his mouth, and he lay dead on the spot. But the hedgehog took the louis-d'or which he had won and the bottle of brandy, called his wife out of the furrow, and both went home together in great delight, and if they are not dead, they are living there still.

The moral of this story is, firstly, that no one, however great he may be, should permit himself to jest at any one beneath him, even if he be only a hedgehog. And, secondly, it teaches, that when a man marries, he should take a wife in his own position, who looks just as he himself looks. So whosoever is a hedgehog let him see to it that his wife is a hedgehog also, and so forth.

Bearskin

There was once a young fellow who enlisted as a soldier, conducted himself bravely, and was always the foremost when it rained bullets. So long as the war lasted, all went well, but when peace was made, he received his dismissal, and the captain said he might go where he liked. His parents were dead, and he had no longer a home, so he went to his brothers and begged them to take him in and keep him until war broke out again. The brothers, however, were hard-hearted.

'What can we do with you?' they said. 'You are of no use to us; go and make a living for yourself.' The soldier had nothing left but his gun; he took that on his shoulder, and went forth into the world. He came to a wide heath, on which nothing was to be seen but a circle of trees; under these he sat sorrowfully down, and began to think over his fate. 'I have no money,' thought he, 'I have learnt no trade but that of fighting, and now that they have made peace they don't want me any longer; so I see that I shall have to starve.'

All at once he heard a rustling, and when he looked round, a strange man stood before him, who wore a green coat and looked right stately, but had a hideous cloven foot.

'I know already what you are in need of,' said the man; 'gold and possessions shall you have, as much as you canst make away with do what you wilt, but first I must know if you are fearless, that I may not bestow my money in vain.'

'A soldier and fear – how can those two things go together?' he answered; 'you can put me to the proof.'

'Very well, then,' answered the man, 'look behind you.' The soldier turned round, and saw a large bear, which came growling towards him.

'Oho!' cried the soldier, 'I will tickle your nose for you, so that you shall soon lose your fancy for growling,' and he aimed at the bear and shot it through the muzzle; it fell down and never stirred again.

'I see quite well,' said the stranger, 'that you are not wanting in courage, but there is still another condition which you will have to fulfil.'

'If it does not endanger my salvation,' replied the soldier, who knew very well who was standing by him. 'If it does, I'll have nothing to do with it.'

'You will look to that for yourself,' answered Greencoat; 'you shall for the next seven years neither wash yourself, nor comb your beard, nor your hair, nor cut your nails, nor say one paternoster. I will give you a coat and a cloak, which during this time you must wear. If you die during these seven years, you are mine; if you remain alive, you are free, and rich to boot, for all the rest of your life.'

The soldier thought of the great extremity in which he now found himself, and as he so often had gone to meet death, he resolved to risk it now also, and agreed to the terms. The Devil (for it was he) took off his green coat, gave it to the soldier, and said, 'If you have this coat on your back and put your hand into the pocket, you wilt always find it full of money.' Then he pulled the skin off the bear and said:

'This shall be your cloak, and your bed also, for thereon shalt you sleep, and in no other bed shall you lie, and because of this apparel shall you be called Bearskin.' After this the Devil vanished.

The soldier put the coat on, felt at once in the pocket, and found that the thing was really true. Then he put on the bearskin and went forth into the world, and enjoyed himself, refraining from nothing that did him good and his money harm. During the first year his appearance was passable, but during the second he began to look like a monster. His hair covered nearly the whole of his face, his beard was like a piece of coarse felt, his fingers had claws, and his face was so covered with dirt that if cress had been sown on it, it would have come up. Whoever saw him ran away, but as he everywhere gave the poor money to pray that he might not die during the seven years, and as he paid well for everything he still always found shelter.

In the fourth year, he entered an inn where the landlord would not receive him, and would not even let him have a place in the stable, because he was afraid the horses would be scared. But as Bearskin thrust his hand into his pocket and pulled out a handful of ducats, the host let himself be persuaded and gave him a room in an outhouse. Bearskin was, however, obliged to promise not to let himself be seen, lest the inn should get a bad name.

As Bearskin was sitting alone in the evening and wishing from the bottom of his heart that the seven years were over, he heard a loud lamenting in a neighbouring room. He had a compassionate heart, so he opened the door, and saw an old man weeping bitterly, and wringing his hands. Bearskin went nearer, but the man sprang to his feet and tried to escape from him. At last when the man perceived that Bearskin's voice was human he let himself be prevailed on, and by kind words Bearskin succeeded so far that the old man revealed the cause of his grief. His property had dwindled away by degrees, he and his daughters would have to starve, and he was so poor that he could not pay the innkeeper and was to be put in prison.

'If that is your only trouble,' said Bearskin, 'I have plenty of money.' He caused the innkeeper to be brought thither, paid him and put a purse full of gold into the poor old man's pocket besides.

When the old man saw himself set free from all his troubles he did not know how to be grateful enough.

'Come with me,' said he to Bearskin; 'my daughters are all miracles of beauty, choose one of them for yourself as a wife. When she hears what you hast done for me, she will not refuse you. You do in truth look a little strange, but she will soon put you to rights again.'

This pleased Bearskin well, and he went. When the eldest saw him she was so terribly alarmed at his face that she screamed and ran away. The second stood still and looked at him from head to foot, but:

'How can I accept a husband who no longer has a human form?' she said. 'The shaven bear that once was here and passed itself off for a man pleased me far better, for at any rate it wore a hussar's dress and white gloves. If it were nothing but ugliness, I might get used to that.'

The youngest, however, said: 'Dear father, that must be a good man to have helped you out of your trouble, so if you have promised him a bride for doing it, your promise must be kept.'

It was a pity that Bearskin's face was covered with dirt and with hair, for if not they might have seen how delighted he was when he heard these words. He took a ring from his finger, broke it in two, and gave her one half, the other he kept for himself. He wrote his name on her half, and hers on his, and begged her to keep her piece carefully, and then he took his leave.

'I must still wander about for three years,' he said, 'and if I do not return then, you are free, for I shall be dead. But pray to God to preserve my life.'

The poor betrothed bride dressed herself entirely in black, and when she thought of her future bridegroom, tears came into her eyes. Nothing but contempt and mockery fell to her lot from her sisters.

'Take care,' said the eldest, 'if you give him your hand, he will strike his claws into it.'

'Beware!' said the second. 'Bears like sweet things, and if he takes a fancy to you, he will eat you up.'

'You must always do as he likes,' began the elder again, 'or else he will growl.'

And the second continued, 'But the wedding will be a merry one, for bears dance well.'

The bride was silent and did not let them vex her. Bearskin, however, travelled about the world from one place to another, did good where he was able, and gave generously to the poor that they might pray for him.

At length, as the last day of the seven years dawned, he went once more out on to the heath, and seated himself beneath the circle of trees. It was not long before the wind whistled, and the Devil stood before him and looked angrily at him; then he threw Bearskin his old coat and asked for his own green one back.

'We have not got so far as that yet,' answered Bearskin, 'you must first make me clean.'

Whether the Devil liked it or not, he was forced to fetch water, and wash Bearskin, comb his hair, and cut his nails. After this, he looked like a brave soldier, and was much handsomer than he had ever been before.

When the Devil had gone away, Bearskin was quite light-hearted. He went into the town, put on a magnificent velvet coat, seated himself in a carriage drawn by four white horses, and drove to his bride's house. No one recognized him, the father took him for a distinguished general, and led him into the room where his daughters were sitting. He was forced to place himself between the two eldest, they helped him to wine, gave him the best pieces of meat, and thought that in all the world they had never seen a handsomer man. The bride, however, sat opposite to him in her black dress, and never raised her eyes, nor spoke a word.

When at length he asked the father if he would give him one of his daughters to wife, the two eldest jumped up, ran into their bed-rooms to put on splendid dresses, for each of them fancied she was the chosen one. The stranger, as soon as he was alone with his bride, brought out his half of the ring, and threw it in a glass of wine which he reached across the table to her. She took the wine, but when she had drunk it, and found the half ring lying at the bottom, her heart began to beat. She got the other half, which she wore on a ribbon round her neck, joined them, and saw that the two pieces fitted exactly together.

'I am your betrothed bridegroom,' he said then, 'whom you saw as Bearskin, but through God's grace I have again received my human form, and have once more become clean.'

He went up to her, embraced her, and gave her a kiss. In the meantime the two sisters came back in full dress, and when they saw that the handsome man had fallen to the share of the youngest, and heard that he was Bearskin, they ran out full of anger and rage. One of them drowned herself in the well, the other hanged herself on a tree. In the evening, someone knocked at the door, and when the bridegroom opened it, it was the Devil in his green coat, who said:

'Look you, I have now got two souls in the place of your one!'

The Master-Thief

One day an old man and his wife were sitting in front of a miserable house resting a while from their work. Suddenly a splendid carriage with four black horses came driving up, and a richly-dressed man descended from it. The peasant stood up, went to the great man, and asked what he wanted, and in what way he could be useful to him? The stranger stretched out his hand to the old man, and said, 'I want nothing but to enjoy for once a country dish; cook me some potatoes, in the way you always have them, and then I will sit down at your table and eat them with pleasure.'

The peasant smiled and said, 'You are a count or a prince, or perhaps even a duke; noble gentlemen often have such fancies, but you shall have your wish.'

The wife went into the kitchen, and began to wash and rub the potatoes, and to make them into balls, as they are eaten by the country-folks. While she was busy with this work, the peasant said to the stranger:

'Come into my garden with me for a while, I have still something to do there.' He had dug some holes in the garden, and now wanted to plant some trees in them.

'Have you no children,' asked the stranger, 'who could help you with your work?' 'No,' answered the peasant, 'I had a son, it is true,

221

but it is long since he went out into the world. He was a ne'er-do-well; sharp, and knowing, but he would learn nothing and was full of bad tricks, at last he ran away from me, and since then I have heard nothing of him.'

The old man took a young tree, put it in a hole, drove in a post beside it, and when he had shovelled in some earth and had trampled it firmly down, he tied the stem of the tree above, below, and in the middle, fast to the post by a rope of straw.

'But tell me,' said the stranger, 'why you don't tie that crooked knotted tree, which is lying in the corner there, bent down almost to the ground, to a post also that it may grow straight, as well as these?'

The old man smiled and said, 'Sir, you speak according to your knowledge, it is easy to see that you are not familiar with gardening. That tree there is old, and misshapen, no one can make it straight now. Trees must be trained while they are young.'

'That is how it was with your son,' said the stranger, 'if you had trained him while he was still young, he would not have run away; now he too must have grown hard and misshapen.'

'Truly it is a long time since he went away,' replied the old man, 'he must have changed.'

'Would you know him again if he were to come to you?' asked the stranger.

'Hardly by his face,' replied the peasant, 'but he has a mark about him, a birth-mark on his shoulder, that looks like a bean.' When he had said that the stranger pulled off his coat, bared his shoulder, and showed the peasant the bean.

'Good God!' cried the old man, 'You are really my son!' and love for his child stirred in his heart. 'But,' he added, 'how can you be my son, you have become a great lord and live in wealth and luxury? How have you contrived to do that?'

'Ah, father,' answered the son, 'the young tree was bound to no post and has grown crooked, now it is too old, it will never be straight again. How have I got all that? I have become a thief, but do not be alarmed, I am a master-thief. For me there are neither locks nor bolts, whatever I desire is mine. Do not imagine that I steal like a common thief, I only take some of the superfluity of the rich. Poor people are safe, I would rather give to them than take anything from them. It is the same with anything which I can have without trouble, cunning and dexterity; I never touch it.'

'Alas, my son,' said the father, 'it still does not please me, a thief is still a thief, I tell you it will end badly.' He took him to his mother, and when she heard that was her son, she wept for joy, but when he told her that he had become a master-thief, two streams flowed down over her face.

'Even if he has become a thief,' she said at length, 'he is still my son, and my eyes have beheld him once more.'

They sat down to table, and once again he ate with his parents the wretched food which he had not eaten for so long. The father said, 'If our lord, the count up there in the castle, learns who you are, and what trade you follow, he will not take you in his arms and cradle you in them as he did when he held you at the font, but will cause you to swing from a halter.'

'Be easy, father, he will do me no harm, for I understand my trade. I will go to him myself this very day.' When evening drew near, the mas-ter-thief seated himself in his carriage, and drove to the castle. The count received him civilly, for he took him for a distinguished man. When, however, the stranger made himself known, the count turned pale and was quite silent for some time. At length he said, 'You are my godson, and on that account mercy shall take the place of justice, and I will deal leniently with you. Since you pride yourself on being a master-thief, I will put your art to the proof, but if you do not stand the test, you must marry the rope-maker's daughter, and the croaking of the raven must be your music on the occasion.'

'Lord count,' answered the master-thief, 'Think of three things, as difficult as you like, and if I do not perform your tasks, do with me what you will.' The count reflected for some minutes, and then said, 'Well, then, in the first place, you shall steal the horse I keep for my own riding, out of the stable; in the next, you shall steal the sheet from beneath the bodies of my wife and myself when we are asleep, without our observing it, and the wedding-ring of my wife as well; thirdly and lastly, you shalt steal away out of the church, the parson and clerk. Mark what I am saying, for your life depends on it.'

The master-thief went to the nearest town; there he bought the clothes of an old peasant woman and put them on. Then he stained his face brown, and painted wrinkles on it as well, so that no one could have recognized him. Then he filled a small cask with old Hungary wine in which was mixed a powerful sleeping-drink. He put the cask in a basket, which he took on his back, and walked with slow and tottering steps to the count's castle. It was already dark when he arrived. He sat down on a stone in the courtyard and began to cough, like an asthmatic old woman, and to rub his hands as if he were cold. In front of the door of the stable some soldiers were lying round a fire; one of them observed the woman, and called out to her, 'Come nearer, old mother, and warm yourself beside us. After all, you have no bed for the night, and must take one where you can find it.'

The old woman tottered up to them, begged them to lift the basket from her back, and sat down beside them at the fire.

'What have you got in your little cask, old lady?' asked one.

'A good mouthful of wine,' she answered. 'I live by trade, for money and fair words I am quite ready to let you have a glass.'

'Let us have it here, then,' said the soldier, and when he had tasted one glass he said, 'When wine is good, I like another glass,' and had another poured out for himself, and the rest followed his example. 'Hallo, comrades,' cried one of them to those who were in the stable, 'here is an old goody who has wine that is as old as herself; take a draught, it will warm your stomachs far better than our fire.'

The old woman carried her cask into the stable. One of the soldiers had seated himself on the saddled riding-horse, another held its bridle in his hand, a third had laid hold of its tail. She poured out as much as they wanted until the spring ran dry. It was not long before the bridle fell from the hand of the one, and he fell down and began to snore, the other left hold of the tail, lay down and snored still louder. The one who was sitting in the saddle, did remain sitting, but bent his head almost down to the horse's neck, and slept and blew with his mouth like the bellows of a forge. The soldiers outside had already been asleep for a long time, and were lying on the ground motionless, as if dead. When the master-thief saw that he had succeeded, he gave the first a rope in his hand instead of the bridle, and the other who had been holding the tail, a wisp of straw, but what was he to do with the one who was sitting on the horse's back? He did not want to throw him down, for he might have awakened and have uttered a cry. He had a good idea, he unbuckled the girths of the saddle, tied a couple of ropes which were hanging to a ring on the wall fast to the saddle, and drew the sleeping rider up into the air on it, then he twisted the rope round the posts, and made it fast. He soon unloosed the horse from the chain, but if he had ridden over the stony pavement of the yard they would have heard the noise in the castle. So he wrapped the horse's hoofs in old rags, led him carefully out, leapt upon him, and galloped off.

When day broke, the master-thief galloped to the castle on the stolen horse. The count had just got up, and was looking out of the window.

'Good morning, Sir Count,' he cried to him, 'here is the horse, which I have got safely out of the stable! Just look, how beautifully your soldiers are lying there sleeping; and if you will but go into the stable, you will see how comfortable your watchers have made it for themselves.' The count could not help laughing.

'For once you have succeeded,' he said, 'but things won't go so well the second time, and I warn you that if you come before me as a thief, I will handle you as I would a thief.'

When the countess went to bed that night, she closed her hand with the wedding-ring tightly together, and the count said, 'All the doors are locked and bolted, I will keep awake and wait for the thief, but if he gets in by the window, I will shoot him.'

The master-thief, however, went in the dark to the gallows, cut a poor sinner who was hanging there down from the halter, and carried him on his back to the castle. Then he set a ladder up to the bedroom, put the dead body on his shoulders, and began to climb up. When he had got so high that the head of the dead man showed at the window, the count, who was watching in his bed, fired a pistol at him, and immediately the master let the poor sinner fall down, and quickly slid back down the ladder and hid himself in one corner. The night was sufficiently lighted by the moon, for the master to see distinctly how the count got out of the window on to the ladder, came down, carried the dead body into the garden, and began to dig a hole in which to lay it.

The thief stole nimbly out of his corner and climbed up the ladder straight into the countess's bedroom. 'Dear wife,' he began in the count's voice, 'the thief is dead, but, after all, he is my godson, and has been more of a scape-grace than a villain. I will not put him to open shame; besides, I am sorry for the parents. I will bury him myself before daybreak, in the garden that the thing may not be known, so give me the sheet, I will wrap up the body in it, and bury him as a dog buries things by scratching.'

The countess gave him the sheet. 'I tell you what,' continued the thief, 'I have a fit of magnanimity on me, give me the ring too – the unhappy man risked his life for it, so he may take it with him into his grave.' She would not gainsay the count, and although she did it unwillingly she drew the ring from her finger, and gave it to him. The thief made off with both these things, and reached home safely before the count in the garden had finished his work of burying.

What a long face the count did pull when the master came next morning and brought him the sheet and the ring.

'Are you a wizard?' said he, 'Who has fetched you out of the grave in which I myself laid you, and brought you to life again?'

'You did not bury me,' said the thief, 'but the poor sinner on the gallows,' and he told him exactly how everything had happened, and the count was forced to own to him that he was a clever, crafty thief.

'But you have not reached the end yet,' he added, 'you have still to perform the third task, and if you do not succeed in that, all is of no use.' The master smiled and returned no answer.

When night had fallen he went with a long sack on his back, a bundle under his arms, and a lantern in his hand to the village-church. In the sack he had some crabs, and in the bundle short wax-candles. He sat down in the churchyard, took out a crab, and stuck a wax-candle on his back. Then he lighted the little light, put the crab on the ground, and let it creep about. He took a second out of the sack, and treated it in the same way, and so on until the last was out of the sack. Then he put on a long black garment that looked like a monk's cowl and stuck a grey beard on his chin. When at last he was quite unrecognizable, he took the sack in which the crabs had been, went into the church, and ascended the pulpit. The clock in the tower was just striking twelve; when the last stroke had sounded, he cried with a loud and piercing voice:

'Hearken, sinful men, the end of all things has come! The last day is at hand! Hearken! Hearken! Whosoever wishes to go to heaven with me must creep into the sack. I am Peter, who opens and shuts the gate of heaven. Behold how the dead outside there in the churchyard, are wandering about collecting their bones. Come, come, and creep into the sack; the world is about to be destroyed!'

The cry echoed through the whole village. The parson and clerk, who lived nearest to the church, heard it first, and when they saw the lights which were moving about the churchyard, they observed that something unusual was going on, and went into the church. They listened to the sermon for a while, and then the clerk nudged the parson and said:

'It would not be amiss if we were to use the opportunity together, and before the dawning of the last day, find an easy way of getting to heaven.'

'To tell the truth,' answered the parson, 'that is what I myself have been thinking, so if you are inclined, we will set out on our way.'

'Yes,' answered the clerk, 'but you, the pastor, have the precedence, I will follow.' So the parson went first and ascended the pulpit where the master opened his sack. The parson crept in first, and then the clerk. The master immediately tied up the sack tightly, seized it by the middle, and dragged it down the pulpit-steps, and whenever the heads of the two fools bumped against the steps, he cried, 'We are going over the mountains.' Then he drew them through the village in the same way, and when they were passing through puddles, he cried, 'Now we are going through wet clouds.' And when at last he was dragging them up the steps of the castle, he cried, 'Now we are on the steps of heaven, and will soon be in the outer court.' When he had got to the top, he pushed the sack into the pigeon-house, and when the pigeons fluttered about, he said, 'Hark how glad the angels are, and how they are flapping their wings!' Then he bolted the door upon them, and went away.

Next morning he went to the count, and told him that he had performed the third task also, and had carried the parson and clerk out of the church.

'Where have you left them?' asked the lord.

'They are lying upstairs in a sack in the pigeon-house and imagine that they are in heaven.'

The count went up himself and convinced himself that the master had told the truth. When he had delivered the parson and clerk from their captivity, he said:

'You are an arch-thief and have won your wager. For once you escape with a whole skin, but see that you leave my land, for if ever you set foot on it again, you may count on your elevation to the gallows.'

The arch-thief took leave of his parents, once more went forth into the wide world, and no one has ever heard of him since.

The Riddle

There was once a king's son who was seized with a desire to travel about the world, and took no one with him but a faithful servant. One day he came to a great forest, and when darkness overtook him he could find no shelter, and knew not where to pass the night. Then he saw a girl who was going towards a small house, and when he came nearer, he saw that the maiden was young and beautiful. He spoke to her, and said:

'Dear child, can I and my servant find shelter for the night in the little house?'

'Oh, yes,' said the girl in a sad voice, 'that you certainly can, but I do not advise you to venture it. Do not go in.'

'Why not?' asked the king's son. The maiden sighed and said, 'My stepmother practises wicked arts; she is ill-disposed toward strangers.'

Then he saw very well that he had come to the house of a witch, but as it was dark, and he could not go farther, and also was not afraid, he entered. The old woman was sitting in an armchair by the fire, and looked at the stranger with her red eyes.

'Good evening,' growled she, and pretended to be quite friendly. 'Take a seat and rest yourselves.'

She blew up the fire on which she was cooking something in a small pot. The daughter warned the two to be prudent, to eat nothing, and drink nothing, for the old woman brewed evil drinks. They slept quietly until early morning. When they were making ready for their departure, and the king's son was already seated on his horse, the old woman said, 'Stop a moment, I will first hand you a parting draught.'

While she fetched it, the king's son rode away, and the servant who had to buckle his saddle tight, was the only one present when the wicked witch came with the drink.

'Take that to your master,' said she. But at that instant the glass broke and the poison spirted on the horse, and it was so strong that the animal immediately fell down dead. The servant ran after his master and told him what had happened, but would not leave his saddle behind him, and ran back to fetch it. When, however, he came to the dead horse a raven was already sitting on it devouring it.

'Who knows whether we shall find anything better to-day?' said the servant; so he killed the raven, and took it with him. And now they journeyed onwards into the forest the whole day, but could not get out of it. By nightfall they found an inn and entered it. The servant gave the raven to the innkeeper to make ready for supper. They had, however, stumbled on a den of murderers, and during the darkness twelve of these came, intending to kill the strangers and rob them. Before they set about this work, they sat down to supper, and the innkeeper and the witch sat down with them, and together they ate a dish of soup in which was cut up the flesh of the raven. Hardly, however, had they swallowed a couple of mouthfuls, before they all fell down dead, for the raven had communicated to them the poison from the horse-flesh. There was no no one else left in the house but the innkeeper's daughter, who was honest, and had taken no part in their godless deeds. She opened all doors to the stranger and showed him the heaped-up treasures. But the king's son said she might keep everything, he would have none of it, and rode onwards with his servant.

After they had travelled about for a long time, they came to a town in which was a beautiful but proud princess, who had caused it to be proclaimed that whosoever should set her a riddle which she could not guess, that man should be her husband; but if she guessed it, his head must be cut off. She had three days to guess it in, but was so clever that she always found the answer to the riddle given her, before the appointed time. Nine suitors had already perished in this manner, when the king's son arrived, and blinded by her great beauty, was willing to stake his life for it.

Then he went to her and laid his riddle before her.

'What is this?' said he, 'One slew none, and yet slew twelve.' She did not know what that was, she thought and thought, but she could not find out, she opened her riddle-books, but it was not in them – in short, her wisdom was at an end. As she did not know how to help herself, she ordered her maid to creep into the lord's sleeping-chamber, and listen to his dreams, and thought that he would perhaps speak in his sleep and discover the riddle. But the clever servant had placed himself in the bed instead of his master, and when the maid came there, he tore off from her the mantle in which she had wrapped herself, and chased her out with rods. The second night the king's daughter sent her maid-in-waiting, who was to see if she could succeed better in listening, but the servant took her mantle also away from her, and hunted her out with rods. Now the master believed himself safe for the third night, and lay down in his own bed. Then came the princess herself, and she had put on a misty-grey mantle, and she seated herself near him. And when she thought that he was asleep and dreaming, she spoke to him, and hoped that he would answer in his sleep, as many do, but he was awake, and understood and heard everything quite well.

'One slew none, what is that?' she asked.

'A raven, which ate of a dead and poisoned horse, and died of it,' he replied.

She inquired further, 'And yet slew twelve, what is that?'

'That means twelve murderers, who ate the raven and died of it,' he answered.

When she knew the answer to the riddle she wanted to steal away, but he held her mantle so fast that she was forced to leave it behind her. Next morning, the king's daughter announced that she had guessed the riddle and sent for the twelve judges and expounded it before them. But the youth begged for a hearing.

'She stole into my room in the night and questioned me, otherwise she could not have discovered it,' he said.

'Bring us a proof of this,' said the judges.

Then were the three mantles brought thither by the servant, and when the judges saw the misty-grey one which the king's daughter usually wore, they said:

'Let the mantle be embroidered with gold and silver, and then it will be your wedding-mantle.'

The Three Little Men
in the Wood

There was once a man whose wife died, and a woman whose husband died, and the man had a daughter, and the woman also had a daughter. The girls were acquainted with each other, and went out walking together, and afterwards came to the woman in her house. Then said she to the man's daughter:

'Listen, tell your father that I would like to marry him, and then you shall wash yourself in milk every morning, and drink wine, but my own daughter shall wash herself in water and drink water.'

The girl went home and told her father what the woman had said.

'What shall I do? Marriage is a joy and also a torment,' said the man. At length as he could come to no decision, he pulled off his boot, and said, 'Take this boot, it has a hole in the sole of it. Go with it up to the loft, hang it on the big nail, and then pour water into it. If it hold the water, then I will again take a wife, but if it run through, I will not.' The girl did as she was ordered, but the water drew the hole together, and the boot became full to the top. She informed her father how it had turned out. Then he himself went up, and when he saw that she was right, he went to the widow and wooed her, and the wedding was celebrated.

The next morning, when the two girls got up, there stood before the man's daughter milk for her to wash in and wine for her to drink, but before the woman's daughter stood water to wash herself with and water for drinking. On the second morning, stood water for washing and water for drinking before the man's daughter as well as before the woman's daughter. And on the third morning stood water for washing and water for drinking before the man's daughter, and milk for washing and wine for drinking before the woman's daughter, and so it continued. The woman became bitterly unkind to her stepdaughter, and day by day did her best to treat her still worse. She was also envious because her stepdaughter was beautiful and lovable, and her own daughter ugly and repulsive.

Once, in winter, when everything was frozen as hard as a stone, and hill and vale lay covered with snow, the woman made a dress of paper, called her stepdaughter, and said, 'Here, put on this dress and go out into the wood, and fetch me a little basketful of strawberries – have a fancy for some.'

'Good heavens!' said the girl, 'no strawberries grow in winter! The ground is frozen, and besides the snow has covered everything. And why am I to go in this paper dress? It is so cold outside that one's very breath freezes! The wind will blow through the dress, and the thorns will tear it off my body.'

'Will you contradict me again?' said the stepmother, 'See that you go, and do not show

your face again until you have the basketful of strawberries!' Then she gave her a little piece of hard bread, and said, 'This will last you the day,' and thought, 'You wilt die of cold and hunger outside, and will never be seen again by me.'

Then the maiden was obedient, and put on the paper dress, and went out with the basket. Far and wide there was nothing but snow, and not a green blade to be seen. When she got into the wood she saw a small house out of which peeped three dwarfs. She wished them good day, and knocked modestly at the door.

'Come in,' they cried, and she entered the room and seated herself on the bench by the stove, where she began to warm herself and eat her breakfast. The dwarfs watched her.

'Give us, too, some of it,' they said.

'Willingly,' she said, and divided her bit of bread in two and gave them the half. They asked, 'What are you doing here in the forest in the winter time, in your thin dress?'

'Ah,' she answered, 'I am to look for a basketful of strawberries, and am not to go home until I can take them with me.' When she had eaten her bread, they gave her a broom and said, 'Sweep away the snow at the back door with it.'

When she was outside, the three little men said to each other:

'What shall we give her as she is so good, and has shared her bread with us?'

'My gift is that she shall every day grow more beautiful,' said the first.

'My gift is that gold pieces shall fall out of her mouth every time she speaks,' said the second.

'My gift is that a king shall come and take her to wife,' said the third.

The girl did as the little men had bidden her, swept away the snow behind the little house with the broom, and what did she find but real ripe strawberries, which came up quite dark-red out of the snow! In her joy she hastily gathered her basket full, thanked the little men, shook hands with each of them, and ran home to take her stepmother what she had longed for so much. When she went in and said good-evening, a piece of gold at once fell from her mouth. Thereupon she related what had happened to her in the wood, but with every word she spoke, gold pieces fell from her mouth, until very soon the whole room was covered with them.

'Now look at her arrogance,' cried the stepsister, 'to throw about gold in that way!' but she was secretly envious of it and wanted to go into the forest also to seek strawberries.

'No, my dear little daughter, it is too cold, you might die of cold,' said the mother. As her daughter let her have no peace, the mother at last yielded, made her a magnificent dress of fur, which she was obliged to put on, and gave her bread-and-butter and cake with her.

The girl went into the forest and straight up to the little house. The three little men peeped out again, but she did not greet them, and without looking round at them and without speaking to them, she went awkwardly into the room, seated herself by the stove, and began to eat her bread-and-butter and cake.

'Give us some of it,' cried the little men; but she replied, 'There is not enough for myself, so how can I give it away to other people?'

When she had done eating, they said, 'There is a broom for you, sweep all clean for us outside by the back door.'

'Humph! Sweep for yourselves,' she answered, 'I am not your servant.' When she saw that they were not going to give her anything, she went out by the door. Then the little men said to each other, 'What shall we give her as she is so naughty, and has a wicked envious heart, that will never let her do a good turn to any one?'

'I grant that she may grow uglier every day,' said the first.

'I grant that at every word she says, a toad shall spring out of her mouth,' said the second.

'I grant that she may die a miserable death,' said the third.

The maiden looked for strawberries outside, but as she found none, she went angrily home. And when she opened her mouth, and was about to tell her mother what had happened to her in the wood, with every word she said, a toad sprang out of her mouth, so that everyone was seized with horror of her.

Then the step-mother was still more enraged, and thought of nothing but how to do every possible injury to the man's daughter, whose beauty grew daily greater. At length she took a cauldron, set it on the fire, and boiled yarn in it. When it was boiled, she flung it on the poor girl's shoulder, and gave her an axe in order that she might go on the frozen river, cut a hole in the ice, and rinse the yarn. She was obedient, went thither and cut a hole in the ice; and while she was in the middle of her cutting, a splendid carriage came driving up, in which sat the king. When he saw her, he caused the carriage to be stopped.

'My child, who are you, and what are you doing here?'

'I am a poor girl, and I am rinsing yarn.'

The king felt compassion, and he saw that she was so very beautiful. 'Will you go away with me?' he said.

'Ah, yes, with all my heart,' she answered, for she was glad to get away from the mother and sister.

So she got into the carriage and drove away with the king, and when they arrived at his palace, the wedding was celebrated with great pomp, as the little men had granted to the maiden. When a year was over, the young queen bore a son, and as the stepmother had heard of her great good fortune, she came with her daughter to the palace and pretended that she wanted to pay her a visit. Once, however, when the King had gone out, and no one else was present, the wicked woman seized the Queen by the head, and her daughter seized her by the feet, and they lifted her out of the bed, and threw her out of the window into the stream which flowed by. Then the ugly daughter laid herself in the bed, and the old woman covered her up over her head. When the king came home again and wanted to speak to his wife, the old woman cried, 'Hush, hush, that can't be now, she is lying in a violent perspiration; you must let her rest to-day.' The King suspected no evil and did not come back again till next morning; and as he talked with his wife and she answered him, with every word a toad leaped out, whereas formerly a piece of gold had fallen out. Then he asked what that could be, but the old woman said that she had got that from the violent perspiration, and would soon lose it again. During the night, however, the scullion saw a duck come swimming up the gutter, and it said:

'King, what are you doing now? Do you sleep, or are you awake?'

And as he returned no answer, it said, 'And my guests, What may they do?'

The scullion said, 'They are sleeping soundly, too.'

Then it asked again, 'What does little baby mine?'

He answered, 'Sleepeth in her cradle fine.'

Then she went upstairs in the form of the queen, nursed the baby, shook up its little bed, covered it over, and then swam away again down the gutter in the shape of a duck. She came thus for two nights; on the third, she said to the scullion, 'Go and tell the king to take his sword and swing it three times over me on the threshold.' Then the scullion ran and told this to the king, who came with his sword and swung it thrice over the spirit, and at the third time, his wife stood before him strong, living, and healthy as she had been before. Thereupon the king was full of great joy, but he kept the queen hidden in a chamber until

the Sunday, when the baby was to be christened. And when it was christened he asked the old woman:

'What does a person deserve who drags another out of bed and throws him in the water?'

'The wretch deserves nothing better,' answered the old woman, 'than to be taken and put in a barrel stuck full of nails and rolled down hill into the water.'

'Then,' said the King, 'you have pronounced your own sentence;' and he ordered such a barrel to be brought, and the old woman to be put into it with her daughter, and then the top was hammered on, and the barrel rolled down hill until it went into the river.

The Juniper-Tree

It is now long ago, quite two thousand years, since there was a rich man who had a beautiful and pious wife, and they loved each other dearly. They had, however, no children, though they wished for them very much, and the woman prayed for them day and night, but still they had none. Now there was a courtyard in front of their house in which was a juniper-tree, and one day in winter the woman was standing beneath it, paring herself an apple, and while she was paring herself the apple she cut her finger, and the blood fell on the snow.

'Ah,' said the woman, and sighed right heavily, and looked at the blood before her, and was most unhappy, 'ah, if I had but a child as red as blood and as white as snow!'

And while she thus spake, she became quite happy in her mind, and felt just as if that were going to happen. Then she went into the house and a month went by and the snow was gone, and two months, and then everything was green, and three months, and then all the flowers came out of the earth, and four months, and then all the trees in the wood grew thicker, and the green branches were all closely entwined, and the birds sang until the wood resounded and the blossoms fell from the trees, then the fifth month passed away and she stood under the juniper-tree, which smelt so sweetly that her heart leapt, and she fell on her knees and was beside herself with joy, and when the sixth month was over the fruit was large and fine, and then she was quite still, and the seventh month she snatched at the juniper-berries and ate them greedily, then she grew sick and sorrowful, then the eighth month passed, and she called her husband to her, and wept and said:

'If I die then bury me beneath the juniper-tree.'

Then she was quite comforted and happy until the next month was over, and then she had a child as white as snow and as red as blood, and when she beheld it she was so delighted that she died.

Then her husband buried her beneath the juniper-tree, and he began to weep sore; after some time he was more at ease, and though he still wept he could bear it, and after some time longer he took another wife.

By the second wife he had a daughter, but the first wife's child was a little son, and he was as red as blood and as white as snow. When the woman looked at her daughter she loved her very much, but then she looked at the little boy and it seemed to cut her to the heart, for the thought came into her mind that he would always stand in her way, and she was for ever thinking how she could get all the fortune for her daughter, and the Evil One filled her mind with this till she was quite wroth with the little boy, and slapped him here and cuffed him there, until the unhappy child was in continual terror, for when he came out of school he had no peace in any place.

One day the woman had gone upstairs to her room, and her little daughter went up too.

'Mother, give me an apple,' she said.

'Yes, my child,' said the woman, and gave her a fine apple out of the chest, but the chest had a great heavy lid with a great sharp iron lock.

'Mother,' said the little daughter, whose name was Marlinchen, 'is brother not to have one too?'

This made the woman angry, but she said, 'Yes, when he comes out of school.'

And when she saw from the window that he was coming, it was just as if the Devil entered into her, and she snatched at the apple and took it away again from her daughter, and said:

'You shall not have one before your brother.'

Then she threw the apple into the chest and shut it. Then the little boy came in at the door, and the Devil made her say to him kindly:

'My son, will you have an apple?' and she looked wickedly at him.

'Mother,' said the little boy, 'how dreadful you look! Yes, give me an apple.'

Then it seemed to her as if she were forced to say to him:

'Come with me,' and she opened the lid of the chest and. 'Take out an apple for yourself,' and while the little boy was stooping inside, the Devil prompted her, and crash! She shut the lid down, and his head flew off and fell among the red apples. Then she was overwhelmed with terror, and thought, 'If I could but make them think that it was not done by me!'

So she went upstairs to her room to her chest of drawers, and took a white handkerchief out of the top drawer, and set the head on the neck again, and folded the handkerchief so that nothing could be seen, and she set him on a chair in front of the door, and put the apple in his hand.

After this Marlinchen came into the kitchen to her mother, who was standing by the fire with a pan of hot water before her which she was constantly stirring round.

'Mother,' said Marlinchen, 'brother is sitting at the door, and he looks quite white and has an apple in his hand. I asked him to give me the apple, but he did not answer me, and I was quite frightened.'

'Go back to him,' said her mother, 'and if he will not answer you, give him a box on the ear.'

So Marlinchen went to him and said:

'Brother, give me the apple.' But he was silent, and she gave him a box on the ear, on which his head fell down. Marlinchen was terrified, and began crying and screaming, and ran to her mother.

'Alas, mother, I have knocked my brother's head off!' she said, and she wept and wept and could not be comforted.

'Marlinchen,' said the mother, 'what have you done? but be quiet and let no one know it; it cannot be helped now, we will make him into black-puddings.' Then the mother took the little boy and chopped him in pieces, put him into the pan and made him into black puddings; but Marlinchen stood by weeping and weeping, and all her tears fell into the pan and there was no need of any salt.

Then the father came home, and sat down to dinner and said:

'But where is my son?'

And the mother served up a great dish of black-puddings, and Marlinchen wept and could not leave off. Then the father again said:

'But where is my son?'

'Ah,' said the mother, 'he has gone across the country to his mother's great uncle; he will stay there awhile.'

'And what is he going to do there? He did not even say good-bye to me.'

'Oh, he wanted to go, and asked me if he might stay six weeks, he is well taken care of there.'

'Ah,' said the man, 'I feel so unhappy lest all should not be right. He ought to have said good-bye to me.' With that he began to eat and said, 'Marlinchen, why are you crying? Thy brother will certainly come back.' Then he said, 'Ah, wife, how delicious this food is, give me some more.' And the more he ate the more he wanted to have, and he said, 'Give me some more, you shall have none of it. It seems to me as if it were all mine.' And he ate and ate and threw all the bones under the table, until he had finished the whole. But Marlinchen went away to her chest of drawers and took her best silk handkerchief out of the bottom drawer, and gathered all the bones from beneath the table, and tied them up in her silk handkerchief, and carried them outside the door, weeping tears of blood. Then the juniper-tree began to stir itself, and the branches parted asunder, and moved together again, just as if someone was rejoicing and clapping his hands. At the same time a mist seemed to arise from the tree, and in the centre of this mist it burned like a fire, and a beautiful bird flew out of the fire singing magnificently, and he flew high up in the air, and when he was gone, the juniper-tree was just as it had been before, and the handkerchief with the bones was no longer there. Marlinchen, however, was as gay and happy as if her brother were still alive. And she went merrily into the house, and sat down to dinner and ate.

But the bird flew away and lighted on a goldsmith's house, and began to sing:

> 'My mother she killed me,
> My father he ate me,
> My sister, little Marlinchen,
> Gathered together all my bones,
> Tied them in a silken handkerchief,
> Laid them beneath the juniper-tree,
> Kywitt, kywitt, what a beautiful bird am I!'

The goldsmith was sitting in his workshop making a gold chain, when he heard the bird which was sitting singing on his roof, and very beautiful the song seemed to him. He stood up, but as he crossed the threshold he lost one of his slippers. But he went away right up the middle of the street with one shoe on and one sock; he had his apron on, and in one hand he had the gold chain and in the other the pincers, and the sun was shining brightly on the street. Then he went right on and stood still, and said to the bird:

'Bird,' said he then, 'how beautifully you can sing! Sing me that piece again.'

'No,' said the bird, 'I'll not sing it twice for nothing! Give me the golden chain, and then I will sing it again for you.'

'There,' said the goldsmith, 'there is the golden chain for you, now sing me that song again.' Then the bird came and took the golden chain in his right claw, and went and sat in front of the goldsmith, and sang,

> 'My mother she killed me,
> My father he ate me,
> My sister, little Marlinchen,
> Gathered together all my bones,
> Tied them in a silken handkerchief,
> Laid them beneath the juniper-tree,
> Kywitt, kywitt, what a beautiful bird am I!'

Then the bird flew away to a shoemaker, and lighted on his roof and sang,

> 'My mother she killed me,
> My father he ate me,
> My sister, little Marlinchen,
> Gathered together all my bones,
> Tied them in a silken handkerchief,
> Laid them beneath the juniper-tree,
> Kywitt, kywitt, what a beautiful bird am I!'

The shoemaker heard that and ran out of doors in his shirt sleeves, and looked up at his roof, and was forced to hold his hand before his eyes lest the sun should blind him.

'Bird,' said he, 'how beautifully you can sing!' Then he called in at his door, 'Wife, just come outside, there is a bird, look at that bird, he just can sing well.' Then he called his daughter and children, and apprentices, boys and girls, and they all came up the street and looked at the bird and saw how beautiful he was, and what fine red and green feathers he had, and how like real gold his neck was, and how the eyes in his head shone like stars.

'Bird,' said the shoemaker, 'now sing me that song again.'

'Nay,' said the bird, 'I do not sing twice for nothing; you must give me something.'

'Wife,' said the man, 'go to the garret, upon the top shelf there stands a pair of red shoes, bring them down.' Then the wife went and brought the shoes. 'There, bird,' said the man, 'now sing me that piece again.' Then the bird came and took the shoes in his left claw, and flew back on the roof, and sang,

> 'My mother she killed me,
> My father he ate me,
> My sister, little Marlinchen,
> Gathered together all my bones,
> Tied them in a silken handkerchief,
> Laid them beneath the juniper-tree,
> Kywitt, kywitt, what a beautiful bird am I!'

And when he had sung the whole he flew away. In his right claw he had the chain and the shoes in his left, and he flew far away to a mill, and the mill went, klipp klapp, klipp klapp, klipp klapp, and in the mill sat twenty miller's men hewing a stone, and cutting, hick hack, hick hack, hick hack, and the mill went klipp klapp, klipp klapp, klipp klapp. Then the bird went and sat on a lime-tree which stood in front of the mill, and sang:

> 'My mother she killed me,'

Then one of them stopped working.

> 'My father he ate me.'

Then two more stopped working and listened to that.

> 'My sister, little Marlinchen,'

Then four more stopped.

> 'Gathered together all my bones,
> Tied them in a silken handkerchief,'

Now eight only were hewing.

> 'Laid them beneath'

Now only five.

> 'The juniper-tree,'

And now only one.

> 'Kywitt, kywitt, what a beautiful bird am I!'

Then the last stopped also, and heard the last words.

'Bird,' said he, 'how beautifully you sing! Let me, too, hear that. Sing that once more for me.'

'Nay,' said the bird, 'I will not sing twice for nothing. Give me the millstone, and then I will sing it again.'

'Yes,' said he, 'if it belonged to me only, you should have it.'

'Yes,' said the others, 'if he sings again he shall have it.'

Then the bird came down, and the twenty millers all set to work with a beam and raised the stone up. And the bird stuck his neck through the hole, and put the stone on as if it were a collar, and flew on to the tree again, and sang:

> 'My mother she killed me,
> My father he ate me,
> My sister, little Marlinchen,
> Gathered together all my bones,
> Tied them in a silken handkerchief,
> Laid them beneath the juniper-tree,
> Kywitt, kywitt, what a beautiful bird am I!'

And when he had done singing, he spread his wings, and in his right claw he had the chain, and in his left the shoes, and round his neck the millstone, and he flew far away to his father's house.

In the room sat the father, the mother, and Marlinchen at dinner, and the father said, 'How light-hearted I feel, how happy I am!'

'Nay,' said the mother, 'I feel so uneasy, just as if a heavy storm were coming.'

Marlinchen, however, sat weeping and weeping, and then came the bird flying, and as it seated itself on the roof the father said:

'Ah, I feel so truly happy, and the sun is shining so beautifully out-side, I feel just as if I were about to see some old friend again.'

'Nay,' said the woman, 'I feel so anxious, my teeth chatter, and I seem to have fire in my veins.' And she tore her stays open, but Marlinchen sat in a corner crying, and held her plate before her eyes and cried till it was quite wet. Then the bird sat on the juniper tree, and sang:

'My mother she killed me,'

Then the mother stopped her ears, and shut her eyes, and would not see or hear, but there was a roaring in her ears like the most violent storm, and her eyes burnt and flashed like lightning,

'My father he ate me,'

'Ah, mother,' says the man, 'that is a beautiful bird! He sings so splendidly, and the sun shines so warm, and there is a smell just like cinnamon.'

'My sister, little Marlinchen,'

Then Marlinchen laid her head on her knees and wept without ceas-ing, but the man said, 'I am going out, I must see the bird quite close.'

'Oh, don't go,' said the woman, 'I feel as if the whole house were shaking and on fire.' But the man went out and looked at the bird:

> 'Gathered together all my bones,
> Tied them in a silken handkerchief,
> Laid them beneath the juniper tree,
> Kywitt, kywitt, what a beautiful bird am I!'

On this the bird let the golden chain fall, and it fell exactly round the man's neck, and so exactly round it that it fitted beautifully. Then he went in and said:

'Just look what a fine bird that is, and what a handsome gold chain he has given me, and how pretty he is!' But the woman was terrified, and fell down on the floor in the room, and her cap fell off her head. Then sang the bird once more:

> 'My mother she killed me.'

'Would that I were a thousand feet beneath the earth so as not to hear that!'

> 'My father he ate me,'

Then the woman fell down again as if dead.

> 'My sister, little Marlinchen,'

'Ah,' said Marlinchen, 'I too will go out and see if the bird will give me anything,' and she went out.

> 'Gathered together all my bones,
> Tied them in a silken handkerchief,'

Then he threw down the shoes to her.

'Laid them beneath the juniper-tree,
Kywitt, kywitt, what a beautiful bird am I!'

Then she was light-hearted and joyous, and she put on the new red shoes, and danced and leaped into the house.

'Ah,' said she, 'I was so sad when I went out and now I am so light-hearted; that is a splendid bird, he has given me a pair of red shoes!'

'Well,' said the woman, and sprang to her feet and her hair stood up like flames of fire, 'I feel as if the world were coming to an end! I, too, will go out and see if my heart feels lighter.'

And as she went out at the door, crash! the bird threw down the millstone on her head, and she was entirely crushed by it. The father and Marlinchen heard what had happened and went out, and smoke, flames, and fire were rising from the place, and when that was over, there stood the little brother, and he took his father and Marlinchen by the hand, and all three were right glad, and they went into the house to dinner, and ate.

Clever Gretel

There was once a cook named Gretel, who always wore shoes with red rosettes on them, and when she walked out with them on, she turned herself this way and that and was very pleased with how she looked, and thought how pretty she was. And when she came home she was pleased to drink a glass of wine, and as wine excites a desire to eat, she tasted the best of whatever she was cooking until she was satisfied, and said, 'The cook must know what the food is like.'

One day the master said to her:

'Gretel, there is a guest coming this evening; so please prepare and cook a two chickens for our meal.'

'I will see to it, master,' answered Gretel.

She killed two fowls, scalded them, plucked them, put them on the spit, and towards evening set them before the fire, that they might roast. The fowls began to turn brown, and were nearly ready, but the guest had not yet arrived. Then Gretel called out to her master, 'If the guest does not come, I must take the fowls away from the fire, but it will be a sin and a shame if they are not eaten directly, when they are juiciest.'

'Quite right Gretel! I will run and fetch the guest,' replied the master.

When the master had turned his back, Gretel moved the spit with the fowls away from the fire, and thought, 'Standing so long by the fire there, makes one hot and thirsty; who knows when they will come? Meanwhile, I will run into the cellar, and take a drink.' She ran down, filled a jug, said, 'God bless it to thy use, Gretel,' and took a good drink, and then another hearty draught.

Then she went and put the fowls down again to the fire, basted them, and drove the spit merrily round.

'They smell so good,' Gretel thought, 'they ought to be tasted to make sure nothing is wrong!' She touched the meat with her finger, and said, 'Ah! how good fowls are! It certainly is a sin and a shame that they are not eaten directly!' She ran to the window, to see if the master was not coming with his guest, but she saw no one, and went back to the fowls, which were beginning to be scorched by the fire.

'One of the wings is burning!' she thought. 'I had better take it off and eat it.'

So she cut it off, ate it, and enjoyed it, and when she had done, she thought that the bird looked rather lop-sided.

'The other must go down too, or else master will notice that something is missing.'

When the two wings were eaten, she went and looked for her master, and did not see him. It suddenly occurred to her, 'Who knows? Perhaps they are not coming at all and have turned in somewhere.'

Then she said, 'Hallo, Gretel, enjoy yourself, one fowl has been cut into, take another drink, and eat it up entirely; when it is eaten you will have some peace, why should God's good gifts be spoilt?' So she ran into the cellar again, took an enormous drink and ate up the one chicken in great glee.

When one of the chickens was swallowed down, and still her master did not come, Gretel looked at the other and said:

'Where one is, the other should be likewise, the two go together; what's right for the one is right for the other; I think if I were to take another draught it would do me no harm.' So she took another hearty drink, and let the second chicken join the first.

While she was just in the middle of eating the second chicken, her master came back!

'Hurry up, Gretel, the guest is coming directly after me!'

'Yes, sir, I will soon serve up,' answered Gretel.

The master looked to see that the table was properly laid, and took the great knife, wherewith he was going to carve the chickens, and sharpened it on the steps. Presently the guest came and knocked politely and courteously at the house door. Gretel ran, and looked to see who was there, and when she saw the guest, she put her finger to her lips.

'Hush! hush!' she said. 'Get away as quickly as you can, if my master catches you it will be the worse for you; he certainly did ask you to supper, but his intention is to cut off your two ears. Just listen how he is sharpening the knife for it!'

The guest heard the knife being sharpened and hurried down the steps again as fast as he could. Gretel was not idle; she ran screaming to her master, and cried:

'You have invited a fine guest!'

'Eh, why, Gretel? What do you mean by that?'

'Yes,' said she, 'he has taken the chickens which I was just going to serve up, off the dish, and has run away with them!'

'That's a nice trick!' said her master and lamented the fine chickens. 'If he had but left me one, so that something remained for me to eat.' He called to him to stop, but the guest pretended not to hear.

Then he ran after him with the knife still in his hand, crying, 'Just one, just one,' meaning that the guest should leave him just one chicken, and not take both. The guest, however, thought no otherwise than that he was to give up one of his ears, and ran as if fire were burning under him, in order to take them both home with him.

The Goose-Girl at the Well

❧ ❧ ❧

There was once upon a time a very old woman, who lived with her flock of geese in a waste place among the mountains, and there had a little house. The waste was surrounded by a large forest, and every morning the old woman took her crutch and hobbled into it. There, however, the dame was quite active, more so than anyone would have thought, considering her age, and collected grass for her geese, picked all the wild fruit she could reach, and carried everything home on her back. Anyone would have thought that the heavy load would have weighed her to the ground, but she always brought it safely home. If anyone met her, she greeted them quite courteously.

'Good day, dear countryman, it is a fine day. Ah! you wonder that I should drag grass about, but everyone must take his burthen on his back.'

Nevertheless, people did not like to meet her if they could help it, and took by preference a round-about way, and when a father with his boys passed her, he whispered to them, 'Beware of the old woman. She has claws beneath her gloves; she is a witch.'

One morning, a handsome young man was going through the forest. The sun shone bright, the birds sang, a cool breeze crept through the leaves, and he was full of joy and gladness. He had as yet met no one, when he suddenly perceived the old witch kneeling on the ground cutting grass with a sickle. She had already thrust a whole load into her cloth, and near it stood two baskets, which were filled with wild apples and pears.

'But, good little mother,' said he, 'how can you carry all that away?'

'I must carry it, dear sir,' answered she, 'rich folk's children have no need to do such things, but with the peasant folk the saying goes, don't look behind you, you will only see how crooked your back is!'

'Will you help me?' she said, as he remained standing by her. 'You have still a straight back and young legs, it would be a trifle to you. Besides, my house is not so very far from here, it stands there on the heath behind the hill. How soon you would bound up thither.'

The young man took compassion on the old woman.

'My father is certainly no peasant,' replied he, 'but a rich count; nevertheless, that you may see that it is not only peasants who can carry things, I will take your bundle.'

'If you will try it,' said she, 'I shall be very glad. You will certainly have to walk for an hour, but what will that signify to you; only you must carry the apples and pears as well?'

It now seemed to the young man just a little serious, when he heard of an hour's walk, but the old woman would not let him off, packed the bundle on his back, and hung the two baskets on his arm.

'See, it is quite light,' said she. 'No, it is not light,' answered the count, and pulled a rueful face. 'Verily, the bundle weighs as heavily as if it were full of cobble stones, and the apples and pears are as heavy as lead! I can scarcely breathe.'

He had a mind to put everything down again, but the old woman would not allow it.

'Just look,' said she mockingly, 'the young gentleman will not carry what I, an old woman, have so often dragged along. You are ready with fine words, but when it comes to be earnest, you want to take to your heels. Why are you standing loitering there?' she continued. 'Step out. No one will take the bundle off again.'

As long as he walked on level ground, it was still bearable, but when they came to the hill and had to climb, and the stones rolled down under his feet as if they were alive, it was beyond his strength. The drops of perspiration stood on his forehead, and ran, hot and cold, down his back.

'Dame,' said he, 'I can go no farther. I want to rest a little.' 'Not here,' answered the old woman, 'when we have arrived at our journey's end, you can rest; but now you must go forward. Who knows what good it may do you?'

'Old woman, you are becoming shameless!' said the count, and tried to throw off the bundle, but he laboured in vain; it stuck as fast to his back as if it grew there. He turned and twisted, but he could not get rid of it. The old woman laughed at this, and sprang about quite delighted on her crutch.

'Don't get angry, dear sir,' said she, 'you are growing as red in the face as a turkey-cock! Carry your bundle patiently. I will give you a good present when we get home.'

What could he do? He was obliged to submit to his fate, and crawl along patiently behind the old woman. She seemed to grow more and more nimble, and his burden still heavier. All at once she made a spring, jumped on to the bundle and seated herself on the top of it; and however withered she might be, she was yet heavier than the stoutest country lass. The youth's knees trembled, but when he did not go on, the old woman hit him about the legs with a switch and with stinging-nettles. Groaning continually, he climbed the mountain, and at length reached the old woman's house, when he was just about to drop.

When the geese perceived the old woman, they flapped their wings, stretched out their necks, ran to meet her, cackling all the while. Behind the flock walked, stick in hand, an old wench, strong and big, but ugly as night.

'Good mother,' said she to the old woman, 'has anything happened to you, you have stayed away so long?'

'By no means, my dear daughter,' answered she, 'I have met with nothing bad, but, on the contrary, with this kind gentleman, who has carried my burthen for me; only think, he even took me on his back when I was tired. The way, too, has not seemed long to us; we have been merry, and have been cracking jokes with each other all the time.'

At last the old woman slid down, took the bundle off the young man's back, and the baskets from his arm, looked at him quite kindly, and said, 'Now seat yourself on the bench before the door, and rest. You have fairly earned your wages, and they shall not be wanting.' Then she said to the goose-girl, 'Go into the house, my dear daughter, it is not becoming for you to be alone with a young gentleman; one must not pour oil on to the fire, he might fall in love with you.'

The count knew not whether to laugh or to cry. 'Such a sweetheart as that,' thought he, 'could not touch my heart, even if she were thirty years younger.'

In the meantime the old woman stroked and fondled her geese as if they were children, and then went into the house with her daughter. The youth lay down on the bench, under a wild apple-tree. The air was warm and mild; on all sides stretched a green meadow, which was set with cowslips, wild thyme, and a thousand other flowers; through the midst of it rippled a clear brook on which the sun sparkled, and the white geese went walking backwards and forwards, or paddled in the water.

'It is quite delightful here,' said he, 'but I am so tired that I cannot keep my eyes open; I will sleep a little. If only a gust of wind does not come and blow my legs off my body, for they are as rotten as tinder.'

When he had slept a little while, the old woman came and shook him till he awoke.

'Sit up,' said she, 'you cannot stay here; I have certainly treated you hardly, still, it has not cost you your life. Of money and land you have no need, here is something else for you.'

Thereupon she thrust a little book into his hand, which was cut out of a single emerald.

'Take great care of it,' said she, 'it will bring you good fortune.'

The count sprang up, and as he felt that he was quite fresh, and had recovered his vigour, he thanked the old woman for her present, and set off without even once looking back at the beautiful daughter. When he was already some way off, he still heard in the distance the noisy cry of the geese.

For three days the count had to wander in the wilderness before he could find his way out. He then reached a large town, and as no one knew him, he was led into the royal palace, where the king and queen were sitting on their throne. The count fell on one knee, drew the emerald book out of his pocket, and laid it at the queen's feet. She bade him rise and hand her the little book. Hardly, however, had she opened it, and looked therein, than she fell to the ground as if dead. The count was seized by the king's servants, and was being led to prison, when the queen opened her eyes, and ordered them to release him, and everyone was to go out, as she wished to speak with him in private.

When the queen was alone, she began to weep bitterly, and said:

'Of what use to me are the splendours and honours with which I am surrounded; every morning I awake in pain and sorrow. I had three daughters, the youngest of whom was so beautiful that the whole world looked on her as a wonder. She was as white as snow, as rosy as apple-blossom, and her hair as radiant as sun-beams. When she cried, not tears fell from her eyes, but pearls and jewels only. When she was fifteen years old, the king summoned all three sisters to come before his throne. You should have seen how all the people gazed when the youngest entered, it was just as if the sun were rising! Then the king spoke, "My daughters, I know not when my last day may arrive; I will to-day decide what each shall receive at my death. You all love me, but the one of you who loves me best, shall fare the best." Each of them said she loved him best. "Can you not express to me," said the king, "how much you do love me, and thus I shall see what you mean?" The eldest spoke. "I love my father as dearly as the sweetest sugar." The second, "I love my father as dearly as my prettiest dress." But the youngest was silent. Then the father said, "And you, my dearest child, how much dost you love me?" "I do not know, and can compare my love with nothing.' But her father insisted that she should name something. So she said at last, "The best food does not please me without salt, therefore I love my father like salt." When the king heard that, he fell into a passion, and said, "If you love me like salt, your love shall also be repaid you with salt." Then he divided the kingdom between the two elder, but caused a sack of salt to be bound on the back of the youngest, and two servants had to lead her forth into the wild forest. We all begged and prayed for her, said the queen, but the king's anger was not to be appeased. How she cried when she had to leave us! The whole road was strewn with the pearls which flowed from her eyes. The king soon afterwards repented of his great severity, and had the whole forest searched for the poor child, but no one could find her. When I think that the wild beasts have devoured her, I know not how to contain myself for sorrow; many a time I console myself with the hope that she is still alive, and may have hidden herself in a cave, or has found shelter with compassionate people. But picture to yourself, when I opened your little emerald book, a pearl lay therein, of exactly the same kind as those which used to fall from my daughter's eyes; and then you can also imagine how the sight of it stirred my heart. You must tell me how you came by that pearl.'

The count told her that he had received it from the old woman in the forest, who had appeared very strange to him, and must be a witch, but he had neither seen nor heard anything of the queen's child. The king and the queen resolved to seek out the old woman. They thought that there where the pearl had been, they would obtain news of their daughter.

The old woman was sitting in that lonely place at her spinning-wheel, spinning. It was already dusk, and a log which was burning on the hearth gave a scanty light. All at once there was a noise outside, the geese were coming home from the pasture, and uttering their hoarse cries. Soon afterwards the daughter also entered. But the old woman scarcely thanked her, and only shook her head a little. The daughter sat down beside her, took her spinning-wheel, and twisted the threads as nimbly as a young girl. Thus they both sat for two hours, and exchanged never a word. At last something rustled at the window, and two fiery eyes peered in. It was an old night-owl, which cried, 'Uhu!' three times. The old woman looked up just a little, then she said, 'Now, my little daughter, it is time for you to go out and do your work.'

She rose and went out, and where did she go? Over the meadows ever onward into the valley. At last she came to a well, with three old oak-trees standing beside it; meanwhile the moon had risen large and round over the mountain, and it was so light that one could have found a needle. She removed a skin which covered her face, then bent down to the well, and began to wash herself. When she had finished, she dipped the skin also in the water, and then laid it on the meadow, so that it should bleach in the moonlight, and dry again. But how the maiden was changed! Such a change as that was never seen before! When the grey mask fell off, her golden hair broke forth like sun-beams, and spread about like a mantle over her whole form. Her eyes shone out as brightly as the stars in heaven, and her cheeks bloomed a soft red like apple-blossom.

But the fair maiden was sad. She sat down and wept bitterly. One tear after another forced itself out of her eyes, and rolled through her long hair to the ground. There she sat, and would have remained sitting a long time, if there had not been a rustling and cracking in the boughs of the neighbouring tree. She sprang up like a roe which has been overtaken by the shot of the hunter. Just then the moon was obscured by a dark cloud, and in an instant the maiden had put on the old skin and vanished, like a light blown out by the wind.

She ran back home, trembling like an aspen-leaf. The old woman was standing on the threshold, and the girl was about to relate what had befallen her, but the old woman laughed kindly, and said:

'I already know all.'

She led her into the room and lighted a new log. She did not, however, sit down to her spinning again, but fetched a broom and began to sweep and scour.

'All must be clean and sweet,' she said to the girl.

'But, mother,' said the maiden, 'why do you begin work at so late an hour? What do you expect?'

'Do you know then what time it is?' asked the old woman.

'Not yet midnight,' answered the maiden, 'but already past eleven o'clock.'

'Do you not remember,' continued the old woman, 'that it is three years to-day since you came to me? Your time is up, we can no longer remain together.'

The girl was terrified, and said:

'Alas! dear mother, will you cast me off? Where shall I go? I have no friends, and no home to which I can go. I have always done as you bade me, and you have always been satisfied with me; do not send me away.'

The old woman would not tell the maiden what lay before her.

'My stay here is over,' she said to her, 'but when I depart, house and parlour must be clean: therefore do not hinder me in my work. Have no care for yourself, you shall find a roof to shelter you, and the wages which I will give you shall also content you.'

'But tell me what is about to happen,' the maiden continued to entreat.

'I tell you again, do not hinder me in my work. Do not say a word more, go to your chamber, take the skin off your face, and put on the silken gown which you had on when you came to me, and then wait in your chamber until I call you.'

But I must once more tell of the king and queen, who had journeyed forth with the count in order to seek out the old woman in the wilderness. The count had strayed away from them in the wood by night, and had to walk onwards alone. Next day it seemed to him that he was on the right track. He still went forward, until darkness came on, then he climbed a tree, intending to pass the night there, for he feared that he might lose his way. When the moon lit the surrounding country he perceived a figure coming down the mountain. She had no stick in her hand, but yet he could see that it was the goose-girl, whom he had seen before in the house of the old woman.

'Oho,' cried he, 'there she comes, and if I once get hold of one of the witches, the other shall not escape me!'

But how astonished he was, when she went to the well, took off the skin and washed herself, when her golden hair fell down all about her, and she was more beautiful than any one whom he had ever seen in the whole world. He hardly dared to breathe, but stretched his head as far forward through the leaves as he dared, and stared at her. Either he bent over too far, or whatever the cause might be, the bough suddenly cracked, and that very moment the maiden slipped into the skin, sprang away like a roe, and as the moon was suddenly covered, disappeared from his eyes. Hardly had she disappeared, before the count descended from the tree, and hastened after her with nimble steps.

He had not gone far before he saw, in the twilight, two figures coming over the meadow. It was the king and queen, who had perceived from a distance the light shining in the old woman's little house and were going to it. The count told them what wonderful things he had seen by the well, and they did not doubt that it had been their lost daughter. They walked onwards full of joy, and soon came to the little house. The geese were sitting all round it and had thrust their heads under their wings and were sleeping, and not one of them moved. The king and queen looked in at the window, the old woman was sitting there quite quietly spinning, nodding her head and never looking round. The room was perfectly clean, as if the little mist men, who carry no dust on their feet, lived there. Their daughter, however, they did not see.

They gazed at all this for a long time, at last they took heart, and knocked softly at the window. The old woman appeared to have been expecting them; she rose, and called out quite kindly, 'Come in – I know you already.'

When they had entered the room, the old woman said:

'You might have spared yourself the long walk, if you had not three years ago unjustly driven away your child, who is so good and lovable. No harm has come to her; for three years she has had to tend the geese; with them she has learnt no evil, but has preserved her purity of heart. You, however, have been sufficiently punished by the misery in which you have lived.'

Then she went to the chamber and called:

'Come out, my little daughter.'

The door opened, and the princess stepped out in her silken garments, with her golden hair and her shining eyes, and it was as if an angel from heaven had entered. She went up to her father and mother, fell on their necks and kissed them; there was no help for it, they all had to weep for joy. The young count stood near them, and when she perceived him she became as red in the face as a moss-rose, she herself did not know why.

'My dear child, I have given away my kingdom, what shall I give you?' the king asked.

'She needs nothing,' said the old woman. 'I give her the tears that she has wept on your account; they are precious pearls, finer than those that are found in the sea, and worth more than your whole kingdom, and I give her my little house as payment for her services.'

When the old woman had said that, she disappeared from their sight. The walls rattled a little, and when the king and queen looked round, the little house had changed into a splendid palace, a royal table had been spread, and the servants were running hither and thither.

The story goes still further, but my grandmother, who related it to me, had partly lost her memory and had forgotten the rest. I shall always believe that the beautiful princess married the count, and that they remained together in the palace, and lived there in all happiness so long as God willed it. Whether the snow-white geese, which were kept near the little hut, were verily young maidens (no one need take offence,) whom the old woman had taken under her protection, and whether they now received their human form again, and stayed as handmaids to the young queen, I do not exactly know, but I suspect it. This much is certain, that the old woman was no witch, as people thought, but a wise woman, who meant well. Very likely it was she who, at the princess's birth, gave her the gift of weeping pearls instead of tears. That does not happen now-a-days, or else the poor would soon become rich.

The Hut in the Forest

A poor wood-cutter lived with his wife and three daughters in a little hut on the edge of a lonely forest. One morning as he was about to go to his work, he said to his wife, 'Let my dinner be brought into the forest to me by my eldest daughter, or I shall never get my work done, and in order that she may not miss her way,' he added, 'I will take a bag of millet with me and strew the seeds on the path.'

When, therefore, the sun was just above the centre of the forest, the girl set out on her way with a bowl of soup, but the field-sparrows, and wood-sparrows, larks and finches, blackbirds and siskins had picked up the millet long before, and the girl could not find the track. Then trusting to chance, she went on and on, until the sun sank and night began to fall. The trees rustled in the darkness, the owls hooted, and she began to be afraid. Then in the distance she perceived a light which glimmered between the trees.

'There ought to be some people living there, who can take me in for the night,' thought she, and went up to the light. It was not long before she came to a house the windows of which were all lighted up. She knocked, and a rough voice from inside cried, 'Come in.'

The girl stepped into the dark entrance and knocked at the door of the room.

'Just come in,' cried the voice, and when she opened the door, an old grey-haired man was sitting at the table, supporting his face with both hands, and his white beard fell down over the table almost as far as the ground. By the stove lay three animals, a hen, a cock, and a brindled cow. The girl told her story to the old man, and begged for shelter for the night. The man said, 'Pretty little hen, pretty little cock, and beautiful brindled cow, what say you to that?'

'Duks,' answered the animals, and that must have meant, 'We are willing,' for the old man said, 'Here you shall have shelter and food. Go to the fire, and cook us our supper.'

The girl found in the kitchen abundance of everything, and cooked a good supper, but had no thought of the animals. She carried the full dishes to the table, seated herself by the grey-haired man, ate and satisfied her hunger. When she had had enough, she said, 'But now I am tired, where is there a bed in which I can lie down, and sleep?'

The animals replied, 'You have eaten with him, you have drunk with him, you have had no thought for us, so find out for yourself where you can pass the night.'

Then said the old man, 'Just go upstairs, and you will find a room with two beds, shake them up, and put white linen on them, and then I, too, will come and lie down to sleep.' The girl went up, and when she had shaken the beds and put clean sheets on, she lay down in one of them without waiting any longer for the old man. After some time, however, the grey-haired man came, took his candle, looked at the girl and shook his head. When he saw that she had fallen into a sound sleep, he opened a trap-door, and let her down into the cellar.

Late at night the wood-cutter came home and reproached his wife for leaving him to hunger all day.

'It is not my fault,' she replied, 'the girl went out with your dinner, and must have lost herself, but she is sure to come back to-morrow.'

The wood-cutter, however, arose before dawn to go into the forest, and requested that the second daughter should take him his dinner that day.

'I will take a bag with lentils,' said he; 'the seeds are larger than millet, the girl will see them better, and can't lose her way.' At dinner-time, therefore, the girl took out the food, but the lentils had disappeared. The birds of the forest had picked them up as they had done the day before and had left none. The girl wandered about in the forest until night, and then she too reached the house of the old man, was told to go in, and begged for food and a bed. The man with the white beard again asked the animals, 'Pretty little hen, pretty little cock, and beautiful brindled cow, what say you to that?'

The animals again replied 'Duks,' and everything happened just as it had happened the day before. The girl cooked a good meal, ate and drank with the old man, and did not concern herself about the animals, and when she inquired about her bed they answered, 'You have eaten with him, you have drunk with him, you have had no thought for us, so find out for yourself where you can pass the night.'

When she was asleep the old man came, looked at her, shook his head, and let her down into the cellar.

On the third morning the wood-cutter said to his wife, 'Send our youngest child out with my dinner to-day, she has always been good and obedient, and will stay in the right path, and not run about after every wild humble-bee, as her sisters did.' The mother did not want to do it.

'Am I to lose my dearest child, as well?' she said.

'Have no fear,' he replied, 'the girl will not go astray; she is too prudent and sensible; besides I will take some peas with me, and strew them about. They are still larger than lentils, and will show her the way.'

But when the girl went out with her basket on her arm, the wood-pigeons had already got all the peas in their crops, and she did not know which way she was to turn. She was full of sorrow and never ceased to think how hungry her father would be, and how her good mother would grieve, if she did not go home. At length when it grew dark, she saw the light and came to the house in the forest. She begged quite prettily to be allowed to spend the night there, and the man with the white beard once more asked his animals, 'Pretty little hen, pretty little cock, and beautiful brindled cow, what say you to that?'

'Duks,' said they. Then the girl went to the stove where the animals were lying, and petted the cock and hen, and stroked their smooth feathers with her hand, and caressed the brindled cow between her horns, and when, in obedience to the old man's orders, she had made ready some good soup, and the bowl was placed upon the table, she said:

'Am I to eat as much as I want, and the good animals to have nothing? Outside is food in plenty, I will look after them first.'

So she went and brought some barley and strewed it for the cock and hen, and a whole armful of sweet-smelling hay for the cow.

'I hope you will like it, dear animals,' said she, 'and you shall have a refreshing draught in case you are thirsty.' Then she fetched in a bucketful of water, and the cock and hen jumped on to the edge of it and dipped their beaks in, and then held up their heads as the birds do when they drink, and the brindled cow also took a hearty draught. When the animals were fed, the girl seated herself at the table by the old man, and ate what he had left. It was not long before the cock and the hen began to thrust their heads beneath their wings, and the eyes of the cow likewise began to blink. Then said the girl, 'Ought we not to go to bed?'

'Pretty little hen, pretty little cock, and beautiful brindled cow, what say you to that?'

'Duks,' the animals answered. 'You have eaten with us, you have drunk with us, you have had kind thought for all of us, we wish you good-night.'

Then the maiden went upstairs, shook the feather-beds, and laid clean sheets on them, and when she had done it the old man came and lay down on one of the beds, and his white beard reached down to his feet. The girl lay down on the other, said her prayers, and fell asleep.

She slept quietly till midnight, and then there was such a noise in the house that she awoke. There was a sound of cracking and splitting in every corner, and the doors sprang open, and beat against the walls. The beams groaned as if they were being torn out of their joints, it seemed as if the staircase was falling down, and at length there was a crash as if the entire roof had fallen in. As, however, all grew quiet once more, and the girl was not hurt, she stayed quietly lying where she was, and fell asleep again. But when she woke up in the morning with the brilliancy of the sunshine, what did her eyes behold? She was lying in a vast hall, and everything around her shone with royal splendour; on the walls, golden flowers grew up on a ground of green silk, the bed was of ivory, and the canopy of red velvet, and on a chair close by, was a pair of shoes embroidered with pearls. The girl believed that she was in a dream, but three richly clad attendants came in, and asked what orders she would like to give.

'If you will go,' she replied, 'I will get up at once and make ready some soup for the old man, and then I will feed the pretty little hen, and the cock, and the beautiful brindled cow.' She thought the old man was up already, and looked round at his bed; he, however, was not lying in it, but a stranger. And while she was looking at him, and becoming aware that he was young and handsome, he awoke, sat up in bed, and said:

'I am a king's son, and was bewitched by a wicked witch, and made to live in this forest, as an old grey-haired man; no one was allowed to be with me but my three attendants in the form of a cock, a hen, and a brindled cow. The spell was not to be broken until a girl came to us whose heart was so good that she showed herself full of love, not only towards mankind, but towards animals – and that you have done, and by you at midnight we were set free, and the old hut in the forest was changed back again into my royal palace.'

And when they had arisen, the king's son ordered the three attendants to set out and fetch the father and mother of the girl to the marriage feast.

'But where are my two sisters?' inquired the maiden.

'I have locked them in the cellar,' he replied, 'and tomorrow they shall be led into the forest, and shall live as servants to a charcoal-burner, until they have grown kinder, and do not leave poor animals to suffer hunger.'

The Singing, Soaring Lark

There was once on a time a man who was about to set out on a long journey, and on parting he asked his three daughters what he should bring back with him for them. Whereupon the eldest wished for pearls, the second wished for diamonds, but the third said, 'Dear father, I should like a singing, soaring lark.'

'Yes, if I can get it, you shall have it,' the father said, and he kissed all three and set out.

Now when the time had come for him to be on his way home again, he had brought pearls and diamonds for the two eldest, but he had sought everywhere in vain for a singing, soaring lark for the youngest, and he was very unhappy about it, for she was his favourite child. Then his road lay through a forest, and in the middle of it was a splendid castle, and near the castle stood a tree, but quite on the top of the tree, he saw a singing, soaring lark.

'Aha, you come just at the right moment!' he said, quite delighted, and called to his servant to climb up and catch the little creature. But as he approached the tree, a lion leapt from beneath it, shook himself, and roared till the leaves on the trees trembled.

'He who tries to steal my singing, soaring lark,' he cried, 'will I devour.'

'I did not know that the bird belonged to you,' the man said. 'I will make amends for the wrong I have done and ransom myself with a large sum of money, only spare my life.'

The lion said, 'Nothing can save you, unless you will promise to give me for my own the first creature to meet you on your return home; and if you will do that, I will grant you your life, and you shalt have the bird for your daughter, into the bargain.'

But the man hesitated and said:

'That might be my youngest daughter, she loves me best, and always runs to meet me on my return home.'

The servant, however, was terrified and said:

'Why should your daughter be the very one to meet you? It might as easily be your dog, or a cat.' Then the man allowed himself to be over-persuaded, took the singing, soaring lark, and promised to give the lion whatever should first meet him on his return home.

When he reached home and entered his house, the first who met him was no other than his youngest and dearest daughter, who came running up, kissed and embraced him, and when she saw that he had brought with him a singing, soaring lark, she was beside herself with joy. The father, however, could not rejoice, but began to weep.

'My dearest child, I have bought the little bird dear,' he said. 'In return for it, I have been obliged to promise you to a savage lion, and when he has you he will tear you in pieces and devour you.' And he told her all, just as it had happened, and begged her not to go there, come what might. But she consoled him.

'Dearest father,' she said, 'indeed your promise must be fulfilled. I will go to the lion and be kind and gentle with him, so that I may return to you safely.'

Next morning she had the road pointed out to her, took her leave, and went fearlessly out into the forest. The lion, however, was an enchanted prince and was by day a lion, and all his people were lions with him, but in the night they resumed their natural human shapes. On her arrival she was kindly received and led into the castle. When night came, the lion turned into a handsome man, and their wedding was celebrated with great magnificence. They lived happily together, remained awake at night, and slept in the daytime. One day he came and said:

'To-morrow there is a feast in your father's house, because your eldest sister is to be married, and if you are inclined to go there, my lions shall conduct you.'

'Yes, I should very much like to see my father again,' she said, and went to the wedding, accompanied by the lions. There was great joy when she arrived, for they had all believed that she had been torn in pieces by the lion and had long ceased to live. But she told them what a handsome husband she had, and how well off she was, remained with them while the wedding-feast lasted, and then went back again to the forest.

When the second daughter was about to be married, and she was again invited to the wedding, she said to the lion:

'This time I will not be alone, you must come with me.'

The lion, however, said that it was too dangerous for him, for if when there a ray from a burning candle fell on him, he would be changed into a dove, and for seven years long would have to fly about with the doves.

'Ah, but do come with me, I will take great care of you, and guard you from all light,' she begged.

So they went away together, and took with them their little child as well. She had a chamber built there, so strong and thick that no ray could pierce through it; in this he was to shut himself up when the candles were lit for the wedding feast. But the door was made of green wood which warped and left a little crack which no one noticed. The wedding was celebrated with magnificence, but when the procession with all its candles and torches came back from church, and passed by this apartment, a ray about the breadth of a hair fell on the king's son, and when this ray touched him, he was transformed in an instant, and when she came in and looked for him, she did not see him, but a white dove was sitting there.

'For seven years must I fly about the world, but at every seventh step that you take I will let fall a drop of red blood and a white feather, and these will show you the way, and if you follow the trace you can release me,' the dove said to her.

Thereupon the dove flew out at the door, and she followed him, and at every seventh step a red drop of blood and a little white feather fell down and showed her the way.

So she went continually further and further in the wide world, never looking about her or resting, and the seven years were almost past; then she rejoiced and thought that they would soon be delivered, and yet they were so far from it! Once when they were thus moving onwards, no little feather and no drop of red blood fell, and when she raised her eyes the dove had disappeared.

'In this no man can help you,' she thought to herself. So she climbed up to the sun, and said to him:

'You shine into every crevice, and over every peak, have you not seen a white dove flying?'

'No,' said the sun, 'I have seen none, but I present you with a casket, open it when you are in sorest need.' She thanked the sun, and went on until evening came and the moon appeared.

'You shine the whole night through, and on every field and forest, have you not seen a white dove flying?' she asked her.

'No,' said the moon, 'I have seen no dove, but here I give you an egg, break it when you are in great need.' She thanked the moon, and went on until the night wind came up and blew on her.

'You blow over every tree and under every leaf, have you not seen a white dove flying?' she asked it.

'No,' said the night wind, 'I have seen none, but I will ask the three other winds, perhaps they have seen it.' The east wind and the west wind came, and had seen nothing, but the south wind said:

'I have seen the white dove, it has flown to the Red Sea, where it has become a lion again, for the seven years are over, and the lion is there fighting with a dragon; the dragon, however, is an enchanted princess.'

The night wind then said to her:

'I will advise you: go to the Red Sea, on the right bank are some tall reeds, count them, break off the eleventh, and strike the dragon with it, then the lion will be able to subdue it, and both then will regain their human form. After that, look round and you will see the griffin which is by the Red Sea; swing yourself, with your beloved, on to his back, and the bird will carry you over the sea to your own home. Here is a nut for you, when you are above the centre of the sea, let the nut fall, it will immediately shoot up, and a tall nut-tree will grow out of the water on which the griffin may rest; for if he cannot rest, he will not be strong enough to carry you across, and if you forget to throw down the nut, he will let you fall into the sea.'

Then she went there and found everything as the night wind had said. She counted the reeds by the sea, and cut off the eleventh, struck the dragon with it, whereupon the lion overcame it, and immediately both of them regained their human shapes. But when the princess, who had before been the dragon, was delivered from enchantment, she took the youth by the arm, seated herself on the griffin, and carried him off with her. There stood the poor maiden who had wandered so far and was again forsaken. She sat down and cried, but at last she took courage and said:

'Still I will go as far as the wind blows and as long as the cock crows, until I find him,' and she went forth by long, long roads, until at last she came to the castle where both of them were living together; there she heard that soon a feast was to be held in which they would celebrate their wedding, but she said, 'God still helps me,' and opened the casket that the sun had given her. A dress lay therein as brilliant as the sun itself. So she took it out and put it on, and went up into the castle, and everyone, even the bride herself, looked at her with astonishment. The dress pleased the bride so well that she thought it might do for her wedding-dress, and asked if it was for sale.

'Not for money or land,' answered she, 'but for flesh and blood.'

The bride asked her what she meant by that.

'Let me sleep a night in the chamber where the bridegroom sleeps,' she said.

The bride would not, yet wanted very much to have the dress; at last she consented, but the page was to give the prince a sleeping-draught. When it was night, therefore, and the youth was already asleep, she was led into the chamber and she seated herself on the bed.

'I have followed after you for seven years. I have been to the sun and the moon, and the four winds, and have enquired for you, and have helped you against the dragon; will you, then, quite forget me?' she said.

But the prince slept so soundly that it only seemed to him as if the wind were whistling outside in the fir-trees. When therefore day broke, she was led out again, and had to give up the golden dress. And as that even had been of no avail, she was sad, went out into a meadow, sat down there, and wept. While she was sitting there, she thought of the egg which the moon had given her; she opened it, and there came out a clucking hen with twelve chickens all of gold, and they ran about chirping, and crept again under the old hen's wings; nothing more beautiful was ever seen in the world! Then she arose, and drove them through the meadow before her, until the bride looked out of the window. The little chickens pleased her so much that she immediately came down and asked if they were for sale.

'Not for money or land, but for flesh and blood; let me sleep another night in the chamber where the bridegroom sleeps.'

'Yes,' the bride said, intending to cheat her as on the former evening. But when the prince went to bed he asked the page what the murmuring and rustling in the night had been? On this the page told all; that he had been forced to give him a sleeping-draught, because a poor girl had slept secretly in the chamber, and that he was to give him another that night.

'Pour out the draught by the bed-side,' the prince said. At night, she was again led in, and when she began to relate how ill all had fared with her, he immediately recognized his beloved wife by her voice, sprang up and cried, 'Now I really am released! I have been as it were in a dream, for the strange princess has bewitched me so that I have been compelled to forget you, but God has delivered me from the spell at the right time.'

Then they both left the castle secretly in the night, for they feared the father of the princess, who was a sorcerer, and they seated themselves on the griffin which bore them across the Red Sea, and when they were in the middle of it, she let fall the nut. Immediately a tall nut-tree grew up, which the bird rested on, and then carried them home, where they found their child, who had grown tall and beautiful, and they lived thenceforth happily until their death.

The Skilful Huntsman

There was once a young fellow who had learnt the trade of locksmith, and told his father he would now go out into the world and seek his fortune.

'Very well,' said the father, 'I am quite content with that,' and gave him some money for his journey.

So he travelled about and looked for work. After a time he resolved not to follow the trade of locksmith any more, for he no longer liked it, but he took a fancy for hunting. Then there met him in his rambles a huntsman dressed in green, who asked whence he came and where he was going. The youth said he was a locksmith's apprentice, but that the trade no longer pleased him, and he had a liking for huntsmanship, would he teach it to him?

'Oh, yes,' said the huntsman, 'if you will go with me.'

Then the young fellow went with him, bound himself to him for some years, and learnt the art of hunting. After this he wished to try his luck elsewhere, and the huntsman gave him nothing in the way of payment but an air-gun, which had, however, this property, that it hit its mark without fail whenever someone shot with it.

Then he set out and found himself in a very large forest, which he could not get to the end of in one day. When evening came he seated himself in a high tree in order to escape from the wild beasts. Towards midnight, it seemed to him as if a tiny little light glimmered in the distance. Then he looked down through the branches towards it, and kept well in his mind where it was. But first he took off his hat and threw it down in the direction of the light, so that he might go to the hat as a mark when he had descended. Then he got down and went to his hat, put it on again and went straight forwards. The farther he went, the larger the light grew, and when he got close to it he saw that it was an enormous fire, and that three giants were sitting by it, who had an ox on the spit and were roasting it. Presently one of them said:

'I must just taste if the meat will soon be fit to eat,' and pulled a piece off, and was about to put it in his mouth when the huntsman shot it out of his hand.

'Well, really,' said the giant, 'if the wind has not blown the bit out of my hand!' and helped himself to another. But when he was just about to bite into it, the huntsman again shot it away from him. On this the giant gave the one who was sitting next him a box on the ear, and cried angrily, 'Why are you snatching my piece away from me?'

'I have not snatched it away,' said the other, 'a sharpshooter must have shot it away from you.'

The giant took another piece, but could not, however, keep it in his hand, for the huntsman shot it out. Then the giant said, 'That must be a good shot to shoot the bit out of one's very mouth, such an one would be useful to us.' And he cried aloud, 'Come here, you sharpshooter, seat yourself at the fire beside us and eat your fill, we will not hurt you; but if you will not come, and we have to bring you by force, you are a lost man!'

On this the youth went up to them and told them he was a skilled huntsman, and that whatever he aimed at with his gun, he was certain to hit. Then they said if he would go with them he should be well treated, and they told him that outside the forest there was a great lake, behind which stood a tower, and in the tower was imprisoned a lovely princess, whom they wished very much to carry off.

'Yes,' said he, 'I will soon get her for you.'

'But there is still something else,' they added. 'There is a tiny little dog, which begins to bark directly any one goes near, and as soon as it barks everyone in the royal palace wakes up, and for this reason we cannot get there; can you undertake to shoot it dead?'

'Yes,' said he, 'that will be a little bit of fun for me.'

After this he got into a boat and rowed over the lake, and as soon as he landed, the little dog came running out, and was about to bark, but the huntsman took his air-gun and shot it dead. When the giants saw that, they rejoiced, and thought they already had the king's daughter safe, but the huntsman wished first to see how matters stood, and told them that they must stay outside until he called them. Then he went into the castle, and all was perfectly quiet within, and everyone was asleep. When he opened the door of the first room, a sword was hanging on the wall which was made of pure silver, and there was a golden star on it, and the name of the king, and on a table near it lay a sealed letter which he broke open, and inside it was written that whoever had the sword could kill everything which opposed him. So he took the sword from the wall, hung it at his side and went onwards: then he entered the room where the king's daughter was lying sleeping, and she was so beautiful that he stood still and, holding his breath, looked at her. He thought to himself:

'How can I give an innocent maiden into the power of the wild giants, who have evil in their minds?' He looked about further, and under the bed stood a pair of slippers, on the right one was her father's name with a star, and on the left her own name with a star. She wore also a great neckerchief of silk embroidered with gold, and on the right side was her father's name, and on the left her own, all in golden letters. Then the huntsman took a pair of scissors and cut the right corner off, and put it in his knapsack, and then he also took the right slipper with the king's name, and thrust that in. Now the maiden still lay sleeping, and she was quite sewn into her night-dress, and he cut a morsel from this also, and thrust it in with the rest, but he did all without touching her.

Then he went forth and left her lying asleep undisturbed, and when he came to the gate again, the giants were still standing outside waiting for him, and expecting that he was bringing the princess. But he cried to them that they were to come in, for the maiden was already in their power, that he could not open the gate to them, but there was a hole through which they must creep. Then the first approached, and the huntsman wound the giant's hair round his hand, pulled the head in, and cut it off at one stroke with his sword, and then drew the rest of him in. He called to the second and cut his head off likewise, and then he killed the third also, and he was well pleased that he had freed the beautiful maiden from her enemies, and he cut out their tongues and put them in his knapsack. Then thought he:

'I will go home to my father and let him see what I have already done, and afterwards I will travel about the world; the luck which God is pleased to grant me will easily find me.'

But when the king in the castle awoke, he saw the three giants lying there dead. So he went into the sleeping-room of his daughter, awoke her, and asked who could have killed the giants.

'Dear father, I know not, I have been asleep.'

But when she arose and would have put on her slippers, the right one was gone, and when she looked at her neckerchief it was cut, and the right corner was missing, and when she looked at her night-dress a piece was cut out of it. The king summoned his whole court together, soldiers and everyone else who was there, and asked who had set his daughter at liberty, and killed the giants.

Now it happened that he had a captain, who was one-eyed and a hideous man, and he said that he had done it. Then the old king said that as he had accomplished this, he should marry his daughter. But the maiden said, 'Rather than marry him, dear father, I will go away into the world as far as my legs can carry me.'

The king said that if she would not marry him she should take off her royal garments and wear peasant's clothing, and go forth, and that she should go to a potter, and begin a trade in earthen vessels. So she put off her royal apparel, and went to a potter and borrowed crockery enough for a stall, and she promised him also that if she had sold it by the evening, she would pay for it. Then the king said she was to seat herself in a corner with it and sell it, and he arranged with some peasants to drive over it with their carts, so that everything should be broken into a thousand pieces. When therefore the king's daughter had placed her stall in the street, by came the carts, and broke all she had into tiny fragments. She began to weep.

'Alas, how shall I ever pay for the pots now?'

The king had, however, wished by this to force her to marry the captain; but instead of that, she again went to the potter, and asked him if he would lend to her once more. He refused.

'No; first you must first pay for the things you have already had,' he said.

Then she went to her father and cried and lamented, and said she would go forth into the world. Then said he, 'I will have a little hut built for you in the forest outside, and in it you shall stay all your life long and cook for everyone, but you shall take no money for it.'

When the hut was ready, a sign was hung on the door whereon was written, 'Today given, tomorrow sold.' There she remained a long time, and it was rumoured about the world that a maiden was there who cooked without asking for payment, and that this was set forth on a sign outside her door. The huntsman heard it likewise, and thought to himself, 'That would suit you. You are poor, and have no money.' So he took his air-gun and his knapsack, with all the things which he had formerly carried away with him from the castle as tokens of his truthfulness still lying in it, and went into the forest, and found the hut with the sign, 'Today given, tomorrow sold.'

He had put on the sword with which he had cut off the heads of the three giants, and thus entered the hut, and ordered something to eat to be given to him. He was charmed with the beautiful maiden, who was indeed as lovely as any picture. She asked him whence he came and whither he was going.

'I am roaming about the world,' he said.

Then she asked him where he had got the sword, for that truly her father's name was on it. He asked her if she were the king's daughter.

'Yes,' answered she.

'With this sword,' said he, 'did I cut off the heads of three giants.' And he took their tongues out of his knapsack in proof. Then he also showed her the slipper, and the corner of the neck-kerchief, and the bit of the night-dress. She was overjoyed at this, and said that he was the one who had delivered her.

On this they went together to the old king, and fetched him to the hut, and she led him into her room, and told him that the huntsman was the man who had really set her free from the giants. And when the aged king saw all the proofs of this, he could no longer doubt, and said that he was very glad he knew how everything had happened, and that the huntsman should have her to wife, on which the maiden was glad at heart. Then she dressed the huntsman as if he were a foreign lord, and the king ordered a feast to be prepared.

When they went to table, the captain sat on the left side of the king's daughter, but the huntsman was on the right, and the captain thought he was a foreign lord who had come on a visit. When they had eaten and drunk, the old king said to the captain that he would set before him something which he must guess.

'Supposing anyone said that he had killed the three giants and he were asked where the giants' tongues were, and he were forced to go and look, and there were none in their heads, how could that happen?'

'Then they cannot have had any,' said the captain.

'Not so,' said the king. 'Every animal has a tongue,' and then he likewise asked what anyone would deserve who made such an answer.

'He ought to be torn in pieces,' the captain replied.

Then the king said he had pronounced his own sentence, and the captain was put in prison and then torn in four pieces; but the king's daughter was married to the huntsman. After this he brought his father and mother, and they lived with their son in happiness, and after the death of the old king he received the kingdom.

Mary's Child

🌱 🌱 🌱

Hard by a great forest dwelt a wood-cutter with his wife, who had an only child, a little girl three years old. They were so poor, however, that they no longer had daily bread, and did not know how to get food for her. One morning the wood-cutter went out sorrowfully to his work in the forest, and while he was cutting wood, suddenly there stood before him a tall and beautiful woman with a crown of shining stars on her head, who said to him, 'I am the Virgin Mary, mother of the child Jesus. You are poor and needy, bring your child to me, I will take her with me and be her mother, and care for her.'

The wood-cutter obeyed, brought his child, and gave her to the Virgin Mary, who took her up to heaven with her. There the child fared well, ate sugar-cakes, and drank sweet milk, and her clothes were of gold, and the little angels played with her. And when she was fourteen years of age, the Virgin Mary called her one day and said:

'Dear child, I am about to make a long journey, so take into your keeping the keys of the thirteen doors of heaven. Twelve of these you may open, and behold the glory which is within them, but the thirteenth, to which this little key belongs, is forbidden you. Beware of opening it, or you will bring misery on yourself.'

The girl promised to be obedient, and when the Virgin Mary was gone, she began to examine the dwellings of the kingdom of heaven. Each day she opened one of them, until she had made the round of the twelve. In each of them sat one of the Apostles in the midst of a great light, and she rejoiced in all the magnificence and splendour, and the little angels who always accompanied her rejoiced with her. Then the forbidden door alone remained, and she felt a great desire to know what could be hidden behind it, and said to the angels,:

'I will not quite open it, and I will not go inside it, but I will unlock it so that we can just see a little through the opening.'

'Oh no,' said the little angels, 'that would be a sin. The Virgin Mary has forbidden it, and it might easily cause your unhappiness.'

Then she was silent, but the desire in her heart was not stilled, but gnawed there and tormented her, and let her have no rest. And once when the angels had all gone out, she thought, 'Now I am quite alone, and I could peep in. If I do it, no one will ever know.' She sought out the key, and when she had got it in her hand, she put it in the lock, and when she had put it in, she turned it round as well. Then the door sprang open, and she saw there the Trinity sitting in fire and splendour. She stayed there awhile, and looked at everything in amazement; then she touched the light a little with her finger, and her finger became quite golden. Immediately a great fear fell on her. She shut the door violently and ran away. Her terror too would not quit her, let her do what she might, and her heart beat continually and would not be still; the gold too stayed on her finger, and would not go away, let her rub it and wash it never so much.

It was not long before the Virgin Mary came back from her journey. She called the girl before her, and asked to have the keys of heaven back. When the maiden gave her the bunch, the Virgin looked into her eyes and said:

'Have you not opened the thirteenth door also?'

'No,' she replied. Then she laid her hand on the girl's heart, and felt how it beat and beat, and saw right well that she had disobeyed her order and had opened the door. Then she said once again, 'Are you certain that you have not done it?'

'Yes,' said the girl, for the second time. Then she perceived the finger which had become golden from touching the fire of heaven, and saw well that the child had sinned, and said for the third time:

'Have you not done it?'

'No,' said the girl for the third time.

Then said the Virgin Mary, 'You have not obeyed me, and besides that you have lied, you are no longer worthy to be in heaven.'

Then the girl fell into a deep sleep, and when she awoke she lay on the earth below, and in the midst of a wilderness. She wanted to cry out, but she could bring forth no sound. She sprang up and wanted to run away, but whichever way she turned herself, she was continually held back by thick hedges of thorns through which she could not break. In the desert in which she was imprisoned, there stood an old hollow tree, and this had to be her dwelling-place. Into this she crept when night came, and here she slept. Here, too, she found a shelter from storm and rain, but it was a miserable life, and bitterly did she weep when she remembered how happy she had been in heaven, and how the angels had played with her. Roots and wild berries were her only food, and for these she sought as far as she could go. In the autumn she picked up the fallen nuts and leaves and carried them into the hole. The nuts were her food in winter, and when snow and ice came, she crept among the leaves like a poor little animal that she might not freeze. Before long, her clothes were all torn, and one bit of them after another fell off her. As soon as the sun shone warm again, however, she went out and sat in front of the tree, and her long hair covered her on all sides like a mantle. Thus she sat year after year, and felt the pain and the misery of the world.

One day, when the trees were once more clothed in fresh green, the king of the country was hunting in the forest, and followed a roe, and as it had fled into the thicket which shut in this part of the forest, he got off his horse, tore the bushes asunder, and cut himself a path with his sword. When he had at last forced his way through, he saw a wonderfully beautiful maiden sitting under the tree; and she sat there and was entirely covered with her golden hair down to her very feet.

He stood still and looked at her full of surprise, then he spoke to her and said, 'Who are you? Why are you sitting here in the wilderness?'

But she gave no answer, for she could not open her mouth.

'Will you go with me to my castle?' the king continued. Then she just nodded her head a little.

The king took her in his arms, carried her to his horse, and rode home with her, and when he reached the royal castle he caused her to be dressed in beautiful garments, and gave her all things in abundance. Although she could not speak, she was still so beautiful and charming that he began to love her with all his heart, and it was not long before he married her.

After a year or so had passed, the queen brought a son into the world. Thereupon the Virgin Mary appeared to her in the night when she lay in her bed alone, and said, 'If you will tell the truth and confess that you did unlock the forbidden door, I will open your mouth and give you back your speech, but if you persevere in your sin, and deny obstinately, I will take your new-born child away with me.' Then the queen was permitted to answer, but she remained hard, and said:

'No, I did not open the forbidden door;' and the Virgin Mary took the new-born child from her arms and vanished with it.

Next morning when the child was not to be found, it was whispered among the people that the queen was a man-eater, and had killed her own child. She heard all this and could say nothing to the contrary, but the king would not believe it, for he loved her so much.

When a year had gone by the queen again bore a son, and in the night the Virgin Mary again came to her, and said:

'If you will confess that you opened the forbidden door, I will give you your child back and untie your tongue; but if you continue in sin and deny it, I will take away with me this new child also.'

'No, I did not open the forbidden door,' the queen said again; and the Virgin took the child out of her arms, and away with her to heaven.

Next morning, when this child also had disappeared, the people declared quite loudly that the queen had devoured it, and the king's councillors demanded that she should be brought to justice. The king, however, loved her so dearly that he would not believe it, and commanded the councillors under pain of death not to say any more about it.

The following year the queen gave birth to a beautiful little daughter, and for the third time the Virgin Mary appeared to her in the night and said:

'Follow me.' She took the queen by the hand and led her to heaven, and showed her there her two eldest children, who smiled at her, and were playing with the ball of the world. When the queen rejoiced at seeing them, the Virgin Mary said, 'Is your heart not yet softened? If you will own that you opened the forbidden door, I will give you back your two little sons.'

But for the third time the queen answered, 'No, I did not open the forbidden door.'

Then the Virgin let her sink down to earth once more, and took from her likewise her third child.

Next morning, when the loss was reported abroad, all the people cried loudly:

'The queen is a man-eater. She must be judged,' and the king was no longer able to restrain his councillors.

Thereupon a trial was held, and as she could not answer, and defend herself, she was condemned to be burnt alive. The wood was got together, and when she was fast bound to the stake, and the fire began to burn round about her, the hard ice of pride melted, her heart was moved by repentance, and she thought:

'If I could but confess before my death that I opened the door.' Then her voice came back to her, and she cried out loudly,:

'Yes, Mary, I did it;' and straight-way rain fell from the sky and extinguished the flames of fire, and a light broke forth above her, and the Virgin Mary descended with the two little sons by her side, and the new-born daughter in her arms. She spoke kindly to her, and said:

'He who repents his sin and acknowledges it, is forgiven.'

Then she gave her the three children, untied her tongue, and granted her happiness for her whole life.

Old Hildebrand

Once upon a time lived a peasant and his wife, and the parson of the village had a fancy for the wife and had wished for a long while to spend a whole day happily with her. The peasant woman, too, was quite willing. One day, therefore, he said to the woman:

'Listen, my dear friend, I have now thought of a way by which we can for once spend a whole day happily together. I'll tell you what; on Wednesday, you must take to your bed, and tell your husband you are ill, and if you only complain and act being ill properly, and go on doing so until Sunday when I have to preach, I will then say in my sermon that whoever has at home a sick child, a sick husband, a sick wife, a sick father, a sick mother, a sick brother or whosoever else it may be, and makes a pilgrimage to the Göckerli hill in Italy, where you can get a peck of laurel-leaves for a kreuzer, the sick child, the sick husband, the sick wife, the sick father, or sick mother, the sick sister, or whoever else it may be, will be restored to health immediately.'

'I will manage it,' said the woman promptly.

Now therefore on the Wednesday, the peasant woman took to her bed, and complained and lamented as agreed on, and her husband did everything for her that he could think of, but nothing did her any good, and when Sunday came the woman said, 'I feel as ill as if I were going to die at once, but there is one thing I should like to do before my end I should like to hear the parson's sermon that he is going to preach today.'

On that the peasant said, 'Ah, my child, do not do it – you might make yourself worse if you were to get up. Look, I will go to the sermon, and will attend to it very carefully, and will tell you everything the parson says.'

'Well,' said the woman, 'go, then, and pay great attention, and repeat to me all that you hear.'

So the peasant went to the sermon, and the parson began to preach and said, if anyone had at home a sick child, a sick husband, a sick wife, a sick father a sick mother, a sick sister, brother or anyone else, and would make a pilgrimage to the Göckerli hill in Italy, where a peck of laurel-leaves costs a kreuzer, the sick child, sick husband, sick wife, sick father, sick mother, sick sister, brother, or whoever else it might be, would be restored to health instantly, and whoever wished to undertake the journey was to go to him after the service was over, and he would give him the sack for the laurel-leaves and the kreuzer.

Then no one was more rejoiced than the peasant, and after the service was over, he went at once to the parson, who gave him the bag for the laurel-leaves and the kreuzer. After that he went home, and even at the house door he cried:

'Hurrah! dear wife, it is now almost the same thing as if you were well! The parson has preached to-day that whosoever had at home a sick child, a sick husband, a sick wife, a sick father, a sick mother, a sick sister, brother or whoever it might be, and would make a pilgrimage to the Göckerli hill in Italy, where a peck of laurel-leaves costs a kreuzer, the sick child, sick husband, sick wife, sick father, sick mother, sick sister, brother, or whosoever else it was, would be cured immediately, and now I have already got the bag and the kreuzer from the parson, and will at once begin my journey so that you may get well the faster,' and thereupon he went away. He was, however, hardly gone before the woman got up, and the parson was there directly.

But now we will leave these two for a while, and follow the peasant, who walked on quickly without stopping, in order to get the sooner to the Göckerli hill, and on his way he met his gossip. His gossip was an egg-merchant, and was just coming from the market, where he had sold his eggs.

'May you be blessed,' said the gossip. 'Where are you off to so fast?'

'To all eternity, my friend,' said the peasant. 'My wife is ill, and I have been to-day to hear the parson's sermon, and he preached that if anyone had in his house a sick child, a sick husband, a sick wife, a sick father, a sick mother, a sick sister, brother or anyone else, and made a pilgrimage to the Göckerli hill in Italy, where a peck of laurel-leaves costs a kreuzer, the sick child, the sick husband, the sick wife, the sick father, the sick mother, the sick sister, brother or whoever else it was, would be cured immediately, and so I have got the bag for the laurel-leaves and the kreuzer from the parson, and now I am beginning my pilgrimage.'

'But listen, gossip,' said the egg-merchant to the peasant, 'are you, then, stupid enough to believe such a thing as that? Don't you know what it means? The parson wants to spend a whole day alone with your wife in peace, so he has given you this job to do to get you out of the way.'

'My word!' said the peasant. 'How I'd like to know if that's true!'

'Come, then,' said the gossip, 'I'll tell you what to do. Get into my egg-basket and I will carry you home, and then you will see for yourself.'

So that was settled, and the gossip put the peasant into his egg-basket and carried him home.

When they got to the house, hurrah! but all was going merry there! The woman had already had nearly everything killed that was in the farmyard, and had made pancakes, and the parson was there, and had brought his fiddle with him. The gossip knocked at the door, and woman asked who was there.

'It is I, gossip,' said the egg-merchant, 'give me shelter this night; I have not sold my eggs at the market, so now I have to carry them home again, and they are so heavy that I shall never be able to do it, for it is dark already.'

'Indeed, my friend,' said the woman, 'you come at a very inconvenient time for me, but as you art here it can't be helped, come in, and take a seat there on the bench by the stove.' Then she placed the gossip and the basket which he carried on his back on the bench by the stove. The parson, however, and the woman, were as merry as possible. At length the parson said, 'Listen, my dear friend, you can sing beautifully; sing something to me.'

'Oh,' said the woman, 'I cannot sing now, in my young days indeed I could sing well enough, but that's all over now.'

'Come,' said the parson once more, 'do sing some little song.'

On that the woman began and sang,

> 'I've sent my husband away from me
> To the Göckerli hill in Italy.'

Thereupon the parson sang,

> 'I wish 'twas a year before he came back,
> I'd never ask him for the laurel-leaf sack.
> Hallelujah.'

Then the gossip who was in the background began to sing (but I ought to tell you the peasant was called Hildebrand), so the gossip sang,

> 'What are you doing, my Hildebrand dear,
> There on the bench by the stove so near?'
> Hallelujah.'

And then the peasant sang from his basket,

> 'All singing I ever shall hate from this day,
> And here in this basket no longer I'll stay.'
> Hallelujah.'

And he got out of the basket, and cudgelled the parson out of the house.

The Queen Bee

There was once a king who had three sons. The eldest two sons went out in search of adventures, and fell into a wild, disorderly way of living, so that they never came home again. The youngest, who was called Simpleton, set out to seek his brothers, but when at length he found them they mocked him for thinking that he with his simplicity could get through the world, when they two could not make their way, and yet were so much cleverer.

They all three travelled away together, and came to an ant-hill. The two elder wanted to destroy it, to see the little ants creeping about in their terror, and carrying their eggs away, but Simpleton said:

'Leave the creatures in peace; I will not allow you to disturb them.'

Then they went onwards and came to a lake, on which a great number of ducks were swimming. The two brothers wanted to catch a couple and roast them, but Simpleton would not permit it, and said:

'Leave the creatures in peace, I will not suffer you to kill them.'

At length they came to a bee's nest, in which there was so much honey that it ran out of the trunk of the tree where it was. The two wanted to make a fire beneath the tree, and suffocate the bees in order to take away the honey, but Simpleton again stopped them and said:

'Leave the creatures in peace, I will not allow you to burn them.'

At length the three brothers arrived at a castle where stone horses were standing in the stables, and no human being was to be seen, and they went through all the halls until, quite at the end, they came to a door in which were three locks. In the middle of the door, however, there was a little pane, through which they could see into the room. There they saw a little grey man, who was sitting at a table. They called him, once, twice, but he did not hear; at last they called him for the third time, when he got up, opened the locks, and came out. He said nothing, however, but conducted them to a handsomely-spread table, and when they had eaten and drunk, he took each of them to a bedroom.

Next morning the little grey man came to the eldest, beckoned to him, and conducted him to a stone table, on which were inscribed three tasks, by the performance of which the castle could be delivered. The first was that in the forest, beneath the moss, lay the princess's pearls, a thousand in number, which must be picked up, and if by sunset one single pearl was wanting, he who had looked for them would be turned into stone. The eldest went thither, and sought the whole day, but when it came to an end, he had only found one hundred, and what was written on the table came to pass, and he was changed into stone.

Next day, the second brother undertook the adventure; it did not, however, fare much better with him than with the eldest; he did not find more than two hundred pearls, and was changed to stone. At last the turn came to Simpleton also, who sought in the moss. It was, however, so hard to find the pearls, and he got on so slowly, that he seated himself on a stone, and wept. And while he was thus sitting, the king of the ants whose life he had once saved, came with five thousand ants, and before long the little creatures had got all the pearls together, and laid them in a heap.

The second task, however, was to fetch out of the lake the key of the king's daughter's bed-chamber. When Simpleton came to the lake, the ducks which he had saved swam up to him, dived down, and brought the key out of the water.

But the third task was the most difficult; from among the three sleeping daughters of the king was the youngest and dearest to be sought out. They, however, resembled each other exactly, and were only to be distinguished by their having eaten different sweetmeats before they fell asleep; the eldest a bit of sugar; the second a little syrup; and the youngest a spoonful of honey. Then the queen of the bees, which Simpleton had protected from the fire, came and tasted the lips of all three, and at last she remained sitting on the mouth which had eaten honey, and thus the king's son recognized the right princess. Then the enchantment was at an end; everything was released from sleep, and those who had been turned to stone received once more their natural forms. Simpleton married the youngest and sweetest princess, and after her father's death became king, and his two brothers received the two other sisters.

The Old Man and His Grandson

There was once a very old man, whose eyes had become dim, his ears dull of hearing, his knees trembled, and when he sat at table he could hardly hold the spoon, and spilt the broth upon the table-cloth or let it run out of his mouth. His son and his son's wife were disgusted at this, so the old grandfather at last had to sit in the corner behind the stove, and they gave him his food in an earthenware bowl, and not even enough of it. And he used to look towards the table with his eyes full of tears. Once, too, his trembling hands could not hold the bowl, and it fell to the ground and broke. The young wife scolded him, but he said nothing and only sighed. Then they bought him a wooden bowl for a few half-pence, out of which he had to eat.

They were once sitting thus when the little grandson of four years old began to gather together some bits of wood upon the ground.

'What are you doing there?' asked the father.

'I am making a little trough,' answered the child, 'for father and mother to eat out of when I am big.'

The man and his wife looked at each other for a while, and presently began to cry. Then they took the old grandfather to the table, and henceforth always let him eat with them, and likewise said nothing if he did spill a little of anything.

The Pink

There was once on a time a queen to whom God had given no children. Every morning she went into the garden and prayed to God in heaven to bestow on her a son or a daughter. Then an angel from heaven came to her and said:

'Be at rest, you shall have a son with the power of wishing, so that whatever in the world he wishes for, that shall he have.'

Then she went to the king, and told him the joyful tidings, and when the time was come she gave birth to a son, and the king was filled with gladness. Every morning she went with the child to the garden where the wild beasts were kept, and washed herself there in a clear stream. It happened once when the child was a little older, that it was lying in her arms and she fell asleep. Then came the old cook, who knew that the child had the power of wishing, and stole it away, and he took a hen, and cut it in pieces, and dropped some of its blood on the queen's apron and on her dress. Then he carried the child away to a secret place, where a nurse was obliged to suckle it, and he ran to the king and accused the queen of having allowed her child to be taken from her by the wild beasts. When the king saw the blood on her apron, he believed this, fell into such a passion that he ordered a high tower to be built, in which neither sun nor moon could be seen, and had his wife put into it, and walled up. Here she was to stay for seven years without meat or drink, and die of hunger. But God sent two angels from heaven in the shape of white doves, which flew to her twice a day, and carried her food until the seven years were over.

The cook, however, thought to himself, 'If the child has the power of wishing, and I am here, he might very easily get me into trouble.' So he left the palace and went to the boy, who was already big enough to speak, and said to him:

'Wish for a beautiful palace for yourself with a garden, and all else that pertains to it.'

Scarcely were the words out of the boy's mouth, when everything was there that he had wished for. After a while the cook said to him:

'It is not well for you to be so alone, wish for a pretty girl as a companion.'

Then the king's son wished for one, and she immediately stood before him, and was more beautiful than any painter could have painted her. The two played together, and loved each other with all their hearts, and the old cook went out hunting like a nobleman. The thought, however, occurred to him that the king's son might some day wish to be with his father, and thus bring him into great peril. So he went out and took the maiden aside, and said, 'Tonight when the boy is asleep, go to his bed and plunge this knife into his heart, and bring me his heart and tongue, and if you dost not do it, you shall lose your life.'

Thereupon he went away, and when he returned next day she had not done it, and said:

'Why should I shed the blood of an innocent boy who has never harmed any one?'

'If you do not do it, it shall cost you your own life,' the cook said once more.

When he had gone away, she had a little hind brought to her, and ordered her to be killed, and took her heart and tongue, and laid them on a plate, and when she saw the old cook coming, she said to the boy:

'Lie down in your bed, and draw the clothes over you.'

Then the wicked wretch came in and said: 'Where are the boy's heart and tongue?'

The girl reached the plate to him, but the king's son threw off the quilt, and said, 'You old sinner, why did you want to kill me? Now will I pronounce your sentence. You shall become a black poodle and have a gold collar round your neck, and shall eat burning coals, till the flames burst forth from your throat.'

And when he had spoken these words, the old man was changed into a poodle dog, and had a gold collar round his neck, and the cooks were ordered to bring up some live coals, and these he ate, until the flames broke forth from his throat. The king's son remained there a short while longer, and he thought of his mother, and wondered if she were still alive. At length he said to the maiden:

'I will go home to my own country; if you will go with me, I will provide for you.'

'Ah,' she replied, 'the way is so long, and what shall I do in a strange land where I am unknown?'

As she did not seem quite willing, and as they could not be parted from each other, he wished that she might be changed into a beautiful pink, and took her with him. Then he went away to his own country, and the poodle had to run after him. He went to the tower in which his mother was confined, and as it was so high, he wished for a ladder which would reach up to the very top. Then he mounted up and looked inside, and cried:

'Beloved mother, lady queen, are you still alive, or are you dead?'

'I have just eaten, and am still satisfied,' she answered, for she thought the angels were there.

'I am your dear son, whom the wild beasts were said to have torn from your arms,' he said, 'but I am alive still, and will speedily deliver you.'

Then he descended again, and went to his father, and caused himself to be announced as a huntsman, and asked if the king could give him a place. The king said yes, if he was skilful and could get game for him, he should come to him, but that deer had never taken up their quarters in any part of the district or country. Then the huntsman promised to procure as much game for him as he could possibly use at the royal table. So he summoned all the huntsmen together, and bade them go out into the forest with him. And he went with them and made them form a great circle, open at one end where he stationed himself, and began to wish. Two hundred deer and more came running inside the circle at once, and the huntsmen shot them. Then they were all placed on sixty country carts, and driven home to the king, and for once he was able to deck his table with game, after having had none at all for years.

Now the king felt great joy at this, and commanded that his entire household should eat with him next day, and made a great feast. When they were all assembled together, he said to the huntsman:

'As you are so clever, you shall sit by me.'

'Lord king, your majesty must excuse me, I am a poor huntsman,' he replied.

But the king insisted on it, and said, 'You shall sit by me,' until he did it. While he was sitting there, he thought of his dearest mother, and wished that one of the king's principal servants would begin to speak of her and would ask how it was faring with the queen in the tower, and if she were alive still, or had perished. Hardly had he formed the wish than the marshal began, and said:

'Your majesty, we live joyously here, but how is the queen living in the tower? Is she still alive, or has she died?'

'She let my dear son be torn to pieces by wild beasts; I will not have her named,' the king replied.

Then the huntsman arose and said, 'Gracious lord father, she is alive still, and I am her son, and I was not carried away by wild beasts, but by that wretch the old cook, who tore me from her arms when she was asleep and sprinkled her apron with the blood of a chicken.' Thereupon he took the dog with the golden collar, and said, 'That is the wretch!' and caused live coals to be brought, and these the dog was compelled to devour before the sight of all, until flames burst forth from its throat. On this he asked if the king would like to see the dog in his true shape, and wished him back into the form of the cook, in the which he stood immediately, with his white apron, and his knife by his side. When the king saw him he fell into a passion, and ordered him to be cast into the deepest dungeon. Then the huntsman spoke further and said:

'Father, will you see the maiden who was my childhood's tender companion and who was afterwards to murder me, but did not do it, though her own life depended on it?'

'Yes, I would like to see her,' the king replied.

'Most gracious father, I will show her to you in the form of a beautiful flower,' the son said, and he thrust his hand into his pocket and brought forth the pink, and placed it on the royal table, and it was so beautiful that the king had never seen one to equal it. Then the son said:

'Now will I show her to you in her own form,' and wished that she might become a maiden, and she stood there looking so beautiful that no painter could have made her look more so.

And the king sent two waiting-maids and two attendants into the tower, to fetch the queen and bring her to the royal table. But when she was led in she ate nothing, and said, 'The gracious and merciful God who has supported me in the tower, will speedily deliver me.' She lived three days more, and then died happily, and when she was buried, the two white doves which had brought her food to the tower, and were angels of heaven, followed her body and seated themselves on her grave. The aged king ordered the cook to be torn in four pieces, but grief consumed the king's own heart, and he soon died. His son married the beautiful maiden whom he had brought with him as a flower in his pocket, and whether they are still alive or not, is known to God.

The Raven

There was once upon a time a queen who had a little daughter who was still so young that she had to be carried. One day the child was naughty, and the mother might say what she liked, but the child would not be quiet. Then she became impatient, and as the ravens were flying about the palace, she opened the window and said, 'I wish you were a raven and would fly away, and then I should have some rest.'

Scarcely had she spoken the words, before the child was changed into a raven, and flew from her arms out of the window. It flew into a dark forest, and stayed in it a long time, and the parents heard nothing of their child. Then one day a man was on his way through this forest and heard the raven crying, and followed the voice, and when he came nearer, the bird said, 'I am a king's daughter by birth, and am bewitched, but you can set me free.'

'What am I to do?' asked he.

'Go further into the forest,' she said, 'and you will find a house, wherein sits an aged woman, who will offer you meat and drink, but you must accept nothing, for if you eat and drink anything, you will fall into a sleep, and then you will not be able to deliver me. In the garden behind the house there is a great heap of tan, and on this you shall stand and wait for me. For three days I will come every afternoon at two o'clock in a carriage. On the first day four white horses will be harnessed to it, then four chestnut horses, and lastly four black ones; but if you are not awake, but sleeping, I shall not be set free.'

The man promised to do everything that she desired.

'Alas,' said the raven, 'I know already that you will not deliver me; you will accept something from the woman.'

Then the man once more promised that he would certainly not touch anything either to eat or to drink. But when he entered the house the old woman came to him and said, 'Poor man, how faint you are; come and refresh yourself; eat and drink.'

'No,' said the man, 'I will not eat or drink.'

She, however, let him have no peace, and said, 'If you will not eat, take one drink out of the glass; one is nothing.' Then he let himself be persuaded, and drank. Shortly before two o'clock in the afternoon he went into the garden to the tan heap to wait for the raven. As he was standing there, his weariness all at once became so great that he could not struggle against it, and lay down for a short time, but he was determined not to go to sleep. Hardly, however, had he lain down, than his eyes closed of their own accord, and he fell asleep and slept so soundly that nothing in the world could have aroused him. At two o'clock the raven came driving up with four white horses, but she was already in deep grief.

'I know he is asleep,' she said. And when she came into the garden, he was indeed lying there asleep on the heap of tan. She alighted from the carriage, went to him, shook him, and called him, but he did not awake.

Next day about noon, the old woman came again and brought him food and drink, but he would not take any of it. But she let him have no rest and persuaded him until at length he again took one drink out of the glass. Towards two o'clock he went into the garden to the tan heap to wait for the raven, but all at once felt such a great weariness that his limbs would no longer support him. He could not help himself, and was forced to lie down, and fell into a heavy sleep. When the raven drove up with four brown horses, she was already full of grief.

'I know he is asleep,' she said. She went to him, but there he lay sleeping, and there was no wakening him.

Next day the old woman asked the man:

'What is the meaning of this? You are neither eating nor drinking anything; do you want to die?'

'I am not allowed to eat or drink, and will not do so,' he replied.

But she set a dish with food, and a glass with wine before him, and when he smelt it he could not resist, and swallowed a deep draught.

When the time came, he went out into the garden to the heap of tan, and waited for the king's daughter; but he became still more weary than on the day before, and lay down and slept as soundly as if he had been a stone. At two o'clock the raven came with four black horses, and the coachman and everything else was black. She was already in the deepest grief.

'I know that he is asleep and cannot deliver me,' she said.

When she came to him, there he was lying fast asleep. She shook him and called him, but she could not waken him. Then she laid a loaf beside him, and after that a piece of meat, and thirdly a bottle of wine, and he might consume as much of all of them as he liked, but they would never grow less. After this she took a gold ring from her finger, and put it on his, and her name was graven on it. Lastly, she laid a letter beside him wherein was written what she had given him, and that none of the things would ever grow less; and in it was also written:

'I see right well that here you will never be able to deliver me, but if you are still willing to deliver me, come to the golden castle of Stromberg; it lies in your power, of that I am certain.'

And when she had given him all these things, she seated herself in her carriage, and drove to the golden castle of Stromberg.

When the man awoke and saw that he had slept, he was sad at heart.

'She has certainly driven by, and I have not set her free,' he said. Then he perceived the things which were lying beside him, and read the letter wherein was written how everything had happened. So he arose and went away, intending to go to the golden castle of Stromberg, but he did not know where it was. After he had walked about the world for a long time, he entered into a dark forest, and walked for fourteen days, and still could not find his way out. Then it was once more evening, and he was so tired that he lay down in a thicket and fell asleep. Next day he went onwards, and in the evening, as he was again about to lie down beneath some bushes, he heard such a howling and crying that he could not go to sleep. And at the time when people light the candles, he saw one glimmering, and arose and went towards it. Then he came to a house which seemed very small, for in front of it a great giant was standing. He thought to himself, 'If I go in, and the giant sees me, it will very likely cost me my life.'

At length he ventured it and went in. When the giant saw him, he said:

'It is well that you have come, for it is long since I have eaten; I will at once eat you for my supper.'

'I'd rather you would leave that alone,' said the man, 'I do not like to be eaten; but if you hast any desire to eat, I have quite enough here to satisfy you.'

'If that be true,' said the giant, 'you mayst be easy, I was only going to devour you because I had nothing else.' Then they went, and sat down to the table, and the man took out the bread, wine, and meat which would never come to an end.

'This pleases me well,' said the giant, and ate to his heart's content.

'Can you tell me where the golden castle of Stromberg is?' asked the man.

'I will look at my map,' said the giant; 'all the towns, and villages, and houses are to be found on it.' He brought out the map which he had in the room and looked for the castle, but it was not to be found on it.

'It's no matter!' said he, 'I have some still larger maps in my cupboard upstairs, and we will look in them.' But there, too, it was in vain. The man now wanted to go onwards, but the giant begged him to wait a few days longer until his brother, who had gone out to bring some provisions, came home. When the brother came home they inquired about the golden castle of Stromberg.

'When I have eaten and have had enough, I will look in the map,' he replied. Then he went with them up to his chamber, and they searched in his map, but could not find it. Then he brought out still older maps, and they never rested until they found the golden castle of Stromberg, but it was many thousand miles away.

'How am I to get there?' asked the man. The giant said, 'I have two hours' time, during which I will carry you into the neighbourhood, but after that I must be at home to suckle the child that we have.'

So the giant carried the man to about a hundred leagues from the castle.

'You can very well walk the rest of the way alone,' he said, and he turned back. But the man went onwards day and night, until at length he came to the golden castle of Stromberg. It stood on a glass mountain, and the bewitched maiden drove in her carriage round the castle, and then went inside it. He rejoiced when he saw her and wanted to climb up to her, but when he began to do so he always slipped down the glass again. And when he saw that he could not reach her, he was filled with trouble, and said to himself, 'I will stay down here below, and wait for her.'

So he built himself a hut and stayed in it for a whole year, and every day saw the king's daughter driving about above, but never could go to her. Then one day he saw from his hut three robbers who were beating each other, and cried to them:

'God be with ye!'

They stopped when they heard the cry, but as they saw no one, they once more began to beat each other, and that too most dangerously. So he again cried:

'God be with ye!'

Again they stopped, looked round about, but as they saw no one they went on beating each other. Then he cried for the third time, 'God be with ye!' and thought, 'I must see what these three are about,' and went thither and asked why they were beating each other so furiously. One of them said that he found a stick, and that when he struck a door with it, that door would spring open. The next said that he had found a mantle, and that whenever he put it on, he was invisible, but the third said he had found a horse on which a man could ride everywhere, even up the glass mountain. And now they did not know whether they ought to have these things in common, or whether they ought to divide them.

'I will give you something in exchange for these three things,' said the man. Money indeed have I not, but I have other things of more value; but first I must try yours to see if you have told the truth.'

Then they put him on the horse, threw the mantle round him, and gave him the stick in his hand, and when he had all these things they were no longer able to see him. So he gave them some vigorous blows.

'Now, vagabonds,' he cried, 'you have got what you deserve, are you satisfied?' And he rode up the glass mountain, but when he came in front of the castle at the top, it was shut. Then he struck the door with his stick, and it sprang open immediately. He went in and ascended the stairs until he came to the hall where the maiden was sitting with a golden cup full of wine before her. She, however, could not see him because he had the mantle on. And when he came up to her, he drew from his finger the ring which she had given him, and threw it into the cup so that it rang. Then she cried, 'That is my ring, so the man who is to set me free must be here.'

They searched the whole castle and did not find him, but he had gone out, and had seated himself on the horse and thrown off the mantle. When they came to the door, they saw him and cried aloud in their delight. Then he alighted and took the king's daughter in his arms, and she kissed him and said, 'Now have you set me free, and tomorrow we will celebrate our wedding.'

The Pied Piper of Hamelin

Once upon a time . . . on the banks of a great river in the north of Germany lay a town called Hamelin. The citizens of Hamelin were honest folk who lived contentedly in their grey stone houses. The years went by, and the town grew very rich.

Then one day, an extraordinary thing happened to disturb the peace. Hamelin had always had rats, and a lot too. But they had never been a danger, for the cats had always solved the rat problem in the usual way – by killing them. All at once, however, the rats began to multiply. In the end, a black sea of rats swarmed over the whole town. First, they attacked the barns and storehouses, then, for lack of anything better, they gnawed the wood, cloth or anything at all. The one thing they didn't eat was metal. The terrified citizens flocked to plead with the town councilors to free them from the plague of rats. But the council had, for a long time, been sitting in the Mayor's room, trying to think of a plan.

'What we need is an army of cats!'

But all the cats were dead.

'We'll put down poisoned food then . . . '

But most of the food was already gone and even poison did not stop the rats.

'It just can't be done without help!' said the Mayor sadly.

Just then, while the citizens milled around outside, there was a loud knock at the door.

'Who can that be?' the city fathers wondered uneasily, mindful of the angry crowds. They gingerly opened the door. And to their surprise, there stood a tall thin man dressed in brightly coloured clothes, with a long feather in his hat, and waving a gold pipe at them.

'I've freed other towns of beetles and bats,' the stranger announced, 'and for a thousand florins, I'll rid you of your rats!'

'A thousand florins!' exclaimed the Mayor. 'We'll give you fifty thousand if you succeed!' At once the stranger hurried away, saying: 'It's late now, but at dawn tomorrow, there won't be a rat left in Hamelin!'

The sun was still below the horizon, when the sound of a pipe wafted through the streets of Hamelin. The pied piper slowly made his way through the houses and behind him flocked the rats. Out they scampered from doors, windows and gutters, rats of every size, all after the piper. And as he played, the stranger marched down to the river and straight into the water, up to his middle. Behind him swarmed the rats and every one was drowned and swept away by the current.

By the time the sun was high in the sky, there was not a single rat in the town. There was even greater delight at the town hall, until the piper tried to claim his payment.

'Fifty thousand florins?' exclaimed the councillors, 'Never . . .'

'A thousand florins at least!' cried the pied piper angrily.

But the Mayor broke in. 'The rats are all dead now and they can never come back. So be grateful for fifty florins, or you'll not get even that . . .'

His eyes flashing with rage, the pied piper pointed a threatening finger at the Mayor.

'You'll bitterly regret ever breaking your promise," he said, and vanished.

A shiver of fear ran through the councillors, but the Mayor shrugged and said excitedly: 'We've saved fifty thousand florins!'

That night, freed from the nightmare of the rats, the citizens of Hamelin slept more soundly than ever. And the strange sound of piping wafted through the streets at dawn, only the children heard it. Drawn as by magic, they hurried out of their homes. Again, the pied piper paced through the town; this time, it was children of all sizes that flocked at his heels to the sound of his strange piping.

The long procession soon left the town and made its way through the wood and across the forest till it reached the foot of a huge mountain. When the piper came to the dark rock, he played his pipe even louder still and a great door creaked open. Beyond lay a cave. In trooped the children behind the pied piper, and when the last child had gone into the darkness, the door creaked shut.

A great landslide came down the mountain blocking the entrance to the cave forever. Only one little lame boy escaped this fate. It was he who told the anxious citizens, searching for their children, what had happened. And no matter what people did, the mountain never gave up its victims.

Many years were to pass before the merry voices of other children would ring through the streets of Hamelin but the memory of the harsh lesson lingered in everyone's heart and was passed down from father to son through the centuries.

Doctor Knowall

There was once on a time a poor peasant called Crabb, who drove with two oxen a load of wood to the town, and sold it to a doctor for two coins. When the money was being counted out to him, it so happened that the doctor was sitting at table, and when the peasant saw how daintily he ate and drank, his heart desired what he saw, and he would willingly have been a doctor too. So he remained standing a while, and at length inquired if he too could not be a doctor.

'Oh, yes,' said the doctor, 'that is soon managed.'

'What must I do?' asked the peasant. 'In the first place buy yourself an A B C book of the kind which has a cock on the frontispiece: in the second, turn your cart and your two oxen into money, and get yourself some clothes, and whatsoever else pertains to medicine; thirdly, have a sign painted for yourself with the words, 'I am Doctor Knowall,' and have that nailed up above your house-door.'

The peasant did everything that he had been told to do. When he had doctored people awhile, but not long, a rich and great lord had some money stolen. Then he was told about Doctor Knowall who lived in such and such a village, and must know what had become of the money. So the lord had the horses put in his carriage and drove out to the village.

'Are you Doctor Knowall?' he asked Crabb.

'Yes, I am,' he said.

'Then you are to come with me and bring back the stolen money,' the rich lord said.

'Oh, yes, but Grethe, my wife, must go too.'

The lord was willing and let both of them have a seat in the carriage, and they all drove away together. When they came to the nobleman's castle, the table was spread, and Crabb was told to sit down and eat.

'Yes, but my wife, Grethe, too,' said he, and he seated himself with her at the table. And when the first servant came with a dish of delicate fare, the peasant nudged his wife, and said:

'Grethe, that was the first,' meaning that was the servant who brought the first dish. The servant, however, thought he intended by that to say, 'That is the first thief,' and as he actually was so, he was terrified, and said to his comrade outside; 'The doctor knows all: we shall fare ill, he said I was the first.'

The second did not want to go in at all, but was forced. So when he went in with his dish, the peasant nudged his wife, and said:

'Grethe, that is the second.' This servant was just as much alarmed, and he got out. The third did not fare better, for the peasant again said:

'Grethe, that is the third.' The fourth had to carry in a dish that was covered, and the lord told the doctor that he was to show his skill and guess what was beneath the cover. The doctor looked at the dish, and had no idea what to say.

'Ah, poor Crabb!' he cried.

When the lord heard that, he cried, 'There! he knows it, he knows who has the money!'

On this the servants looked terribly uneasy, and made a sign to the doctor that they wished him to step outside for a moment. When therefore he went out, all four of them confessed to him that they had stolen the money, and said that they would willingly restore it and give him a heavy sum into the bargain, if he would not denounce them, for if he did they would be hanged. They led him to the spot where the money was concealed. With this the doctor was satisfied, and returned to the hall, and sat down to the table.

'My lord, now will I search in my book where the gold is hidden,' he said.

The fifth servant crept into the stove to hear if the doctor knew still more. The Doctor, however, sat still and opened his A B C book, turned the pages backwards and forwards, and looked for the cock. As he could not find it immediately he said:

'I know you are there, so you had better show yourself.'

Then the fellow in the stove thought that the doctor meant him, and full of terror, sprang out, crying:

'That man knows everything!'

Then Dr. Knowall showed the count where the money was, but did not say who had stolen it, and received from both sides much money in reward, and became a renowned man.

but she did not touch it. Next day she again went out with her goat, and left the few bits of broken bread which had been handed to her, lying untouched. The first and second time that she did this, her sisters did not remark it at all, but as it happened every time, they did observe it.

'There is something wrong about Two-Eyes, she always leaves her food untasted, and she used to eat up everything that was given her,' they said. 'She must have discovered other ways of getting food.'

In order that they might learn the truth, they resolved to send One-Eye with Two-Eyes when she went to drive her goat to the pasture, to observe what Two-Eyes did when she was there, and whether any one brought her anything to eat and drink. So when Two-Eyes set out the next time, One-Eye went to her and said, 'I will go with you to the pasture, and see that the goat is well taken care of, and driven where there is food.' But Two-Eyes knew what was in One-Eye's mind, and drove the goat into high grass.

'Come, One-Eye, we will sit down, and I will sing something to you,' she said when they got there. One-Eye sat down and was tired with the unaccustomed walk and the heat of the sun, and Two-Eyes sang constantly,

> 'One eye, are you waking?
> One eye, are you sleeping?'

until One-Eye shut her one eye, and fell asleep, and as soon as Two-Eyes saw that One-Eye was fast asleep, and could discover nothing, she said:

> 'Bleat, my little goat, bleat,
> Cover the table with something to eat,'

and seated herself at her table, and ate and drank until she was satisfied, and then she again cried:

> 'Bleat, bleat, my little goat, I pray,
> And take the table quite away,'

and in an instant all was gone. Two-Eyes now awakened One-Eye.

'One-Eye, you want to take care of the goat, and go to sleep while you are doing it, and in the meantime the goat might run all over the world. Come, let us go home again,' she said. So they went home, and again Two-Eyes let her little dish stand untouched, and One-Eye could not tell her mother why she would not eat it, and to excuse herself said, 'I fell asleep when I was out.'

Next day the mother said to Three-Eyes:

'This time you shall go and observe if Two-Eyes eats anything when she is out, and if any one fetches her food and drink, for she must eat and drink in secret.'

So Three-Eyes went to Two-Eyes, and said: 'I will go with you and see if the goat is taken proper care of, and driven where there is food.' But Two-Eyes knew what was in Three-Eyes' mind, and drove the goat into high grass.

'We will sit down, and I will sing something to you, Three-Eyes.'

Three-Eyes sat down and was tired with the walk and with the heat of the sun, and Two-Eyes began the same song as before, and sang:

> 'Three eyes, are you waking?'

but then, instead of singing,

> 'Three eyes, are you sleeping?'

as she ought to have done, she thoughtlessly sang,

> 'Two eyes, are you sleeping?'

and sang all the time,

> 'Three eyes, are you waking?
> Two eyes, are you sleeping?'

Then two of the eyes which Three-Eyes had, shut and fell asleep, but the third, as it had not been named in the song, did not sleep. It is true that Three-Eyes shut it, but only in her cunning, to pretend it was asleep too, but it blinked, and could see everything very well. And when Two-Eyes thought that Three-Eyes was fast asleep, she used her little charm,

> 'Bleat, my little goat, bleat,
> Cover the table with something to eat,'

and ate and drank as much as her heart desired, and then ordered the table to go away again,

> 'Bleat, bleat, my little goat, I pray,
> And take the table quite away,'

and Three-Eyes had seen everything. Then Two-Eyes came to her, woke her and said:

'Have you been asleep, Three-Eyes? You are a good care-taker! Come, we will go home.'

And when they got home, Two-Eyes again did not eat, and Three-Eyes said to the mother:

'Now, I know why that high-minded thing there does not eat. When she is out, she says to the goat,

> "Bleat, my little goat, bleat,
> Cover the table with something to eat,"

and then a little table appears before her covered with the best of food, much better than any we have here, and when she has eaten all she wants, she says,

> "Bleat, bleat, my little goat, I pray,
> And take the table quite away,"

and all disappears. I watched everything closely. She put two of my eyes to sleep by using a certain form of words, but luckily the one in my forehead kept awake.'

'Do you want to fare better than we do?' cried the envious mother. 'The desire shall pass away,' and she fetched a butcher's knife, and thrust it into the heart of the goat, which fell down dead.

When Two-Eyes saw that, she went out full of trouble, seated herself on the ridge of grass at the edge of the field, and wept bitter tears. Suddenly the wise woman once more stood by her side.

'Two-Eyes, why are you weeping?' she said.

'Have I not reason to weep?' she answered. 'The goat which covered the table for me every day when I spoke your charm, has been killed by my mother, and now I shall again have to bear hunger and want.'

'Two-Eyes, I will give you a piece of good advice,' said the wise woman. 'Ask your sisters to give you the entrails of the slaughtered goat, and bury them in the ground in front of the house, and your fortune will be made.'

Then she vanished, and Two-Eyes went home and said to her sisters:

'Dear sisters, do give me some part of my goat; I don't wish for what is good, but give me the entrails.'

'If that's all you want, you can have it,' they said, and they laughed.

So Two-Eyes took the entrails and buried them quietly in the evening, in front of the house-door, as the wise woman had counselled her to do.

Next morning, when they all awoke, and went to the house door, there stood a strangely magnificent tree with leaves of silver, and fruit of gold hanging among them, so that in all the wide world there was nothing more beautiful or precious. They did not know how the tree could have come there during the night, but Two-Eyes saw that it had grown up out of the entrails of the goat, for it was standing on the exact spot where she had buried them. Then the mother said to One-Eye:

'Climb up, my child, and gather some of the fruit of the tree for us.'

One-Eye climbed up, but when she was about to get hold of one of the golden apples, the branch escaped from her hands, and that happened each time, so that she could not pluck a single apple, let her do what she might.

'Three-Eyes, do you climb up; you with your three eyes can look about you better than One-Eye,' the mother said then.

One-Eye slipped down, and Three-Eyes climbed up. Three-Eyes was not more skilful, and might search as she liked, but the golden apples always escaped her. At length the mother grew impatient, and climbed up herself, but could get hold of the fruit no better than One-Eye and Three-Eyes, for she always clutched empty air.

'I will just go up, perhaps I may succeed better,' said Two-Eyes.

'You indeed, with your two eyes, what can you do?' cried the sisters.

But Two-Eyes climbed up, and the golden apples did get out of her way, but came into her hand of their own accord, so that she could pluck them one after the other, and brought a whole apronful down with her. The mother took them away from her, and instead of treating poor Two-Eyes any better for this, she and One-Eye and Three-Eyes were only envious, because Two-Eyes alone had been able to get the fruit, and they treated her still more cruelly.

It so befell that once when they were all standing together by the tree, a young knight came up.

'Quick, Two-Eyes,' cried the two sisters, 'creep under this, and don't disgrace us!' and with all speed they turned an empty barrel which was standing close by the tree over poor Two-Eyes, and they pushed the golden apples which she had been gathering, under it too. When the knight came nearer he was a handsome lord, who stopped and admired the magnificent gold and silver tree.

'To whom does this fine tree belong?' he asked the two sisters. 'Anyone who would bestow one branch of it on me might in return for it ask whatsoever he desired.'

Then One-Eye and Three-Eyes replied that the tree belonged to them, and that they would give him a branch. They both took great trouble, but they were not able to do it, for the branches and fruit both moved away from them every time.

'It is very strange that the tree should belong to you,' the knight said, 'and that you should still not be able to break a piece off.'

They again asserted that the tree was their property. While they were saying so, Two-Eyes rolled out a couple of golden apples from under the barrel to the feet of the knight, for she was vexed with One-Eye and Three-Eyes, for not speaking the truth. When the knight saw the apples he was astonished, and asked where they came from. One-Eye and Three-Eyes answered that they had another sister, who was not allowed to show herself, for she had only two eyes like any common person. The knight, however, desired to see her.

'Two-Eyes, come forth,' he cried.

Then Two-Eyes, quite comforted, came from beneath the barrel, and the knight was surprised at her great beauty.

'You, Two-Eyes, canst certainly break off a branch from the tree for me,' he said.

'Yes,' replied Two-Eyes, 'that I certainly shall be able to do, for the tree belongs to me.'

And she climbed up, and with the greatest ease broke off a branch with beautiful silver leaves and golden fruit, and gave it to the knight.

'Two-Eyes, what shall I give you for it?' asked the knight.

'Alas!' answered Two-Eyes, 'I suffer from hunger and thirst, grief and want, from early morning till late night; if you would take me with you, and deliver me from these things, I should be happy.'

So the knight lifted Two-Eyes on to his horse, and took her home with him to his father's castle, and there he gave her beautiful clothes, and meat and drink to her heart's content, and as he loved her so much he married her, and the wedding was solemnized with great rejoicing. When Two-Eyes was thus carried away by the handsome knight, her two sisters grudged her good fortune in downright earnest.

'The wonderful tree, however, still remains with us,' thought they, 'and even if we can gather no fruit from it, still everyone will stand still and look at it, and come to us and admire it. Who knows what good

things may be in store for us?' But next morning, the tree had vanished, and all their hopes were at an end. And when Two-Eyes looked out of the window of her own little room, to her great delight it was standing in front of it, and so it had followed her.

Two-Eyes lived a long time in happiness. Once two poor women came to her in her castle, and begged for alms. She looked in their faces, and recognized her sisters, One-Eye, and Three-Eyes, who had fallen into such poverty that they had to wander about and beg their bread from door to door. Two-Eyes, however, made them welcome, and was kind to them, and took care of them, so that they both with all their hearts repented the evil that they had done their sister in their youth.

The Fox and the Horse

A peasant had a faithful horse which had grown old and could do no more work, so his master would no longer give him anything to eat.

'I can certainly make no more use of you,' he said, 'but still I mean well by you; if you prove yourself still strong enough to bring me a lion here, I will maintain you, but now take yourself away out of my stable,' and with that he chased him into the open country.

The horse was sad, and went to the forest to seek a little protection there from the weather. There he met a fox who said:

'Why do you hang your head so, and go about all alone?'

'Alas,' replied the horse, 'avarice and fidelity do not dwell together in one house. My master has forgotten what services I have performed for him for so many years, and because I can no longer plough well, he will give me no more food, and has driven me out.'

'Without giving you a chance?' asked the fox.

'The chance was a bad one. He said, if I were still strong enough to bring him a lion, he would keep me, but he well knows that I cannot do that.'

'I will help you,' said the fox. 'Just lay yourself down, stretch yourself out, as if you were dead, and do not stir.'

The horse did as the fox desired, and the fox went to the lion, who had his den not far off.

'A dead horse is lying outside there, just come with me, you can have a rich meal,' he said to the lion.

The lion went with him, and when they were both standing by the horse the fox said:

'After all, it is not very comfortable for you here. I tell you what – I will fasten it to you by the tail, and then you can drag it into your cave, and devour it in peace.'

This advice pleased the lion: he lay down, and in order that the fox might tie the horse fast to him, he kept quite quiet. But the fox tied the lion's legs together with the horse's tail, and twisted and fastened all so well and so strongly that no strength could break it. When he had finished his work, he tapped the horse on the shoulder.

'Pull, white horse, pull,' he said.

Then up sprang the horse at once, and drew the lion away with him. The lion began to roar so that all the birds in the forest flew out in terror, but the horse let him roar, and drew him and dragged him over the country to his master's door. When the master saw the lion, he was of a better mind, and said to the horse, 'You shall stay with me and fare well.'

And he gave him plenty to eat until he died.

The Six Servants

In former times there lived an aged queen who was a sorceress, and her daughter was the most beautiful maiden under the sun. The old woman, however, had no other thought than how to lure mankind to destruction, and when a wooer appeared, she said that whoever wished to have her daughter, must first perform a task, or die. Many had been dazzled by the daughter's beauty, and had actually risked this, but they never could accomplish what the old woman enjoined them to do, and then no mercy was shown; they had to kneel down, and their heads were struck off.

A certain king's son who had also heard of the maiden's beauty, said to his father, 'Let me go there, I want to demand her in marriage.'

'Never,' answered the king; 'if you were to go, it would be going to your death.'

On this the son lay down and became sick, unto death, and for seven years he lay there, and no physician could heal him. When the father perceived that all hope was over, with a heavy heart he said to him:

'Go thither, and try your luck, for I know no other means of curing you.'

When the son heard that, he rose from his bed and was well again, and joyfully set out on his way.

And it came to pass that as he was riding across a heath, he saw from afar something like a great heap of hay lying on the ground, and when he drew nearer, he could see that it was the stomach of a man, who had laid himself down there, but the stomach looked like a small mountain. When the fat man saw the traveller, he stood up.

'If you are in need of any one, take me into your service,' he said.

'What can I do with such a great big man?' the prince asked.

'Oh,' said the Stout One, 'this is nothing, when I stretch myself out well, I am three thousand times fatter.'

'If that's the case,' said the prince, 'I can make use of you, come with me.'

So the Stout One followed the prince, and after a while they found another man who was lying on the ground with his ear laid to the turf.

'What are you doing there?' asked the king's son.

'I am listening,' replied the man.

'What are you listening to so attentively?'

'I am listening to what is just going on in the world, for nothing escapes my ears; I even hear the grass growing.'

'Tell me,' said the prince, 'what you hear at the court of the old queen who has the beautiful daughter.'

'I hear the whizzing of the sword that is striking off a wooer's head,' he answered.

'I can make use of you,' the king's son said, 'come with me.'

They went onwards, and then saw a pair of feet lying and part of a pair of legs, but could not see the rest of the body. When they had walked on for a great distance, they came to the body, and at last to the head also.

'Why,' said the prince, 'what a tall rascal you are!'

'Oh,' replied the Tall One, 'that is nothing at all yet; when I really stretch out my limbs, I am three thousand times as tall, and taller than the highest mountain on earth. I will gladly enter your service, if you will take me.'

'Come with me,' said the prince, 'I can make use of you.'

They went onwards and found a man sitting by the road who had bound up his eyes.

'Have you weak eyes, that you cannot look at the light?' the prince asked him.

'No,' replied the man, 'but I must not remove the bandage, for whatever I look at with my eyes, splits to pieces, my glance is so powerful. If you can use that, I shall be glad to serve you.'

'Come with me,' replied the king's son, 'I can make use of you.'

They journeyed onwards and found a man who was lying in the hot sunshine, trembling and shivering all over his body, so that not a limb was still.

'How can you shiver when the sun is shining so warm?' said the king's son.

'Alack,' replied the man, 'I am of quite a different nature. The hotter it is, the colder I am, and the frost pierces through all my bones; and the colder it is, the hotter I am. In the midst of ice, I cannot endure the heat, nor in the midst of fire, the cold.'

'You are a strange fellow,' said the prince, 'but if you will enter my service, follow me.'

They travelled onwards, and saw a man standing who made a long neck and looked about him, and could see over all the mountains.

'What are you looking at so eagerly?' said the prince.

'I have such sharp eyes that I can see into every forest and field, and hill and valley, all over the world,' the man replied.

'Come with me if you will, for I am still in want of such an one,' the prince said.

And now the king's son and his six servants came to the town where the aged queen dwelt. He did not tell her who he was, but said:

'If you will give me your beautiful daughter, I will perform any task you set me.'

The sorceress was delighted to get such a handsome youth as this into her net, and said, 'I will set you three tasks, and if you are able to perform them all, you shall be husband and master of my daughter.'

'What is the first to be?'

'You shall fetch me my ring which I have dropped into the Red Sea.'

So the king's son went home to his servants.

'The first task is not easy,' he said. 'A ring is to be got out of the Red Sea. Come, find some way of doing it.'

'I will see where it is lying,' said the man with sharp sight, and he looked down into the water. 'It is sticking there, on a pointed stone.'

The Tall One carried them thither, and said, 'I would soon get it out, if I could only see it.' 'Oh, is that all!' cried the Stout One, and lay down and put his mouth to the water, on which all the waves fell into it just as if it had been a whirlpool, and he drank up the whole sea till it was as dry as a meadow. The Tall One stooped down a little, and brought out the ring with his hand. Then the king's son rejoiced when he had the ring, and took it to the old queen. She was astonished.

'Yes, it is the right ring,' she said. 'You have safely performed the first task, but now comes the second. Do you see the meadow in front of my palace? Three hundred fat oxen are feeding there, and these must you eat, skin, hair, bones, horns and all, and down below in my cellar lie three hundred casks of wine, and these you must drink up as well, and if one hair of the oxen, or one little drop of the wine is left, your life will be forfeited to me.'

'May I invite no guests to this repast?' inquired the prince, 'no dinner is good without some company.' The old woman laughed maliciously.

'You may invite one for the sake of companionship, but no more,' she replied.

The king's son went to his servants and said to the Stout One:

'You shall be my guest today, and shall eat your fill.'

Hereupon the Stout One stretched himself out and ate the three hundred oxen without leaving one single hair, and then he asked if he was to have nothing but his breakfast. He drank the wine straight from the casks without feeling any need of a glass, and he licked the last drop from his finger-nails. When the meal was over, the prince went to the old woman, and told her that the second task also was performed. She wondered at this.

'No one has ever done so much before,' she said, 'but one task still remains,' and she thought to herself, 'you shall not escape me, and will not keep your head on your shoulders!' Out loud she said: 'This night, I will bring my daughter to you in your chamber, and you shall put your arms round her, but when you are sitting there together, beware of falling asleep. When twelve o'clock is striking, I will come, and if she is then no longer in your arms, you are lost.'

'The task is easy,' the prince thought. 'I will most certainly keep my eyes open.' Nevertheless he called his servants, told them what the old woman had said, and remarked, 'Who knows what treachery lurks behind this? Foresight is a good thing keep watch, and take care that the maiden does not go out of my room again.'

When night fell, the old woman came with her daughter, and gave her into the prince's arms, and then the Tall One wound himself round the two in a circle, and the Stout One placed himself by the door, so that no living creature could enter. There the two sat, and the maiden spake never a word, but the moon shone through the window on her face, and the prince could behold her wondrous beauty. He did nothing but gaze at her, and was filled with love and happiness, and his eyes never felt weary. This lasted until eleven o'clock, when the old woman cast such a spell over all of them that they fell asleep, and at the self-same moment the maiden was carried away.

Then they all slept soundly until a quarter to twelve, when the magic lost its power, and all awoke again.

'Oh, misery and misfortune!' cried the prince, 'now I am lost!' The faithful servants also began to lament, but the Listener said:

'Be quiet, I want to listen.' Then he listened for an instant and said, 'She is on a rock, three hundred leagues from here, bewailing her fate. you alone, Tall One, can help her; if you will stand up, you will be there in a couple of steps.'

'Yes,' answered the Tall One, 'but the one with the sharp eyes must go with me, that we may destroy the rock.' Then the Tall One took the one with bandaged eyes on his back, and in the twinkling of an eye they were on the enchanted rock. The Tall One immediately took the bandage from the other's eyes, and he did but look round, and the rock shivered into a thousand pieces. Then the Tall One took the maiden in his arms, carried her back in a second, then fetched his companion with the same rapidity, and before it struck twelve they were all sitting as they had sat before, quite merrily and happily. When twelve struck, the aged sorceress came stealing in with a malicious face, which seemed to say, 'Now he is mine!' for she believed that her daughter was on the rock three hundred leagues off. But when she saw her in the prince's arms, she was alarmed.

'Here is one who knows more than I do!' she said. She dared not make any opposition, and was forced to give him her daughter. But she whispered in her daughter's ear:

'It is a disgrace to you to have to obey common people, and that you are not allowed to choose a husband to your own liking.'

On this the proud heart of the maiden was filled with anger, and she meditated revenge. Next morning she caused three hundred great bundles of wood to be got together, and said to the prince that though the three tasks were performed, she would still not be his wife until someone was ready to seat himself in the midst of the wood, and bear the fire. She thought that none of his servants would let themselves be burnt for him, and that out of love for her, he himself would place himself upon it, and then she would be free. But the servants said, 'Every one of us has done something except the Frosty One, he must set to work,' and they put him in the middle of the pile, and set fire to it. Then the fire began to burn, and burnt for three days until all the wood was consumed, and when the flames had burnt out, the Frosty One was standing amid the ashes, trembling like an aspen leaf, and saying, 'I never felt such a frost during the whole course of my life; if it had lasted much longer, I should have been benumbed!'

As no other pretext was to be found, the beautiful maiden was now forced to take the unknown youth as a husband. But when they drove away to church, the old woman said:

'I cannot endure the disgrace,' and sent her warriors after them with orders to cut down all who opposed them, and bring back her daughter. But the Listener had sharpened his ears, and heard the secret discourse of the old woman.

320

'What shall we do?' said he to the Stout One. But he knew what to do, and spat out once or twice behind the carriage some of the sea-water which he had drunk, and a great sea arose in which the warriors were caught and drowned. When the sorceress perceived that, she sent her mailed knights; but the Listener heard the rattling of their armour, and undid the bandage from one eye of Sharp-eyes, who looked for a while rather fixedly at the enemy's troops, on which they all sprang to pieces like glass. Then the youth and the maiden went on their way undisturbed, and when the two had been blessed in church, the six servants took leave.

'Your wishes are now satisfied, you need us no longer, we will go our way and seek our fortunes,' they said to their master.

Half a league from the palace of the prince's father was a village near which a swineherd tended his herd, and when they came thither the prince said to his wife:

'Do you know who I really am? I am no prince, but a herder of swine, and the man who is there with that herd, is my father. We two shall have to set to work also, and help him.' Then he alighted with her at the inn, and secretly told the innkeepers to take away her royal apparel during the night. So when she awoke in the morning, she had nothing to put on, and the innkeeper's wife gave her an old gown and a pair of worsted stockings, and at the same time seemed to consider it a great present.

'If it were not for the sake of your husband,' she said, 'I should have given you nothing at all!'

Then the princess believed that he really was a swineherd, and tended the herd with him, and thought to herself:

'I have deserved this for my haughtiness and pride.'

This lasted for a week, and then she could endure it no longer, for she had sores on her feet. And now came a couple of people who asked if she knew who her husband was.

'Yes,' she answered, 'he is a swineherd, and has just gone out with cords and ropes to try to drive a little bargain.'

'Just come with us, and we will take you to him,' they said, and they took her up to the palace, and when she entered the hall, there stood her husband in kingly raiment. But she did not recognize him until he took her in his arms, kissed her, and said:

'I suffered much for you and now you, too, have had to suffer for me.'

And then the wedding was celebrated, and he who has told you all this, wishes that he, too, had been present at it.

Iron John

❧ ❧ ❧

There was once on a time a king who had a great forest near his palace, full of all kinds of wild animals. One day he sent out a huntsman to shoot him a roe, but he did not come back.

'Perhaps some accident has befallen him,' said the king, and the next day he sent out two more huntsmen who were to search for him, but they too stayed away. Then on the third day, he sent for all his huntsmen.

'Scour the whole forest through,' he said, 'and do not give up until you have found all three.' But of these also, none came home again, and of the pack of hounds which they had taken with them, none were seen more. From that time forth, no one would any longer venture into the forest, and it lay there in deep stillness and solitude, and nothing was seen of it, but sometimes an eagle or a hawk flying over it. This lasted for many years, when a strange huntsman announced himself to the king as seeking a situation, and offered to go into the dangerous forest. The king, however, would not give his consent.

'It is not safe in there,' he said. 'I fear it would fare with you no better than with the others, and you wouldst never come out again.'

'Lord, I will venture it at my own risk, of fear I know nothing,' the huntsman replied.

The huntsman therefore betook himself with his dog to the forest. It was not long before the dog fell in with some game on the way, and wanted to pursue it; but hardly had the dog run two steps when it stood before a deep pool, could go no farther, and a naked arm stretched itself out of the water, seized it, and drew it under, When the huntsman saw that, he went back and fetched three men to come with buckets and bale out the water. When they could see to the bottom there lay a wild man whose body was brown like rusty iron, and whose hair hung over his face down to his knees. They bound him with cords, and led him away to the castle. There was great astonishment over the wild man; the king, however, had him put in an iron cage in his courtyard, and forbade the door to be opened on pain of death, and the queen herself was to take the key into her keeping. And from this time forth everyone could again go into the forest with safety.

The king had a son of eight years, who was once playing in the courtyard, and while he was playing, his golden ball fell into the cage. The boy ran thither and said:

'Give me my ball out.'

'Not till you have opened the door for me,' answered the man.

'No,' said the boy, 'I will not do that; the king has forbidden it,' and ran away. The next day he again went and asked for his ball.

'Open my door,' said the wild man, but the boy would not.

On the third day the king had ridden out hunting, and the boy went once more and said:

'I cannot open the door even if I wished, for I have not the key.' Then the wild man said, 'It lies under your mother's pillow, you can get it there,' the wild man said.

The boy, who wanted to have his ball back, cast all thought to the winds, and brought the key. The door opened with difficulty, and the boy pinched his fingers. When it was open the wild man stepped out, gave him the golden ball, and hurried away. The boy became afraid.

'Oh, wild man, do not go away, or I shall be beaten!' he cried after him. The wild man turned back, took him up, set him on his shoulder, and went with hasty steps into the forest. When the king came home, he observed the empty cage, and asked the queen how that had happened. She knew nothing about it, and sought the key, but it was gone. She called the boy, but no one answered. The king sent out people to seek for him in the fields, but they did not find him. Then he could easily guess what had happened, and much grief reigned in the royal court.

When the wild man had once more reached the dark forest, he took the boy down from his shoulder, and said to him, 'You will never see your father and mother again, but I will keep you with me, for you have set me free, and I have compassion on you. If you do all I bid you, you shall fare well. Of treasure and gold have I enough, and more than anyone in the world.'

He made a bed of moss for the boy on which he slept, and the next morning the man took him to a well.

'Behold,' he said, 'the gold well is as bright and clear as crystal, you shall sit beside it, and take care that nothing falls into it, or it will be polluted. I will come every evening to see if you have obeyed my order.'

The boy placed himself by the margin of the well, and often saw a golden fish or a golden snake show itself therein, and took care that nothing fell in. As he was thus sitting, his finger hurt him so violently that he involuntarily put it in the water. He drew it quickly out again, but saw that it was quite gilded, and whatsoever pains he took to wash the gold off again, all was to no purpose. In the evening Iron John came back, looked at the boy, and said, 'What has happened to the well?'

'Nothing, nothing,' he answered, and held his finger behind his back, that the man might not see it. But he said, 'You have dipped your finger into the water, this time it may pass, but take care you do not again let anything go in.'

By daybreak the boy was already sitting by the well and watching it. His finger hurt him again and he passed it over his head, and then unhappily a hair fell down into the well. He took it quickly out, but it was already quite gilded. Iron John came, and already knew what had happened.

'You have let a hair fall into the well,' said he. 'I will allow you to watch by it once more, but if this happens for the third time then the well is polluted, and you can no longer remain with me.'

On the third day, the boy sat by the well, and did not stir his finger, however much it hurt him. But the time was long to him, and he looked at the reflection of his face on the surface of the water. And as he still bent down more and more while he was doing so, and trying to look straight into the eyes, his long hair fell down from his shoulders into the water. He raised himself up quickly, but the whole of the hair of his head was already golden and shone like the sun. You may imagine how terrified the poor boy was! He took his pocket-handkerchief and tied it round his head, in order that the man might not see it. When he came he already knew everything, 'Take the handkerchief off,' he said. Then the golden hair streamed forth, and let the boy excuse himself as he might, it was of no use.

'You have not stood the trial, and can stay here no longer. Go forth into the world, there you will learn what poverty is. But as you have not a bad heart, and as I mean well by you, there is one thing I will grant you; if you fall into any difficulty, come to the forest and cry, "Iron John," and then I will come and help you. My power is great, greater than you think, and I have gold and silver in abundance.'

Then the king's son left the forest, and walked by beaten and unbeaten paths ever onwards until at length he reached a great city. There he looked for work, but could find none, and he had learnt nothing by which he could help himself. At length he went to the palace, and asked if they would take him in. The people about court did not at all know what use they could make of him, but they liked him, and told him to stay. At length the cook took him into his service, and said he might carry wood and water, and rake the cinders together.

Once when it so happened that no one else was at hand, the cook ordered him to carry the food to the royal table, but as he did not like to let his golden hair be seen, he kept his little cap on. Such a thing as that had never yet come under the king's notice, and he said, 'When you come to the royal table you must take your hat off.'

'Ah, Lord, I cannot; I have a bad sore place on my head,' he answered. Then the king had the cook called before him and scolded him, and asked how he could take such a boy as that into his service; and that he was to turn him off at once. The cook, however, had pity on him, and exchanged him for the gardener's boy.

And now the boy had to plant and water the garden, hoe and dig, and bear the wind and bad weather. Once in summer when he was working alone in the garden, the day was so warm he took his little cap off that the air might cool him. As the sun shone on his hair it glittered and flashed so that the rays fell into the bed-room of the king's daughter, and up she sprang to see what that could be. Then she saw the boy, and cried to him:

'Boy, bring me a wreath of flowers.'

He put his cap on with all haste, and gathered wild field-flowers and bound them together. When he was ascending the stairs with them, the gardener met him.

'How can you take the king's daughter a garland of such common flowers?' he said. 'Go quickly, and get another, and seek out the prettiest and rarest.'

'Oh, no,' replied the boy, 'the wild ones have more scent, and will please her better.' When he got into the room, the king's daughter said, 'Take your cap off, it is not seemly to keep it on in my presence.' He again said, 'I may not, I have a sore head.'

She, however, caught at his cap and pulled it off, and then his golden hair rolled down on his shoulders, and it was splendid to behold. He wanted to run out, but she held him by the arm, and gave him a handful of ducats. With these he departed, but he cared nothing for the gold pieces. He took them to the gardener.

'I present them to your children, they can play with them,' he said.

The following day the king's daughter again called to him that he was to bring her a wreath of field-flowers, and when he went in with it, she instantly snatched at his cap, and wanted to take it away from him, but he held it fast with both hands. She again gave him a handful of ducats, but he would not keep them, and gave them to the gardener for playthings for his children. On the third day things went just the same; she could not get his cap away from him, and he would not have her money.

Not long afterwards, the country was overrun by war. The king gathered together his people, and did not know whether or not he could offer any opposition to the enemy, who was superior in strength and had a mighty army. Then said the gardener's boy:

'I am grown up, and will go to the wars also, only give me a horse.'

The others laughed, and said, 'Seek one for yourself when we are gone, we will leave one behind us in the stable for you.' When they had gone forth, he went into the stable, and got the horse out; it was lame of one foot, and limped hobblety jig, hobblety jig; nevertheless he mounted it, and rode away to the dark forest. When he came to the outskirts, he called 'Iron John,' three times so loudly that it echoed through the trees. Thereupon the wild man appeared immediately.

'What do you desire?' he asked.

'I want a strong steed, for I am going to the wars.'

'That you shall have, and still more than you asked for.'

Then the wild man went back into the forest, and it was not long before a stable-boy came out of it, who led a horse that snorted with its nostrils, and could hardly be restrained, and behind them followed a great troop of soldiers entirely equipped in iron, and their swords flashed in the sun. The youth made over his three-legged horse to the stable-boy, mounted the other, and rode at the head of the soldiers. When he got near the battle-field a great part of the king's men had already fallen, and little was wanting to make the rest give way. Then the youth galloped thither with his iron soldiers, broke like a hurricane over the enemy, and beat down all who opposed him. They began to fly, but the youth pursued, and never stopped, until there was not a single man left. Instead, however, of returning to the king, he conducted his troop by bye-ways back to the forest, and called forth Iron John.

'What do you desire?' asked the wild man. 'Take back your horse and your troops, and give me my three-legged horse again.' All that he asked was done, and soon he was riding on his three-legged horse.

When the king returned to his palace, his daughter went to meet him, and wished him joy of his victory.

'I am not the one who carried away the victory,' said he, 'but a stranger knight who came to my assistance with his soldiers.' The daughter wanted to hear who the strange knight was, but the king did not know.

'He followed the enemy, and I did not see him again,' he said.

She inquired of the gardener where his boy was, but he smiled, and said, 'He has just come home on his three-legged horse, and the others have been mocking him, and crying, "Here comes our hobblety jig back again!" They asked, too, "Under what hedge have you been lying sleeping all the time?" He, however, said, "I did the best of all, and it would have gone badly without me." And then he was still more ridiculed.'

'I will proclaim a great feast that shall last for three days,' the king said to his daughter, 'and you shall throw a golden apple. Perhaps the unknown will come to it.' When the feast was announced, the youth went out to the forest, and called Iron John.

'What do you desire?' asked he.

'That I may catch the king's daughter's golden apple.'

'It is as safe as if you had it already,' said Iron John. 'You shall likewise have a suit of red armour for the occasion, and ride on a spirited chestnut horse.'

When the day came, the youth galloped to the spot, took his place among the knights, and was recognized by no one. The king's daughter came forward, and threw a golden apple to the knights, but none of them caught it but he, only as soon as he had it he galloped away.

On the second day Iron John equipped him as a white knight, and gave him a white horse. Again he was the only one who caught the apple, and he did not linger an instant, but galloped off with it. The king grew angry.

'That is not allowed; he must appear before me and tell his name,' he said. He gave the order that if the knight who caught the apple should go away again they should pursue him, and if he would not come back willingly, they were to cut him down and stab him.

On the third day, he received from Iron John a suit of black armour and a black horse, and again he caught the apple. But when he was riding off with it, the king's attendants pursued him, and one of them got so near him that he wounded the youth's leg with the point of his sword. The youth nevertheless escaped from them, but his horse leapt so violently that the helmet fell from the youth's head, and they could see that he had golden hair. They rode back and announced this to the king.

The following day the king's daughter asked the gardener about his boy.

'He is at work in the garden; the queer creature has been at the festival too, and only came home yesterday evening; he has likewise shown my children three golden apples which he has won.'

The king had him summoned into his presence, and he came and again had his little cap on his head. But the king's daughter went up to him and took it off, and then his golden hair fell down over his shoulders, and he was so handsome that all were amazed.

'Are you the knight who came every day to the festival, always in different colours, and who caught the three golden apples?' asked the king.

'Yes,' answered he, 'and here the apples are,' and he took them out of his pocket, and returned them to the king. 'If you desire further proof, you may see the wound which your people gave me when they followed me. But I am likewise the knight who helped you to your victory over your enemies.'

'If you can perform such deeds as that, you are no gardener's boy; tell me, who is your father?'

'My father is a mighty king, and gold have I in plenty as great as I require.'

'I well see,' said the king, 'that I owe thanks to you; can I do anything to please you?'

'Yes,' answered he, 'that indeed you can. Give me your daughter to wife.' The maiden laughed, and said:

'He does not stand much on ceremony, but I have already seen by his golden hair that he was no gardener's boy,' and then she went and kissed him. His father and mother came to the wedding, and were in great delight, for they had given up all hope of ever seeing their dear son again. And as they were sitting at the marriage-feast, the music suddenly stopped, the doors opened, and a stately king came in with a great retinue. He went up to the youth, embraced him and said:

'I am Iron John, and was by enchantment a wild man, but you have set me free; all the treasures which I possess, shall be your property.'